PH...
va...

Af...
an... ...iovel, *Dece*...
Ne... ...d and was made into a ...
M... ...*stmas* starring Kristin Chenoweth and Josh ...
As ...ippa Croft, she also wrote the Oxford Blue series – *The Firs...*
Time We Met, *The Second Time I Saw You* and *Third Time Lucky*.

Phillipa lives in a Staffordshire village and has an engineer husband and scientist daughter who indulge her arty whims. She runs a holiday-let business in the Lake District, but a big part of her heart belongs to Cornwall. She visits the county several times a year for 'research purposes', an arduous task that involves sampling cream teas, swimming in wild Cornish coves and following actors around film shoots in a camper van. Her hobbies include watching *Poldark*, Earl Grey tea, Prosecco-tasting and falling off surf boards in front of RNLI lifeguards.

🐦 @PhillipaAshley

The Christmas Holiday

Phillipa Ashley

avon.

Published by AVON
A division of HarperCollins*Publishers* Ltd
1 London Bridge Street
London SE1 9GF

www.harpercollins.co.uk

HarperCollins*Publishers*
1st Floor, Watermarque Building, Ringsend Road
Dublin 4, Ireland

A Paperback Original 2022

1

First published in Great Britain by HarperCollins*Publishers* 2022

A catalogue copy of this book is available from the British Library.

ISBN: 978-0-00-849432-2

Typeset in Birka by Palimpsest Book Production Limited, Falkirk,
Stirlingshire
Printed and Bound in the UK using
100% Renewable Electricity at CPI Group (UK) Ltd

To Janice
Happy Birthday, best buddy
xxx

Prologue

It was the biggest Christmas tree Krystle had ever seen: twice as tall as her, and topped by a glittering star that almost touched the ceiling. You could barely see the branches for the shiny baubles, stripy candy canes, strings of beads and wooden toys.

It was swathed with tinsel in the colours of a peacock's feathers, shimmering in the light of the fire. Underneath there were presents in every shape and size, wrapped in paper and tied with ribbon and bows.

The room reminded Krystle of a Christmas card that her Auntie Linda had sent her and her mum the previous year. The card showed a family gathered around a tree in a huge room, opening the gifts in front of the hearth.

Standing on tiptoes, she peered through the old-fashioned window. Her feet sank into the soil and water squelched into her trainers. Auntie Linda had loaned Mum the money to buy them but they hadn't lasted long in the rocky, muddy places she'd been to in the Lake District over the past few days.

The instructors at the Outdoor Centre spoke in soft northern accents and smiled a lot. They'd made jokes about the pink trainers and lent her 'proper footwear' for some of the activities. Krystle knew they meant to be kind, but she hated the stiff boots, shaped by someone else's feet. She'd rather have wet socks.

Actually, she'd rather be inside full stop . . . It was already almost dark even though they hadn't had their lunchtime sandwiches so very long ago. Some of the stars were already twinkling and lights peeped out from the tiny cottages in the Thorndale valley.

Krystle was supposed to be waiting at the edge of the village for the bus. All the kids were tired and cold after another long walk, eating crisps and chattering about what might be for dinner at the Outdoor Centre where they all had to sleep in bunk beds.

No one had noticed her slip away from the others towards the grand house with stone pillars. She had been drawn to its glowing windows like she was to the big stores in London that she loved to visit with Auntie Linda. A quick look wouldn't do any harm, would it? Better than standing in the cold while the rain fell and being told to 'keep their chins up' by the teachers, whatever that meant.

She pulled off her mitten and spread her palm over the pane, hoping to feel the warmth of the fire. The glass was cold but she could hear the faint crackle and hiss as the flames leapt. She'd never been in front of a fire inside a house. Auntie Linda had told her they were 'very nice to look at but a lot of trouble' and Mum had said they were too dangerous to have in a flat.

Here in this huge house, the fire looked safe and inviting. Where were the people who owned it? Why weren't they enjoying their beautiful room like the family in the card? If it were Krystle's house, her mum would be curled up on the sofa with a magazine and a glass of wine. Auntie Linda would be in the armchair, her feet on the footstool, a sherry in her hand. Krystle would lie on the rug, reading a book, toasting by the fire, wondering what the presents contained.

It was such a contrast to her real life, which was like a ride on the Southend rollercoaster that Auntie Linda had treated her to. Krystle loved rollercoasters but she didn't want to be on one all the time.

Linda said that Mum was 'doing her best', and Krystle did believe it. She loved her mother but she was often cross and impatient, always short of money and very unhappy. As long as Krystle could remember, they'd moved from flat to flat or 'B&Bs' with peeling walls and the smell of other people's cooking.

As for school, she'd had to change so many times, she'd lost count. Just as she'd made friends, she was uprooted to another place because her mum had fallen out with her boss – and Krystle didn't blame her as they sounded horrible – or refused to 'keep her daughter in this skanky hole any longer'.

Yet things were about to change again. Just not for the better.

Her mother had a new boyfriend, Gus, and they were moving in with him by Christmas. It filled her with dread. He wasn't violent – in fact he largely ignored her – but she felt he'd cast a giant shadow over her life that having a permanent home didn't make up for. Gus made jokes about old people, reeked of aftershave and often had food stuck in his beard.

He also had twin daughters a year older than Krystle, who laughed at her clothes and called her a 'chav'. The Terrible Twins shared a room so Krys would have to sleep on the sofa bed in Gus's 'office', and have to tidy it away every night so that no trace of her was left in his 'workspace'.

The girls had made it clear they hated the idea of sharing their house as much as much she did, especially since she'd pushed one of them in a puddle for teasing her for having free school meals.

If only they could live with Linda . . . but her mum was mad on Gus and told Krys she'd have to make the best of it.

Krystle was tired of making the best of it. She didn't want to wear someone else's boots and she didn't want to go back to London. If only they could move here to the Lake District and live in this house, her mum and Auntie Linda, maybe a dog and a cat too.

She pressed her face to the glass, squashing her nose to the pane, willing herself to be magicked inside the fairy tale world of the Christmas card.

'Krystle Jones, what on earth are you doing?'

The booming voice startled her and she fell backwards into the border with a squelch. She wasn't hurt – didn't think she was – but the shock had made her heart thump hard and made her out of breath.

Above her, a woman towered over her, hands on hips.

'Come away from there! This is someone's private property!'

Miss Braithwaite's bushy eyebrows faced off like two warring caterpillars. She looked taller and wider than ever from ground level. The rain had turned icy and sharp, like tiny needles against Krystle's face.

'S-sorry, Miss Braithwaite.' Krystle pushed herself up on her elbows, feeling the damp seep through her coat to her jumper.

'The minibus is here. We almost went back to the centre without you!'

Krystle let out a squeak of alarm. 'No!'

Miss Braithwaite's frown melted into a kinder smile. She reached down and took Krystle's hand, pulling her to her feet.

'Come on, madam. Of course, we wouldn't leave you behind but a lot of people have gone to a lot of trouble to organise this trip. It's not fair to keep them waiting, is it?'

'No, miss.' She tried to brush the mud from her jeans but ended up smearing it into the denim.

Miss Braithwaite rolled her eyes. 'Don't worry about your clothes. We can pop them in the machine at the centre.' She pursed her lips. 'But those silly trainers are soaked. I'll put them in the drying room for a few days. Don't worry, you can wear your boots for the rest of the week.' She clapped her gloves together. 'Now, chop chop! The driver's not too pleased at being kept waiting, I can tell you.'

With a silent sigh, she squelched behind Miss Braithwaite towards the minibus which was parked at the end of the drive to the house. She glanced back, imagining she could see shadows at the windows; the family returning from a walk to enjoy hot chocolate with squirty cream and little pink marshmallows. Maybe the children would be allowed to open a present early, even though it wasn't Christmas for a few weeks yet. If Krystle was their mum, that's what she would do: let them have one little gift now, just one . . .

'Hallelujah! The wanderer returns!' Miss Braithwaite announced as Krystle climbed into the bus. Some of the boys jeered but a few kids slid admiring glances at her for having escaped, even temporarily.

Far from being annoyed, the driver didn't even look up from his newspaper when Krystle slunk past him. She wrinkled her nose. The bus smelled of wet clothes and fishpaste sandwiches.

Her new friend, Harriet, moved aside so she could take the window seat. 'You're wet,' she whispered.

'Sorry. Better keep away from me.'

Harriet smirked. 'I bet Miss Braithwaite was pissed off.'

'A bit.' Krystle nodded and they both stifled giggles.

The engine rumbled and the bus lurched forward.

Wiping away the condensation on the window, Krystle watched the glow of the house fading away into the dusk. Soon, it was only a memory, lost amid the white flakes falling on the stone walls and fields.

Harriet offered Krystle a Haribo. Her tongue was lime green. 'Where did you go?' she whispered.

'The Christmas card house,' Krystle said, delving into the packet. 'And one day, I'm going to live in a place just like it.'

Chapter One

TWENTY-FOUR YEARS LATER

November 1st

'For God's sake, does it ever stop raining in this bloody place?'

'It's called the Lake District. I guess they need rain to fill up the lakes,' Krys answered, watching the wipers thrash across the Porsche's windscreen.

'Obviously.' Brett fiddled with the wiper stalk. 'Why aren't these things working?'

'They're already on maximum. I don't think they can go any faster. It's your car. Haven't you read the manual?'

'Of course I haven't read the manual. Who reads a manual to find out how the wipers work? It should be obvious. Jesus! What was that?'

Krys couldn't answer for a second. Her teeth were still rattling after the car had lurched forward, crashing down onto the track.

'I think it was a rock. Be careful, Brett. Why don't you slow down a bit? This car's not made for rough terrain like this.'

'It's a four-wheel drive. It's made for off-road driving, though when I bought it, I never intended to be careering down a cart track to the back of beyond. If I don't get a move on, we'll never get to this manor house before dark.'

Better than not getting there at all, Krys thought, steadying herself with a hand on the dashboard. She told herself not to be annoyed at Brett for moaning. Arguing before they'd even reached Holly Manor was not the way to start a 'make-or-break' holiday that was meant to mark a fresh start in their relationship.

Besides, she was the one who'd booked the manor, fully aware it was a mile off the public roads at the head of the Thorndale Valley. She'd read the description on the rental site, although she'd hardly been in a fit state to take in every last detail, with so many conflicting emotions surging through her when she'd pressed 'Book Now'.

If you're in search of glorious solitude in a picture-postcard setting, Holly Manor is your dream holiday retreat, the online description had read. *Immerse yourself in the majesty of the remote western Lake District, while enjoying the luxury and comfort of this traditional Lakeland manor house.*

A drone picture had shown the grand old house standing proud at the head of a lush valley, surrounded by England's highest mountains with its deepest lake virtually on the doorstep.

In the photos, a cosy fire burned in the sitting room, with blankets (almost certainly artisan) draped over the squishy sofa. Vases of wildflowers stood on the antique tables while the kitchen had a gleaming Aga, scrubbed oak table and a dresser full of artfully mismatched china, perfectly in keeping with the age of the property. Krys was impressed by the styling, but it was the emotional connection that mattered.

Even after almost twenty-five years, and the filter of a child desperate for a sprinkle of magic, it *had* to be the Christmas card house. Finally, she was in a position to get inside; the tragedy was it had taken the death of her beloved auntie to finally make her childhood dream come true.

She'd never forget the 'chat' she'd had with Linda, not long before she passed away, not that either of them had expected it to happen so soon. Linda hadn't even been ill, apart from a few minor ailments, as far as Krys knew. She'd lain awake long into the night after their conversation, not wanting to face up to the prospect of losing someone who'd been the rock of her life.

Linda had sat her down in her North London flat over a mug of tea. 'You know this place is rented so I can't leave you much but I've got a little nest egg put by. Now, let's not have any silly comments about spending the money on myself. You're the closest I've ever had to a granddaughter and a daughter too . . .'

'No! I don't want anything!'

'I said "no silly comments".' She gave Krys a stern look. 'So I want you to do something exciting with the money when you get it: nothing sensible or practical. Something you've always dreamed of. Spend it on something that makes you smile – or scares you – anything that you'll remember forever.'

'*You* should treat yourself. I can manage now and I have a good life. Thanks to you.'

'Well, I plan on sticking around for a good while longer,' Linda said. 'But when the time comes, I want you to do something that reminds you of me. Have some fun. God knows, you deserve it after the start you had in life.'

Now, Krys thought, what could be better than spending the legacy on the kind of house that had inspired her all those years ago?

She'd recently finished a stint as Christmas buyer for a big store chain, a job that had provided cover for someone on parental leave. Linda's death in May had hit her hard but there had been no time to grieve properly. Now, the contract had come to an end. Krys had another temporary one lined up after the New Year, but the two-month break was desperately needed. She was on her knees physically and emotionally, and she and Brett had neglected their relationship.

A long holiday in the peace of the Lake District would give them the space and time to focus on each other, even if Brett would have to go back to London for some of the weekdays.

When Krys had searched online for a holiday house in the Lake District, she'd almost fallen off her chair when Holly Manor itself had popped up. The write-up said it had only recently been 'totally refurbished and transformed into a luxury holiday home'. To Krystle, it was as if the manor had been put on the site just for her, a message from Linda to go for her dream.

It would also be the ultimate symbol of how far she'd come, not that she would ever share that with Brett. He was part of the new phase in her life, now she was a successful, independent career woman.

A tingle of excitement shot through her as they drew closer to the manor. After all these years, she was minutes from stepping into her fantasy – if Brett didn't run into a stone wall first.

His knuckles were white on the wheel but he risked a glance at her. 'Remind me again why you were so keen for it to be *this* property?'

'Because I searched for it for *ages*. Because it will be wonderful to decorate it for Christmas.'

'You're supposed to be taking a break from work, sweetheart.'

'This isn't work. It's *fun*. As well you know.'

He gave an indulgent roll of the blue eyes that had attracted her when she'd met him while working on her most recent contract. He was a senior exec with the marketing agency running the store's Christmas ad campaign and they'd hit it off right away. He was handsome, charming and ambitious, and hadn't had a privileged upbringing: not as tough as her own, but nonetheless, his determination appealed to her.

They'd been seeing each other since the spring, and more or less living in each other's flats. There'd been vague chat about them maybe moving in together but nothing concrete had been decided: they'd both been far too busy, flitting about the country and abroad, working long hours and fitting each other in around their jobs.

He'd supported her when Linda died, but within a week, it was back to the daily grind for both of them, a whirlwind of hotel stays and late nights at the screen. Lately, Krys had been thinking that there had to be more to life. With her current role ending anyway, she'd decided to take a couple of months to live – to breathe – after the turmoil of the recent past.

Brett had agreed that they both needed to devote more time to each other or what was the point of staying together? He was also well aware of how important Christmas was to her: how could he not be when Christmas was her actual *job*.

In the dozen or so years since she'd left uni, she'd made a name for herself as a seasonal buyer, sourcing decorations for department stores, garden centres and interiors shops. The Christmas schemes she found and put together adorned dozens of stores but the process always started the previous January. As soon as one Christmas was done, it was time to start the cycle again, visiting trade fairs across Europe, then placing orders and launching the ranges to her own in-store team in the spring, before unveiling it all to the press in July.

She was a real-life 'Mrs Christmas' and yet since Linda had died, the lustre of her dream job had dimmed somewhat and the glitter had fallen off.

In any other year, Krys would have taken her great-aunt to see 'her decorations' in the shops. But this year, she hadn't the heart to go and see them on her own and Brett was too busy.

Linda was also the only person who knew about the Christmas card house. There was no way Krys was telling Brett about that dark afternoon when she was a kid. She'd never spoken to him about her background, how tough it had been growing up in a dingy room with peeling walls, wrapped in a duvet because her mum couldn't afford the electric bill.

He'd no idea how it had felt to be taken on your first and only holiday to the Lakes by well-meaning people and feeling you had to be grateful when you only felt how different your life was from the people helping you. Now she was an adult and her fortunes had changed, by dint of hard work and a slice of luck, she'd made several secret donations to the charity but she still stung from wearing someone else's boots.

She wriggled her toes. She was in a designer pair today and a padded coat that had cost the equivalent of a lot of electricity, even these days. Brett had treated her to the boots and bought a new Barbour for himself.

'You know,' he said, glancing at her as he drove down a rutted track. 'I wish I'd bought that flat cap to match this coat.'

'Why didn't you?' Krys asked.

'That would be going too far down the hipster route,' he said. 'The next thing you know I'd be trading in the Porsche for a scooter and jacking in my job to run a vegan cat café.'

She giggled and Brett laughed back. He could be very amusing, when he wasn't stressed out over work. He took one hand off the wheel to pat her thigh.

'Brett! Watch out!'

'Jeez!' Just in time, he swerved to avoid a huge pothole full of water.

Her pulse raced and she caught sight of her shocked face reflected in the wing mirror. 'Are you absolutely sure this is the right track?' she said.

He tightened his hands on the wheel. 'Snooty satnav woman says so.'

'But the directions didn't.' Krys was running short on patience. 'They said to take the surfaced track off the B road and ignore the s-satnav.'

He cursed as the wheels hit another rock. 'I paid a mint for a decent satnav so I'm bloody well going to trust it. Anyway, we can't turn round now. This track's barely wide enough for the car and snooty satnav woman claims we're only five minutes away.'

Through the rain pouring down and the darkening leaden November sky, Krys searched the fields for a glimmer of light that could be the manor. There was nothing. She was growing worried.

'You know what? I think we should find somewhere like a field entrance or a gateway to turn around and go back to the lane so we can follow the directions.'

'No. We're almost there. Look! Isn't that the house over the fields?' He slowed down to walking pace.

Ahead of them, a stream crossed the road and a few hundred yards beyond it there was indeed a large stone house with lights glowing on the ground floor. Krys wound down the window for a better look, got a face full of sleet and shut it again.

'It looks like it,' she said warily.

'I'm sure it is. Look at those bloody big chimneys. They're the ones you were raving about.'

He was right. The house was topped by four chunky Lakeland chimneys. 'It does look like it but we can't get to it this way. There's a stream across the track. Look!'

'It's only a trickle and it says "Ford" on that sign,' Brett declared. 'And this is a four-wheel drive. It's made for exactly this situation.'

Yes, but . . . The Porsche Cayenne might have been made for splashing through a trickle but it definitely wasn't made for the torrent flowing in front of them that seemed to be swelling by the minute.

'Brett. No. Don't try it. You don't know how deep it is or what might be in it.'

'Like what?'

'Rocks and trees and, um, debris.'

'Since when did you lose your sense of adventure, Krys? That's why I like you! A little stream isn't going to stop us now. Not when we're so close.'

She wrinkled her nose. The stream didn't look *too* bad and there was a makeshift rocky ramp leading down into it. The lights were on in the manor, which meant someone must have reached it safely, and it was a *very* long way back to the road to retrace their steps.

She imagined opening the door to the crackle of a fire, being enveloped by warmth and perhaps the aroma of mince pies that had been baked in the Aga and left for them. It had been a very long drive from North London and it would be *so* lovely to reach the house before dark.

'I suppose we could try it if we're very careful.'

It was all he needed. 'I can't wait to put my feet up with a beer.'

Before she could say another word, he'd put the Porsche into drive mode and plunged down the slope to the stream. Krys stifled a 'wait!' and held on to the seat, telling herself not to be a wuss. It was going to be OK. The Porsche cut through the water and was already moving out of it when it juddered to a halt.

Brett let out a groan. 'Shit.'

Feeling the vehicle shudder with the weight of water around its wheels, Krys tried to stay calm. 'What's that?'

'Feels like a rock under the rear tyres. Damn it, I thought we were out of here.'

Setting his mouth in a determined line, he pressed the accelerator. The car stubbornly refused to move, while the engine screamed in protest.

'Brett. Stop. Just stop. We're stuck. Revving the engine won't help.'

'I have to try.' Brett floored it. The noise of the water was almost as loud as the engine.

'Stop!' Krys shouted. 'Why did you drive in here?' By which she really meant, why did she let him drive her in there.

'Why did you bring us to this godforsaken place?' he snapped.

'Because it isn't godforsaken. We're the ones who've been stupid, but arguing won't help. The important thing is what are we going to do about the situation now?'

He took his hands off the wheel and clapped them on his head. 'Wait for help?'

'No. It's too dangerous, and anyway, who's going to rescue us?'

'The RAC?' He grabbed his phone and swore. 'There's no signal! Bloody hellhole.'

'You knew there was no mobile coverage around here.'

'It's not the Outback, though! There must be a signal somewhere nearby.'

I wouldn't bank on it, Krystle thought. A thud against the door tore her attention away from Brett. Outside, a scarily large tree branch floated past the car at an alarming speed. The stream might not be *very* deep but the current was moving fast.

'I think we need to get out of here. We'll have to unload our stuff and walk to the manor and use the house phone.'

'What?' He snorted in disbelief. 'We can't simply abandon the car in the middle of this river.'

Peering out of the window, she felt her heart beat a little faster. The water was almost lapping the door sills. She could swear the level had climbed much higher in the past minute or so.

'I think we should get out of here now,' she said firmly.

He hesitated and then glanced out of his window. When he turned back to her, he seemed a little paler. 'Maybe you're right, but you stay in the car. I'll go for help.' He hesitated before grasping the door handle.

With a struggle, he opened the door and slipped into the water, cursing. 'It's not raining quite as hard,' he called back. 'Stay dry while I walk up the hill a bit and try to get a signal.'

'Brett. No!'

It was too late. He hadn't heard her above the noise of the stream tumbling past. Krys watched him scramble up the bank and slither down the other side, before vanishing in the rain. She sat for half a minute, imagining how mad he'd be when he returned, his hair plastered to his head, his new boots covered with mud.

'Oh!'

She was sure she'd felt the car tremble.

Goosebumps popped up on her skin and another glance at the water level decided it: she wasn't waiting in the car for him a moment longer. Even if it meant being drenched, she would try to unload some of the bags from the rear seat, in case the water rose even higher. At the very least, she would make sure her overnight bag and some of the boxes of decorations were safe. If possible, she'd also retrieve their suitcases from the boot.

She opened the door although it seemed stiffer than she'd first thought. Then she realised that the water had risen above the sill and was slopping into the car.

Handbag slung over her body, she slid down from the car with a squeak of shock. The water was above her knees, dark brown and icy cold. The bottom of the stream was slippery and uneven and her foot slipped into a cleft between the rocks, causing the water to wet the top of her jeans. Somehow, she managed to pull her overnight bag from the rear seat and sling it onto the bank. However, two of the boxes of decorations were on the driver's side of the car and the water was now swirling around her thighs. Brett's case was in the boot so there was no hope for that.

She hauled herself into the rear seat, reaching for the plastic box with her favourite baubles. She had her hands on the edge of it when the car lurched sideways, leaving her legs dangling from the rear door. She screamed. The car was shaking with the force of the water and the noise was terrifying. She had no choice but to abandon everything.

Chapter Two

'*G*et out! Now!'
    A voice came from behind her and she felt two hands on her legs. Neither of them were Brett's.

She twisted to see a man standing in the stream, holding her by the knees. 'Come on! Before this thing's carried off downstream!'

The water raged around the car and was surging up the slope of the ford.

'Slide down into the water. I'll make sure you won't fall.'

He'd mistaken her reluctance for fear when she was just as worried about her suitcase and, if she was honest, the decorations.

'All our stuff's in the car!' Krys shouted.

'Leave it. There's no time. This isn't a game. It's life-threatening.' The tone softened a little. 'I'm behind you. Slide down backwards.'

A second later, Krys dropped into the chilly grip of the stream. The cold made her gasp and the water closed around her waist. With the current swirling past, she struggled for footing on the rocks.

Next to her, the car groaned and lurched again. Krys let out a yell and the stranger grabbed her arm, pulling her against him. His face was a dark blur in the rain.

'Come on,' he urged, guiding her by the elbow towards the edge of the ford – or where it had once been. The waters surged around her, so powerful she knew she'd be swept away if she let go of him. She stumbled but he caught her and stopped her from falling.

Her heart pounded. 'Sorry!' she said.

'No time for apologies,' he growled. 'Come on. We're almost there.'

Unceremoniously, he pushed her ahead of him, out of the clutches of the stream, which was swelling by the second. She staggered up the other side of the ford then spotted her overnight bag a few feet away, about to be carried off.

'My bag!'

A second before the water reached it, Krys lunged at her bag and scrambled back up the side of the ford, thanking her lucky stars to have her feet on dry land again. Although 'dry' was a relative term. The track was thick with mud and the rain was lashing down from a sky the colour of gunmetal.

She was soaked to the skin yet she was safe. Breathing heavily, she clutched her bag to her chest and found the man next to her.

'You OK?' he said, with eyes full of concern. 'That was a close one.'

'I'm fine, thanks, but I had no idea how fast the water could come up like that!'

'Really?' His expression hardened. 'What were you thinking of, driving into a beck in these conditions?'

'I w-wasn't driving!' she shot back, taking him in properly for the first time. Dripping hair clung to his skull and hung over the collar of his coat. His clothes – an old waxed jacket, jeans and wellies – were all as sodden as Krys's own. He also sounded very pissed off.

'You weren't driving?' Bushy eyebrows met in the middle. 'Who was, then?'

'Brett.'

'And where is this Brett?'

'He went to find help. He thought he might get a signal higher up the lane.'

'What?' The eyebrows shot up. 'He left you in the middle of a river?'

'To get *help*,' Krys repeated. 'We're not stupid.'

'Oh no. Of course not. You drive down a farm track in a flooded area and straight through a beck in spate. Then your husband leaves you to drown.'

Krys fired up with indignation. It was good to have been helped but that's as far as her gratitude went. She *was* angry but not so much with this wild-looking rescuer as with Brett and herself. She should have stopped him, insisted he turn back or taken the wheel herself. She should never have let herself be badgered into taking the short cut – or been persuaded by her own foolish desire to live out her Christmas fantasy.

None of that mattered now. All the decorations and most of their stuff was still in the car.

'Thanks for helping me, but it's too late to change anything now,' she said haughtily. 'What matters is finding Brett.'

The man opened his mouth then shut it. 'OK. I didn't mean to be *rude,* but I can't understand why . . . oh, never mind. You wait in my Land Rover – if that's OK with you – and I'll go and find him.'

'What about our car?'

'Nothing we can do about it for now. It'll have to stay there. Get in, and I'll find your husband.'

'He's not my husband, he's my boyfriend.'

'Whatever. Brett, you say?'

'Yeah. Brett.' Krys didn't mean to be ungracious, but this was not the time for niceties, not that the man seemed used to polite conversation. She followed him up the slope to his Land Rover, which was as rough round the edges as its owner.

Still, she felt bad about soaking the seats until she saw the state of the interior. The seats were muddy and covered in grey fur. The vehicle smelled of dog too. While the man went round to the rear, she climbed inside and sat down, shivering with the cold.

'Oh my God!'

She suddenly felt hot meaty breath against her neck, and something licking it. She whipped around to find a border collie grinning at her, its tongue lolling.

The man was back at the door. 'Ah, you found Jake! Come on, boy. Job for you.'

Jake wriggled through the gap between the seats. His claws dug into her legs as he used Krys as a human springboard to bound out of the door.

'Don't worry, Jake will find Brett,' the man said, adding grimly, 'Or he'll die trying. He was training to be a search and rescue dog until last year but he failed the course.'

'Great. V-very r-reassuring,' Krystle said.

'You're shivering. Could be a sign of hypothermia. Make sure you stay here. We won't be long.'

We? It had come to this. Krys hugged herself to stop from shaking. The reality of the situation had hit her. Brett could be injured – or worse – and here she was alone at the mercy of the Wild Man of Thorndale and his incompetent dog. The lights of her dream Christmas card house glimmered through the gathering gloom; a tantalising glimpse of a fairy tale that once again seemed out of her reach.

With a tormented scrape, the Porsche succumbed to the torrent and was carried downstream, clattering against rocks until it finally crashed against a footbridge.

Krys wasn't a crier: she'd learned long ago that tears were useless to change any situation. However, it was all she could do not to let out a wail as the car tilted on its side. Through the open door, her suitcase fell into the river, followed by several boxes of decorations.

She held her hand over her mouth in horror as the boxes tipped over, spilling out their cargo of glass angels, vintage baubles, wooden stars – gifts from Linda, junk-shop finds and pocket-money treats. The torrent had no mercy and no regard for sentiment and memories. It took everything away, carrying the precious decorations – and all they meant to her – on the swirling waters.

Chapter Three

'Arghhh! Owww!'

'Lean on me. We'll soon be at the car.' Max tightened his arm around Brett's back as he limped back towards the Landy.

'Should I be moved in this condition?' Brett wailed. 'Ow!'

Max gritted his teeth. The man hadn't stopped moaning since he'd found him sitting on the fellside barely fifty metres from the car, waving his phone in the air. He'd obviously been trying to find a mobile signal. Max could have told him he'd no chance. Luckily, Jake had found Brett, though his greeting – a full face-wash with a hot tongue – hadn't gone down too well, especially as Jake had had liver for breakfast.

'The main thing is to get you into shelter.' Max said. 'It's probably going to snow.'

'Oh really? You could have fooled me,' Brett said sarcastically.

Mustering his patience, Max reminded himself that Brett was, technically, a casualty even though he was a pain in the arse.

'Let me help you down to my car.'

'That's OK, we just need a bit of a tow out of the stream,'

Brett said, as they shuffled down the short slope towards the Land Rover. 'My girlfriend is still in there.'

'No, she isn't,' Max said, his patience evaporating. 'It wasn't safe so I helped her out. She's waiting in my car.'

'Oh . . .' Brett seemed puzzled. Initially, Max hadn't had the heart to tell him that the Porsche was a write-off. However, on hearing that Brett had thought it was safe to leave his partner inside the vehicle in a flooded stream, he changed his mind.

'Your car's a goner, mate.'

Brett stopped, his expression agonised, though, it transpired, not with pain. 'A "goner"! What do you mean?'

'Carried downstream from what I saw just before I found you. Fortunately your girlfriend decided to get out before it was swept away. It's wedged against the footbridge.'

'Wedged under a bridge?' Brett swore, then let out a gasp. 'Oh my God. Krys might have been drowned!'

'If she'd stayed in there, it's a possibility, but she's OK so you can relax.'

'*Relax?* You're joking, pal. My car's a wreck, my clothes are soaked, all our stuff's ruined and I've broken my ankle.'

'It's not broken.'

'Are you a trained medical professional?'

'No, but I've been on some mountain rescues and if it was broken, it would really hurt.'

'It *does* really hurt!'

'Sprains can be very painful but I don't think it's fractured.' Max had done a rudimentary exam before he'd helped Brett to his feet.

'Thanks but I'd rather get it X-rayed and have a doctor look at it. Can we call out a rescue team? Air ambulance, maybe?'

'I'm afraid not. The MRTs all over the Lakes are on flood rescues and the helo's been tasked to a life-threatening emergency on Helvellyn.'

24

'Helo?' Brett frowned.

'The rescue helicopter.' Max smiled at Brett; after all, the man was way out of his comfort zone and in genuine discomfort with his twisted ankle, even if he was a prat. 'I'm sorry to break it to you, but I'm all you've got for now.'

'Brett!'

Having spotted them, Krys rushed out of the Land Rover and up the slope towards them. She seemed far more concerned about Brett than he was about her. Or perhaps he was being too cynical, Max thought. It had become his default reaction of late.

'Oh my God! What happened? Are you badly hurt?' Krys took Brett's arm.

'I slipped and hurt my ankle.' Brett put on a surprisingly brave smile. 'It's not too bad and according to Max here, it's not broken.'

'*Max?*' Krys stared at him.

'Yes. Sorry. Didn't have time to introduce myself. I'm Max. Now, let's get you both out of this rain. You sit in the middle.'

Krys opened the Landy door, but before they could help Brett inside, he spotted his car further downstream. It was lying on its side against the stone bridge, water flowing over and round it. Max hoped it wouldn't take the bridge itself out, or that would block one of the routes for the farmer.

'Jesus Christ,' Brett murmured.

Krys rubbed his arm. 'I know. Your lovely car and all our stuff . . .' Her voice wobbled a little. 'My decorations are all gone too. I saw them floating away.'

Brett swore. 'You can get some more. As for the car, I can claim on the insurance, and after all,' he grasped Krys's hand, 'all that matters is that you're safe.'

Finally, thought Max.

'I'll help you in,' he said gruffly, as realisation dawned that these people were now his responsibility and that they probably weren't going to like what he had to say.

'You have to be kidding?' Brett said when Max explained that he and Krys wouldn't be able to stay at Holly Manor that evening. The three of them were sitting in the front bench seat of the Land Rover, with Jake in the back, panting with excitement at all the drama.

'B-but the house is only a little way away. I can *see* the lights. We're on the right side of the stream now, aren't we?'

The hope in Krys's voice softened Max's response.

'Yes, but there's another river between us and the house. You can't see it but it's much bigger than this beck. The bridge over that is almost under water too. I can't risk it.'

'So – so what are we going to *do*?' Brett sounded like a scared child.

'I'm afraid we'll have to wait until morning and hope the water levels go down.'

'Morning?' Brett was white-faced. Max thought he must be in shock.

Krys cut in, a little shaky but clearly ready to make the best of things, unlike Brett. 'OK, it's not ideal but we have to deal with the situation as it is now. Is there a B&B we can stay at? Or a farmhouse that will put us up for the night?'

'I'm afraid not,' Max said, summoning people skills he'd barely used for years. 'This track leads to the head of the valley. There's only one property between here and Scafell Pike.'

'What's that? Some abandoned hovel, I bet!' Brett curled his lip. 'I suppose you're going to say we'll have to stay in a pigsty!'

'No one keeps pigs round here,' Max snapped. 'Only sheep.'

26

'I don't care if they keep fucking unicorns. What the hell are we going to do?'

'Brett! I'm *sure* Max is only trying to help us.' Krys turned to Max. 'Look, this has been a bit of an ordeal, and while we're very grateful for your help, you said there's a house around here?'

'I said "property". It's pretty basic.'

'We don't care. We'd be happy to stay anywhere.'

Brett grunted, then muttered, 'What have we done to deserve this? Will someone tell me?'

Max relented and decided to stop winding him up. 'The property is mine and you're welcome to stay with me for the night.' His heart sank even as he issued the invitation. 'Though I warn you, it's not what you might be used to. It's an old Bothy and it doesn't have many home comforts but it's watertight and you'll be able to get some rest while you dry out.'

'Watertight . . . that's something to be grateful for,' Brett muttered. 'Though we can't dry out our clothes because my bags are in the bloody car.'

'I can lend you some stuff,' Max said, reining in his annoyance. If he hadn't happened to be venturing to the village to collect some supplies, this barmy couple might have been out all night in the storm, or God forbid, even worse.

'We *are* grateful,' Krys said. 'It's been a shock, that's all.'

'I know, and that's why it's important for you to get to shelter.'

'If you're in the mountain rescue, don't you have some radio thing we can use to call for help?' Brett said.

'I'm not in the local team. I only help out occasionally, and anyway, they don't keep radios in their houses. They have pagers and they're only issued with radios when they're on a shout. In a genuine emergency,' Max added.

'Jesus.'

'Brett!' Krys cut in. 'I'm sorry, Max. We're not au fait with how things operate up here.'

'Why would you be?' Max said, feeling sorry for Krys. Brett might be an idiot, but he was willing to make allowances for her – for now.

'First thing tomorrow, as long as the water level has gone down, I'll drive you to where you can find a signal and you can let the police, your family and the Holly Manor housekeeper know what's happened. If not, I'll walk until I get a signal and I can arrange for your car to be retrieved and have you on your way. If anyone does happen to see your car in the river, they'll be worried and might call the emergency services.'

'Thanks,' Krys said. 'You *do* look very pale, Brett, and it's freezing. I think we should accept Max's kind offer and let everyone know we're OK.'

Brett nodded. 'Yeah, sure,' he grunted then swore. He rubbed his face and flinched away from the dog, who panted happily inches from his face.

'He's called Jake,' Krys said, with a glance at Brett. 'It's only his way of making friends.'

Before he could start laughing, Max shoved the Landy into gear, wishing he could magic his unexpected guests into the luxurious surroundings of the manor so he could be alone again. He wasn't sure how he was going to cope with making small talk with anyone after so long, let alone two entitled metropolitans. The woman didn't seem too awful but he'd have been happy for Brett to vanish in a puff of smoke.

'Hold on,' he said, as the Landy lurched forward with a tortured crunch. 'It could be a bumpy ride.'

Chapter Four

'And you're sure there's no other alternative?'

Krys winced at Brett's comment when Max stopped the 'Landy' outside his cottage. Although, while she was determined to make the best of things, even she thought 'cottage' was being very generous to the single-storey building. Its thick stone walls resembled more a barn or a cow shed. As for Max, he made no secret of the fact he didn't want them there.

'Believe me,' he said. 'If there was the remotest possibility of finding you somewhere else, I'd have driven you there this instant. Stay here.' He got out, then, possibly realising he'd spoken to them as if they were unruly collies, added: 'Please.'

'Ow!' Brett yelled.

Unable to wait to be released from the rear, Jake had squeezed through the seats and used Brett's lap to launch himself out of the driver's door.

Once Max was out of earshot, Brett closed his eyes and said: 'What are we doing in this dump?'

'Keeping warm and safe in an emergency,' Krys said, rubbing a space on the Landy window so she could take a closer look at the 'dump'.

The slated roof looked in good repair and the metal chimney sticking out of it was definitely a good sign. She'd also spotted a log store and a couple of other small outbuildings towards the rear of the Bothy.

'For all we know, this guy might be a serial killer,' Brett said.

'I doubt it. He may be a bit grumpy but he *does* help out with the mountain rescue. They don't employ psychopaths.'

'They don't employ anyone. They're volunteers.'

Krys turned back to Brett. 'Then he must be OK and we don't have much option other than to trust him. Why don't you google him or see if anyone's gone missing round here lately?' she added wickedly.

'I can't. There's no wi-fi. No phone. No one knows we're here. Classic serial killer scenario.'

'That's Netflix. This is real,' Krys shot back. 'Seriously, he said we can speak to Holly Manor first thing and then we'll be able to let the local police know we're safe.'

'We might not be safe by morning.'

They waited another few minutes but there was no sign of their host.

'Now, where is Mad Max . . .' Brett said with a smirk. Even though she was shivering, Krys had to smile. They heard barking and snarling from one of the outbuildings. 'And his killer hound,' Brett added.

'Jake's a big softy,' Krys said then heard footsteps behind the car. 'Shh! He's back.'

Max pulled open the door and her heart rate rocketed.

'Jesus Christ!' Brett shouted.

Max was brandishing an axe.

'We need more firewood,' he said morosely. 'I was putting diesel in the generator so there's light and power in the Bothy. While I was in there I chopped some more wood for the fire.'

He managed a smile that was more of a snarl. 'So you won't have to sit in the cold.'

Krys burst out laughing in relief and because she felt silly, but Brett simply closed his eyes. He was soaked and probably had a sore leg and she felt sorry for him.

'I also managed to get a text out to the local MRT base so they know you're safe,' Max said. 'And won't worry about the car.'

He handed Krys his phone and she saw the reply from 'Thorndale MRT Team Leader': *Thanks for letting us know. Will inform police and Nikki at cottage co.*

'Thank goodness something's gone right today,' Brett muttered.

'Thanks,' Krys said, pleased to recognise the name of the Holly Manor housekeeper.

'No problem. You're lucky I could send a text in this weather. Now, let's go inside.'

He helped Brett out of the car and into the Bothy, with a degree of care Krys hadn't expected.

Luxurious it wasn't, but it was dry and hopefully would be cosy. The main room was larger than it looked and divided into two spaces. The thick stone walls had been plastered and whitewashed. At one end was a kitchen area, with an old cooking range, sink and rather ancient looking fridge. The seating was arranged around a wood burning stove which still seemed to be giving off some warmth. There was a sagging sofa and a high-backed leather chair, which had clearly been occupied by Jake, as the cushion was covered with dog hair.

'Down, boy!' Max called when Jake tried to reclaim his customary seat.

With a confused glance at his master, Jake did as he was told and lay down near the stove.

'First things first. You can change in the bathroom,' Max said, indicating a door. 'It's through that wooden door next to the fridge. If you want to leave your wet stuff in the shower cubicle, I'll sort it out in a minute.'

'Thanks,' Krys said. 'I'll let Brett go first then take my case in there and put some dry stuff on.'

'If you leave your boots here, I'll put them by the fire. Brett, I'll find you something to wear. I can't guarantee it will be stylish but it should fit.'

While Max went into his room, Krys helped Brett off with his boots, and took her own off, along with her soggy socks. Brett was shivering and uncharacteristically subdued.

'It'll be OK,' she said to him.

'Yeah,' was all he could manage, eyeing the room. 'Remind me again that I'm not having a nightmare?'

'It's all too real,' Krys said, kissing his cheek. 'You'll feel better with dry clothes on.'

The door squeaked open and Max emerged. He'd changed out of his dripping clothes into faded jeans, torn at the knee, and a fisherman's sweater that had seen better days, judging by the hole at the hem. He'd also combed his hair. Krys did a double take. He looked less like the Wild Man of Thorndale now and a little more like a model from an outdoor sports catalogue. It normally took an awful lot of expensive styling to achieve that tousled rugged look, she thought, deciding not to mention it to Brett. He spent a fortune trying to get his hair just right, and she'd had to move half of her own toiletries from the bathroom cabinet to make room for his 'products'. She dreaded to think what would happen when he saw himself in the mirror, though personally, she preferred the natural look.

Max handed over a pile of folded clothes and two old towels. 'They're Jake's,' he said. 'The towels, that is, not the clothes.

They're all clean. I don't have visitors so I don't keep much spare linen.'

Brett stared at the towels. Krys took one from the top of the pile. 'Thanks, Max.'

The briefest of nods. 'Clothes should fit you. Best I could do, I'm afraid. Why don't you use my room while Brett's in the bathroom? Bring your wet stuff out and I'll sort it.'

'Thanks. We're, um, very grateful.'

Carrying the towel and clothes, Brett hobbled into the bathroom.

Leaving Max stoking up the wood burner, Krys went into his bedroom.

It wasn't as cosy as the living area but it was equally neat and plain, with thick white walls and a slate floor. There was an iron bedstead with a dark blue duvet and a similar woven blanket to the ones Krys had spotted in the pictures for Holly Manor. A handmade rug in fir green softened the flagged floor and a pile of books was stacked on the oak bedside table. Together, these little comforts added a touch of homeliness to the otherwise spartan room that reminded Krys of a monk's cell.

A cupboard with double doors was set in one wall opposite the window, where she presumed Max kept his clothes. The small window, set deep in the walls, had no curtains. It was dark outside but Krys assumed that with no neighbours for miles, Max had no need to cover the windows.

Even so, it was weird stripping off in front of the bare glass and she hurried the task, even though it was tricky taking off her soaking jeans and jumper. After drying herself on the towel, she dug out a long-sleeved tee and sweatshirt and a pair of trousers from her salvaged bag.

Her mind went back to the river, where her main suitcase must by now be underwater with all her 'best' clothes in it.

Clothes she'd carefully chosen and cherished . . . There was no point crying over them. What could she do about it now?

Of course, Brett could claim for the clothes and jewellery on the insurance. She'd have to as she couldn't afford to replace the necklace he'd given her, a bracelet and glamorous coat that she'd treated herself to.

Other things were lost forever and that hurt far more. While some of the decorations had been high-end, free samples, others were irreplaceable, because of the memories attached to them.

Those trinkets were way more precious than designer labels and diamonds. Some had been gifts from Auntie Linda and Harriet, even her mother . . . then there was the little wooden rocking horse she'd bought with an unexpected fifty pence she'd found in the street when she'd been on her way to a Saturday job in the chip shop . . . and a fabulous glass Eiffel Tower that she'd brought home from her first foreign business trip to Paris. That had been a symbol of how hard she'd worked to achieve her hopes and dreams.

Now they were all gone, shattered against the rocks, their shards flowing into the lake.

Maybe she would go down there tomorrow, once they were at Holly Manor, and try to find them. You never knew, they might be retrievable, possibly repairable.

Once more, Krys hardened her heart against the threat of tears. She should count her blessings, as Linda used to say – and she had many these days, the most important of which was that she and Brett weren't in the car when it was swept away.

Suppressing a shiver, she sat on Max's bed and hastily pulled on some reindeer socks and a pair of ballet pumps, the only item of footwear in her overnight case. She checked her other precious possession: her iPad, saying a silent thank you that it was snug inside its waterproof case. Her book, a hardback edition, was there too.

Krys picked it up: Dickens's *A Christmas Carol*.

To Krys
Happy Christmas my darling girl
This is the original Christmas fairy tale
Auntie Linda XXX

At fourteen, she'd warmly thanked her auntie, while in secret thinking she'd no interest in reading a book written two centuries before. She liked reading, but if she was honest, she loved crafting far more.

Krys hadn't got on with her mum's new partner, Gus, and after a year of trying to share his home with his own twin daughters, she'd found it unbearable.

Gus's Ghouls (as she'd nicknamed them) had no time for an impostor who wore funny clothes, some of which Krys had made herself or adapted from charity shops. They thought she was 'a weirdo' for spending her time making 'stupid rubbish' and said she 'needed therapy' for her obsession with Christmas decorations.

One night, Krys had packed her bags and gone round to Linda's, begging her to take her in. It turned out to be the best decision she'd made. At first she'd missed her mum and continued to see her. But gradually, she'd had less and less contact with her mum and while she'd felt guilty for being happier with her great-aunt, the situation was better for everyone.

With her own room, and peace and quiet, she had had time to focus on her crafts. Linda had taken her to a craft fair and she'd fallen for the little felted decorations. She'd learned how to make her own and turned out tons of cute woodland animals, flowers and Christmas characters as well as brooches, key rings and tree decorations.

She'd had a stall at the school Christmas fair and sold the lot, much to the disgust and envy of Gus's Ghouls. After buying a gift for Linda, Krys had saved the profits and invested them in more materials. Soon, before she'd even been to art school, she'd got a nice little business going at local craft fairs and fetes.

Her mother had moved to the other side of London with Gus and co, and after that, Krys rarely saw her. The phone calls dwindled. Linda tried to get her mum to make more contact: Krys overheard some of their conversations, but she knew the truth. Her mother had made a new life, and Krys wasn't part of it.

She was hurt, deep down, more than she ever let on. Like the borrowed boots, she didn't fit into her mother's new life, so she shut the door on the past and focused on the future and reinventing herself as Krys.

With the help of a scholarship from a charity trust, and a good result in her A Level Art, she'd won a place at a prestigious London Arts college to study a degree in interior design.

Since leaving, she'd had jobs with two stores and a garden centre chain, where she'd bought and supervised products for the seasonal displays and eventually become a senior buyer. The job had involved everything from buying the Christmas decorations to overseeing the organisation of a dozen Santa's Grottos at all the branches.

Her latest role had been a whirl of trade fairs in the UK and abroad, meetings, presentations, long hours, late nights, launches and wining and dining clients. It was her dream job – unimaginable when she'd first peered through that window – and she was living it. Then Auntie Linda died.

She'd realised since that she was already surviving on fumes even before Linda had passed away. She never seemed to get enough sleep, was always grabbing meals, constantly running on adrenaline and saying yes to everything.

Then came the funeral. Instead of reuniting her in grief with her mother, it only deepened the rift between them.

With no other close relatives except her mum, it had fallen to Krys to organise everything. Her mother hadn't even offered to help; claiming she was 'rushed off her feet' with her job and her growing family of step-grandkids.

Her comment when Krys had asked if she wanted to be involved was: 'You're much better at dealing with this stuff, Krystle.'

Somehow, Krys had got through the funeral, dealt with Linda's small estate and carried on with her round of work and launches. By September, the store branches were starting to display her stock.

However, the sparkle had gone. For the first time ever, she had no Linda to take into the store and say: 'Those are my decorations.' There was no one to explain to where each had come from, or why she'd chosen it. There was no one to treat to a champagne afternoon tea in a posh hotel afterwards, and no Linda to dress the tree with.

She didn't want to spend Christmas in London and that's when she'd had the idea of renting Holly Manor.

Brett had been dubious at first about her 'bunking off to the far north', but when she'd explained, he'd understood.

'It could be fun and you need the rest. You deserve it. I can spare a week at the start of November and then I can pop back a couple of times and come up for a proper Christmas. You won't be too lonely without me, will you?'

'No, because I plan to spend the time decorating the house in my own time at my own pace. My way. I can take some pictures and visit the local area, the quirky little shops, and chill out. And we can walk.'

He'd laughed. 'I'll pack my boots! You'll need a car, you know, after I've left.'

Although she could drive, Krys didn't possess a car. There was no point when her flat was two minutes' walk from a Tube station and she'd nowhere to park it anyway.

'I'll hire one when we get there but I might just chill out for a few days. Read a book . . .'

She realised she'd been sitting on Max's bed, still staring at the dedication on the title page.

She really would read it again, now she had so much time on her hands. With Brett away in the week, she'd have a lot of it. She shivered, and for the first time realised what a remote place this was. With the sleet pattering on the windows of the Bothy, and no one within reach, she wondered if she'd made a mistake in coming to Thorndale and expecting it to solve so many of her problems.

Chapter Five

As she stooped to put the hardback back in her case, Krys's eye was drawn by the books stacked neatly on Max's bedside table. Mountaincraft, basic first aid, a DIY manual and a biography of Beethoven.

OK, she probably hadn't expected any romance or comedy but it was all very dry reading matter. She was ready to return to the living area when she spotted something lying behind the books. It was a photo frame, face down, almost slipping off the edge of the table.

It seemed to have been tucked away out of view, and hastily. Had Max hidden it while he changed, knowing that he'd have to let Krys in? She itched to turn it over and see what was in the picture, but when she did, she found the frame was empty.

Who kept a photo of – nothing?

Unless the picture had been hastily removed?

Despite her curiosity to know more about their uncommunicative host, she left it as it was. With any luck, they'd find out more from Max during the course of the evening . . . then again, she had a strong suspicion that he would only reveal the bare minimum. A man who chose to live in a glorified shack in a remote area, like a hermit, couldn't be very keen on socialising.

Once again, Brett's remark about Max being a serial killer popped into her mind and disturbed her. She didn't think he was a murderer, but it wasn't beyond the realms of possibility that he might have *had* to live away from people . . . or be seeking an escape from something or someone.

She brushed her hair, left it loose and draped the towel around her shoulders to keep her top dry. She wondered what Brett would be wearing and how sore his ankle was.

When she emerged, the wood stove was crackling and Max was pouring boiling water into three mugs. The aroma of instant coffee had never smelled so good. Brett wouldn't touch it normally but she hoped he was going to be suitably grateful now.

'Brett's having a shower,' he said and held up a bottle of amber liquid. 'Medicinal tot?'

'Definitely. Thanks.'

He poured a slug into each mug 'I made a lamb hotpot yesterday. I was going to make it last, but we can have it all tonight with some bread. I warn you, it's not gourmet . . . You're not veggies, are you?'

'Neither of us are and we're very grateful.'

With a grunt that could have meant anything, he handed a mug to Krys and she sat on the sofa, cradling it in her hands. Alcoholic steam rose from it.

'This is delicious. Wow.'

'It's only from a distillery down the dale but it's not bad.'

'You can say that again. I'll have to get some as presents for friends.'

'I'll give you directions to the place,' he said. 'So you won't get lost.'

Unsure whether to be amused or annoyed, Krys exchanged a look with him and a flicker of a smile passed over his lips. 'So, you've rented Holly Manor until Christmas?' he asked.

'Yes. I'm taking a break from my job.'

He nodded but didn't enquire further as to what she did.

Krys felt obliged to elaborate, in the hope it might draw him out. 'I'm a buyer. I specialise in sourcing and designing seasonal displays for luxury lifestyle stores and garden centres. You know, Easter, summer and Christmas, of course. They call me Mrs Christmas in the trade.'

She added a smile that wasn't returned.

'Mrs Christmas?' Max grimaced. 'I would have thought this was one of your busiest periods.'

Jake lay at his feet, watching Krys through brown eyes.

'Yes and no. By this stage all the hard work is done. The decorations and displays are all in the shops, or on sale. The cycle starts again in January, and by July, the Christmas goods are launched to the press. They're available in some shops by September.'

'As you can probably tell, I've no call for shops, particularly the luxury lifestyle ones.'

He was so deadpan as he said it, it was impossible for Krys to tell if he was being humorous or just bluntly honest. Probably the latter.

'Not even at Christmas?' she said, deciding to call his bluff.

He downed a glug of whisky. 'Especially not at Christmas.'

Krys gave a deep inner sigh.

A moment later, the door to the bathroom squeaked and Brett slunk out, a sheepish look on his face. It was all Krys could do not to giggle. The borrowed jeans were an inch too short and, it had to be said, a little snug around the waist. The sweatshirt bore the logo 'Thorndale Country Show: Steward' and his feet were clad in hiking socks.

41

'N-nice to be in dry clothes,' she managed, almost shaking with suppressed laughter.

'That's about all you can say,' Brett muttered. 'Stupid question, but I don't suppose you've got any moisturiser, mate?'

'I've got some axle grease in the workshop,' Max replied.

'Very funny,' Brett grunted and Max grinned, though Krys might just as easily have described it as a snarl.

Brett hobbled to the settee, grimacing.

'I'll find you some painkillers,' Max said. After rummaging in a kitchen cupboard, he handed them over with a glass of water.

With a grunt of thanks, Brett took them and leaned back, with his eyes closed. He looked shattered. The sore leg and loss of his car had hit him hard and she left him to rest while she helped Max in the kitchen area, half expecting him to snap at her to leave him alone.

'Do you get called out often with the mountain rescue team?' she dared to ask while he put the casserole in the Aga to warm up.

'Not often. Like I said, I'm not officially a team member, but I'm here if they're short of hands. I'm not formally trained but I know the area well and I've friends from the village who are proper members.'

He *did* have friends, then, Krys thought, so perhaps he wasn't as isolated as they'd first assumed.

'If they need me,' he went on, 'they call in on their way to the Pike. The main car park isn't far and they often rendezvous there. Obviously, I report anything too, if I'm worried.'

Krys pressed on, relieved to have found a topic he did seem willing to talk about. 'You said Jake was a search and rescue dog?'

'He completed part of the course when he was a pup, but he wasn't suited. He's too excitable and easily distracted though he's got a hell of a nose for sniffing people out. Sadly, his owner passed away suddenly, so I took him on.'

'I think he's lovely,' she said.

A fleeting smile passed over his lips. 'Yes, he's a good boy, aren't you, mate?'

Jake appeared at Krys's side. 'He knows we're talking about him,' she said.

'Or he can smell the food.' Max ruffled his fur. 'Have you got a dog?' he asked.

'Oh no. Never have done. We couldn't have pets when I was younger,' she replied. 'Never in one place long enough.'

'That's a shame . . .'

'Maybe I will, one day. I live in a flat at the moment though and I'm away an awful lot with my job. I travel all over the country and sometimes abroad.'

Krys surprised herself. She hadn't thought of getting a pet until – well, until Max had asked her. Her lifestyle had made it out of the question, but Linda's passing had opened up so many 'what ifs?' and alternative paths her life might take. She'd fully assumed she would simply have her two months off then resume her life in the New Year as Mrs Christmas . . . start the whole festive merry-go-round all over again.

She already had two trips planned to Europe, and meetings with suppliers at trade shows. Time, tide and Christmas waited for no man or woman.

'I've been super busy,' she said, finally realising how exhausting the past few months had been.

'Even Mrs Christmas must need a break,' Max murmured.

They balanced their dinner on their laps, watched by Jake. The hotpot was fragrant with herbs, with lamb melting off the bone and winter vegetables. Max provided hunks of crusty bread to soak up the sauce. Glasses of tap water were produced but even that tasted sweet and purely delicious, which was odd considering Krys had had enough Lakeland water to last a lifetime.

'Is this sourdough?' Brett asked, dipping a hunk in the hotpot with a relish Krys hadn't expected.

'It is,' Max said. 'A bakery van delivers to the stores in Thorndale. We're not total barbarians.'

Krys giggled.

A trickle of gravy ran down Brett's chin and into his goatee. 'Yes, but it must be lonely out here in the back of beyond?' he said.

'It suits me.'

'How long have you lived here?' Krys asked, thinking of the photo. That must have had a person in it, family at least, if not a partner? Though why someone would hide a photo of a mate, she wasn't sure. She didn't think it would be a picture of Jake, somehow.

'A few years now,' Max said.

'You've been here *years*?' Brett raised an eyebrow. 'Never tempted to go back to civilisation?'

'I've tried it and I'm happier with my own company.'

'But what if something goes wrong?' Brett sounded incredulous.

'Like driving into a stream?' Max shot back, a glint of mischief in his eye.

Brett raised his water glass. 'Touché.'

'I've survived so far. The Bothy may not be luxurious but I've got all I need.'

'I can see that,' Krys said, feeling tension crackling between the two men. 'It's very comfortable here.'

'Like I say, I've all I want. It's surprising how you cope when you strip away the unnecessary fripperies, even the so-called essentials.' He caught her eye.

'Believe me,' she said. 'I understand *exactly* what you mean.'

Max seemed about to reply – possibly to contradict her – but thought better of it. She'd expected him to mention her job, the decorations, the 'fripperies', but something in her tone must have stopped him.

Good job, because she would have been drawn into telling him why she understood what it was like to live without luxuries, without Christmas presents and without even a roof over her head as basic as the Bothy. He spoke as if he had once had a life very different to the one he lived now. Had he made a 'lifestyle choice' to hole up like this? Or had it been forced upon him by circumstances?

'Hmm,' he said.

They finished the rest of the meal in relative silence. After dinner, Max got out the whisky bottle again for the three of them. Normally no whisky drinker, Krys had water in hers but Brett and Max had it neat.

Max held up the bottle. 'Another?'

Brett waggled his glass. 'Don't mind if I do. After all, it is medicinal. It's surprisingly good, considering it's not an actual single malt.'

Krys winced but was happy that Brett seemed reasonably content, even though the whisky and the pills were probably not the best combination.

Max left the cap off the bottle. 'Krys?'

'No, I'm OK, thanks. I might go to bed soon. We mustn't keep Max awake,' she said with a hard stare at Brett.

'I'll get this down me then grab some sleep. If I can . . .'

Ten minutes later, Brett's glass was still half full but he was spark out, head back, eyes closed and mouth open.

'Best leave him,' Max said softly. 'You can have my bed. I'll sleep on the floor.'

'No, I couldn't turn you out of your own bed.'

Brett let out a snicker but was clearly out for the count.

Max picked up a blanket. 'Let's not argue and wake him up, eh? He needs the rest. I'll change the sheets for you.'

'But you'll be on the hard floor,' she whispered, secretly not having relished the prospect herself.

'I've slept in far worse places,' he said softly, laying the blanket over Brett.

While Max changed the bed, Krys used the bathroom. It was basic but clean. No signs of frippery. No bath oils and lotions, eau de toilettes and grooming products. Just a shower, basin and loo and a bar of soap to wash her face with. Actually, the soap was rather a surprise and there were several others stacked on the slate window ledge. They were of the handmade artisan variety tied with raffia and a tiny card that read: Thorndale Natural Soap Company. One even had rose petals embedded in it and another had a cinnamon stick tied to it. Krys closed her eyes and sniffed it, inhaling the scent of the season, imagining herself in the roll top bath at Holly Manor, with a glass of fizz and carols playing from her iPhone.

She knew it was probably sexist, but she felt as if a woman had given Max the toiletries, and she wondered who it was.

She opened her eyes to see sleet pattering the window pane and beyond only impenetrable darkness. Auntie Linda had always loved describing places outside London as 'the back of beyond'. This truly was. A frisson of excitement travelled through her.

Now that they were safe, she'd decided to embrace the adventure again. It had something of the spirit of her trip to the Lakes when she was young, being dragged out of her comfort zone and hating some of it – the cold, the wet, the rucksack – but finding it impossible to forget.

Everything was going to be OK: apart from the car, of course. This trip had been meant to help them bond, but had so far only widened some of the cracks in their relationship. They'd have to work hard to mend those, starting with recovering Brett's precious car, a symbol of his hard work.

After hastily brushing her teeth, she went back to the sitting room, thinking of how she and Brett were going to deal with the recovery and insurance people in the morning. They certainly couldn't relax until the car was retrieved and they'd hired a replacement.

Brett snored beneath the blanket, under the watchful eye of Jake, who seemed about to lick his hand then thought better of it.

With a smile, Krys ventured into Max's room to find him standing by the cupboard in the wall. He closed the latch on the door and turned to her, with a surprised expression on his face as if he'd forgotten she and Brett were there. *It must be a shock to have guests, or intruders,* she thought.

There was faded linen on the bed, but smelling fresh and aired.

'Are you sure about this? I feel I've taken over your space,' she said again.

'I wouldn't have offered if I wasn't sure.' He picked up a foam mat and a mummy-style sleeping-bag from the side of the bed. 'At least I don't have to sleep under a bivi, and I'll have Jake to keep me warm. Now, goodnight. Get some rest. You've had quite an ordeal.'

Krys climbed into bed and switched off the lamp. A sliver of light showed beneath the door to the main room, but within a minute that was extinguished and she was plunged into total darkness. She lay there, trying and failing to make out shapes.

Nothing pierced the night. No street lights, moonlight, not even the blue or red of chargers, routers, nightlights or TV standby. She felt for her bag by the bed, seeking her phone, simply for reassurance that if she needed to get up, she would be able to see if the lamp somehow failed.

Stretching lower, her fingers brushed the floor and closed around something smooth and hard that was definitely not her phone. It was rounded and felt as if it were made of wood . . . She switched on the lamp, blinking in the glare.

The object was a miniature spinning top, made of hand turned wood. It was grooved, solid but somehow delicate, made of a wood that graduated from a rich brown to blond. It must have rolled under the bed.

Carefully, she placed it on the bedside table and switched off the lamp again, snuggling under the down duvet as the sleet pattered against the pane. From the living room came the sound of Brett snoring from time to time and Jake snuffling, but other than the three of them there wasn't the slightest hint of human activity beyond the stone walls of the Bothy.

Still, Krys felt safe. With civilisation within reach – at least by morning – her limbs relaxed. They could soon be out of the way of their reluctant host and start their holiday.

Chapter Six

Max tossed and turned in the sleeping bag. With Jake yipping in doggy dreamland, he hadn't expected to get much sleep. However, it wasn't the canine snuffles keeping him awake, it was the presence of other humans. He hadn't had another person to stay overnight since he'd moved into the Bothy two-and-a-half years previously.

Hardly anyone had crossed the threshold apart from the builders initially, and on a couple of occasions, members of the mountain rescue team in need of a place to shelter.

Pressure on his legs told him Jake had decided to act as a footwarmer. The dog's eyes reflected the dying embers of the stove. He probably sensed something was different, and he wanted to protect Max from the strangers in the house.

Being honest, it hadn't been as awful as he'd expected to share a meal and a drink with his guests. Brett had irritated him and he couldn't really understand why Krys was with the guy. They seemed mismatched; out of step.

Even soaked to the skin, worried and understandably annoyed with both Brett and Max, Krys was a very attractive woman.

Even more so, standing in her reindeer socks, her dark brown hair falling over her shoulders, ready to climb into his bed. As for Brett, Max supposed he might be considered good-looking by some women: he was tall and looked like he went to the gym but he was also self-obsessed and more worried about his precious car and clothes than her.

Mystifyingly, Krys seemed to care deeply for the guy whereas Brett cared only about himself, in Max's opinion.

He couldn't respect a man who'd left his partner at the mercy of a flooded stream, though he suspected Krys wouldn't thank him for saying that. She wasn't looking for chivalry, that was for sure, and had certainly put him in his place when he'd – patronisingly – talked about managing without home comforts. After all, it *was* his choice to live his stripped-back lifestyle and he wished he hadn't made the comment.

While Brett spoke in smooth accentless tones, Krys had a North London twang that she didn't try to hide. Her clothes were new and he'd seen the labels when he'd hung them to dry by the range: a decent jacket, a nice pair of boots. Yet she had the look of someone who'd been through the fires, clawed their way up and developed a tough shell. Almost being swept away and losing her suitcase hadn't upset her as much as it might have. The only thing that seemed to have brought her near to tears was the loss of the Christmas decorations.

As Jake shifted to lie across his knees, Max allowed himself a smile. He was making a lot of assumptions about his unexpected guests.

He could only imagine the assumptions they were making about *him*.

* * *

'It's snowed!' Krys declared the moment Max opened the door into the Bothy the next morning. Jake shook himself, scattering icy clods over the flagstones.

'First snow of the winter,' he said, finding her excitement infectious despite himself. 'A skittering down here but the high fells are covered.'

'I saw through the window. They look amazing.'

Max had to agree. The sky was a washed-out blue, the fell tops thickly covered from five hundred metres, the snow sparkling in the morning sunlight. Her face lit up with delight, like a kid on Christmas morning. She wore the same expression as his little brother – the same one Max himself must have had – walking into the sitting room at his family home all those years ago to find the tree surrounded by gifts. His parents had made a big deal of the season, and Max had loved Christmas then . . . back when he was innocent and untainted by loss and self-reproach.

He stamped his feet on the mat. 'It'll bring out the thrill seekers. The MRT will be swamped with city-types who hare up here at the first snowflake, without the right equipment.'

'I can promise you we've no intention of haring up any mountains,' Krys retorted.

'Good.' He unlaced his boots, ashamed of his crabbiness.

'Is it unusual to have snow at the start of November?' she said tightly. 'Obviously, I wouldn't know, being a city-type.'

Max softened his tone. Since when had he become such a grouch?

'We can have snow on the tops for eight months of the year, on and off,' he said, hardly able to meet her eye. He noticed the sofa was empty and a rumpled blanket on the cushions.

'How's Brett? I left him asleep when I took Jake out before dawn.'

'He's changing in your room,' she replied archly. 'I trust that meets with your approval?'

'Were his clothes dry?'

'Not too bad, but he asked if he could borrow the jeans a few hours longer. We'll have them laundered at Holly Manor and return them. Then we can be out of your hair.'

'Forget it. Keep them. I can buy some more.'

'I thought you didn't go shopping.' Her gaze was shrewd, her voice teasing. Max rather liked it: it had been a long time since any woman had teased him, unless you counted the mountain rescue team, where banter was a requirement of the job.

'I can use an online store,' he said. 'Though that may be hard to believe. I've been meaning to get some new stuff – as you might have noticed, I'm hardly on trend. I'll put some breakfast on. I've not got much in but plenty of eggs and a bit of bacon. I can do a fry-up.'

'Great. It's been ages since I had bacon and eggs. My aunt loved a cooked brekkie. She always treated me and my mum on a Sunday morning . . . and when I moved in with her we had bacon butties every weekend.'

'Your aunt sounds like a woman after my own heart,' Max said, relieved that Krys seemed to have called a verbal truce, which was more than he deserved. He was also more intrigued by her past than before.

While the bacon sizzled in the pan, and Krys opened a tin of food for Jake, he thought of her comment about her auntie. She'd obviously had to leave the family home for some reason and live with this aunt, which confirmed his guess she'd had a less than ideal start in life. He didn't probe further, however, partly because he didn't want to pry and also because it would have meant forging more of a connection – relationship – than he dared risk.

How sad was that? Not asking any questions so he didn't have to listen to the answers or empathise? It was self-preservation, he reminded himself. He came here to avoid intimacy – of all kinds.

He slid the bacon onto a plate to keep warm in the oven and broke the eggs into the hot fat.

Krys offered to slice the loaf so Max found her the bread knife and board.

'How do you cope here?' she asked, cutting the loaf carefully. 'Without any proper communication or tech, I mean? I couldn't do without being connected, for my job or in normal life.'

'I manage. I do have a mobile and I can use the wi-fi at the pub or a café if it's essential, though I've never been one for social media anyway so when I moved here, I didn't miss it.' Obviously he knew what Instagram, Facebook and Twitter were from his previous life, but when he'd stepped out of the rat race to live at the Bothy, he'd made a conscious effort to avoid the Internet as much as possible.

'What about the TV?'

'I don't miss that either. I have a digital radio to keep up with the news and I listen to the odd classical programme. Mostly, though, I'm busy maintaining the Bothy . . . or doing other stuff out of doors.' Just in time, he stopped himself from being more specific. 'I like to get up into the hills as much as possible.'

'I was right when I said I won't be haring up any mountains but you'll probably see us around while we're at the manor, or at least see me. I want to make the most of the great outdoors, unplug from tech and connect with the local area. So we do have something in common.'

Max broke a few more eggs into the pan and the sizzle was loud. 'Hmm.'

'In fact, I was hoping to support local businesses while I was here and get involved in the community,' she went on, standing back from a board full of neat slices. 'Are there any Christmas events in Thorndale? Craft fairs, carol service, party at the pub – all the usual jollity?'

'I wouldn't know. Like I said, I don't do Christmas, not even vicariously. I'm the last person to ask about jollity.'

'I think I've worked that out. Sorry for asking you.'

Again, he'd been rude, almost without meaning to – as if it had become a habit. Or perhaps he needed to nip any further conversation about Christmas – about anything – in the bud. He didn't want to be friendly with the neighbours, however attractive one of them might be.

Max slid the eggs onto the plates. 'Your breakfast's ready. As soon as we've eaten, we'll have you on your way. I'm sure you're desperate to get out of here.'

'Not as desperate as you,' Krys retorted and Max could find no way of contradicting her that sounded sincere.

Chapter Seven

Krys could barely contain herself when the fat chimneys of Holly Manor came into view, peeping above a stand of fir trees. She wanted to jump out of the Land Rover and walk – run – the rest of the way shouting 'Yay!!' With Brett's injured ankle, that was impossible, and anyway, she didn't think either he or Max would appreciate such a display of childish delight.

After breakfast, Max had driven them there, along with their few remaining possessions. It had only taken ten minutes, via the ford, which was now back to a stream. Brett had cursed when they'd seen the Porsche was still lying against the bridge so Krys had squeezed his hand tightly.

As they'd reached the lane, Brett finally found a signal so he could phone his insurer and the local garage to sort out the recovery. He tapped away on his phone, sending messages to a bunch of people.

'Will the stream flood again?' she asked Max once they were safely through the ford.

'The snowmelt will raise the rivers but most of the snow is on the tops and will work its way down over the next day or so. It shouldn't cause a flash flood like the downpours we've had this past week,' he said.

'That's a relief.'

'If you're worried about your holiday, the forecast is dry for a few days but I'm sure you'll see every kind of weather between now and Christmas.'

With an inner sigh, Krys didn't bother trying to make small talk again. She'd tried to be civil to Max and he'd rebuffed her. Perhaps there was a pleasant person lurking deep under the frosty exterior, but she wasn't going to waste time trying to dig him out. Looking sexy and knowing how to cook a decent breakfast didn't make up for being grumpy and rude.

Her Christmas card house was her sole focus now – and it was almost in touching distance. It was as if a magical being had waved a wand over the landscape and transformed it from a grim backwater to a postcard stunner. The mountain tops were covered in snow like a pure white cloth with lacy edges. The valley itself had a sprinkling of snow, but it was already melting.

A short while later, they were turning off the lane, over a cattle grid and up a bumpy gravel track towards two stone pillars.

Engraved on the left-hand pillar were the words: HOLLY MANOR.

The excitement bubbled over. 'We're here! The Christmas card house.'

Brett looked up from his phone. 'The *what*?'

'Nothing. I just think that this place looks like it should be on a Christmas card,' Krys said hastily.

Max hadn't taken any notice and was already on the drive.

'I'll help you out with your stuff,' he said, rather grudgingly.

'What's left of it . . .' Brett muttered.

He seemed too busy brooding on what he'd lost to appreciate the beauty that lay in front of him.

The traditional Lakeland house – over two hundred years old – was her memory made into reality, and she knew why it had made such an impression on her.

By any standards, child's or adult's, it was a gorgeous place to live. The stone façade was double-fronted, with sash windows either side of a navy front door and a row of three windows above. The morning sun glinted off the glass and the remains of the snow glittered with sun sparkles on the driveway. Melting snow dripped from the holly bushes and yew trees, with the softest of sounds.

'It's wonderful.'

Brett limped forward to join her, Max carrying her bag behind.

Brett stared up at the house. 'Hurrah! Civilisation at last!' he declared.

He shook Max's hand, more enthusiastically than Krys had expected. 'Thanks, mate. You've been a lifesaver.'

'Hardly,' Max muttered.

The front door opened and a tall, wiry woman in her mid-forties hurried down the steps. 'Oh, you poor things. What an ordeal you've had. Come inside and get warm. I'm Nikki, I run the housekeeping team for the letting agency.'

'Hi there, are we glad to see you,' Brett said.

'I bet you are. I've got the manor all cosy for you.' She turned to Max. 'You're a hero saving my guests from the beck!'

'I don't think Krys and Brett will describe me as a hero after they've had to spend a night at the Bothy.'

'Rubbish! I bet it was super cosy. Better than spending a night out in the snow.'

'It was.'

'Shame our car's still under water,' Brett said.

'But we're safe, which is what matters. Thanks to Max,' Krys added.

'I heard you had a narrow escape. News travels fast round here,' Nikki said. 'Welcome to Thorndale.'

'Bet we're the laughing stock,' Brett mumbled.

'On the contrary, everyone's glad you're OK.' Nikki was being very diplomatic, in Krys's opinion. 'Now, come inside and make yourselves comfortable.'

Brett hobbled after Nikki but Krys lingered at the foot of the steps. She wanted to thank Max even though she knew he'd hate it.

'Thanks so much for helping us. We won't forget it.'

Impulsively she reached for his hand to shake it.

He didn't flinch but there was a look of great surprise on his face, and he did take her hand in a brief but firm handshake. 'You're welcome.'

'Maybe we'll see you around?' Krys said.

'I doubt we'll be able to avoid each other. Goodbye.'

He got into the Land Rover and finally Krys walked into Holly Manor, with the rumble of the engine in her ears, before it faded away. She prided herself on being a 'people person' but Max was a lost cause. She saw him drive off with a mix of regret that he'd stayed deep in his crusty shell, and relief that she could now relax and enjoy her stay with Brett.

And one look at Holly Manor banished Max from her mind as she was dazzled by the size and character of the house. It had been worth every penny of Linda's legacy. Her auntie would have adored it. Once again, Krys squashed down any tears, hearing Linda in her ear, saying: *What are those tears for, you daft thing? You're here, you made it. Now, get on with enjoying it.*

'I've lit a fire in the drawing room,' Nikki said cheerfully. 'Why don't you go in there and warm yourselves? Tea or coffee?'

'Coffee please,' Krys said.

'Any chance of a cappuccino?' Brett's voice lifted in hope.

'Of course. I'll pop the machine on. I'll bring some gingerbread in too. I don't normally greet guests in person, but after what happened to you, I thought I'd make up a fire and see if you needed any help. The wi-fi code's in the information book on the coffee table,' Nikki added. 'Do you want a tour or do you want the coffee first?'

'Coffee, first. I need to make some calls. Think I'll put my feet up in front of that fire,' Brett said.

'I can't wait to look round,' Krys said, itching to explore the rest of the house but feeling loyal to Brett. 'Why don't I come into the kitchen and help with the drinks while Brett calls the insurer?'

Nikki seemed glad of the help and Krys followed, eager to scope out more of the house.

'Wow. This is even bigger than I'd expected.'

The room was airy, with high ceilings and two big windows looking out onto the garden, with its hollies and beech trees, still clinging to shrivelled leaves. Copper foliage littered the lawn and a squirrel scampered across it.

'That's a red squirrel!' Krys cried.

'It is. They're becoming rare now but they will still come to the bird feeders on cold days like this.'

Nikki loaded the coffee machine with a cappuccino pod. It was bright red and gleaming, one of a number of shiny appliances. The oak units were of a traditional design but the appliances looked brand new. She imagined decorating the hearth over the Aga with holly and greenery from the garden for her Instagram feed. Maybe she'd bake some mince pies and create a Christmassy scene . . . Actually, make that gingerbread . . .

Nikki had opened a paper wrapper and was arranging the slices, dusted with brown sugar, on a plate.

'This room is huge,' Krys said. 'Has it always been the kitchen?'

'Oh yes, right from seventeen ninety-five when the manor was built, though it was several rooms up until the sixties apparently. The owners knocked the scullery and laundry room into the cooking area to create this space. It's been refitted many times since then, of course.'

Nikki arranged the plate on a tray while Krys made herself a cafetiere of coffee.

'There's a welcome hamper on the table,' she said. 'And some fresh food in the fridge, so you won't go hungry on your first day. If you're stuck, I can pop to the stores.'

'No, don't go to any more trouble. We'll manage with what's here. We're very grateful to have finally made it in one piece.'

Nikki laughed. 'Yes, this must seem the lap of luxury after the Bothy.'

'Yes, though Max did his best to look after us. It could have been a lot worse.'

'He does his best. Actually, you can see the Bothy from the upstairs rooms,' Nikki said. 'Along with the lake and the Scafells. I always think the Bothy looks like it's hiding in the shadow of the mountain though it's stunning on a day like this.'

'It must be lonely for him,' Krys said, shivering at the idea of the mountain's shadow creeping over the little house as the sun went down.

'That's the way he likes it. He has Jake to keep him company and I think that's all he needs. Max likes to keep everything he does under wraps . . . I shouldn't say anything but it's true that still waters run deep.'

'Oh. In what way?' she asked.

'Well . . . the truth is, I don't know *that* much. No one does, apart from Amina perhaps. She runs the post office and stores,' Nikki explained. 'He turned up about three years ago and bought the Bothy. It was in a terrible state but he renovated it almost single-handed and lives in it off-grid.'

'I noticed,' Krys said, amused and intrigued.

'The villagers have given up trying to get him to join in any community events and he doesn't welcome visitors.' Nikki smiled. 'As a rule. He has been known to pitch in when the mountain rescue need an extra pair of hands. He goes to the pub most Saturday evenings and visits the stores but he's not a joiner, if you know what I mean.'

'I realised he liked his private space. It was very good of him to help us.'

'Oh, he helps anyone who needs it. He's been on searches, provided shelter for the teams when they've been out on a shout, and he does a bit of maintenance on their vehicles. It's only through Amina that we know anything of his past. Apparently, her cousin's friend used to work with him down south. Some tech business or other. They say he had a breakdown, decided to quit the rat race and come back up here.'

'So he's from here originally?'

'He did mention he was born in the Lakes and left when he was a teenager. He's polite and helpful, in his own gruff way, but we've given up pushing him about his previous life. It's not fair on the man when he's come up here for some peace and quiet. Many people come here seeking an escape and I respect that.'

'Of course.' Krys was still processing the news. No wonder Max had seemed gruff when he'd had to play host to two city-types, especially a woman who styled herself Mrs Christmas.

'Oh dear. I promised not to gossip and now I've done just

that. Poor Max. If he came to escape from people, he chose the wrong place, eh?'

Nikki said it lightly enough, but Krys could tell she felt guilt for talking about Max. She left soon after, reiterating her offer to call her if they needed anything.

Krys looked back on their stay at the Bothy with a fresh perspective and decided not to pass on the information to Brett. They wandered around the house together and ended in the master bedroom, where Krys went over to the window and gazed out. It overlooked the rear of the house, where the lawned gardens gave way to fields edged with dry stone walls that scrambled up the fellsides at crazy angles. Eventually even the walls stopped and the barren rocky slopes rose to the summit of Scafell Pike, England's highest mountain.

A sunray broke through high clouds, bathing the valley in light and making the lake glitter.

'It might sound silly,' she said. 'But I feel as if Linda's here with us.'

Brett's arms encircled her. 'Not all the time, I hope.'

He was smiling at her, his eyebrows raised, a hint of mischief in his eyes.

'Definitely not.' Krys was pleased to see his sense of humour back. He was a kind man, and generous, under the shell he'd built around himself. Krys knew he'd felt he had to prove himself and he sometimes gave the impression of being a rich boy.

He'd lavished gifts on her and taken her to swanky restaurants and the opera. It was a lifestyle she could never have dreamed of when she was younger.

Many people would have been delighted, and she was very thankful to be able to enjoy such comforts, but it gave her far more satisfaction to pay her own way. Modest luxuries, bought with her own money – hard earned from her own efforts – meant much more than expensive presents.

'This is more like it,' he said, stretching out on the leather sofa with his leg on the footstool. 'The insurance are sorting things out. I'm waiting to hear back from them about a hire car but they say we should have one delivered here tomorrow.'

'That's good. I'll have to see about hiring some wheels for myself before you leave.'

He took her hand. 'Thanks for taking care of me. I know I was a pain but I wanted this trip to be perfect for you. I blame myself for driving into that stream. It was stupid and you could have been hurt.'

'Forget it. We're here now. We'll have to go out and buy some new clothes.'

He slid her a cheeky look. 'We've no transport so we'll have do without them for today.' He pulled her to him and she thrilled at the twinkle in his eyes. His spark was back and she could never resist that handsome face.

'Absolutely.' As the morning wore on, Krys was still pinching herself to believe she was at Holly Manor. After they'd made love, she'd walked around the upstairs of the house gazing out of every window, her jaw dropping at the view from all sides.

There were three other bedrooms, and the two at the front overlooked the driveway. Krys wandered into the larger and sat in the window seat.

There were more fields and walls, but also several streams winding their way into Wastwater, England's deepest lake, which she'd read had been carved out by a glacier in the Ice Age. The hills on one side plunged down a thousand feet and were so steep that they were walls of scree – bare rocks sliding down from the fell tops. The lake itself was a mirror, reflecting the mountains. It was dramatic and awe-inspiring.

'Now I know why,' she'd murmured to herself, thinking of how it had been voted as the UK's favourite view a few years before.

She longed to pull on her boots and set off on a walk but Brett had no clothes that were dry enough. Nikki had found him an old pair of 'garden clogs' from the boot room, much to Krys's amusement. They'd have to wait until the hire car arrived and they could go into the nearest town for some new outdoor gear.

Brett was in the sitting room, talking on his phone in front of the fire. He'd done a pretty good job for one with no experience of making up a fire and was amusingly proud of himself. He'd rustled up some toasties from the local cheese, bread and chutney in the hamper and Krys was now in the kitchen, scrolling through her phone to see what she could make from eggs, sausage and potatoes.

She'd decided on a Spanish style tortilla and was taking down the copper frying pan from a rack above the central island when she noticed a small wooden object nestled on the shelf.

It was a bird – a robin judging by the ruby wood on its chest. It looked hand-turned, like the top she had found in Max's bedroom. It nestled in the palm of her hand, two beady eyes gazing back at her. Krys had seen thousands of hand-crafted pieces in her time, and knew instinctively that it was by the same person who'd made the spinning top in the Bothy.

The workmanship was unmistakeable. Resolving to ask Nikki if she knew who'd made it, Krys replaced it and set to work making the tortilla.

Brett opened a bottle of wine from the hamper and they sat in front of the fire demolishing the tortilla before getting an early night.

The following morning, Krys took a long soak in the tub, using the handmade toiletries from the local soap company and thinking – weirdly – of Max.

When she came downstairs, Brett was in a bathrobe, tapping away on his laptop in the small room that served as a study.

Wrapped up warmly herself, she made a hot chocolate and took it into the gardens. Beech leaves crunched under her boots after the overnight frost, and scarlet berries shone like jewels in the holly trees. She found a bench in a sunny spot and sat there cradling her mug, drinking in the fells, which were criss-crossed with stone walls and dotted with sheep. Closer to home, the gardens had some flower borders, though almost everything lay dormant, ready for the northern winter to come.

However, there was still plenty of rich colour in the autumn leaves and the evergreens. Her decorator's eye lighted on the emerald of holly, ivy and yew in the grounds and the brown of pine cones scattered on the grass. As Christmas drew nearer, it would be lovely to decorate the house with fresh foliage, gathered from the garden and countryside.

She thought of how she might style the house once she'd managed to get hold of some new decorations – and a tree of course. She'd read about a Christmas tree plantation at Firholme House, a country estate near Keswick. They delivered larger trees in the local area and Krys was determined to have one that did justice to the high ceilings of Holly Manor.

It would need a lot of decorations . . . and her quest to replace her lost ones would have to start almost immediately, both online and at local shops and craft fairs.

After sitting for a while, she took her mug to the kitchen. Brett was engaged in a heated conversation – hopefully not on Zoom, given that he was still wearing his bathrobe. With any luck, he would be done soon, so they could relax and get outdoors.

Krys went back into the garden with her mobile and snapped a few photos on her phone, meaning to upload them to her

Instagram account at some point. However, for now, she revelled in the luxury of being unplugged, listening to the jackdaws in the yew trees and watching a friendly robin pecking around the bird feeders.

She wondered if Brett might go for a walk after lunch . . . they needed food and his courtesy car was due to arrive any time so they could venture out. She went back inside, where he'd finished his call and was standing in the sitting room, mobile in hand, staring out of the window.

She walked up behind him and slipped her arms around his waist. 'Oh good. Your call's finished. I've been thinking: the hire car should be here anytime. Let's go out and get some proper outdoor gear.'

Brett turned around and hugged her to him. 'I just got a call from the car company. It'll be here in ten minutes.'

'Great! We need food and I'd love to explore.'

'Ah, Krys, I'd love to explore too but . . .' He screwed up his face and alarm bells rang.

'"But" what?' Her skin prickled.

'I need to get dressed.'

She laughed in relief. 'I should hope so. You don't want the car people to see you like that.'

'True.' His smile melted away and he took her hand. 'But I need to go back to London too.'

It was a bolt from the blue and threw her off kilter for a moment. 'What do you mean?' she managed. 'You have to go back to London? When?'

'This afternoon, I'm afraid.'

She let go of his hand. 'What? We've only just arrived.'

'I'm gutted, babe, and if there was any way of avoiding it, I'd stay. There's a crisis at work. Our biggest client has had cold feet about the TV campaign we proposed and is threatening to pull out altogether. How will it look if the marketing director is swanning around on holiday?'

'There's video conferencing . . .' she said, still trying to process that he was leaving so soon.

'This can't be sorted over a screen. I need to show up in person and read the body language. There's bound to be something behind their jitters: in fact, I've a nasty feeling that another agency might be trying to muscle in. It's hanging by a thread now. How would it look if we lost the contract because I couldn't be bothered to pop back to London?'

Krys understood about the need to meet people in person. You needed to see people's reactions and body language, respond to that and build relationships outside of the office. However, 'popping' back three hundred miles after two nights away? 'But your ankle . . .'

'It's much better, and you're here for the next two months. I can be back by next weekend, promise, maybe sooner if we can steer the project back on track.'

She nodded. She wasn't going to whine and certainly not beg. It was disappointing, especially given their shaky start.

Now she'd be rattling around Holly Manor on her own.

'I'd better get my own wheels sorted straightaway,' she said firmly.

Brett pulled her to him and kissed her. He pushed her hair out of her eyes. 'This is why I love being with you so much. You're strong, capable. Nothing fazes you. I admire that. And I can collect some of your clothes from your place – and mine – while I'm in London.'

'Good thinking. Can't have you running around naked,' she said, hiding her disappointment with humour she didn't feel.

'Oh, I don't know . . .'

Krys laughed but slipped out of his embrace. The very last thing she felt like was consolation sex.

A few hours later, she stood at the doorstep with him, trying to put on a brave face. He was in his own clothes now. Max's jeans and sweatshirt had been abandoned in the laundry room, the pair of garden clogs had been left in the boot room.

'I'll be back before you know it,' he said. 'You'll be OK here on your own?'

'Of course, I've spent nights on my own in far worse places than this.'

'I know, darling.' He kissed her. 'You're amazing.'

'Am I?' Krys said the words in her own head while he jogged to the car and jumped in. She didn't feel amazing. She felt abandoned, which was ridiculous when she'd managed on her own for so long. It was the contrast between her hopes and plans and reality that stung. This was meant to be a fantasy that included Brett. It wasn't going to be half so much fun with no one to share it with.

He closed the car door and drove off, without even a wave out of the window.

She was being silly and yet, as the engine faded away between the high stone walls, she was thinking about his words that morning.

Loved being with her. Admired her. Strong and capable.

She should have been flattered. She'd striven to be strong and capable. It was great to be admired and have someone enjoy – love – your company.

Saying he loved being *with* her wasn't the same as that he loved *her*, though.

The question was: did she *want* to be loved by Brett?

Only two people had loved her as far as she knew. Her mum

– who still did love her but very rarely told her so – and Auntie Linda, who'd said it every time she'd seen or spoken to her.

Now there was only one.

Was it wrong to want – hope – that one day, in the not-too-distant future, there might be another?

She'd always been too busy for a serious relationship. Never looking for it until . . . now?

She shook herself back to reality and common sense. Brett was gone and she'd be fine. She hoped he'd be careful and his ankle would hold up on the long drive back to London. Max had strapped it up at the Bothy and Krys had rebandaged it with supplies from the manor's first aid box.

Turning back to the house, she gazed up at the grand facade. For now, she had the place completely to herself. In all her life she'd never been so far from other people.

She wasn't sure whether to be excited or terrified.

Chapter Eight

Krys was up early the next morning, ready to walk into Thorndale to buy a few supplies and explore the village. Her first night alone hadn't been quite as restful as she'd expected. Owls had hooted and the wind rustled the trees. There had also been some eerie cries from the garden that she assumed – hoped – were the local wildlife.

She already had a craving to see other humans, so armed with a walking app and an OS map, she set off through the gates of the manor and onto the track.

It was cold but the sun was out, lighting up the russet and orange of the fells. A few pockets of snow clung on to the mountains, while ribbons of water tumbled down their flanks into the becks. Under a pale blue sky, breathing in clear air, it felt great to be unplugged.

Gradually her thoughts wandered from when the hire car would arrive and how she'd ever replace her decorations, to how beautiful the bracken was and how cute the sheep were, with their heart-shaped faces and curious stares as she strolled by.

She almost took a wrong turn before checking the app and

eventually finding the stile that took her on the footpath that led by the edge of the river to the village. To her relief, she couldn't see the wrecked Porsche from her route.

Brett had said the recovery company would retrieve it and he'd message her when they were on their way. Even better, he'd be back at the weekend too, and in the meantime she could finally indulge in some 'me time'. With the birds flying across her path under vast open skies, she felt a peace and exhilaration that had been missing in the months since Linda had passed away.

Smoke spiralling from chimneys signalled that the village wasn't far off. Just as the cottages came into view, she passed a modern stone building with a large sign saying: Thorndale Mountain Rescue Team.

It had a radio mast and two large doors like an ambulance station, one of which was open, showing the specially adapted Land Rovers. Krys shuddered to think that the team might have been called out to rescue her and Brett. She really would have been ashamed to show her face in the village if that had happened.

Turning away, she headed on to Thorndale centre. When she and Brett had arrived, they'd been so busy following the satnav in the foul weather that they'd hardly noticed the cluster of grey buildings.

Under this morning's bright sky, the place looked straight from a Beatrix Potter tale. Twenty or so homes huddled around a small green in the centre, all made of the same grey stone as Holly Manor, although on a smaller scale. The fragrant scent of woodsmoke hanging in the air made her nose twitch.

As well as the cottages, there was a village inn called The Cock (she pictured Brett sniggering) and a post office with stores. It occupied a building with a shop on one side and what must be the proprietor's home on the other, judging by the garden.

Several wooden tables were stacked by the house wall, and through the window of a glass lean-to, Krys could just make out a counter with a chrome coffee machine on it. An 'A board' was folded up by the gate, with faded chalk announcing coffee and drinks. The café was clearly closed for now.

A red pillar box stood on the pavement at the front, next to a little shed stocked with bundles of firewood, and containers of anti-freeze and de-icer. Clearly the residents were hunkering down for a hard winter, and Thorndale Stores was the place to find everything.

With a childlike sense of anticipation, Krys stepped inside. A bell rang as she did so, making her smile. It reminded her of the shop on the corner of Auntie Linda's road. It had closed when Krys had been a teenager but she still recalled it vividly.

And Linda would have *loved* this place too.

It was a real Tardis, with odd rooms shooting off it, accessed by steps marked with hazard tape. The postmistress was serving a couple from behind her screen, while her assistant, a spindly young guy, sold a lottery ticket to a man who was wearing cargo shorts despite the cold.

Krys took the chance to wander round, passing racks of postcards and displays of Kendal Mint Cake. There were walking sticks, waterproofs and fleecy mittens alongside batteries, mobile chargers and the day's newspapers. A shelf of books held everything from *Fifty Shades of Grey* to *Best Routes up the Pike*.

Remembering her main reason to visit the shop, Krys grabbed a basket and ventured into the food area. She collected a sourdough loaf, some milk, cheese, yoghurt and berries, remembering just in time that she'd have to walk almost two miles home to Holly Manor. A proper shop would have to wait until her car arrived the following day.

The gift area held racks of Christmas cards and a range of what Linda had called 'knick-knacks', and her eye settled on some very pretty soaps tied with raffia. They were the same brand that she'd been surprised to find in Max's frugal bathroom, as well as her own at the manor.

They were so pretty, in jewel-like translucent shades, that she decided she'd buy some as gifts before she left. They'd make a great stocking fillers for a couple of her favourite suppliers and her London friends.

She spotted a mini bottle of the whisky that Max had given her and Brett. It was so small, she decided to add it to her basket, along with a packet of homemade gingerbread . . . it would go very nicely with the whisky while she was curled in front of the fire alone.

She might also make up a parcel of Lakeland treats for Harriet, who she still saw regularly. They'd kept in touch since they'd met on the Outward Bound holiday. Harriet had trained as a nurse and worked at one of the big London teaching hospitals. She was married with two little children now. The local goodies would make a lovely reminder of how they met and the bond they'd formed.

With her basket growing heavy, and mindful of the trip home, Krys decided to call it a day. She was about to leave the gift area when her eye caught more temptations.

One corner of the display was given over to wooden ornaments, almost certainly made by the same craftsperson who'd made Max's spinning top and the robin in the manor kitchen. Krys picked them up, enjoying the smooth surfaces and the warmth of the colours. She sniffed them, inhaling the subtle scent of wood.

And oh! – she caught her breath. There was a tiny angel and several mini Christmas trees, all with cord threaded through the top.

Her heart beat faster. It was an omen.

She *had* to have them. They would be the first step to replacing the precious items lost in the flood. She knew she'd have to order most of the stuff online, and that a lot of it would come from far flung places or be free samples from suppliers, but it would mean so much more to rebuild her stock of handmade, personal decorations.

She looked around for a label or any information to reveal who the maker was, but found none, so she added the decorations to her basket in case they were snapped up by someone else.

Determined not to be tempted by anything else, she headed straight for the counter. The postmistress, who reminded Krys of a glamorous TV presenter from a countryside programme, had swapped places with her assistant and was now working the till.

'Hello, can I help you?' she said.

Noting a name badge that read 'Amina', Krys heaved her basket onto the counter. 'Thanks.'

'It's an eclectic mix,' she said, as Amina scanned the milk and the angel.

'It always is in this place.' Amina smiled, and rang up the whisky and wedge of local cheese. 'Are you staying locally?'

'Yes, at Holly Manor.'

Amina froze, the scanner poised over the robin. 'You must be one of the people who almost drowned in the beck. You had a close shave there.'

'I know . . .' Krys felt herself blush. 'Almost drowned' sounded very dramatic. 'We were very lucky that Max came along.'

'He's a star!' Amina exclaimed.

'Hmm. He – um – told you what happened, then?'

'God, no! Max wouldn't have told us. He hates attention. No, Nikki's brother was with the team leader when Max texted to say you were OK. Everyone in the village knows about it now.'

Of course, Krys thought, *obviously*.

'I'm sorry. The gossip in this place . . . we were all very relieved for you,' Amina went on. 'Though it must be a right pain in the arse to hear everyone talking about it. It's worse than *EastEnders* round here.'

Krys had to smile too. 'We were grateful to Max,' she admitted. 'I'm hoping the recovery people will come out to remove the car later.'

'If not, the farmer would shift it with his tractor, but I'm not sure your insurer would be impressed.'

'Maybe not!'

'So, was all your luggage in the car?' Amina asked.

'Virtually. I managed to save my overnight bag and our phones but my suitcase and a load of Christmas decorations must be in the lake by now.'

'Ouch. I am sorry.'

Amina scanned the wooden trees.

'That's why I've bought these, to replace the lost ones,' Krys said, adding them to her bag. 'The decorations had a lot of sentimental value,' she explained, in case Amina thought she was being trivial in chattering about a few bits of tinsel. 'Some were from my auntie and she died earlier this year.'

'I'm sorry for your loss.' Amina looked as if she meant it. 'Were you very close?'

'Yes. She practically brought me up. She loved Christmas and so do I.'

Amina gave a sympathetic frown. 'It's our busiest time of year and I'm knackered by Christmas and glad it's all over.'

There was now no one but Krys in the shop so she said, 'Do you know who makes the wooden ornaments? They're so lovely. There's one in the manor kitchen and I saw one at Max's place.'

'You found one at Max's place?'

'Yes . . .' Krys didn't want to admit she'd found it in Max's bedroom. Even if everyone knew she and Brett had stayed at the Bothy, it seemed far too personal a detail to admit she'd slept in his bed. 'I did wonder if he makes them.'

Amina seemed taken aback but then laughed out loud. 'Can you really see Max making wooden ornaments?'

'Well . . . no, if I'm honest.' Krys felt foolish for even thinking it but also slightly miffed that Amina had made her astonishment so obvious. She must know Max well to make a statement like that.

'It was only an idea because I know he has an outbuilding and woodshed at the Bothy.' The image of the axe came back to her again, making her cringe a little.

'Oh, I think he just keeps firewood in there,' Amina said. 'From what I gather.' She pushed the miniature whisky over to Krys. 'No, these are made by an old guy from the local area who likes to keep himself to himself. He doesn't want the limelight, only to make enough to live on.'

'I see.' Krys took out her card to pay for her haul.

'I don't think he has much else in his life,' Amina said. 'He lives in the middle of nowhere, poor man. We've given up asking him to join in with any of the community events.'

'And you don't know his name?' Krys said, swiping the card over the reader. 'Because I might buy some more. They're so sweet and beautifully made. Quite unique.'

'It's Dave,' came a deep voice from the shop entrance.

Krys spun round to find a familiar figure behind her.

Max hovered a few feet away, with a loaf in his arms and Jake at his heels.

'His name's Dave,' he said. 'The old guy who makes the turned ornaments.'

Her heart sank a little. Trust Max to turn up when she'd

bought a load of Christmas gifts, even though it was no business of his.

'Oh,' Krys said with cool politeness. 'Does he have a studio I can visit?'

Max shrugged. 'Not as far as I know.'

'He seems to sell all his stuff through local shops,' Amina said, adding, 'Hello, Max.'

Max smiled at her. 'Hello, Amina.'

They exchanged a knowing look over Krys's shoulder, the kind that definitely excluded anyone but themselves. *Hmm*. However, Krys wasn't going to be put off, even if she did suspect Max and Amina would rather like to talk without her present.

'Oh, OK . . . so do you think you'll be getting any more of Dave's pieces in, because I'd really like to buy some more before Christmas?'

'I might, but he's not terribly reliable,' Amina said, a little too vaguely for Krys's liking.

'In that case, I'll keep checking,' Krys said firmly. 'I'm sure to be in quite often for my shopping. I'm expecting the delivery of a hire car tomorrow. Oh, sorry, that's my phone.' She pulled it out of her pocket. 'It's Brett. I'd better take it. Bye, both.'

She tossed her phone into the shopping bag and carried it outside the shop, with the phone's urgent ringing making her heart beat faster. She needed to answer the call as it was sure to be about the Porsche and she didn't want to miss it.

It bothered her that their car was rammed against a bridge in that beautiful landscape . . . a beacon that reminded people for miles around that two clueless city-types had tried to battle with the forces of nature and lost. That car was not only a hazard but a symbol of humiliation and – if she was honest – loss. The sooner it was shifted, the better.

Depositing her shopping on a table outside the shop, she answered the call just as Brett declared: 'I was about to give up on you.'

'No, I was in the post office. I'm glad I caught you.'

Brett passed on the news that the recovery people were on their way, and in fact it would only be half an hour before they were at the beck. He told Krys he missed her and said he'd be back at the weekend before dashing off to 'another boring meeting'.

Krys picked up the bag from the table and the bottom ripped, sending most of her purchases rolling onto the pavement straight to the boots of Max.

'Here, let me help you.'

Cursing inwardly, she gathered up her purchases and put them on the table. Fortunately, the milk hadn't exploded and the wooden ornaments, wrapped in a piece of tissue by Amina, seemed OK.

Jake sniffed at the cheese and gingerbread.

'Jake!'

He slunk back to Max, who picked them up from the pavement. The cheese wrapper was soggy. 'Don't worry, it'll dry out.'

'I don't intend on keeping it long enough for that.' Krys said, drawing a brief smile from Max that lit up his eyes. They were brown, flecked with amber. He was clean shaven and his dark brown, almost black hair, shot through with the tiniest threads of grey, curled onto the collar of his jacket. Close up, his rugged features were even more striking than she remembered. He might not be an axe murderer but he certainly had killer looks.

She shook herself back into reality. 'Um. I'll have to go back inside and buy a bag.'

'Don't waste your money. I keep some in the boot. Even

recluses have to go to the shops to get their sourdough and artisan spirits sometime.'

He said it so deadpan that Krys had to smile. Perhaps he was in the mood to build bridges after their unpromising start. Even so, she was wary of his changeable moods.

He went to the Land Rover which was parked outside and collected a jute shopping bag.

'Thanks.' Krys started packing the bag.

Max added the milk, but the decorations were still on the table.

'Here you go,' he said, holding out the decorations in his palm. It was rough, with callouses, a healing cut and clean but broken nails. Brett's hands were smooth, from his monthly manicure at the spa next to his office.

Krys nestled the items on top and hoisted it into her arms.

Max's deep caramel gaze swept from her face to her boots – new but muddy – finally settling on the bag. 'It's a fair way to Holly Manor with shopping. Would you like a lift? Or is Brett coming to pick you up?'

'No, actually he's had to go back to London unexpectedly.'

His face was filled with confusion.

'An emergency at work. Something to do with a client that he had sort out in person.'

'Shame he had to interrupt his holiday,' Max said.

'Tell me about it.' Krys sighed. 'It couldn't be avoided. He was meant to stay for the rest of this week. Never mind, he'll be back on Friday night for a long weekend. My hire car arrives tomorrow so I'll be mobile again but I fancied a walk today. I never expected to buy so much.'

He nodded. 'I'm more than happy to give you a lift if it would help.'

'It's not really on your way . . .' she began, then had an afterthought. 'Are you going back to the Bothy via the ford?'

'Yes. Why?'

'The recovery people are on their way now to remove the car. Obviously there's no need for me to be there but I wondered if there was a chance of rescuing any of my stuff. I know we can claim on the insurance but some of it had sentimental value. I'd at least like to try and salvage a couple of things. If you wouldn't mind dropping me off, I can ask them.'

'It's worth a try though I doubt the recovery crew will let you anywhere near the car once they start. It might be best to get over there before they arrive and start spouting health and safety rules. The water levels are down so we might get access.'

Krys was surprised. 'That sounds dodgy.'

'A lot of things are dodgy but if you don't take a chance, you'd never do anything. These things mean a lot to you, right?'

'Yes,' she said, primed to leap on any remarks about 'fripperies'.

Instead, he said, 'Then jump in and we'll try and beat them to it.'

Chapter Nine

Ten minutes later, the Land Rover was once again bumping down the track towards the ford. Jake had taken the middle seat, sitting between her and Max, tongue lolling as if he was in on their plans. Krys half-expected him to start commenting on the idiocy of Londoners who'd driven into a raging torrent.

Instead, he contented himself with a series of little yips as the car slowed.

'Good. They're not here yet,' Max said, climbing swiftly out of the vehicle, followed by Jake and Krys.

The Porsche was a sorry sight, still wedged across the arch of the footbridge. The water level had dropped so low that almost the whole of the vehicle was exposed, branches poking out of the rear windscreen, which had been smashed by the force of the water.

'I don't think we'll be able to open the tailgate,' Max said, as he and Krys made their way down the bank towards the battered shell.

'The things I really wanted were on the back seat,' she said. 'Though they'll have been inundated.'

Today, the water gurgled like a contented baby; it was impossible to imagine the beck had had the power to lift a tonne of metal and sweep it away. Although the stream was low, Krys was still prepared to get her boots and jeans soaked in the process.

She stood on the bank, hands on hips, working out if she could climb on top and how she was going to open the door – if she could at all. It looked risky but it might be her only chance to retrieve some of her precious memories.

'Do you want me to take a look inside?' Max said.

'I can't let you do that on your own. This is my mad idea.'

'I seem to remember suggesting it myself.'

'What if something happened to you while you were trying to grab a few decorations . . .' she said.

'Don't worry, I won't sue.'

'I meant I don't want you to be hurt,' Krys said sharply.

'I was joking. Look, I've done far stupider things than this, I assure you. This stuff means a lot to you, right?'

'Yes.' Krys sighed, softening a little. 'I know it sounds crazy, but those decorations – some of them – are a link to my past . . . my childhood. If I can save a few, I'd feel so much better.'

'In that case, please accept the help.'

He hadn't dismissed her or laughed at her, which was progress.

'OK, then. I wouldn't mind a hand . . . I'm worried the doors will be jammed *if* we can even climb up.'

'Two of us might be able to,' he said. 'Though it'll mean getting wet again.'

'I think I can live with that,' Krys shot back. 'If it means salvaging some of my things.'

'OK, let's give it a try.'

With a shopping bag in hand, they climbed onto the rocky bank and onto the side of the car. The metal was slippery with water and weed but Max managed to wrench open the door. Krys had a moment when her heart was in her mouth as the car juddered under their weight.

'I can't help thinking this is a bad idea,' she said.

'We should definitely get a move on in case it shifts, but we're so close now, let's go for it. I'll hold the door. Be careful.'

Krys didn't need his warning to know how mad the escapade was for a few Christmas decorations. She lowered herself inside, finding it disorienting to be in a car on its side, the bottom of which was under six inches of brown water. The interior stank of rotting carpet and the leather was stained and crammed with twigs, leaves and mud. Surely nothing could have survived that onslaught. The plastic boxes that had held the decorations were upended and some of the items bobbing around, while others had rolled underwater.

At first, she didn't know what to salvage, if anything, then she spotted a silver reindeer that Linda had given her. It was plastic and filthy but could be washed. She put it in the shopping bag and decided to simply grab whatever bits she could and worry about cleaning them later. In a few minutes, she'd rescued a couple of dozen decorations, some of them broken, all of them thick with mud and sopping wet.

'Whoa!' The car trembled a little as if it might move again.

'I think we'd better leave,' Max called down. 'I can see the recovery truck at the top of the track.'

'OK.'

Krys abandoned the search and handed her bag of sopping booty to him. He helped her out of the door and to slide down off the side of the car and into the stream and up the bank. They'd reached the Land Rover when the truck arrived. Krys spoke to the crew and put on a brave face at their banter about the car.

They told her they would be 'a good while' moving it and, being wet and cold yet again, she accepted Max's offer to take her back to Holly Manor. The sky had darkened and you could no longer see the tops of the high fells for slate grey clouds. She felt as if the mountains were pressing down on her.

'Thanks for helping me out,' she said, carrying her bag of decorations while he brought the shopping to the door. The house suddenly seemed looming rather than grand, and Krys felt very alone. It was ridiculous when she'd craved an escape from her busy life, but the lack of any other human for miles weighed on her.

'Um . . . would you like to come in for a hot drink?' she said. 'I have hot chocolate and some nice coffee,' she added, wondering why she was even bothering to ask him in when he'd made it plain he shunned company. Maybe she felt she owed him something for helping her retrieve even a few of her precious memories. He'd probably refuse again but at least she'd done her duty.

'I'm filthy and so's Jake. We'll only mess up your carpets.'

'You can take your boots off,' she said. 'Well, Jake can't, but you know what I mean.'

'I – Oh, OK, why not? Hold on.'

Still slightly shellshocked that he'd accepted her invitation and a little worried about whether she really wanted him to come in at all, Krys waited while he fetched a towel from the boot.

'It's for Jake,' he said.

'Well, I didn't think it was for you.'

At the entrance to the hallway, he used the towel to clean Jake's paws as best he could before removing his own boots and socks.

Krys loaded a pod into the coffee machine before dashing

upstairs to change into dry clothes, not that she had many. Downstairs, Max was calling to Jake, who'd wandered into the kitchen.

When she came down, Max was in the kitchen feeding a dog treat to Jake.

'Sorry,' he said. 'He's a great dog but he will wander off sometimes, especially if he's on the trail of a tempting scent.'

'I had a bacon sandwich this morning. Maybe he can smell some of the rind and fat in the bin.'

She took the coffee mug from the machine. 'Milk?'

'Thanks.'

His feet were bare on the flagstone floor. 'You know I haven't been in here before,' he said.

'Really?' She handed over the mug. 'You know Nikki, the housekeeper, though?'

'Yes, she's in the MRT, but I've never been inside. No reason to.' He leaned against the worktop and looked around. 'It's a hell of a place. Looks to be early nineteenth century.'

'Even older. Late eighteenth.'

'I should have known by the chimneys. These old Lakeland manors have so much character. I'd have loved a place like this . . . at one time,' he added.

So there had been a time when Max was entranced by places like Holly Manor, Krys thought.

'It is gorgeous,' she said. 'And very big. It seems strange to be here on my own though I'll be able to reach civilisation and buy some proper outdoor clothes tomorrow.'

'And replace your decorations?' His expression was hidden by his mug. Krys wasn't sure if he was teasing her so decided to call his bluff.

'Yes, if I see any. I plan on getting a tree for the manor. Even though I'm on a break, I've always wanted to have time to really go to town on my own home. Or rather, someone else's home. My flat's too small for the sort of extravaganza I'd love to create.'

Max curled his lip. '*Extravaganza*? Do people really go to that much trouble?'

'They do,' Krys said, sensing his incredulity and ready to fight her corner. 'Some clients love to have a different theme every year. They'll see a new range in a store and want the whole tree-ful. Others call in professional decorators.'

His eyes widened in disbelief. 'People pay for someone to hang tinsel on their Christmas trees?'

Krys laughed at the horror in his voice. 'Don't sound so shocked. It's no different to having the painters in, or getting someone to help with the garden. They're too busy and they want their houses to look great – or maybe they don't have an eye for décor. The professional firms do hotels and businesses in November and then move on to people's homes.'

'Bloody hell. I'd worked out that contractors did the shops and hospitality venues, but not actual private houses.'

'Maybe I'd better not invite you here when I've had a chance to decorate this place, then . . .'

'Oh, I've no objection to other people sticking giant Santas on the roof,' he said. 'If that's what makes them happy.' He cradled the mug and Krys's eyes were drawn again to the hands that held it. She'd seen hands like it before, on scores of craft-speople she'd met in the course of her job. Working hands, bearing the marks of every piece they'd devoted their lives to producing.

'We tend to offer alternatives to the inflatable Santa these days,' she said smoothly. 'There's a huge choice of outdoor décor now though I tend to focus on the interiors, on luxe and artisan decorations. Most of them are mass-produced but I'm always on the lookout for beautiful and unusual pieces.'

'I'm sure everything you select is all very tasteful.' There was only a hint of a curl of the lip.

'Actually, the provenance of the items is very important to me and the customers,' she said, determined to fight her corner. She took down the bird from the island alcove, and cradled it in her palm. 'Like Dave's robin, for instance. This would be exactly the kind of artisan piece I'd love to see in one of my displays.'

Max's gaze flickered briefly over the toy then back to Krys and he smiled. 'I'm sure he'd be very flattered.'

'You think?'

'I've really no idea. Apart from his name, I know nothing about the man.'

Krys gave up and laid it next to her new purchases. 'There were such lovely things in the post office. Handmade soaps, jewellery, these wooden decorations. I'll ask Nikki if there's a Christmas craft fair coming up locally in case Dave turns up at one.'

Max levered himself off the worktop and put his mug down. 'Like I said, I don't do Christmas.'

'But Dave clearly *does*, if he's lavishing so much time on these hand-crafted ornaments. He should really raise his prices. These would sell for at least twice as much in a high-end store. He could make more than he does now.'

'Perhaps he doesn't do it for the money.'

'Even so, I assume he still has to make ends meet?'

'Like I said, you can manage on far less than you imagine if you streamline your life.' Max held her gaze, both unwilling to back down.

What was he trying to imply? That she was indulging herself – or selfish – in renting the manor and filling it with Christmas decorations. If he was, his attitude irked her. She was sure he'd had money once. She could tell by his voice, his education, the books, the whisky in the Bothy – the few luxuries he chose to keep. She could smell it from years of experience of people with everything – and nothing – no matter how he chose to live now.

'I know, Max. I *have* been there. For the first thirteen years of my life, I had no home to call my own and my dad was never a part of my life. Me and my mum lived in a succession of flats, bed and breakfasts and on relatives' floors. It was only because of Auntie Linda that we had any stability at all. So,' she finally drew breath, shocked at her outpouring, 'I *have* managed with "very little" and I know what it's like to be counting every penny, so if this Dave is struggling, I can help him.'

Despite the polite smile on his face, Max's body language was stiff with discomfort.

'I'm sorry for being rude and for patronising you. I shouldn't have jumped to conclusions or made assumptions about you – or anyone. And I've really no idea if Dave, whoever he, she or they are, is struggling. People round here are proud and tend to keep their troubles to themselves. In my experience if the guy is anything like the rest of the local populace, he'd rather keep on doing exactly as he does now.'

He called to Jake.

'Come on, boy. We'd best be getting home.'

Jake lifted his snout as if to ask, 'Do I have to leave now?' but it was a small crumb of comfort to Krys, who thought she'd been making progress with Max.

He'd made her world seem slightly tawdry, a feeling Krys wasn't used to, and she wasn't amused. His coffee mug was still half full but he was on his way, so Krys showed him out of the house, with Jake kept firmly to heel.

'Thanks for the lift and help with the car,' she said, determined to be polite, once he'd pulled his boots on over bare feet and retrieved his damp socks from the hall radiator.

'You're welcome,' was the gruff reply.

With that, he trotted down the steps and she got a quick raise of the hand through the Land Rover window before he drove off.

Even though she knew a lot about people in general, she clearly had a lot to learn about Max in particular. It was unlikely she was going to find out, anyway, as judging by his reaction, he'd practically erected 'keep out' barriers around him.

Chapter Ten

'So are you going to the pub tomorrow night, or are you going to spend another night watching *Strictly*, with Jake for company?'

Max's friend, Davy, grinned as Max handed him a wrench. Max had agreed to help replace the winch on the MRT Land Rover. While he wasn't a trained mechanic, he knew Landys and it would save the team money, which was vital when the whole team was entirely dependent on public donations. All of it had to be raised by the individual team as there was no national organisation to distribute cash. It meant a continuous effort on the part of the volunteers and supporters.

'I don't watch *Strictly*,' Max said. 'I don't have a TV.'

'Sorry, mate. I forgot. So, are you coming to the pub?'

Max hesitated. He did often go to The Cock on Saturday nights for a drink with whoever happened to be there: always at least half a dozen members of the MRT and more often than not Amina and some of the other villagers. He might be living like a hermit, but he wasn't a total recluse. However, his encounter with Krys earlier that week had reminded him of how unfit – or unused – to unexpected company he was. He'd been churlish and dismissive about her job and now he could have kicked himself.

Not that he need worry she'd be at the pub, with Brett arriving for the weekend. They'd be holed up at the manor, probably sipping champagne in the tub, to the aroma of scented candles and rose petals. It was a thought that made him a little queasy – on Krys's account, not Brett's.

'Yeah, I'll probably drop by.'

If he wanted a pint, he always walked there with Jake, who loved lying by the fire in the bar and meeting other dogs. Max smiled: it had come to this. His only outing consisted of taking his pet on a play date.

Davy stared at him. 'What's so funny?'

'Nothing. You know I'll be there. Shall we get on with repairing this winch?'

When Max walked into The Cock, several familiar faces were already gathered in their usual haunt: a large table with a settle and stools near to the fire in the bar. The pub – so named because of its alleged cock-fighting pit – was a traditional Lakeland inn, originally built to host weary travellers to what would have been a wild and dangerous corner of the country in the seventeenth century. It still was wild and dangerous, though its unwitting visitors fell prey to the mountains rather than highwaymen these days.

Sometimes, people who'd been rescued offered a thank you donation, though it was never expected and rarely covered the cost of the callout. Occasionally, people seemed affronted to have been helped at all, with no clue of the extreme danger they'd been in. They simply looked on the MRT as if it was a taxi service . . . a bit like Brett.

Reminding himself to rein in his cynicism, he ducked his head under the doorway that led from the porch to the bar, savouring the tang of woodsmoke and ale. The place rang with laughter and chat. Half of Thorndale was in there, along with a handful of outsiders who'd ventured to the area for a long weekend or a visit to their holiday homes.

The vast majority were familiar faces and smiled at him, or ran a hand over Jake's fur as he gave a little yip of greeting to a doggy friend at the MRT table.

Krys and Brett were hunkered down in the next booth. *So,* thought Max, *he's deigned to come up from London at the weekend, then?*

Max still didn't understand what had been so urgent that it couldn't be dealt with via the wonders of video conferencing. If he'd been Brett, he'd never have wasted a precious chance to spend the week with Krys.

However, Brett hadn't had the perspective that Max had been given. He probably had no idea how precious every moment was, when it came to spending time with those you loved. How every second was to be treasured far beyond any jewel.

She caught his eye and said 'hello' and Brett nodded and flashed his teeth in a smile before returning to the menu. Max caught a whiff of Krys's perfume, a citrussy floral which reminded him of Provence . . . A memory surfaced, unbidden and unwanted. He hadn't been to the South of France since . . .

'Max! Hello! And Jake too!' The greetings came from members of the MRT and gave Max a warm glow inside, despite his grumpiness. He raised a hand in reply before Jake disappeared under the table with his canine chums. The dogs were blissfully happy. If only life was that simple, Max thought.

Davy was at the bar so Max joined him while he ordered the drinks.

'Evening,' Davy said. 'You decided to grace us with your presence then?'

'Jake needed a walk.'

Davy raised an eyebrow. 'Sure he did, mate.'

Krys came up to the bar and nodded a hello at Max.

He did a double take at the sight of her close up. She was dressed in a cream polo neck sweater with skinny jeans and knee-high boots that emphasised the length of her legs. That luxuriant brown hair was caught up in a claw clip and she wore pale peach lip gloss.

Max's tongue seemed to have turned numb.

'Hi, Max,' she said cheerfully. 'Didn't expect to see you here.'

'I um – sometimes come here on a Saturday.'

'Oh? Well, we decided to give The Cock a try too.' A smile played at the corner of her lips, where a strand of hair had escaped from her ponytail and caught in her lip gloss. Max had an insane urge to reach out and brush it away.

'It's a decent place,' he said hoarsely. 'Not gourmet but the goulash is good.'

'I'll take your word for it. I came to collect a menu actually.'

'I can help.' Max reached over to the end of the bar and found one.

'Thanks.'

'How's the car?' he asked.

'My hire car? It's great. I decided to get a four-wheel-drive.'

'Good idea. And you've been – um – OK at the manor?' He almost added 'on your own' but realised how patronising that would be. If he'd been that worried about her, he'd have called in and not been so rude when he'd last seen her.

'Fine. Absolutely fine. I've had some lovely walks and I've been into Keswick for some new gear.'

'Nice,' said Max, as tongue-tied as the university student

93

who'd met another beautiful woman at a wedding party all those years before. He'd fallen hard that night and he had the same sense of inevitability now, but it could not happen again. It was sacrilege for it to ever happen again. It would kill him, if it happened again.

'And how are your decorations?' he said, trying his hardest to be pleasant.

She wrinkled her nose. 'I managed to clean and dry a few out in the airing cupboard. Half are beyond help, but I can't bear to get rid of them. The memories . . .' Her voice tailed off.

'I can understand that sentiment,' he said.

She frowned in surprise, and Max felt bad. She was probably genuinely astonished that he might show empathy after his previous rudeness.

'Max!' Davy blundered in, like an enthusiastic Labrador scattering everything in his path. The foam from the pints dripped down his big hands.

He handed one to Max. 'And this is?'

'I'm Krys.' Krys greeted them warmly enough, still clutching the menu.

'I'm David,' Davy said before Max could make the introduction.

Her eyes widened in surprise. 'So you're Dave.'

'Max has already told you about me?' Davy sounded equally amazed.

'Um. Not in so many words.' She exchanged a glance with Max, who couldn't think of a reply.

Fortunately Davy wasn't so shy. 'I answer to "Dave" sometimes, though Davy's more my style. My surname's Crockett, you see.'

'You're joking!'

'Only half. It's Crockford.'

Krys joined in with the laughter, which included a wry smile from Max. 'Got me,' she said, pointing a manicured finger at Davy.

'Sorry, I couldn't resist. Let me make it up to you. Can I get you a drink?'

She threw him a dazzling smile. 'Thanks, but my boyfriend just got a round in and we need to order our food.' She waggled the menu at them both. 'Nice to see you, Max, and to meet you, Davy.'

With that, she walked over to the table next to the MRT gang.

'That went well,' said Davy, lingering by the bar.

'Extremely,' said Max. 'I didn't know you were interested or I'd have told you about the boyfriend.'

'You might have warned me. How did you know, anyway?'

'A – you didn't give me chance, and B – they're the pair I helped out of the beck the other day.'

Davy stared at Krys's table, where a waitress was taking their order. 'Serious between them, is it?'

'They're a couple, yes, but I've no idea about the state of the relationship. He's called Brett and she's called Krys. They both work in London. If you hadn't been off beating the crap out of people for the past week, you'd know the gossip.'

'Hey, mate. It's called being a professional rugby player. I get paid to beat the crap out of people. So this Krys and Brett will be gone soon enough?'

'She's staying until New Year. She rented Holly Manor for two months.'

Davy whistled. 'With The Dapper Gent over there?'

Max was amused. 'Sometimes. He's been back and forth to London.'

'You mean he leaves her here on her own?'

'She's a grown woman, Davy. More than capable of taking care of herself.'

He raised an eyebrow. 'Do you think I should drop round for tea?'

'Not if you don't want to be arrested.'

'I was joking. I wouldn't do anything of the kind, unless she was single and I was invited.'

'Well, she's not and you won't be. Besides, she prefers coffee.'

Davy scrutinised him. Max wished he hadn't added the throw-away line about the coffee because his friend's eyes gleamed as if he'd scented prey. 'You must have got pretty close to them if they stayed the night.'

'I got close to Brett, seeing as we were both sleeping in my living room with Jake. Krys had my bed.'

'Very noble.'

Krys's laughter rang out from the pub table. Brett planted a lingering kiss on her lips.

Davy sighed. 'She's a cracker. Lights up the place, if you know what I mean. Shame she's with him.'

Max knew exactly what Davy meant and thought the same, but crushed both of these thoughts and any more questioning from his friend by thrusting his glass into Davy's hand: 'Take my drink to the table, would you, mate? I'm going to the gents.'

A while later, Max got talking to some of the members of the team who were sitting on the next table to Brett and Krys. Brett had his arm around her back and every so often nuzzled her ear. Max tried to look away.

The group included the Thorndale medic, Katya, and the leader of nearby Bannerdale MRT, Will, who was on a training weekend with Thorndale. He was a strapping, fit guy who'd been born and brought up on the Lakeland fells, and you'd never know he was fifty. A veteran of thousands of rescues, he already had the MBE for the service he'd given to the team.

Max stood by the table with Davy, joining in the banter about 'shouts' and the recent weather, hoping that no one mentioned the plonkers who'd driven their Porsche into the beck. The MRT were meant to not judge but that was largely for the PR. Privately, Davy had already told him exactly what he thought of the incident.

'So, when are you going to become a proper member of the team?' Will said to Max, handing him a pint.

Here we go, thought Max, wondering if the 'king's shilling' would be at the bottom of the tankard. He knew that in olden times, that was how the Royal Navy used to press gang unwitting drinkers into joining up without realising it.

Davy laughed. 'You've no chance, Will, mate. We keep asking him but he won't sign up.'

'I help out,' said Max. 'I'm here when you need me. I don't need to do all the official training and courses.'

Will sipped his pint before responding. 'You're right, but they'd only be a formality for you. Your mountain craft is top-notch and more importantly, you know this place like the back of your hand.'

'Not as well as you lot. I wasn't born round here.'

'You may as well have been,' Davy said.

Max felt uncomfortable. He liked Davy, and the whole MRT. They were a friendly bunch and, generally speaking, respected his need for privacy but tonight seemed like a charm offensive. Out of the corner of his eye, he spotted Krys watching and probably listening. Brett was nowhere to be seen. Probably re-gelling his hair, thought Max, unable to suppress a smile.

'Thing is, we're short of volunteers at the best of times and it would be great if we could have an extra pair of hands to call on,' Will went on. 'You're virtually one of us already, you live next to the mountain and you seem to be reasonably human.'

Max laughed. 'I wouldn't be too sure about the human part.'

'Honest, it's only a couple of navigating and first aid courses,' Will said, smooth as butter. He paused to sip his pint casually.

'Bit of rope work, practising with the stretchers. You've already done most of it on a casual basis.'

'That's a bit different to being on call,' Max said, aware that he was rapidly running out of excuses. The others all had day jobs – medics, teachers, and in Will's case, he owned a chain of outdoor equipment stores. Nikki had her cottage housekeeping job, and even Amina, who was so busy with the post office, helped out when she could. He had nothing to do with his time; nothing he would admit to, anyway. It looked cowardly to refuse.

'Tell you what,' said Will, clearly sensing a chink in Max's armour. 'We've an introductory course starting next week. It'll cover winter skills, search and rescue protocols. To be honest,' he said with an eye-roll, 'from what I hear from this lot here, you could teach it yourself.'

Davy patted Max on the back. 'No pressure, mate.'

None at all, thought Max, yet his resistance was melting away. He had a feeling this was a battle that it might be better to lose to keep them off his back.

Krys was now watching them intently, in the way of someone who was following a conversation closely without realising that their fascination had been noticed.

Max sipped his own pint. 'A short course?' he said.

Davy nodded. 'Just a couple of nights. Plus the candidates' challenge, at some point, of course.' He grinned. 'That'll be easy for you, carrying a typical rescue load up the fell at rescue speed and showing off your navigation skills.'

'Ease you in gently,' Will added with a gleam in his eye.

'Of course . . .' Max said, knowing that the candidates' trial was called a challenge for a good reason. He met Will's eyes, knowing he'd been reeled in by a master. 'What nights?'

'Tuesday and Wednesday,' Davy cut in. 'At the base.'

Max scratched his chin, realising that Krys was still listening. 'Well, I was planning on washing my hair and ironing my tux but I suppose I could put those off for another night.'

Davy banged the table with his fist so hard that Max's pint almost flew off the table. 'Eu-bloody-reka!'

Will held out his hand. 'Thanks. You won't regret it.'

Max shook it. 'I only hope you don't.'

He glanced over at Krys while Davy and Will drank their pints with glee. She threw him a smile, though whether it was approval or merely politeness, Max wasn't sure.

Amina and Nikki joined them at the table to be informed that Max had been persuaded to at least attend a couple of training sessions. Amina slapped him on the back and Nikki asked him if he'd had his arm twisted. Max was already nervous about having been drawn in but to his relief, the chatter turned to funds, and the forthcoming Winter Ball at the base to raise cash and allow the team to let their hair down.

'Ball' was a rather grandiose title from what Max could work out, but it seemed a popular event. Nikki and Amina were chief organisers of the yearly bash where everyone in Thorndale put on their glad rags and danced the night away to help raise the cash for the many and constant needs of the team, such as new Land Rovers, roof repairs and updated equipment. At least everyone except Max, that is, who had turned down invitations to the last two events.

'We've sold twenty tickets already but we need to flog a lot more,' Nikki said. 'At a push, we can accommodate sixty.'

Max sought refuge in his pint, longing to avoid an invitation. He had nothing against fundraising and had, unbeknown to anyone else, made several anonymous donations via the webpage. It was the ball he wanted no part in: the idea of dressing up, dancing and partying made him feel almost physically ill. The once a week at the pub was as much as he could handle, and it had taken him a year to even start going to that.

'I'll print off some leaflets and keep them by the till,' Amina said. 'The weekenders are sure to come.'

'I'll ask Emma to persuade some of her mates,' Will said. 'And we'll definitely be there with some of the Bannerdale lot. Put me down for a table,' he added.

'That's almost doubled attendance,' Nikki joked. 'Now we need some lots for the auction.'

'I could offer an outdoor pursuits weekend,' Will said.

Max listened in, knowing Will was a wealthy guy and a generous one at that. He felt uncomfortable.

'I can find you some bits and bobs from the post office stores,' Amina offered.

Nikki spoke. 'I'm working on the cottage letting company to stump up a weekend away, though that would be a busman's holiday for anyone who actually lives here!'

Laughter rang around the table.

'I can offer some auction lots,' Max said.

Eyes swivelled in his direction, and the amazement in their expressions shocked him.

'Oh, Max. We don't expect anything.' Amina regarded him closely.

'Don't worry about it, mate,' Davy said.

'We don't want people to feel under pressure.' Nikki smiled at him indulgently. 'You've offered to volunteer. That's more than enough.'

Plans and laughter flew over his head. Max listened and sought refuge in his pint, yet inside he had shrunk a little more. Tonight had shone a light on the man he'd become and he wasn't sure he liked what he'd seen. Was he considered such a recluse that he'd had to be manipulated into joining the MRT – and the more he thought about it, the more he was convinced he'd been asked not for the team's benefit but for his own. He might not even have said yes to that, if Krys hadn't been watching and listening so intently.

Had he been influenced by Krys's interest in the conversation? Did she even care if he said yes? Why did he care if she did?

As for the ball, no one had actually invited him this time. They'd all assumed he wouldn't say yes – and he certainly didn't want to – but on that score, they'd given up on him.

All of that was bad enough, but the question of the donation to the auction had made him squirm the most. His kind friends clearly considered him as a project, an eccentric character who needed support even more than their own organisation did.

They knew even less about him than they thought.

While the others chatted, Max's attention was drawn by Brett and Krys, sitting in front of two empty plates. He couldn't fail to overhear Brett declare in a loud voice to Krys:

'Sorry, babe, got talking to some bloke at the bar. Works for one of our suppliers and has a second home in the next village. Small world, eh? Can I get you another drink or would you rather I took you home to bed?'

Chapter Eleven

It was beginning to look a lot like Christmas, or rather, it soon *would* be, Krys hoped, climbing into Nikki's car at the manor ready for a trip to her first festive market.

She and Nikki had been chatting in The Cock and Nikki had invited her to go with her to the Keswick Christmas Fair on her day off, a Tuesday.

'I can't find anyone else as enthusiastic about Christmas shopping as I am,' she'd said, much to Krys's amusement. 'And I'm determined to get in early this year instead of saving it all until the last minute. Last year, I left it until the twenty-third and then I was called out on an all night rescue! Everyone got Amazon vouchers and whatever chocs and booze were left in the post office.'

'Well I still need to do mine,' Krys said. Although she didn't have many people to buy for: a couple of colleagues and she always exchanged gifts with Harriet and a few of her London friends. This year she might have to post everyone's unless she made a trip back down south.

There would be no Linda to buy for, of course, and that cut

deep. She and her mother hadn't exchanged gifts for years and after the row over Linda's funeral, they weren't about to start.

However, there was Brett and he enjoyed receiving – and giving – gifts so that would be fun.

However, her other main objective was to find some unique decorations to replace the ones she'd lost in the flood. As she'd told Max, she'd managed to salvage around a dozen glass and wooden items, carefully washing and drying them. A favourite 'clip-on' feathered peacock had also miraculously survived, albeit with his tail now a little scraggy.

The ruined ones were still in a cardboard box. She couldn't bear to chuck them out, and Max seemed to have understood why.

Being honest, she wasn't expecting to see anything on the stalls and in the shops that she hadn't seen before. Much of it would be what she'd looked at herself the previous January and February so she already knew the trends and colour themes.

The vast majority of it would also be imported, but on the other hand, she was always ready to be surprised. Sometimes the only way to find unique ideas was to get out there and see what local craftspeople were producing: to touch it and feel it, imagine it on a tree or someone's mantelpiece. You just never knew what you might come across in the most unexpected places.

Like Dave's robins and angels.

Nikki collected Krys from Holly Manor before dawn and they set off to Keswick, with the sun rising over the sea. While it was only fifteen miles as the crow flew, England's two highest mountains stood in between Thorndale and the town, so the journey took almost an hour, skirting the coast before heading inland.

'No one gets anywhere in a hurry in the Lakes,' Nikki said, expertly negotiating the single-track roads out of the vale.

When she wasn't managing her team of housekeeping and cleaning staff, she'd told Krys she was in a fell running club. This seemed to consist of dashing up impossible slopes and hurtling down them at terrifying speeds. Krys thought it sounded like madness but Nikki's eyes lit up when she spoke about it, the same as Krys's did when she saw a store full of Christmas decorations.

Each to their own, thought Krys, as Nikki enthused about an upcoming race called the Ice Breaker 20, consisting of a twenty kilometre 'outing' around local fells.

'You can come and watch if you like,' she said.

'As long as I *do* only have to watch,' Krys said, laughing.

She wasn't keen on running herself, preferring a bit of power walking around city parks and YouTube pilates videos she could do anywhere.

'Oh, we won't make you run. Though you could start, if you fancied it. We have a beginners' club.'

'No. No!'

'Only winding you up.' Nikki grinned wickedly. 'Come along and see a load of sweaty people doing bonkers things. You probably saw Katya from the MRT at the pub. She's a local GP and volunteers as the team doctor. And she's in the running club.'

'I heard her name mentioned. It sounds exhausting.'

'So does your lifestyle. All that jet-setting and Christmas twenty-four seven. I don't know how you do it.'

'I wouldn't call it jet-setting but I do get to travel abroad several times a year. February is when it all kicks off big time, with trade fairs in the UK at Birmingham and Harrogate, but they also have them in Porto in Portugal and I once went to one in Mexico which was amazing.'

'That sounds very glamorous.'

'Well, they're working trips really, so you don't get that much time to sightsee. The suppliers from all over the world gather to showcase their festive decorations for the following season. The big daddy of them all is in Frankfurt at the start of February. I'm booked into that one. It's called Christmas World and it has every kind of Christmas decoration you could dream of and then some!'

'February!'

'Oh yes, it's my busiest time of the year. When everyone else is all out of festive feeling, I have to get all excited and enthusiastic for Christmas World.'

'It sounds . . . a mixture of heaven and hell if I'm honest,' Nikki said.

'I suppose it is. Heaven for me, but for anyone who hates Christmas, I should imagine it would be their idea of hell.' Max immediately sprang to mind. He would have probably rather run naked up the Pike than go within a hundred miles of Christmas World.

'Just how Christmassy are we talking?' Nikki asked.

'Ma-hoo-sively, over the top Christmassy on an Everest-style scale,' Krys said.

She found it hard to describe her first visit to the Christmas World show, as a junior buyer with a big store chain.

'It has all the indoor and outdoor decorations that end up in the shops plus much bigger things; the kind of decorations you see in shopping centres, city streets and hotels. As well as the big trade stands, large areas are set up with cabins like you get at Christmas markets. It's where all the buyers go to hunt for new trends and colour themes.'

'Wow. I can't believe all this starts so soon after New Year.'

'Harrogate is actually in late January. Most of the big store buyers go along in person. I look around, order samples, look at prices and present what I think the latest trends are. Then we make a decision because most of the large manufacturers are located abroad and make to order.'

'Wow. You really are a full time Mrs Christmas. Will you expect to find anything in the Lakes?'

'I don't know. I hope so . . . and I'd love to find out who makes the wooden pieces. Who Dave really is.'

'Dave?'

'Amina said he was called Dave and that he's very shy. Um – I probably shouldn't ask this but is he – are Max and Amina together?'

'Max and Amina?' Nikki laughed. 'Whatever gave you that idea?'

'Oh, nothing really. Only that I went in the post office and they seemed . . . close.' When Nikki didn't say anything, Krys felt sheepish, and more than a bit nosy. 'I'm probably way off the mark. Ignore me.'

'No, sometimes it takes an outsider to see what's under your nose. I suppose they *are* very friendly, or as friendly as Max gets with people. And they are both single, and let's face it, the two most attractive people in Thorndale, so yes, it's not impossible they're an item and hiding it very well.' She smiled.

Krys smiled too. Max was a very attractive man, and if she were being generous she might call him enigmatic – although awkward and anti-social were more accurate.

Laughing off Nikki's comment, she said, 'What am I like? Here in Thorndale five minutes and spreading gossip about my neighbours. I think I should stick to decorating, rather than matchmaking.'

'I'll definitely stick to housekeeping,' Nikki said. 'I'm *always* wrong about who's with who.'

Krys spotted the sign at the entrance to the town, whose grey buildings were nestled in a bowl of huge snow-topped fells. 'Here we are!' she said, relieved to move on to a less contentious topic.

'Yes and from what you've told me, I think you're going to enjoy this.' They waited at a crossing while people poured across the road. 'Looks busy already. Let's find a spot and you can show me how Mrs Christmas rocks Keswick!'

It might not be Christmas World, but Krys was enchanted by the little Lakeland town's festive fair. The stalls were lined up on either side of the main street around a grey stone building with a square tower.

'That's the Moot Hall,' Nikki explained when Krys asked what it was. 'It was a market and a courthouse way back, but it's the tourist info centre now.'

With the snow-topped fells behind it, the hall made the perfect centrepiece for the traders huddled around it. Krys's nose twitched at the aromas of cheese, fish and pies on the food stalls. Others were selling jams and chutneys, Lakeland ales, gins and whisky. Soon her jute bag was bulging with goodies for the larder at Holly Manor and a bottle of whisky for Brett.

So often, she saw little treats that would have been perfect for Auntie Linda: handmade chocolates, a miniature of damson gin, a matching scarf and hat knitted by the stallholder herself, some luxurious bath goodies. There was no Linda to buy them for, so Krys bought some chocolates and toiletries for Harriet and a couple of other friends. She also treated herself to a woolly bobble hat.

Nikki had gone to a deli on the market square, leaving Krys to mooch around the remaining traders. Finally, she found what she'd actually come for: several stalls dedicated to festive decorations. One was cheap and cheerful with tinsel and imported stuff. There was no shame in that; Krys was all too aware that decorations were expensive and not everyone could afford the high-end pieces that ended up in posh stores.

She'd never forgotten the isolation that had come from peering into a world she could never be a part of. She always tried to make sure her store stocked a range of decorations to suit more modest budgets.

Leaving that stall aside, she moved on to the next, stacked with glass baubles with vintage Lakeland district scenes printed on them. They were a bit kitsch but you couldn't be a Christmas buyer without loving a bit of kitsch so she bought one for herself, and one to add to Harriet's Christmas parcel.

Another stall had woodland themed garlands and decorations, including some turned bowls and ornaments. None of them were as exquisitely made as Dave's.

Nikki appeared through the crowds, with a bulging bag.

'You look as if you've been busy,' Krys said.

With a grin, Nikki patted the bag. 'I think I bought half the shop. I got treats for my parents, nieces and nephews and most of the rescue team.'

Nikki hadn't mentioned a partner and Krys didn't like to ask. She felt she'd already pried too much about Max and Amina.

'How have you got on? I see you've already been spending.'

'Mostly on anything but decorations,' Krys said, showing Nikki her purchases. 'I did buy a couple of baubles with Lakeland scenes on them.'

'I see enough of those out of my window,' Nikki said wryly. 'But I do need more stuff for some of the properties. Several of the owners asked us to decorate their properties for big Christmas bookings. I've had a go with my team in the past, but I'm no professional like you.'

'I'm not an actual professional Christmas decorator. That's a specialist job, but obviously I know how I want the room to look. You've no fear at Holly Manor, I'm looking forward to doing my own decorations, and don't worry, I'll take them all home with me when I'm done after New Year.'

Nikki laughed. 'You can give me a few tips. No, please don't feel you have to. That would make today a busman's holiday.'

'I never need a break from Christmas, not on a personal level. That's why I hired Holly Manor, so I could relax and enjoy the season for a while – with Brett too, of course. I only wish Auntie Linda could be with me.' Krys's gaze trailed over the mountains again. They were topped with snow. 'She'd have loved it here.'

'Close, were you?'

'Very. My mum and I were homeless for a while and ended up living with Linda. Then Mum met a new guy and we didn't hit it off so I moved out to live with my auntie permanently from when I was around fourteen. We don't have much contact now.'

'That sounds difficult.'

'It was – for all of us. My dad did a vanishing act when I was a baby. Mum worked a load of jobs to try and keep a roof over our heads but we ended up in B&Bs. Linda only had a small flat herself but she was always there to help.'

'When did you lose her?'

'May.'

'I'm so sorry.'

Krys's chest tightened. 'She wouldn't have wanted me to be gloomy and miserable even though I miss her like I'd never dreamed. Linda would've wanted me to look forward to my life and enjoy it.'

'She sounds like a wonderful woman and I'm sure she'd want you to enjoy yourself,' Nikki said kindly. 'On that note, I know of a lovely little gift shop by the lake that I think you'll like.

They showcase Lakeland arts and are bound to have lots of Christmassy stuff. Let's go and have a mooch.'

After lunch, they strolled down to Derwentwater with hot chocolates from the lakeside café. The clouds had rolled in over the mountains, turning the sky and lake grey. However, nothing could dampen Krys's mood. She'd found some pretty handmade garlands in the gift shop, plus two beautiful pairs of leather gloves that she would post to a work colleague and another friend whom she saw regularly. Feeling very festive, she started talking about the weekend with Nikki.

'When's Brett back?' Nikki asked, as they stood by the boat hire centre on the lake. There was snow on the fell tops opposite.

'This Friday, hopefully in time for dinner. He had to miss last weekend because he has a business trip to Paris.' Krys was looking forward to showing him her haul. In fact, an idea was brewing for a surprise that would give him a proper welcome.

'It must be a big contrast with your busy life in London. It's so quiet here, it can drive you mad – and I'm used to it. It's why we rely on the community so much. It can be claustrophobic but we all depend on each other.'

Krys thought about Max: it seemed a strange place to escape to, in one way. He might have been far more anonymous in a big city. She could understand he wanted solitude and beautiful surroundings but when it came to avoiding attention, she wondered why he'd chosen Thorndale.

'It must be lonely rattling round the manor on your own. Why don't you come to the MRT on Thursday evening?'

'The MRT? I thought it was only for members.'

'It's for anyone who wants to help. We always have tea and cake. It's my turn to bring those this week. In fact, don't let me

110

forget to visit the cake stall on the market. I'll be drummed out of town if I turn up empty handed. I don't have time to make my own; I'm no Domestic Goddess.'

Krys laughed. 'I haven't baked mince pies for ages but I'm planning on trying.'

'I'm hopeless at baking,' Nikki declared. 'Come along, and not only for the cake. You might enjoy it and the search and rescue dogs come too: they're always fun to meet.'

'Like Jake?' Krys said.

'Well, better behaved than Jake though Max *will* probably bring him. We've managed to persuade him to come to a training session and we're hoping he'll hang around for a brew afterwards.'

Krys thought of another night on her own channel surfing at the manor and decided. 'If you really think I wouldn't be in the way, I'd love to. The cute search dogs have swung the deal.'

'Great . . . Oh, and you might be interested in something else,' Nikki said, delving in her handbag. 'We're having a bit of a brainstorm about the Winter Ball.'

'The ball?'

'Our big winter charity do.' She pulled out a crumpled leaflet. 'Maybe you and Brett might want to come?'

Krys read the handout.

GRAND WINTER BALL
in aid of Thorndale MRT
at the Mountain Rescue Base
December 20th
Disco. Band. Buffet.
7 'til late
Dress to impress

'Wow. Grand Winter Ball. That sounds exciting.'

'Well, I wouldn't get *too* excited! It's called a ball but may not be a ball as you know it. I'm sure you've been to some swanky events.'

'Not as many as you'd think,' she said tactfully, having been to several black-tie events with Brett, and in the course of her own work. Parties, launches and posh do's that she could only ever have dreamed of at one time.

'It may not be your thing, of course, we're hardly the Ritz.'

'I think it sounds fun. I'm sure Brett would love to come,' she said, crossing her fingers and hoping he'd be up for it. The idea of a Christmas event up here 'in the wilds' was too tempting to pass up. They could dress up and dance the night away . . . it would be a wonderful finale to their holiday before settling in for the big day itself.

'In fact, if you have time, you could help us glam up the base a bit for the do?'

Krys was too taken aback to reply. She hadn't expected to be sucked into the life of the village so quickly.

'Oh sorry, here I am.' Nikki grimaced. 'You're meant to be a guest and I'm handing you a list of jobs as long as your arm.'

'No, I don't mind, I'm happy to have something to do. Do you already have your own decorations?'

'Um, the odd bit of tinsel, and we'll buy a tree of course. We always mean to have a theme and really go to town, but we end up dragging the same sad old stuff out of the cupboard.'

'I've ordered some new decorations for the Manor and I'm always being offered free samples. I could spare some of those.'

'Oh? I didn't mean to scrounge!'

'You're not, and if you wanted, I could come over earlier and help out with the decorating.'

'That would be amazing. Any help is always really welcome.

We're a small team and it's becoming harder and harder to get volunteers.'

'Really?' Krys thought of the way Max had been cajoled into joining.

'You don't have to have knowledge of the mountains to help us. There are lots of roles in fundraising, manning the phones, looking after relatives waiting for news.'

'If I did live here, I'd definitely volunteer, but I'm only around until New Year so I don't think I can do much.'

'If you can spare some time to help at the ball, that would be more than enough. Now, it's getting dark already. If you've had enough retail therapy, shall we head home?'

It was totally dark by the time Nikki dropped Krys at the manor, with the stars and moon hidden under a thick layer of clouds. Krys took her shopping inside, lit the lamps, drew the curtains and made up the fire. Outside, owls hooted and the wind gusted through the trees.

The old house creaked and there were some bloodcurdling cries from the garden which she now knew were amorous foxes, after mentioning them to Nikki on the way home.

Even though she told herself the noises were only the wind, the wildlife and the building's heating system, she felt a little bit spooked and longed for Brett to return on Friday. There were only so many walks you could make alone without someone to share them with and she couldn't wait to tell him about the ball.

He'd told her that he'd sorted the issue with the wavering client then had to go to Paris to finalise a contract with the French branch of a new US-based client. He was planning to drive straight from the airport to the Lakes to spend a long weekend with her.

She decided that she would definitely carry out her plan to surprise him by decorating the sitting room and hallway.

She had no tree yet; Nikki had said that the local tree centre opened on the last weekend in November. Besides, she'd like to choose a tree with Brett: he'd need some serious TLC when he arrived for the weekend. However, she could make a start on the rest of the sitting room and hallway as soon as her online order of decorations arrived. Making a mental note to gather some greenery from the garden, she grabbed a glass of wine and called him on Zoom, excited to tell him all her 'adventures' and plans and about the ball.

'Hello, babe.'

Krys did a double take.

Brett was slumped in his chair, with his top three buttons undone and a haggard expression. It could have been the lighting in his hotel room but he looked haunted with stress to a degree she hadn't seen before.

'You look as if you've been working hard. How's this new deal going?'

'It's the biggest deal we've ever secured and they're on the cusp of signing it. I just need to nudge them over the line. One of their directors is wavering about using a London based firm, though.'

'At this late stage?'

'Tell me about it.' He swore and rubbed his eyes. 'I've been up since four, fine-tuning our presentation to address this guy's worries. Everyone else is on side. I can only hope they go for it.'

'When will you find out?'

'Couple of days' time. I'll catch the early flight and it's straight from Heathrow to you.'

'You look done in, Brett. I'm sure you'll ace it, and whatever happens, you can only do your best.'

'My best?' he scoffed. 'That won't be enough to keep my job

if this deal goes tits up. There's no prize for trying your best in our business. This isn't a bit of tinsel and a few glittery reindeer.'

'You know what I mean,' she said, annoyed at him belittling her role.

'Yeah. Sorry.' He dragged his hand across his eyes. 'I'm tired and grouchy. I didn't mean to be a git. How's your day gone?'

She softened a little. He did look awful. 'Good. I went into Keswick with Nikki. Did some shopping and found some interesting pieces for next year.' She felt a bit guilty about saying what a relaxing day she'd had, even though she had no need to. 'I'll tell you all about it at the weekend.'

Brett managed a smile before a terrifying screech made him lean forward abruptly.

'Jesus, what was that?'

'Shagging foxes,' Krys said, chuckling at his horrified face. 'Not a serial killer.'

'I'm still not so sure about that Max,' he said. 'He'd better not be waiting outside with his chopper.'

'I doubt it,' Krys said, amused. 'He's probably tucked up with Jake.'

'I wish I was tucked up with you.'

Krys smiled, pleased to see him more like his old self. She kissed her fingers and held them to the screen.

'Well, don't stay up too late,' she said, a little disappointed that this didn't seem a good time to tell him about the ball.

'Ha ha! I wish I could take to my bed but I can't. Gotta grab a quick shower and head back down to the bar with the rest of the team, see if there's anything else we can do. It's high stakes stuff.'

'Take care anyway. Oh, by the way, I'm going to invite Harriet for a visit. As I'm here on my own,' she added pointedly.

'Good idea,' said Brett, sounding relieved. 'Take care. Don't let Max rope you into any more escapades.'

'He won't!'

But Brett was gone.

Krys thumped the pillow with an 'oomph' of frustration. She wasn't exactly angry at Brett because she understood the kind of pressure he was under. She'd worked very hard to carve out her own career and gain a reputation for the trends she spotted and displays she organised. The bottom line was shown in the customers' reactions and at the retailers' tills.

Although she was meant to be on a hiatus, she couldn't afford to completely relax. She had to make preparations for the next contract, which began in the new year, and had already booked her hotel and meetings with suppliers at Frankfurt and Birmingham.

Most of the pieces she found were presented to her by contacts or at the trade fairs, but she was always on the hunt for something new and different. It didn't look like Dave was interested in scaling up his production in any way – even if she could track him down.

Chapter Twelve

To Krys's delight, Harriet was as keen to visit as Krys was to see her.

'I've been waiting for an invitation!' she cried when Krys called. 'In fact, how do you fancy some company later this week? I've got some days owing that I have to take by the end of the year. Can't promise to arrive in a Porsche though.'

'I wouldn't care if you turned up on a penny farthing!'

'A penny farthing?' Harriet giggled. 'That's the sort of thing Miss Braithwaite would ride. Is she still around?'

'I doubt it. Probably retired by now. I haven't been near the Outdoor Centre,' Krys said. 'Are you sure George and the kids can spare you?'

'They'll have to. I need some me-time and I've already spoken to George. He's going to visit the outlaws with them, so I've escaped that dubious pleasure!'

Krys laughed. Harriet's rather snooty in-laws had once asked her why she hadn't trained to be a hospital consultant instead of 'settling for nursing'. Her husband, George, was a lovely guy but Krys could understand why Harriet would grab any excuse to get out of a visit.

'OK. Will you drive?'

'I'd rather not be stuck in the traffic for hours. Is there a train?'

'Yes, but I'll come over to Kendal to collect you, save you a very long journey round to this side of the Lakes.'

'Are you sure?' Harriet asked.

'One hundred percent. I can't wait to show you Thorndale.'

'I can't wait to see it again.'

'Harriet!' Krys managed before her friend cut the call. 'Bring some proper boots.'

'Oh, thanks for the heads-up. I was going to wear my sparkly pink trainers.'

Laughing, Krys ended the call, a glow of warmth spreading through her. She was really looking forward to seeing her friend and reminiscing about old times. Without Brett, they'd be able to have a good old catch-up. She'd better stock up on wine . . .

The following day brought more pleasures: her replacement decorations had finally been delivered to Holly Manor and unboxing them was like unearthing buried treasure.

Even though they were items she'd seen many times and actually chosen for the store display, it was still a thrill to finally see them in their rightful place: her fantasy Christmas card house. Already, she envisaged them on the Christmas tree she was going to buy in a couple of weeks' time. The swags and garlands, however, could be installed immediately on the front door, windowsills and mantelpiece.

Carefully, she removed each bauble from the boxes, laying them out on the dining table.

She'd chosen two themes in keeping with her temporary Lakeland home. One was centred around a fantasy ice palace while the other was inspired by a whimsical woodland motif.

Soon, the table was covered with forest creatures, icicles and snowy swags. She had planned to make a real garland for the door, but it probably wouldn't last until New Year so the faux one was a better solution for now. It was a real beauty, with dark green, almost blue spruce, dotted with frosted berries and 'snow'.

She was securing it to a small nail above the knocker when there was a familiar rumble behind her.

Max and the Landy.

Max strode over, with Jake at his heels. He wasn't smiling but that meant nothing. He could have won the lottery or the Bothy had been hit by a meteorite, for all Krys knew. Jake, on the other hand, ran straight up to her and rolled over at her feet, offering his belly for a stroke.

Crouching down, Krys rubbed his tum. 'Hey, boy. Great to see you too.'

With a yip, Jake shot off to explore the gardens so she turned her attention to his owner.

'Hi there, this is a surprise.'

'Is it inconvenient?' he asked.

'No. I wasn't busy. Or rather I wasn't busy with work. I was hanging up the door wreath. As you can see. My replacement decorations came this morning.'

His brow furrowed. 'But it's still November.'

'I know, but I like to start early.'

Again, a blank expression. Krys wasn't about to explain herself. It was pointless to a self-confessed Christmas-phobe.

'Would you like to come in?'

A moment's hesitation then he nodded. 'Thanks. Jake!'

'He's enjoying himself,' she said. 'There were foxes outside last night.'

'He'll probably roll in fox poo.'

Secretly hoping Jake did, Krys laughed. 'I'm sure he'll enjoy having a bath later.'

Max grimaced. 'I won't enjoy it.'

'Come in.'

The moment he stepped into the hallway, his jaw dropped.

'Wow. This really is,' he was clearly struggling for the right words, 'Christmassy.'

She laughed. 'It's only a small selection of the ranges I bought for the stores. These are my favourite pieces from two key trends.'

He stepped over a box of woodland garlands and picked up a jolly looking squirrel. 'Is this honestly what people are hanging on their trees this year?'

She braced herself for his scorn, determined to fight her corner, no matter how grouchy he was. 'These are the key themes in our stores, yes. The squirrel is part of the Woodland Wonders range, but we're also offering the Neon City, Ice Palace and Christmas by the Sea motifs. That was inspired by a coastal theme, with pastel colours, and baubles in the shape of mermaids and shells.'

'Neon mermaids,' he said, raising an eyebrow. 'How very festive.'

'No, mermaids and Neon City,' Krys explained, unable to resist winding him up. 'They're separate ranges. The neon series is aimed at the younger, urban buyers and has tech themes like mobile phones and cameras.'

'Phones?' He wrinkled his nose. 'Like I said, how very festive.'

'They are. The customers love them. They also love the neon penguins and Santas that you can hang on the wall. We sell a lot of pre-lit, pre-decorated trees to that demographic who might have less space.'

'This is a whole new world . . .' he muttered.

'The Ice Palace collection is spectacular, based around a palette of white and silver with cool blue accents,' she said. 'You should see the whole scheme of icicles, snowflakes and polar bears on a tree. As for the door-scaping, that's spectacular.'

'Door-scaping? What the hell's that?'

'Oh, it's *huge* these days,' Krys went on, almost enjoying his obvious disgust. 'It's all about the trend for decorating your front door with garlands, swags and wreaths – but that's not all. You can add arches and figures.'

'Figures?' Max looked dazzled. 'Of what?'

'Anything. Lifesize Nutcracker models to guard the entrance of your home. Our Ice Palace range included two silver unicorns.'

'And people actually part with their hard-earned cash to buy glittery unicorns?'

'And the rest,' Krys added with relish. 'Some people see a display in a magazine or online and they want the whole look.'

He shook his head. 'It sounds very expensive.'

'I'm afraid it can be. It seems a bit strange but a lot of people have come to appreciate their homes more than they used to. They want to push the boat out, and in some stores, there are customers around who want to spend lavishly.'

She faltered because he'd asked a question that she'd asked herself many times. 'Personally, I'm a traditionalist and like to add all the pieces I've gathered from over the years along with some new ones. Of course, I'm incredibly lucky to be given a lot of free samples.'

He was still dumbfounded.

'Max, you did ask me . . .'

He nodded. 'Yeah. I suppose it's your job. More than a job. It's your passion. I do get it.'

'You don't have to get it. It's OK to hate the whole commercial idea of it. I learned long ago that Christmas – or this version of it – is Kryptonite to a lot of people. The important thing is that I love it and I want to share it.'

'Aren't you—'

'Exploiting them?'

'Making them think they need this stuff to have a happy Christmas.'

'I hope not. Look, people have had a hard time lately. They want to bring some magic into their lives and if they want to do it with a glittery unicorn or a neon penguin, then why not?'

'There's really no answer to that,' he said.

Krys despaired of his cynicism but he'd answered one niggling suspicion. She was crazy to even have imagined Max might be the craftsman behind the wooden decorations.

'Is there any particular reason for this visit?' she said frostily.

'Yes. I came over to bring this.' He dipped a hand in his pocket and pulled out a small golden hoop. 'You left it in my bedroom.'

'Oh. My earring. I'd been wondering what happened to it. I'd assumed it must have been lost in the flood.'

She took it from him.

'It had rolled under the bedside table. Found it when I was cleaning earlier.'

'Really?' Krys knew exactly when it might have happened: when she was looking at the photo on the table and found the wooden top. 'Thanks,' she said, hoping Max would assume it had simply rolled under the table by accident.

Max stuck his hands in his pockets, leaving her waiting for him to impart any other revelations.

'Are you going to the base tonight?' he asked.

'Yeah. I was planning to. Nikki invited me. What about you?'

'I'm doing the candidates' challenge this afternoon. It ends with a debrief tonight so I've no choice but to go, and I don't think they'd let me join if I failed to turn up for the most important part of the process.'

'It sounds pretty tough to me,' Krys said, remembering she wasn't supposed to have overheard the team conversation in the pub.

'It's no picnic but it's crucial that you can help carry a stretcher off the hill and find your own way about up there. I'd be lying if I said I wasn't a bit nervous but the team will give plenty of support.' He sighed. 'Whether I want it or not.'

'Good luck with it,' Krys said, adding generously, 'Thanks for bringing the earring.'

'It was on my way,' he murmured. 'I'd better collect Jake before he gets into any more trouble. Enjoy your decorating.'

Calling to the dog, he strode down the steps of the manor towards the car.

That evening, the headlamps of Krys's hire car swept over a familiar vehicle when she turned into the entrance to Thorndale mountain rescue base after dinner. She could hardly get lost: the red lights on the radio mast must be visible for miles around.

To her relief, Nikki's car was already parked outside.

Despite having introduced herself at scores of events where she knew no one, intruding on a tight-knit community, even when she had met a few of the people, gave Krys butterflies.

She messaged Nikki to say she'd arrived and climbed out of the car to find her almost at the car.

'Hello! I was on the lookout for you.'

'Great. I do feel a bit like a cuckoo in the nest.'

'No way. Everyone's looking forward to seeing you. Come on, let's meet the gang.'

Inside, the base was much bigger than it looked from the outside, with double doors leading through to a large room from the foyer where dozens of serious mountain coats had been hung on pegs. Muddy boots were stacked on racks.

'It looks brand new.'

'It's only a couple of years old. The CEO of a company donated it in gratitude for us helping their family member.'

'That was generous of them.'

'Yes. Before that we had to manage in a ramshackle place that had been farm buildings. The farm bungalow was demolished and we built this place. Now we have a proper training room, garages for the vehicles, a canteen, a control room and the new mast. The stone barn at the side was listed so it was refurbished. We use it for training and open days, and with the canteen and the barn, we can also throw a half decent party.'

'It looks much bigger than I'd thought. Loads of character too,' Krys said, admiring the beams and stone walls. She already had ideas for decorating it: maybe an ice palace theme, or an Alpine chalet? She wondered if she could call in some suppliers to donate samples to decorate it. She was owed a few favours. For now, she kept that to herself. No use making promises you couldn't keep.

'It must cost a lot to run,' Krys observed, as they walked into the main room.

'We still have to fundraise for day-to-day costs and we're always keen to make people aware of our work. You'd be amazed how many people set off on a mountain walk without so much as a bottle of water. We even have people trying to ascend the Pike in flip-flops!'

'You're joking?'

'No. It happened once to a group in the summer. They made it to around two thousand feet before calling us, but we don't judge. We only want to help.' Nikki had a glint in her eye. 'As you'll find out. Here we are. Thorndale MRT gang.'

There must have been around twenty people chattering away, most with mugs in their hands. She recognised a few faces from the pub immediately, including Davy and Katya, the team medic.

There was no sign of Max, and her heart sank a little. What if he had decided not to turn up for the candidates' challenge, not because he was scared but because he'd backed out of becoming a formal part of the team? She wouldn't wish that on him.

A few faces turned in her direction, eyeing her with curiosity. Others smiled.

Nikki ushered her forward. 'Let's start with the pub gang as you've met them already.'

It wasn't as bad as she'd expected. Of course it wasn't. Everyone was welcoming and she was soon into her stride in the way she would have been meeting any new group of people. She wasn't on show here either, no need to make an impression. Even so, she was aware that her unusual job was a source of intrigue – even astonishment – to some.

Nikki brought her a coffee and introduced Krys to one of the search and rescue dogs, a sweet border collie called Star, who allowed herself to be stroked.

While she fussed the dog, Max walked into the room and was immediately surrounded by people. She could tell by the laughter and banter that things had gone well. Davy slapped him on the back and several people shook his hand.

Max looked awkward and kept shaking his head. Krys guessed he was actually rather pleased.

He caught her eye and she mouthed 'well done' before forcing her full attention back to her new friends, who were talking about some of their rescues. They had plenty of false alarms but some sounded incredibly dangerous, involving abseiling down cliffs and helicopter airlifts.

'Then there are the people who decide to climb to the top of a fell to photograph the sunset,' Davy said. 'But hadn't thought how they'd find their way down in the dark after said event had occurred.'

Krys let out a gasp. 'You're kidding me now?'

He laughed deeply. He was a handsome guy, though she hoped he wouldn't renew his offer of a drink, as he had in the pub. It was unlikely, given he now knew she had a boyfriend. 'No, we've seen everything,' he said. 'Some of it ends happily, some of it is tragic.'

'The worst shouts are the ones where we end up finding a body,' Dr Katya explained. 'People are drawn to the peace and tranquillity of the fells, and who can blame them? Trouble is, they can also be dangerous and there are always a few poor souls who don't want to be found, and choose remote places like this to vanish.'

'That's awful. Those poor people ending their lives all alone.' Krys shivered. She'd known plenty of friends with mental health issues and had suffered bouts of anxiety herself. It had been terrifying but she'd got through it with the help of Linda, and the support of friends. It gave her a new perspective on the mountains: a place of great beauty but also of menace.

The doctor pressed her lips together then said. 'It's beyond sad. It always affects us but all we can do is find the unfortunate person and at least bring them home so their loved ones have some closure and a funeral.'

Krys shook her head. 'I don't know how you do it.'

'Because we love the fells. We want people to enjoy them safely and we love helping people. Sounds corny, but that's why we do it and we couldn't imagine not lending a hand.'

'Besides, it gives us a great excuse to bunk off work,' Davy put in to general laughter.

'You all have day jobs?' Krys said.

'Yes.' Nikki nodded at the team chattering in the canteen area. 'We've a doctor, of course.'

Katya gave a little bow and laughed.

'And a professional rugby player,' Davy said, with a wink.

Nikki rolled her eyes good-humouredly. 'Always comes in handy if we want to practise our scrums on top of the Pike.'

Davy pouted. 'I'm hurt.'

'We also have a sculptor, a butcher, hairdresser, chef, nuclear engineer, bar staff, a vicar.' Nikki ticked them off on her fingers.

'Sounds like Happy Families!' Krys joked.

'Ah, but I don't think Happy Families ever featured a drag artiste. Though it should,' Nikki added.

'A drag artiste!'

Nikki smiled. 'It's true. One of our number made it to the final stages of the RuPaul auditions. He's a paramedic in his day job.'

Krys automatically scanned the room, to see if she could spot the famous drag queen/medic. Was it the very tall man in the Harry Potter specs? Or the red-haired Viking lookalike chatting to Max?

However, with almost everyone wearing nondescript outfits in their fleeces and jeans, it was impossible to even hazard a guess. Besides, she'd met enough people in the course of her job and daily life to realise that making judgements based on appearance was pointless. Look how she and Brett had judged Max: as an eccentric wild man, possibly an axe murderer. They'd certainly been wrong about the second. He was no wild man, either, though eccentric might still fit the bill.

'I'll keep you guessing,' Nikki said.

'I'm sure Hector will be more than happy to tell you himself,' Katya put in.

'Then we'll definitely buy a ticket,' Krys said.

Max had moved closer. Krys wondered if he was as nervous as she'd been. Katya and Nikki were called away by the team leader so left Krys to Davy and Max.

127

'Hey, Max. You're not the only rookie tonight,' Davy said.

Max's brow furrowed in confusion.

'We have another new recruit,' Davy said mischievously.

'Oh, I'm not an actual recruit! Nikki asked me to help out with the decorations at the ball. I won't be hauling stretchers down the Pike.'

Davy laughed. 'So, you are coming to the ball. Will Brett be there too?'

'I haven't asked him yet,' Krys said. 'But yes, he will.'

'Must be lonely in that big place on your own.'

'Actually, *no*. I've plenty to keep me occupied. Finally I've had time to do some shopping, read a book, relax and take lots of walks. And Brett's home at the weekends,' Krys said firmly. 'Most of the weekends.'

'I'm sure Krys doesn't need company,' Max said bluntly.

And certainly not Davy's kind of company, she thought.

'Well, if you don't try, you don't get anywhere,' he said cheekily. 'I'll take it as my cue to get myself a coffee and leave you two to it.'

'I apologise for Davy,' Max said the moment his friend had left. 'He's a good bloke but he's hopeless at taking a hint.'

'Yet he knows I'm in a relationship?'

'Yeah, and he should have accepted that. He won't bother you again.'

'He wasn't bothering me. It's just that it's a bit . . . awkward to have to hammer home the point.'

'He needs it. Not the most tactful person. Again, I apologise on his behalf.'

'No need. It's not your fault. It's good to see you, though,' she said lightly. 'Well done on completing the challenge.'

His eyes lit up with genuine pleasure, but he said, 'The team may live to regret my success.'

'I – um – couldn't help overhearing the conversation in the pub the other weekend. It must have been difficult to say yes to joining the team.'

Max seemed surprised that she'd noticed but there was an ironic twist of the lips. 'They've tried to persuade me to join before, but when Will Tennant weighed in, I was left with no choice. Besides . . . there's only so long you can hide away from the world.'

He turned his deep brown gaze on her, as if he was daring her to contradict him. It was as if a veil had been drawn back on the frosty man who'd so reluctantly given them shelter in his home.

'Do you want to hide away?' she asked carefully.

'Sometimes. Most times.'

'Though not all?'

The smile again: vanishing as quickly as water over a fall. 'Not all. Not lately. And from now on . . . it looks like I'll have no choice but to be a bit more sociable.'

'I'm sure it won't be as painful as you think.'

'We'll see.'

Again, the world-weary smile that held very little mirth. Max had allowed her a glimpse of a different man; one who might once have been the first to put up his hand when his help was needed and thrived in the spotlight.

'How's Brett?' he said, switching the focus away from himself. 'Ankle OK?'

'Back to normal though I haven't seen him since the other weekend. He's trying to seal a big contract at work.'

'Oh?' His frown deepened. 'That's a shame.'

'Yes, but I understand what it's like. I've been there myself. Work comes first.'

'I've been there too and I promise you, it should *never* come at the expense of a relationship,' he snapped.

Wow. That was emphatic.

'It's only for a few weeks. It'll be done soon and then I'm sure he can relax. He's coming back this weekend,' Krys said, defending Brett and a little annoyed with Max's vehement response.

'I hope so.' Max heaved a sigh. 'Look, I'm sorry for foisting my opinions on you. I shouldn't have said anything. I'm being as much of a pain in the arse as Davy. It's none of my business.' He turned to leave.

Instinctively, Krys laid a hand on his arm.

He glanced down at it, as if amazed at the human contact. Krys didn't think anyone had touched him – apart from in a rescue, perhaps – let alone got close to him, in a very long time.

She withdrew her hand. 'Max, wait.'

He stopped and looked at her. This time, his eyes held only pain.

'Ignore me. I'm no use to anyone.'

'No use? That can't be true.'

'Oh, it is.'

'Max. If you want to talk to someone – an outsider – I can be a good listener. You only have to ask. We could go for a walk with Jake, if it helps.'

Jake glanced up at the mention of his name, as if he was waiting for Max to make a decision. Max was wavering.

'Right, guys! Listen up!'

A shout from the control room door shattered the moment. A second later, loud beeps pierced the room as pagers went off in a dozen pockets.

Hazel, the team leader, strode in. 'I need your full attention!' she called.

The room fell silent and every eye was intent on her.

'There's been a major incident. Three students haven't returned from a climbing expedition on the Pike. They left their route at

Thorndale YHA with an intended return time of five p.m. They haven't been heard of or contactable since, so the YHA manager has phoned us. Let's hope they've managed to make their own way down but we can't afford to assume that. It's a full-scale search operation. We need all the hands we can get.'

Chapter Thirteen

Krys's conversation with Max ended abruptly. The atmosphere had changed from laughter and chatter to deadly serious.

All eyes were on Hazel.

'We've already called Bannerdale MRT and four of their members are on the way. We've also alerted the Coastguard but visibility is poor and the winds are gusting force seven up on the tops. Probably some sleet and ice up there too, as you'll all be aware.'

Heads nodded, murmurings of agreement.

'I need all trained personnel to join me in the control room for a briefing. Max, can you join Davy and help load and prepare the vehicles?

'Will do,' said Max and Davy nodded.

Swiftly, people were assigned tasks, and words like 'casualties', 'stretcher' and 'airlift' were bandied about in quick succession. Krys heard the wind swirl around the base and rain pattering against the panes. It had been chilly enough here at sea level. What must it be like high up on the fells? Lost in the pitch darkness? The students must be terrified.

A few minutes later, people began to flow out of the room into the kit room, the vehicle bay and control room.

Max lingered a moment. 'Looks like I'm going to be needed sooner than I'd hoped.'

'Can I do anything?' Krys asked.

'I'm sure you can. Ask Nikki, she'll sort you out. I'll see you later.' He smiled. 'Look after Jake for me, will you? Make sure he doesn't get into any trouble.'

'I'll try,' she said.

'Stay with Krys, mate.' Max crouched beside him and ruffled his ears. 'I'll be back soon.'

'See you later,' he said to Krys.

He hurried through to the control room, abandoning her to organised chaos.

See you later? Did he mean that evening – or on the walk he'd been on the verge of agreeing to? She'd been sure he was going to say yes.

It was trivial now. Lives were at stake: Krys had never been in a remotely similar situation before and could feel the adrenaline surging. Her heart was beating faster, strung as tense as a wire, almost twitching to be given a task to ease the tension.

Nikki was deep in conversation with Davy but Krys didn't wait. If she was in the way, she'd leave now, but if she could help, she was staying.

Davy left just as Krys reached her. 'Nikki. Is there anything I can help with?'

'Definitely if you're up for it. We'll need hot drinks and food ready for when the team get back or new teams swap over. We might have cold, wet and frightened young people arriving. Adults too. Fingers crossed,' Nikki added. 'They'll need re-assuring and calming, as well as feeding and warming up, but that could be hours away. The early hours or even morning. It'll be a very long night.'

'I'm staying,' Krys declared.

'Thanks. Why don't you go into the kitchen and I'll find someone to familiarise you with the place? I have to go up into the hills myself.'

Krys shuddered. 'Be careful,' she said. 'All of you.'

'Don't you worry about us.' Nikki zipped her jacket to her chin. 'See you later. There's no time to lose.'

Although Krys was kept busy initially, she was soon involved in a waiting game. Having heard about the incident, Amina had arrived with a box of biscuits when Krys walked into the kitchen.

'I never expected this,' Krys said.

'You never know what's going to happen next in this game,' Amina said.

'What else can I do to help?'

'I brought some fresh supplies from the stores. Wanna give me a hand to unload them from the van?'

'Sure.'

Krys helped bring in several litres of milk, tea bags, cereal bars and bananas. Amina gave her a quick run-through of the hot water urn, showed her where the mugs were and then they went to collect some blankets and put them in a smaller room equipped with a couple of sofas.

'This is a relatives' room though it can also be used for the team to get some rest. It's where people can wait for news, or in the worst case have some peace if they've had bad news.'

Mindful of what she'd heard earlier that evening, Krys suppressed a shudder. This was not a job for the faint-hearted. In fact it wasn't a job at all, given no one was paid a penny for helping out, yet they risked their safety anyway.

'Prepare for the worst but hope for the best. It usually turns out OK,' Amina said, picking up on Krys's anxious expression. 'Bet you anything those students have made their own way down and they're snug in some dale bar, sinking a few pints.'

'Does that happen?'

'More times than you'd believe. People descend into the wrong valley and they can't face or afford an exorbitant taxi ride back to their start point. They might be lodged in a different YHA or a pub and have forgotten to tell the person they left their emergency details with. Folk can do funny things or not think straight when they're under pressure.'

When they'd chatted about the team and the weather, Krys sat down at the table and checked her phone while Amina went off into the main room.

Krys had wondered whether to message Brett but it was now past eleven and a bit too late to disturb him. He'd find it hard to believe she was at the MRT base, helping out – in her small way – with a search and rescue operation. She had to admit there was a buzz about it, as well as anxiety, and felt guilty. Was that normal?

A broad-shouldered man with chiselled cheekbones and a square jaw came up and spoke to Amina.

'Hey, Amina. Do you know where the sugar is? We seem to get through tons of it.'

'Top cupboard next to the fridge, Hector.'

So *this* was Hector. He was definitely built like a Trojan warrior.

'I keep telling the team it's bad for them but no one listens to my health advice.' He rolled his eyes. He certainly looked in great shape to Krys, as if he spent hours in the gym lifting weights.

'How's the gig gone in Cockermouth?' Amina asked him.

'Pretty good. It was me and two mates and eighty mostly ladies. Lots of Prosecco was consumed and it went down a storm. Did you see Max went out with the team?' Hector said to Amina with a raised eyebrow. 'Quite the turn-up that he agreed to join at all.'

'Possibly.' Amina's eyes were mischievous over the rim of her mug.

'So you're not that surprised. You know him best though.'

'Hardly.'

'Come on, he talks to you more than any of us,' Hector said to Krys's keen interest. 'What's made him suddenly change his mind about joining us?'

'I've no idea. He has been emerging from his shell more lately. He's started coming to the pub and down to the village more. When he first moved in, he'd come along once every couple of weeks, hardly make eye contact and leave. Things change a little when I told him Jake needed a home last winter.'

'You credit Jake with bringing him out of his cave?' Hector seemed amused.

'It helped,' Amina said. 'And we got talking and he said he'd help out with the rescues if we were ever desperate.'

Jake pricked up his ears at the mention of his name then settled down again by Krys's feet. She stroked his head and sipped her coffee, intrigued. She was more convinced than ever that there was definitely more to Max and Amina's relationship than 'just friends'.

'Max hasn't had the happiest time in the past,' Amina said, as if she needed to explain the conversation to Krys. 'Although none of us really know what happened, I think there was a family tragedy. That's all we can gather.'

'Unless he's spoken to you?' Hector said, eyeing Krys closely.

'No . . . He hardly knows me,' Krys said, taken aback by the very suggestion. 'We worked out he likes to keep himself to himself. I wouldn't pry into his private life.'

'No, of course not,' Amina said.

Puzzled, Krys returned to her drink. Either no one genuinely knew why Max was in Thorndale, or they weren't saying. Ditto his relationship with Amina, *if* there was a relationship: she didn't give the impression she knew much more about him than Krys herself. Either that or there was a conspiracy of silence around Max.

The crackle of static drew Hector to the radio room but he returned with no concrete update on the search. Krys decided to keep herself busy.

'I may as well scope out the room for the Christmas decorations,' she told Amina and explained that her latest delivery had arrived that morning.

Amina took her through to the training room, a cavernous space with open rafters that betrayed its barn origins. 'What do you think?' she said, as they stood in the middle.

'It's a great space. I'm sure we can do something,' Krys said, ideas forming in her mind. Brett would have laughed at the mere idea of it hosting a ball, which would make it all the more delicious when they turned up on the night and she showed him the transformation. She was itching to get started on it.

'Good, because I'm hopeless at visualising rooms. It's as much as I can do to arrange the stock on the shelves. I've been dying to hear more about your job. It's not every day you meet a real-life Mrs Christmas.'

Amina seemed genuinely interested in her work, so Krys told her about her career, how she'd got into it, and about Auntie Linda.

In return, Amina explained how she'd taken over the post office stores after she'd seen the house and business up for sale five years previously.

'I was born and bred in the Lakes but I went to uni in North London and stayed there, working in retail management. I loved the bright lights and buzz of the city. The place never slept and neither did I when I was younger.'

'I know what you mean. I love London and the cities I visit. I get up early and walk around as a place wakes up.'

'I have trouble getting up,' Amina joked. 'But while I was in the Smoke, I met a guy and we got married but it didn't work out. One day I was back visiting my folks, and they mentioned this place had come up. Part of me was worried about coming home to Thorndale, but in other ways, it felt so right. I was burnt out from working. My soul was weary too, after the split from my husband.'

Amina hadn't mentioned anyone else. Was Max the new person to light up her life? He'd arrived three years ago, from what Krys could work out.

'Thorndale healed me,' Amina went on. 'It sounds corny but it was exactly what I needed at the right time. But you have Brett. Lucky you.'

'Yes . . .' Brett would never have moved to Thorndale. She was having trouble getting him to stay more than a weekend. He was busy, of course, that was the reason, and he'd promised to add the week he was owed onto the Christmas break he'd already booked.

Krys had already realised that you needed at least a few days to fully decompress from working so hard. It had taken her almost a week to settle into the new rhythm of Thorndale: to stop checking her phone every five minutes when she was out, or be anxious she didn't have a signal. Now she'd ceased to fear that blank space on the screen where the signal bar should be and felt only relief.

Instead, she'd focused on the hills, the russet of bracken, the crunch of a leaf under her boots, the high-pitched mew of a buzzard, the tiny forest of lichen on a wall. Anytime she wanted to return to her online world, she had the manor where her friends were on the end of a WhatsApp call. It was just refreshing not to be available every second of her life.

The control room radio crackled and there was a flurry of animated conversation.

'Well, well,' Hector said, abandoning his mug on the worktop. 'Something's happening at last.'

Amina held up her crossed fingers, with a grimace. Krys's pulse spiked again. She didn't know the students but she was almost as edgy as if they were personal friends. She couldn't tell if the news was good or bad from the noises from down the corridor.

Hector called from the door to the canteen. 'Well, the good news is they've been found. The bad news is one of them has sustained a fractured ankle. He's being airlifted off. The others can be walked down.'

Amina blew out a breath. 'That's a relief. Could have been a lot worse. A fracture in those conditions is considered life-threatening, though, so no one will relax until the casualty's safe in hospital. It also could be another couple of hours until the team's back. You don't have to wait if you want to get home to your bed,' she said. 'It's past one already.'

'I've been here this long. I think I'll see it out,' Krys said.

'Good on you. We can afford to chill out for a wee bit longer before we start getting ready.'

It was three a.m. before anyone came back from the mountain, heralded by headlights in the car park and tired bodies pouring into the canteen. Krys found herself hoping that Max would be in the first group, but he wasn't.

Despite the late night, there was a lot of laughter and huge relief. The helicopter had taken the injured student to hospital and the others had been met by paramedics and taken to the local hospital for a check-up. News had come through that the student was 'comfortable' and would be OK.

Hector went outside to help unload the kit so the others could have some hot food and 'decompress'.

Krys was in charge of the tea urn, dispensing drinks and handing out biscuits and cereal bars.

'It's too early for breakfast, otherwise we'd be dishing up bacon butties,' Amina whispered.

Shortly afterwards, Max arrived, dishevelled and tired but – surprisingly – smiling. Catching sight of Krys, his amazement was obvious.

'You're still here?' he said, accepting a mug of coffee with a heartfelt thanks.

'Yes. I lost track of the time. Then it got so late, it didn't seem worth going to bed. How was it?'

'Honestly? I was bricking it at times, worried that I'd make an arse of myself or trip over and have to be rescued. It's one thing helping out as an amateur, quite another when you're meant to be one of the "professionals".'

Krys smiled. 'You did OK, though, and the casualties are safe and well.'

'Almost. The lad's messed up his ankle pretty badly but he'll heal.'

'Hey, Max! You did well, mate. For a novice.'

Max almost staggered forward under Davy's slap on the back. 'I survived. So did the casualties.'

'You didn't kill anyone or yourself. First rule.'

'He was brilliant,' Hazel said, joining them and shaking Max's hand. 'Well done. Good to have you on board.'

Max could not keep the grin off his face.

'He won't be able to get out of the door if you keep giving him a big head,' Davy said, then became more serious. 'Honestly, mate, your knowledge of the fells round here is as good as anyone's. Your suggestion to head for that hidden gully was inspired. We'd have taken longer to locate them if you hadn't.'

'It was an educated guess, given their description of their location,' Max said, looking a little embarrassed by the attention.

'It saved a lot of time,' Hazel said. 'I'm glad you decided to join us. Now, let's grab some hot drinks and then we can all go home to our beds.'

Krys listened intently, intrigued by Max's reaction to the praise. Davy didn't renew any offers to take her out and kept his conversation to the rescue. Nikki returned and the team leader thanked Krys for staying to help.

Max laughed out loud several times, his eyes lighting up. She might have been mistaken, but he almost seemed happy. She knew she certainly was, and she'd have loads to tell Brett when he came home.

The moment Krys set foot in Holly Manor, her phone beeped with several messages, as if it was annoyed she'd dared venture out of signal range. Which might have been true because they were all from Brett asking – demanding – she call him. When she looked at the times, three were before ten p.m. then one at midnight. He must have really wanted to talk to her.

Well, it was way too late now. She dragged herself upstairs, pulled off her jeans and jumper and got into bed in the rest of her clothes. Not even screeching foxes or hooting owls would keep her awake now.

Unexpectedly, the night had turned into one of the most exciting and rewarding experiences of her life: in a different way to landing her first job or a big contract. Deeply satisfying with a sense that, in however small a way, she'd made a contribution to potentially saving someone's life.

She lay awake, recalling Max's words to her after Hazel had thanked her for helping out.

'I only made the tea,' she'd said, embarrassed.

'Yeah, but you stayed here, gave up your bed and your time for a bunch of people you hardly know,' Max had replied. 'We don't think people are better because they go up the mountain. Everyone is an important part of the group.'

Krys wasn't so sure. Standing behind the urn and handing out biscuits was hardly dicing with death.

Even so, it had been an amazing evening. Max had been chatting. Max had been smiling. Max had been laughing. Whatever had kept him away from human company, he was back.

Krys was as buzzed as any of them. She didn't think she'd sleep at all, and wait until she told Brett, when she spoke to him the next morning.

He'd never believe it . . .

Chapter Fourteen

The insistent buzzing of the phone on the bedside table was a rude awakening for Krys. Weak sunlight streamed through a chink in the curtains which meant it was pretty late – then she caught sight of the phone.

She fumbled for the answer button, pushing herself up on the pillows, relieved he hadn't video called her.

'Brett. M-morning.'

'Krys! Where've you been? I've been trying to get hold of you since last night. I'm calling before I head off for a lunch meeting.'

'Lunch?' Krys groaned. 'It's half-eleven, I hadn't realised . . .' she said, still rubbing sleep from her eyes. 'I was out on a shout.'

'I called you at *midnight*. Hang on . . . did you say you were "out on a shout"? As in a rescue? Jesus, Krys, you weren't out in the dark on the mountains? Is this anything to do with Mad Max?'

'No, I was at the base, waiting for the casualties and making tea. Why would it have anything to do with Max?'

'I don't know, only that it's exactly the kind of thing that oddball would rope you into. What do you want to get involved in all that for?'

Now wide awake, Krys was losing patience at Brett's comments about Max. It didn't seem so funny now she'd seen how he and the team had put themselves at risk to go after the students.

'Nikki invited me. She asked if I'd lend a hand decorating the base for the ball. Then the call came through about the casualties and they needed all the help they could get. We rescued three students. They'd have died otherwise.'

'We?' he echoed. 'Well I suppose it's a good thing you're making friends.'

'Yes . . .' She swung her legs from under the duvet so she was sitting upright. Somehow she felt better able to deal with Brett while she wasn't actually in bed. OK, he was busy but she was a bit annoyed with his tone. It was none of his business what she did with her spare time while he was in London. 'Like I say, I went along to talk about helping with the Winter Ball. I've bought two tickets. I didn't have a chance to ask you and I didn't think you'd mind.'

She waited for the answer but got only silence. One that stretched and stretched like a bungee cord.

'Brett? Are you still there?'

'Yes. I'm still here . . .'

'These tickets for the ball. I thought it would be fun and it's the weekend before Christmas. So you'll have finished work and can relax. It's all for a good cause. We can talk about it when you're home this weekend, if you really want to, but I know it'll be a lot of fun . . .'

'Krys . . .'

'They need funds to keep the place running. Can you believe they give all their time and risk their safety for nothing?

Just to help people who've got into trouble in the hills. It's the least I can do to buy a couple of tickets and spare some time for them.'

'Krys!'

She held the phone away from her ear.

'What's the matter? You sound angry.'

'I'm not angry and yes to the ball but . . .' His voice tailed off. 'I'm really sorry but I won't be home this weekend.'

She stood up abruptly. 'Why not?'

'Because I'm – I don't know how to say this and I *have* been trying to get you but – I'm going to the States tomorrow.'

She clamped the phone to her ear, unsure of what she'd heard. 'The States? How long for?'

'A week, maybe two. It's as much of a surprise to me as to you. After we won the Paris contract, the boss called me in and said they want someone experienced to oversee it from the US side. He promised the client he'd find the right guy – or woman – but they asked for me. They know me, they trust me and so the boss asked if I'd go to the New York office and finalise the deal from there.'

'New York? Wow . . . and they asked for you personally?'

'Yes. I can hardly refuse, can I? If it goes well, I'll be in line for a seat on the board, according to my boss. I'm really sorry to leave you in that godforsaken place for the next couple of weeks, but I *have* to take this opportunity.'

'Yes . . . yes, I see.'

Krys saw but she didn't have to like it. The whole point of renting Holly Manor had been to spend some quality time together and now the exact opposite seemed to be happening.

'I – I'll miss you,' she said.

'I know, babe. If there was any other way, believe me I wouldn't go, but I've no choice.'

'No.'

She tried to understand: she travelled a lot for her own job, sometimes at short notice. It was part of the job but Brett's absence still stung, because she'd pinned so many hopes on this break, on spending cosy nights in front of the fire. Since she'd been sucked more into the life of the community, she'd invested even more in it. She so wanted Brett to get to know the area and people a little better. She was sure he might grow to appreciate them more and see that there was a different life beyond the non-stop one they'd been living.

'Krys, are you still there?'

'Yes. I'm here.'

'Look, I'll definitely be home in a couple of weeks and this ball sounds like a laugh. I'll pay for the tickets.'

'There's no need . . .' It seemed scant consolation.

'I insist. My treat, and it's great you won't be too lonely, with your new mountain rescue mates.' There was amusement in his voice, but Krys didn't feel like laughing.

'Actually,' she said, 'I won't be lonely at all because Harriet's coming up for a few days.'

'Sounds great. Two girls together. Enjoy hitting the bright lights, will you?'

'In Thorndale? It's hardly New York,' she said, not ready to let him off so lightly, even if she would have a great time with Harriet.

He laughed. 'I'll be working or schmoozing clients every waking minute,' he said. 'Now, I have to go, I need to pack and grab a few hours shut-eye before I have to head to the airport. Take care, I'll video call when I get to the Big Apple. I promise to bring you back some decorations from Macy's.'

I'd rather have you.

Brett had ended the video call before she voiced her thoughts out loud, or maybe she was too disappointed with him to say them anyway.

She didn't know how to feel or react to this latest let-down.

For a few seconds, she stood in the window gazing out over the fell tops. Clouds scudded over the snow-topped mountains. Crows cawed in the trees and a deer had wandered into the garden and was nibbling a shrub. It was an idyllic scene but she felt acutely lonely.

No matter how much she'd started to join in with the community, she didn't belong here. No matter how much she tried to understand that Brett had to meet his work demands, she felt hurt and disappointed. It was going to be a long two weeks until he returned . . .

As she watched, the post van turned into the driveway.

Her mood immediately lifted when the postman jumped out and retrieved a large box from the rear. It had to be her latest batch of Christmas decorations. She'd ordered even more when Nikki had asked her to decorate the base, just to be on the safe side.

Hopping about, she pulled on jeans and a sweatshirt and scurried downstairs. She couldn't stay gloomy long with a new batch of baubles on the doorstep. She'd have a great time with Harriet, throw herself into decorating the manor and base and Brett would be back before she knew it. They could make the ball a spectacular finale to her Christmas holiday.

Chapter Fifteen

It was a three hour round trip to collect Harriet from the station at Kendal, but Krys was happy to have the extra precious time to catch up together. She'd kept herself busy over the past few days, planning how to decorate the manor, visiting the lantern parade in Ambleside and taking part in The Cock's quiz night. Yet she was still missing Brett and longing for the company of her old friend.

Harriet emerged from the station entrance as Krys arrived, eagerly scanning the car park for a familiar face.

Buzzing with excitement, Krys jogged over and they threw their arms around each other.

'Oh, how amazing to see you!' Harriet was beaming as ever.

Krys hugged her. 'It really, really is,' she said, feeling far more emotional than she'd expected. Perhaps it was because it was the first time they'd ever been back to the scene of their first meeting. 'Sorry it's raining,' she said.

'I wouldn't have expected anything less!'

As they drove west along the coast road, the rain cleared and the winter sun came out, turning the vast expanse of Morecambe Bay into a shimmering bowl of light.

'This is a-mazing,' Harriet said, her ginger ponytail bobbing enthusiastically. 'And look at those mountains! I can hardly believe it's the same place. It seemed a minging dump when I was little.'

'Probably because you felt sick on the minibus,' Krys said.

'Yes, having to stop in a layby to throw up isn't the best start to a holiday, not that it was a holiday.'

'More like a sentence.' Krys laughed. 'We were so ungrateful.'

'We were kids,' Harriet said.

'That's how I feel again now. I'm so excited to see you. Thanks for coming.'

'It's me who should thank you. I'm getting a wonderful mini break in a gorgeous house with the bonus of avoiding a visit to the Snooty Outlaws.' She squeaked. 'Oh, is that snow on the mountain?'

'It is,' Krys said with pride. 'Wait until you reach Thorndale. The tops are completely white.'

Harriet was suitably gobsmacked by Holly Manor. Krys lit a fire and they settled down in front of it.

'It looks gorgeous. I love a bit of bling,' said Harriet, tucking her feet under her on the sofa, holding a glass of mulled wine that Krys had bought from the market. 'Who would have ever believed it? The two of us, here in this place.'

Krys felt more relaxed than she had for days. 'I'd say I could never have imagined it, but I did.'

Harriet nodded. 'Same. It's about time we saw each other more often, but with busy lives, families, partners . . .'

'Brett?' Krys said.

'Yes. You two don't get much time together so I didn't want to muscle in.'

'Muscle in any time, whoever I'm with. Though it is nice to be able to say what we feel without anyone around.'

'And how do you feel?' Harriet said. 'About Brett being away?'

'I was disappointed and a bit annoyed at first and I do miss him but,' Krys took a deep breath, 'I can take care of myself. I've joined the local mountain rescue team.'

'Nooooo wayyyy!'

'Yes, way. Well, not exactly "joined", though I have been to a couple of meetings and offered to help decorate their base for their fundraising ball. You'd have loved the last one, it was about first aid.'

'Oh no, I'm on holiday,' Harriet declared. 'Please don't tell them I'm a nurse or I'll be roped in too.'

'Don't worry, I won't. I doubt we'll bump into anyone while you're here apart from Nikki, the Holly Manor property manager.'

'And she's in the MRT as well?'

'Oh, yes. They all have other jobs, apart from Max of course.'

'Ah Max. Now, I *do* hope we bump into him.'

'Why?' Krys asked, knowing that sly smile well.

'Because you have mentionitis about him.'

'No, I do not!' Krys exclaimed.

'Well, he always seems to creep into our conversations somehow. "Max popped in with Jake . . ." or "Max saved us from certain drowning" or "Max hates Christmas but he's got a heart of gold really".'

'I have never said any of those things, Harriet Taylor!'

Harriet shrugged. 'Not the exact words but pretty close.' She topped up her wine glass. 'You know, I would love to meet this Max.'

'I can't guarantee that.'

'OK, and there's something else that might be easier to guarantee.'

'What?'

'I'd like to see the Outdoor Centre. It is quite near here, isn't it? I've been on Google maps.'

'It's on the other side of the lake to here,' Krys said. 'I haven't been yet.'

'Why not?'

She shrugged. 'Not sure, really. Scared of how it will make me feel.' Krys didn't want any more intense emotional experiences after the past few months.

'What's there to fear?' Harriet asked. 'You're a super successful career woman, doing what you love, despite a rough start.'

'We both are. You have George and two great kids.'

'True. I'd have been very happy if I could have seen into the future on that dark day outside the manor here.'

Krys hesitated. She'd have been very happy too, as long as the future had stopped short of Linda dying.

'Although I had some happy times and met you and it inspired me to go for what I wanted, still, it reminds me of a past I've left behind me.'

'Nothing to be ashamed of. Those times were tough and maybe you associate it with all that. Your loss is still new too, Krys. Be kind to yourself. We don't have to go there.'

'Do you mind if we don't? I don't want to waste any time revisiting it while you're here. I tell you what, I would love to show you the mountain rescue base and we can walk there.'

With the weather crisp and dry the following morning, Krys and Harriet wrapped up and headed towards the village.

'Those mountains. They look gorgeous. There's even more snow!'

'They are beautiful.'

'It always seemed to rain when we were kids.'

'That's because it really did rain for a week. We're very lucky to have some sunshine at all at the end of November.'

They had lunch in The Cock before setting off for home as

the shadows lengthened, passing the base on the way. 'I couldn't believe how dark and quiet it was last night,' Harriet said.

'The sun sets by four at this time of year,' Krys said. 'And there's no light pollution.'

'It is beautiful,' Harriet said, linking arms with Krys, reminding her of their childhood bond. 'Now, come on, show me this mountain rescue base. You know you want to, really . . . and if you do, I can let you have a green Haribo.'

Smiling, Krys led her friend into the car park of the base.

Harriet blew out a breath. 'Wow. It's pretty smart. I'd kind of expected a shack.'

'It's pretty impressive though they have to do a lot of fundraising to keep it like that.'

Hector was standing by a Land Rover and shouted a hello to Krys.

Krys waved back.

Harriet raised an eyebrow. 'He seems nice – if *very* tall.'

'He's a paramedic,' Krys said. 'And a drag artiste.'

'*And* in the mountain rescue? What's wrong with these people?' Harriet joked. 'Don't they have homes to go to? Phew. From someone who's in the job professionally, I am in awe that they do this for free and out in all weathers.'

They'd almost reached the manor when they met Max and Jake walking towards the village.

He managed a smile and Jake immediately ran up to them, looking for fuss which was duly given.

'He'll stand any amount of that,' Max said.

'Oh, so this is Jake, is it? Oh, a border collie! Isn't he gorgeous?' Harriet rubbed his ears. 'You handsome fella. I've heard so much about you from Krys.'

Krys caught Max's eye. 'Harriet likes dogs,' was all she could manage.

'I do. I adore them. I have three chihuahuas,' she said. 'Small but very mighty.'

Max smiled. 'I bet.'

Max chatted for a few minutes about Harriet's journey and how she was enjoying the manor and then he left, presumably on his way to the post office or pub.

'So that was Max!' Harriet declared, once he was safely out of hearing. 'He is lush. Bloody hell, Krys, you never said *that*.'

'Actually I think he's a bit scruffy,' Krys said wickedly, silently agreeing with Harriet that Max was pretty gorgeous when he wanted to be.

'Scruffy? What about ruggedly handsome, totally hot and brooding?'

Krys laughed. 'Rugged and morose. Moody and a little bit strange . . .'

'Oh, *intriguing*. I want regular reports on him from now on. You do know that he couldn't take his eyes off you?'

'What? Now you're winding me up.'

'No, I was watching him while you stroked the dog. He looked like he was wishing you'd do the same to him and he had that suppressed look of longing on his face. You know, like Mr Darcy when he's watching Elizabeth Bennet and doesn't want her to know he's totally mad on her.'

Krys let out a gasp, that became a giggle. 'That's in a movie, not real life, and Max is about as far from being Mr Darcy as I am from being a swooning heroine in a corset.'

Harriet nodded. 'That is true. About *you*, I mean, but I definitely get the Mr Darcy vibes off *him*.'

'Harriet Taylor!' Krys declared, with mock outrage. 'If you keep on like this, I won't crack open that bottle of champagne I'd been saving specially for you.'

Actually, she'd been saving it for Brett but as he was living it up in New York, she was bloody well going to enjoy it with her old friend.

Harriet had been back in London for a couple of days when the doorbell rang while Krys had her arms elbow deep in flour, having decided to make mince pies for the first time in years.

Having been expecting a delivery of sample garlands from a Dutch supplier, she was surprised to find Nikki and Amina on the step, shiny-eyed and smiling broadly, as if they were about to convert her to something.

'Hello!' they trilled together.

Nikki piped up. 'We want to ask a favour.'

'Another one,' Amina added with a grin. Krys wondered how she had the ability to look absolutely stunning in the teeth of a gale.

'Come into the kitchen,' she said, rather pleased to have the company, while wondering what the favour might be.

'We've interrupted your baking,' Nikki said.

'It's OK. I was going to chill the pastry for a little while. That's what it suggests in the recipe, anyway. Do you want a coffee?'

Nikki and Amina perched on stools at the breakfast bar while Krys rustled up cappuccinos. She was a dab hand at playing barista now.

'I'm meant to be your housekeeper. Really, I should be making these,' Nikki said when Krys handed over the mugs.

'It's your day off. Both of you, and it's not as if I'm rushed off my feet.'

With the pastry in cling film in the fridge, Krys made a drink herself and leaned against the worktop. Behind her visitors, two tall windows looked over the garden with the fells in the distance.

She thought of Max and Nikki climbing them in the dark with the MRT and Brett, horrified at the idea of Krys herself venturing up there.

'So, how can I help you?' she asked.

'Remember that you mentioned that in one of your previous jobs, you used to be in charge of organising Santa's Grotto?' Nikki said.

'I did,' said Krys, cautiously. 'Though that was a few years ago, now.'

'Even so, you know a lot more about it than we do,' Amina continued.

'You see, the MRT has connections to the local outdoor centre,' Nikki explained. 'We sometimes give safety talks, we take the search dogs to visit and a couple of the staff there help us out on rescues.'

'Thorndale Outdoor Centre?' Krys echoed.

'Yes,' Nikki said. 'It's a few miles away in the next valley.'

Krys could picture it. The dorms, the boot room, the canteen smelling of overcooked cabbage and minced beef.

'Anyway, we usually help organise a Christmas party for some of the kids who are staying and some local children too. We have games, food, a disco and a Santa's Grotto for the young ones – though it hasn't happened for the past couple of years, so this year we want it to be bigger and better than ever.'

'It's the day before the ball, though, so you might be too busy enjoying yourself with Brett,' Amina said.

'But if you possibly can spare the time, it would be such a boost for the centre. Most of the kids who'll be there have really missed out on treats like this for one reason and another, so we'd like to push the boat out for them and make sure they have an amazing time,' Nikki continued. 'Sooo . . .' She shared a glance with Amina, who took up the thread.

'We kind of wondered if you'd decorate the place and help us organise it?'

'I know you're already helping at the base but this is probably even more important,' Nikki added.

Krys had been on the alert for the request since the words 'Santa's Grotto' had been mentioned; even so, it sounded quite a challenge. She'd always had big budgets and suppliers to call on and with that kind of support, it was relatively easy to make a place look amazing. Here, she'd have no professional resources and certainly no budget. She'd already called in a lot of favours and gone on the scrounge.

However, lack of budget wasn't the only reason why she was prevaricating. 'I haven't been in charge of running the grotto for a few years now. When I worked for the garden centre chain, I did order the decorations.'

'You know more about it than we do.'

Their faces were so hopeful and Harriet's words came back to her: *What have you got to fear? You're a super successful career woman, doing what she loves, despite a rough start.*

'I wouldn't want to raise your expectations too high, or the children's hopes . . .' Krys said warily. 'Or the staff's.'

What if Miss Braithwaite was still in charge? Even after all these years, she wasn't sure she could work with the woman – or *for* the woman, even as a volunteer.

'Um. You said the staff sometimes work with the MRT. Is it anyone I know?' she asked, angling for an answer.

'It's Jo and she's lovely. She'll just be ecstatic that a professional is stepping into the breach. If you're too busy, though, please do say. We know you're already committed to help with the ball.'

Krys's heart sank but seeing these two expectant faces in front of her, it was going to be almost impossible to say no.

What kind of a person was she if she couldn't agree to help out a kids' party? They were probably children just like she'd been, longing for a bit of sparkle to brighten up tough times. Amina and Nikki gave so much time to the MRT team. It would be something else to throw herself into now that she'd be at a loose end until Brett's return.

'Of course, we don't want to disrupt your break,' Amina said. 'You and Brett deserve some time together.'

'Brett's not here at the moment. He's had to make an unexpected trip to New York and won't be back for a while.'

'Unexpected trip to New York. How glamorous,' Amina said.' I wish someone would beam me out of the post office to New York.'

'He will be back for the ball, though, won't he?' Nikki asked.

'Absolutely,' said Krys. 'OK, I'll help if I can.' Her mind was already whirling with how she could possibly stretch the decorations for two events.

'Hurrah! Thank you so much,' Amina said.

'And the good news is Jo says there might already be some stuff for the grotto,' Nikki added brightly.

'That's good,' Krys said, trying to focus on the positives and sweeping aside her misgivings.

'You might want to take a look at them though; they've been in storage for a couple of years.'

'OK,' she said, wondering where she could scrounge even more decorations for two large spaces including a Santa's Grotto. She was owed a few favours, she thought, maybe she could call them in. She'd been a good customer of several large decoration suppliers. They *might* have some display samples or damaged stock. A thought suddenly occurred to her.

'This grotto. Who's going to play Santa?' she asked, praying that wouldn't be part of the deal.

'Oh that's easy!' Nikki piped up. 'Hector does it. He's incredible. Even we don't recognise him.'

She gave an inner sigh of relief. 'I'd like to see that.'

A while later, Krys closed the door and took a few deep breaths. Her Christmas holiday was turning into anything but a holiday, in every sense of the word.

Chapter Sixteen

Quelling the butterflies in her stomach, Krys headed for the Outdoor Centre trying to recognise landmarks from two decades before. The weather was very different on this December day, towering clouds scudding over a washed-out blue sky, rather than unremitting grey.

Back then, Thorndale had all been seen through the prism of a young girl who hadn't much wanted to be there and longed for the lights and crowds of London. Never could she have imagined turning up one day to help decorate the place.

She hadn't told Brett about her 'commission' to help out with the children's party as well as the ball. She'd save that for when he was home. He'd video called her twice, looking very tired, but wired about the contract he was setting up. The city sounded noisy, exciting and 'crazy busy' according to Brett. Krys wasn't sure whether to be envious or relieved she wasn't there. The slower, quieter pace of life in Thorndale was like a drug to her, as much as the frantic city seemed to be to him – only with the opposite effects.

'So will you be home for next weekend?' she asked.

'Should be . . . if not, it would only be another couple of days or so,' he replied. 'But not too long. Promise I'll be back in dull old Thorndale soon. I'll probably need to sleep for a week.'

'It's not that dull,' Krys said, feeling uneasy at his vagueness about his return – and annoyed at his comments about Thorndale. 'Harriet and I had a great time.'

'I'm sure you did. I hope you behaved . . . oh, shit. Must go. Their VP is on my mobile.'

'OK. Brett, I bought the ball tick—'

He never heard her news; he'd ended the call before she could say any more.

With a sigh, she turned into the car park of the Outdoor Centre, steeling herself. She waited a few minutes, allowing the memories to wash over her. A group of children, around the age she had been, milled around a minibus parked near the reception. They were kitted out in identical coats . . . how many of them felt like fish out of water or resented wearing borrowed clothes?

It hit her how fortunate she was despite the past few months. How far she'd come . . . and yet she felt more alone than ever. So many things only had value if you had someone special to share them with.

Her fingers tightened around the wheel. She took a deep breath: this place was bound to bring back mixed emotions but she was here for a happy purpose. Time to be professional.

This was no good. She couldn't stay in the car all day . . . With a deep sigh, she got out and walked towards the building, finding her dismay replaced by surprise. The façade seemed smart and modern, with a climbing wall on one side and picnic benches at the front.

She didn't remember any of that, only dark walls under grey

skies. Had the building always been like this or did it seem so grim because she was seeing it through the eyes of a scared and unhappy ten-year-old?

A group of teenagers stood at the bottom of the climbing wall watching two instructors give them a briefing. Krys shuddered. She was glad they hadn't had a climbing wall when she'd stayed. The walks had been scary enough, under louring mountains with fast flowing streams.

A gust of wind had literally knocked a boy off his feet. He'd been unhurt but it had scared some of the younger kids. The boy had become a legend for the rest of the week, however, and every time the tale was told, it was embellished until the rumour went around the centre that he'd sailed into the air like Mary Poppins and was only saved by Miss Braithwaite grabbing his trouser leg and wrestling him to the ground.

The memory brought a grin to Krys's face. That had been one of her happier recollections and she and Harriet had giggled over it when she'd visited.

The closer Krys got, the more she realised the centre must have recently had a refurb. A cheery wooden squirrel held a welcome sign by the entrance, but it was inside that had undergone the biggest transformation. She barely recognised the reception area, now opened out and populated with squidgy sofas, a pool table, giant bean bags and a café area. Several children ran through, laughing and waving at a young woman in an Outdoor Centre fleece.

Feeling a little less apprehensive, Krys approached the woman, whose name badge read 'Jo'.

'Hello . . .' she said, hearing the edge of croakiness in her voice. 'I'm Krys. Nikki – um – suggested I might be able to help out with the Christmas party.'

Jo's rather bemused expression morphed into a grin. 'Oh yes.

I've been expecting you. We are so relieved you offered to help. Nikki said you're a proper Mrs Christmas.'

Krys laughed, relaxing another notch. 'That's a nickname they gave me at work. I'm happy to help in any way I can.'

'Shall I show you around?'

'That would be great.' Krys hesitated. She was brim-full of conflicting emotions yet Jo seemed so lovely. 'You know, I stayed here once many years ago.' Unexpectedly, the words tumbled out.

Jo's eyes widened in surprise. '*You* stayed here?'

'Yes. I came here with a bunch of other kids from London. The place was run by a Miss Braithwaite then.'

'Braithwaite?' Jo frowned before recognition dawned. 'Oh, you must mean Cathy Braithwaite?'

'Was it? We never learned her first name. I don't think we even knew she had one.'

Jo laughed. 'It was a bit more formal then, I expect. We're all on first name terms now, but I do know Cathy slightly. She's retired. She goes to WI with my mum.'

'Your *mum*?'

Krys realised Jo was only around twenty-five.

'Yup. I think Cathy is the president or something. I dunno, I don't go.' She grinned. 'Come on, let's have a tour and you can tell me how it's changed. I think you'll have quite a surprise.'

Jo showed Krys the new dormitories, still with bunk beds but now with thick duvets and cheerful covers rather than slippery sheets and scratchy blankets. The flashing strip light had gone, replaced with soft lights, and the walls were covered in posters and artwork drawn by the kids. Everywhere seemed cosy too, rather than damp and chilly. Clearly, some money had been invested in the place over the past few years.

The canteen was also bright, with long tables and windows looking over the fells. It smelled of coffee rather than cabbage.

'This is where we'll have the party. Obviously we push all the tables back.

'Nikki mentioned you had some decorations.'

'Did she? Oh dear. They've been in storage for a couple of years. I dug the box out this morning.' Jo wrinkled her nose. 'Don't expect too much.'

She pushed open the door and flicked on a light in a storeroom under the stairs. It had bare stone walls and smelled very musty. She lugged a box into in the corridor.

'I hope the damp hasn't got to them.'

Krys opened the lid of the box. She hadn't expected much but the sight that greeted her was a sorry one. The box contained some strands of moulting tinsel, baubles with broken fasteners and squashed foil garlands.

'Is it that bad?' Jo asked, then peered into the box. 'Oh dear, they're even worse than I thought earlier.'

Krys put on a brave face. 'Don't worry. We can sort it.' She started thinking on her feet. 'Where were you thinking of having the grotto?' she asked, moving the conversation on.

'We usually use the staff room but it means moving all our stuff.'

'Would it be OK to have a look in there?'

'Sure. Come on. Ignore the pizza boxes and dirty glasses. We had a takeout last night and I haven't had a chance to clear away.'

Krys had no issue with the mess, it was the size of the room that bothered her. Barely more than a large storeroom, it had a sink, kettle area and microwave squeezed in one corner. Even she couldn't imagine it being a magical grotto: Santa Hector would take up most of it.

Using all her tact, she suggested to Jo that it was a shame to make the staff move their stuff out and asked if there were any other possibilities. It really needed somewhere rustic and magical, or at least somewhere that could be transformed into somewhere magical.

After ruling out a storeroom full of cleaning equipment, they went out to the rear of the building. It had a courtyard with some outbuildings. Behind those was a large field with snow-topped fells rising high into the sky.

She asked Jo what the outbuildings were used for.

'The larger one is an equipment store but it's packed with hiking and climbing gear so we can't use that.'

Adjacent to it was a smaller, older stone building with a stable door.

'What's that one?'

'Old stable block from back in the day. We use it for storing the winter grit, the log chipper and mower . . . though they're due for a service. I've been meaning to ask the grounds team to book them in for ages so now's as good a time as any.' Jo gave the stable block another glance, and nibbled her lip. 'I warn you it's very basic inside and probably full of spiders!'

'I'm not a huge spider fan,' Krys said, though she was becoming more and more excited by the idea of turning the little hut into a winter wonderland. It had exactly the right rustic, ramshackle atmosphere.

Jo slid back the wooden door to reveal the interior and flicked a switch to reveal a space divided by a stall with the equipment to one side. Apart from the cobwebs and dried grass, its stone walls and rafters gave Krys goosebumps of excitement.

'I told you it was a mess.' Jo brushed a cobweb off her hair. 'Yuk.'

Krys stared up at the rafters. 'It's perfect! It would make an amazing grotto. We could rig up a black curtain with fairy lights as a backdrop – that would cost next to nothing. Outside, we could install an archway with illuminated figures so the kids would be dry while they waited to see Santa. We could get some hay bales for Santa to sit on, and it would be *so* cosy and atmospheric.' She caught Jo's look of alarm. 'It would need some work but I'd be happy to come over and help clear it out. I know you must be busy.'

'We're much quieter than in the summer, and apart from the party kids, we don't have any other groups booked in that week. We usually spend the time sorting out repairs and paperwork. It's just that . . . well, let's say you have a much better imagination than I do!'

'It will be fine, I promise you. More than fine.'

'In that case, I'll ask the groundsman to shift the grit bags, book the equipment in and we'll all help tidy it up.' Jo smiled to herself. 'Maybe I can picture Hector sitting in there, in his beard and red outfit.'

'He'll love it to bits.'

'I've ended up being his helper a couple of times in the past.' She rolled her eyes. 'You should see my ears and pixie boots.'

Krys laughed. 'I've been a Santa's helper too a few times.'

'I don't mind, really,' Jo said with a grin. 'The children's faces make it all worthwhile, even if some of them aren't too sure.'

'I know exactly what you mean. My aunt took me to see Santa in the local community hall a couple of times. I still remember how excited I was so I know what it can mean.'

'Thanks for doing this.'

'You're welcome. It'll be fun.' Krys checked herself. She could barely believe what she'd just said. 'I'm glad I came back to see the changes.'

'Good. From what I've heard, it sounds as if it was all a bit grim back in those days. The staff did their best but they had hardly any funds. We're lucky to have benefactors and grants now and we've moved on a lot in the way we care for and support children and young people. I hope it's a much more professional and welcoming place now.'

'Everyone tried to be kind, I'm sure,' Krys said. 'Though I was dead set against coming here in the first place. At times, I couldn't wait to go home but I was only a kid. Since then, I've thought a lot about the place. It changed my life but perhaps not in the way that was intended.'

Jo's interest was piqued. 'Oh?'

'It showed me another world outside London,' Krys said, once again peeping through the windows of the house into a life that seemed way beyond her reach. 'I definitely wouldn't have been doing what I do now if I hadn't come to Thorndale.'

'How? If you don't mind me asking.'

'Let's just say that being here inspired me to go for what I wanted in life, so if I can make these kids' lives happier for a little while and give them some positive memories, it'll be a privilege. How many people are coming?'

'Around thirty kids, age three to nine, and a bunch of adults. Some of the kids are from the local area but some are residential. We've arranged transport for the local ones. For a few, this might be the only Christmas party and presents they get. Times are very tough for families these days, even when parents are in full time work.'

'I can imagine,' Krys said, her comment coming straight from the heart. 'Where do you find the gifts from?'

'Businesses, community groups like the MRT and local residents' donations. We try to find out what each child would really like, and within reason they receive that gift and a little surprise. We provide party food, an entertainer for the younger ones and a mini disco. We're relying on a handful of staff and volunteers to help out on the day.'

'I'll be here if you want me to, of course,' Krys said.

'I'm counting on it!'

Back inside the centre, Krys made some notes, and made arrangements to come back to check out the stable/grotto when Jo and her staff had finished clearing it out. She didn't want to make any specific promises about the décor but was secretly buzzing with ideas.

However, her wilder visions of a living nativity scene soon went out of the window. It would cost far too much. She'd have to come up with other ideas to make it special and some lighting and figures would go a long way towards that. They could be reused for years to come too.

'Your job sounds amazing. How did you get into it?' Jo asked.

Krys gave her a quick rundown of how she'd become a Christmas buyer.

'My mum's into the whole Christmas thing. She loves getting the decorations down every year. Some are as old as the hills.'

'That's what it's all about for many people. They love the tradition: a treasured decoration or bauble reminds them of childhood, and if it was a gift from a loved one, it evokes really special memories.'

'That sounds like Mum. She has an angel from my grandma that dates back to the fifties. I guess you have all new stuff every year.'

'Oh no!' Krys said. 'Obviously I like to collect new bits and pieces. It's my job to be on the lookout for the latest trends and I get samples or treat myself, but I still love to get out the old ones each year.' Linda came into her mind, as ever. 'Some people do like to follow the new trends though, and have a different theme every year.'

'Surely not *every* year?' Jo sounded horrified.

'A few people, yes, though it's more common to change every few seasons.'

'That sounds very expensive.'

'It can be, particularly when they want all the decorations from the range,' Krys said. It was part of her job to make customers crave the whole look on a tree or display but she didn't say anything to Jo. She felt awkward about it, considering the circumstances.

'You can also hire professional decorators to do a whole room or house worth of decorations,' she said.

'Oh my God. You mean there are people whose job it is to put up tinsel?'

'Well, it's a bit more involved than that.' Krys smiled. 'There are several companies devoted solely to Christmas decorating. In November, they generally do commercial venues like shopping malls, hotels and city centres. They wrap tree branches in lighting, and install large scale displays and Christmas trees. In December they move on to homes.'

Jo shook her head. 'Ordinary people have professionals in to trim their tree?'

'They might have a huge house, be too busy to decorate, want to put on a show for a party, or can't cope with going up ladders and handling electrics.'

'I can understand that.'

'So they call in a dedicated team. The advantage is that you can hire all the decorations, and then return them to the company. That way you can definitely have a different theme each year.'

Jo sighed. 'I don't think that kind of budget will work here.'

'No . . . and while it would look spectacular, even if you had all the money in the world, I don't think it would be the right thing because the kids themselves need to get involved. After all, it's all about them, isn't it?' Krys smiled. 'When I worked at the garden centre, we used to employ crafters to do workshops in the school holidays. Would that work here?'

'We have craft sessions from time to time. There's a brilliant local crafter called Sasha who was here at Easter. She took the kids out and made things out of leaves, twigs and berries. They turned them into collages and artwork . . .' Jo sighed. 'The problem is, we've used up our budget for the year.'

'Don't worry about that,' Krys said, planning on scrounging as many freebies as she could and contributing towards the rest. 'Would you mind getting in touch with Sasha? Let me know her fee and how much the materials would be?'

'That's very kind, but you've already given your time. We can't let you pay for everything too.'

'Why not? Call it my Christmas present to the centre. And if I'm honest, it will give me far more pleasure than spending it on gifts that might . . . be unwanted.' No Linda to buy for, she thought, and she and her mother certainly didn't exchange presents. She was lucky if she received a card lately.

When they'd finished talking, Krys went into the car park and checked her phone. She had a message from one of the suppliers asking her to call them and one from Nikki asking how it had gone with the Outdoor Centre.

With a sigh, she returned to Holly Manor. By half-past three, on a grey afternoon, it was already almost night and the dark windows of the imposing house seemed very melancholy. Her footsteps echoed on the parquet floor.

After switching on the lights in the downstairs rooms and drawing the heavy curtains, she put on the TV for company. To pass the time, she made a full-on assault on the suppliers who might be able to help her, firing off emails. With the foxes at it outside, she made some pesto pasta and turned up the TV to drown out their howls of passion while she ate it: at least someone was enjoying a sexy night in. She grabbed a glass of wine and was just starting to wonder whether she should have yet another early night when her phone rang.

'Hello. It's Max.'

'Max?' Krys wondered how he'd got hold of her number.

'Yes.'

'You're on your phone . . .'

'It happens. Actually, I'm parked outside the pub. Nikki gave me your number. I hope that's OK?'

'I – yes, I suppose so,' she replied.

'Good,' Max barked back. He paused. 'I was just wondering if you might be going to the MRT meeting this week?'

'Um . . .' Taken aback, Krys hesitated. She wanted to go but felt she would have to make excuses for Brett not being around – again. 'I hadn't decided.'

'It's up to you,' Max said, rather gruffly, Krys thought. 'Only it's dog training night and we need some casualties.'

Krys wasn't sure whether to be amused or flattered. 'Are you suggesting I should be one of them?'

'I dunno. It was only an idea I had on the spur of the moment. You don't have to.'

'What do I have to do?' Krys said, enjoying winding him up and surprised Max did anything 'on the spur of the moment'.

'Lie around in the dark and cold, waiting for a collie to sniff you out. There's sleet forecast too, so wrap up warm.'

'You make it sound so tempting.'

'If you don't have other plans, that is . . .' he said. 'I don't like to make assumptions.'

'Oh, really?' Krys said, then decided. 'OK, you're on. After all, what else am I going to do on a wet night in the back of beyond?'

Chapter Seventeen

Krys curled into a ball, making herself as small as she possibly could. It had started to rain, and it wouldn't take much of a drop in temperature for that rain to turn to sleet at any moment.

She was trussed up like a mummy in several layers, waterproof jacket and waterproof trousers. Even so, the wind was howling over her head and her cheek was freezing as she hunkered down in a peaty hollow on the fellside.

She didn't dare check her phone; she didn't want the light or movement to give away her location. She'd probably been lying there for twenty minutes but it felt like hours since Max had driven her out to a location above the base and guided her another ten-minute walk up a rough path. Without his torch and knowledge, she'd have fallen several times.

Then Max had abandoned her. It had been eerie to see the beam of his head torch fading away, leaving her quite alone. Thank goodness the Lakes didn't have bears or wolves, she thought. The same boy who'd been blown off his feet had tried to convince her and some of the other kids that the Lakes still did have wolves left alive in the remote areas. Miss Braithwaite had told him not to be silly, that the last wolves had been killed four hundred years before . . .

Yet lying here in the dark and cold, she could imagine them still roving the fells. For what seemed like an age, there was no human sound to be heard, and all she could see above her were the stars, while the wind whistled eerily though the grass.

'Oh my God!' Her heart rate rocketed.

Eyes glowed in the darkness and a furry creature leapt on her.

It started barking and licking her face.

'Star! Hey there!'

Krys fussed the dog, who was wildly excited and barking loudly.

'Star!'

The voice of its handler was followed by more barking.

Krys scrambled to her knees, praising the dog. 'Well done, girl! I didn't even hear you coming.'

Max arrived with Star's owner, their torch beams sweeping over her.

She pushed herself up, feeling stiff from lying on the wet ground, but exhilarated that Star had found her.

'I never heard a thing. She just appeared from nowhere.'

'She's a good lass,' her owner said, producing a rubber toy and playing tug-of-war with Star as her reward.

They walked down the fell and Max drove Krys back to the base.

'How was that?'

'Cold. A bit disorienting. I'd hate to be lost on the fells.'

'It can be pretty scary.'

'Scary?' She was surprised. 'Don't tell me you've ever got into trouble?'

'Once or twice. I've been caught out in a snowstorm while I was descending the Pike. I managed to find my way down, though. And once, I took a wrong turn in some fog. Ended up far too close to a two-hundred-foot drop for comfort.'

'That sounds horrendous.'

'It was the closest I've ever come to calling out the MRT myself. I did have a bar of signal but you can never rely on it. You're mad if you go up there – or anywhere on the fells – without knowing how to use a map and compass. GPS is all very well but it isn't always reliable. People have come to rely on technology and apps but mobile phones can run out of battery, they get dropped on rocks and into becks. It's not worth the risk.'

'No . . . I can see the lure of the mountains though. I'm glad I've gone along to the MRT nights. I felt I knew next to nothing about the dangers up there. Stuff I'd never thought of: those down draughts that can knock you off your feet. Being benighted, and cragfast.' She smiled. 'Lovely words for terrifying situations. At least I now know what to carry in my rucksack. Nikki gave me a survival bag, head torch and whistle and I had no problem stuffing my pack with extra snacks.'

The lights of the base came into view and Max drove on to the car park, but instead of getting out, he turned to Krys.

'I'm glad the MRT nights have made you feel safer. You can pass your knowledge on to Brett when he's up here at the weekend.'

'I will. I mean I would, but Brett's not going to be here this weekend.' Again, she thought. As she'd suspected, his 'few days' had turned into an extra week. 'He's away in the States on business.'

'Oh?' Max frowned.

'Yes, he's involved in finalising a new project and the client wanted him to work from the New York office for a while. Apparently, he's irreplaceable.'

'In my opinion, no one is irreplaceable,' Max shot back. 'Not at work, anyway. Loved ones are a different thing.'

Krys's turn to frown. Her annoyance at Max's sharp response was replaced by curiosity at the second part of his comment.

'If you mean loved ones like Linda, then yes, I agree. No one can replace her. I only meant that no one else could do Brett's job.'

'Good for Brett,' Max said. 'I won't keep you any longer. It's late. Thanks for being such a good casualty. I'm sure I'll see you around.'

Krys went back to the manor, intrigued yet again by Max's mercurial ways. Had he lost a loved one? Nikki had said there had been a tragedy in his life and he'd had a breakdown. Short of asking him directly or interrogating other team members, that side of his life would have to remain a mystery, unless she got to know him better.

She went to bed but was woken as she was dropping off by a WhatsApp message from Brett.

Might be stuck in NYC for a while longer. Next weekend looking dodgy too. REALLY sorry. Will be in touch. B x

She tried to call him back but then realised it was the middle of the working day on the East Coast. She would contact him later and find out more about the meaning of his message. She didn't have a good feeling about it.

Where Brett was concerned, their chances of spending a Christmas holiday together were fast disappearing down the drain. The ball wasn't that far away and she pinned all her hopes on that.

She woke to a voice mail from Brett, apologising for being delayed and blaming 'last-minute brinkmanship' on the part of his client before they decided to finally sign off the contract.

She swore softly. A message and a voice mail. He hadn't even had the courage to tell her personally. OK, he was busy, and this was a key moment in his career, and yet . . . he'd known how important this holiday was. All she was getting were excuses. She hadn't seen him for over three weeks now.

The days were flying by, each one a precious chance to spend time together, and the thought made her stomach knot with regret.

It was a dry and bright day so she put on her rucksack and headed towards the Scafell path, intending to walk up the side of the stream and explore its lower slopes a little. It had been mild so there was no snow on the tops and as she walked up the path, the clouds rolled over and hid the top from view. Several people overtook her, wishing her a good morning. They had baskets of stones, picks and spades in their hand.

Krys stopped at a small knoll that gave a tremendous view back over the Thorndale Valley and Wastwater. The sunlight glittered off the windows of the mountain base, and the stream tumbled past. It was so beautiful, but she felt very alone.

'Woof!'

Familiar barks made her turn round to find Jake and Max walking up the path. Max had a rucksack and a basket of stones which he put on the ground.

'Hello!' she said. 'Fancy seeing you here.'

He smiled. 'Actually, I'm on my way to help out the path menders.'

'And here's me thinking you wanted to carry a load of rocks up here for fun.'

'I know how to party,' he said, deadpan.

She laughed, feeling ridiculously pleased to see him.

'Are you going all the way up the Pike?' he said, frowning.

'No. I think the summit's a bit beyond me at the moment.'

'I don't see why,' Max said. 'You're properly equipped.' He nodded at the rucksack. 'You could show Brett how it's done when he's back next week, if the weather's looking fair.'

'I'd love to,' she said, thinking that Brett would take a lot of persuasion even if she herself dared. 'But I can't see when, to be honest.' She sighed. 'He's been delayed again and he won't be home this weekend.'

Max frowned. 'By work?'

'Yes.'

'I'm sorry to hear that.' He sounded genuine, she thought.

'So am I, and as for the Pike, I think I'll stop at exploring part of the way,' Krys said. As she did so, the clouds parted to reveal the fell top three thousand feet above. She was filled with a sense of longing and of need to be up there. 'It must be incredible to be up there looking down on the world . . .' she said.

Max followed her gaze. 'It is . . . I could take you, if you wanted to.'

She turned to him, astonished. 'You?'

'Yes, me, if you could bear it. It's more than worth the effort. Although the days are short, there's a calm weather window over the weekend. Now you're not busy . . .' He corrected himself. '*If* you're not busy, and you'd like to, we could go up and do some compass and navigation work . . .' He paused. 'Unless you want to wait until Brett's back.'

'No,' she said too quickly. 'We might miss the weather window.'

Krys sat there, astonished at the offer and quietly amused that Max's idea of a good time was some 'compass and navigation work'. She'd also never have a better chance of going with an experienced guide. She'd be safe with Max.

'Of course, it isn't everyone's cup of tea.' He was in gruff mode again, possibly readying himself to be rejected. 'It'll be a long day; tiring too. Your muscles will know you've been up there and back.'

'I'd *love* to do it,' she said, hastily, before he could withdraw the offer.

'We'll have to make an early start, to be sure of getting back in daylight.'

'I'm used to early starts.'

'Of course.' He smiled.

'Will Jake come too?' she asked.

'No, I'll leave him behind. I don't want to risk him running off. He gets very excited. *Too* excited. If he gets in among the boulder field, he might hurt his pads. It's happened before.'

She nodded, thinking Jake couldn't get as excited as she was about the prospect of climbing her first mountain. It was the perfect antidote to being disappointed about Brett.

It was still dark when Max picked up Krys from Holly Manor and took her back to the Bothy. Her new rucksack was packed with extra layers, water, snacks and her survival bag, whistle and compass. Brett would be amused, no doubt – or perhaps not so amused by the idea of Max taking her up the mountain. Yet it was only a walk, and besides, Brett wasn't there. Krys was torn: disappointed that he wasn't around and yet, if he was, she wouldn't have this opportunity to spend an exciting day with Max. Was that disloyalty? Was it . . . cheating?

Laughing at herself, she brushed such thoughts aside and focused on enjoying the day.

With Max carrying an even bigger rucksack than hers, they set off as the sun was tinging the sky pink in the east. Krys hadn't slept much, she was so excited – and a little nervous – about the adventure.

To her relief, Max explained they were taking the easiest and most straightforward route, but that it would still take at least six hours and be pretty challenging, but she'd be 'just fine'.

The sun rose and the fell tops revealed themselves under a gorgeous blue sky.

'Will there be snow up there?' she asked, while they walked up the side of a gill at the base of the mountain.

'There might be a few pockets but not on the route I've chosen,' he said. 'So, you shouldn't need your ice axe and crampons.'

'Good, because I haven't brought any.'

He grinned. 'We'd better stay clear of any proper climbing, then.'

Krys rolled her eyes. Their chat soon subsided, or at least her ability to reply did as they climbed relentlessly beside the gill. There were steep sections, with rocky steps cutting into the pathway. Soon she was breathing hard and feeling warm. Her rucksack was heavy and she had to take off her padded jacket and stuff into her backpack.

Max slowed down and after about an hour's steady climb uphill, they reached a flatter area and stopped for a drink and a PowerBar not far from a large metal box on legs. Painted blue, it stood out against the fellside: an incongruous sight about the size of a very large sofa.

'What's that over there?' Krys asked, pointing to it.

'It's the MRT stretcher box. It's full of rescue equipment. Years ago, before mountain rescue teams were established, there used to be boxes over the Lakes so mountain-goers could help themselves and their mates in an emergency. Some of them are still in use – they save us carrying too much kit up here.'

'That makes sense. I've felt the weight of those metal stretchers on the training nights. I can see why you'd want to keep some equipment on the fellside.' She shuddered. 'No matter how beautiful it is today, it gives me the shivers to think of being stuck up here in the dark.'

'Hopefully we won't have to resort to any of the rescue kit today. Come on, let's get going again. The path's going to be a bit rougher from here on, but not quite as steep and unrelenting.'

They set off again, with the views becoming more breath-taking – and the path more lung-sapping – as they climbed higher. At one point, they had to traverse a narrow path across a slope above a drop that made Krys's heart beat faster than she wanted it to. Max was at her back, asking if she was OK, and at one point offering a helping hand over a high rocky step.

When she did stop for breath, though, the views were jaw-dropping. The valley of Thorndale spread out before them far below, with the dark lake glittering in the winter sunshine. You could see exactly how a glacier had scoured it out in the Ice Age.

Shading her eyes, she peered into the far west towards a shimmering horizon. 'The Celtic Sea.'

'Yes. We should be able to see the Isle of Man from the top.' He tipped his water flask to his mouth. 'Make sure you drink plenty.'

Krys was still in her fleece, her jacket having been stuffed in her backpack. She took a long swig of water. 'It's hot work, climbing continuously.'

He smiled. 'For now, but it's going to be at least five degrees cooler at the summit, probably more, and the winds could be pretty strong and cold. I promise you'll need all those layers by the time we get up there.'

Krys found it hard to believe but as they climbed higher, her ears popped and the wind grew keener. She put her coat, hat and gloves back on, and tried to resist the urge to ask Max: 'Are we nearly there yet?'

When she felt she couldn't go another step without her legs giving way, they stopped for another refuel. Max produced a large slab of fruit cake to go with her coffee.

'Who made this?' she said after a few bites of the gooey cake.

'Who do you think? Jake?'

She laughed. 'Well done. It's delicious.'

'Thanks.' He gave a little bow and his eyes twinkled. Krys didn't think she'd ever seen him so relaxed or at ease. He was clearly in his element.

'Come on, final push,' he said, taking her mug from her and stashing it in his rucksack. 'It'll be worth it.'

She hoped so because the final mile to the summit involved a hard scramble through a boulder field that made her legs and arms ache. The vegetation and grassy areas had gone, replaced by bare rockfaces and steep sided gullies with fast-flowing streams. Amazingly, the sky was still free of clouds, though a bitter breeze was blowing from the sea. They'd been walking for almost three hours and her calves and thighs were screaming for a rest when finally Max announced, 'That's the summit cairn, just up there.'

'Are you sure? I've thought it was in sight so many times.'

He grinned. 'No, that's definitely it. It'll all have been worth it, I promise.'

With renewed energy, she spotted the pile of rocks that marked the summit and felt a rush of adrenaline. She had actually climbed a real mountain – and not just any mountain, but England's highest peak.

There were a couple of other walkers at the top. The wind was blowing and very cold. Tiny ice crystals had formed between some of the rocks, but there was no snow. The sun shone down from air that seemed pure and gin-clear.

'I can't believe I'm literally standing on top of England.'

'Believe it. On a clear day you can see the four nations of the UK. So they say: Northern Ireland, Wales, Scotland and the Isle of Man.'

Max pointed out Scotland, on the other side of Solway Firth and the Isle of Man in the sea to the west. Sadly, Ireland and

Wales were hidden in the haze. Even so, the 360-degree panorama took her breath away. She wanted to hold her arms out and twirl round like when she was child. It was very, very tempting to shout 'I'm the Queen of the World' but she wasn't sure Max would appreciate it.

Max pointed out the landmarks including the other highest peaks, Helvellyn and Skiddaw, as well as most of the lakes, which radiated from the mountains like the spokes of a wonky wheel.

'It is truly amazing.' Krys turned to Max, standing with his hands on his hips and a massive grin on his face. 'Thanks for bringing me up here.'

'Don't thank me. You got up here all by yourself.'

She laughed. 'At times, I wasn't sure I'd manage it.'

'Yet you have. Now, let's have some lunch and a rest because at some point, we're going to have to go down.'

They shared sandwiches. Max had brought doorstop ones with wedges of local cheese and chutney. Krys had made hers with farm shop ham and mustard from the post office. He produced some Grasmere gingerbread and she had some hot chocolate made by the velvetiser in Holly Manor and some mince pies.

He enjoyed both with an appreciative smack of the lips. 'This is a bit better than my usual rations.'

'I thought we'd need a treat at the top. Or rather I would.'

'Who made the pies?'

'Who do you think?' She laughed. 'I did! I've had – um – some time on my hands so I've been practising my baking skills.'

'Well, they're very moreish. Too moreish . . .'

They both laughed and finished their lunch in companionable silence. She couldn't resist a secret glance or two at him. Even wind-blown and unshaven, he had a rugged handsomeness that was straight from the cover of the climbing magazines in the manor.

She could no longer deny her physical attraction to him, nor the pleasure she took in his friendship, however grudgingly given at times. She shivered. Max was staring into the distance. She had no idea where he was, but she had a hunch it wasn't here with her on the top of a mountain.

He was somewhere it was impossible to reach.

While they put their rucksacks back on, Max urged her to be careful, saying that most accidents happened on descents when people were tired. This wasn't reassuring, but she guessed it was necessary.

Her calves began to tremble as her legs tired on the descent and she stopped more frequently than on the way up, at Max's suggestion. She knew he could tell she was flagging, and she didn't mind. Energy drinks and PowerBars were produced from his rucksack. No wonder it looked so big, it was full of supplies, but she wasn't complaining.

'Whoa!'

His cry came a fraction after her boot slipped on loose gravel on the rocky step. She stumbled forward, but he grabbed her arm from behind and pulled her back, steadying her.

Her heart thumped wildly but both feet were back on the ground. His fingers were still around her arm, lightly reassuring her. She was surprised he couldn't hear her heart beating. She wouldn't have fallen far but it would have hurt a lot, possibly have done some serious damage to her legs or back.

'You're OK,' came his soothing voice. 'Take a moment.'

'I'm – OK.' She looked at him and saw his eyes full of concern, and – tenderness, even. She thought of Harriet's comments about him. Was it possible that Max really did *like* her? As more than a friend?

He let go of her arm and she laughed, feeling awkward and embarrassed.

'Sorry, I didn't realise how big a step down that was. I was in a world of my own.' Her heart rate stopped bouncing around quite so much but she was still shaken.

'Don't worry. It happens,' he said gruffly. 'You're bound to be tired. I'll be glad to be down myself.'

Krys let that pass, knowing that Max could probably have gone back up to the top and down again if he'd wanted to. So could Nikki or any of the team. This was their element.

'I'll be glad too,' she said. 'But it's been brilliant.'

'I'm pleased it hasn't been too awful,' he said in his usual way. 'We should be back at the car in half an hour, but like I say, take your time. We'll be on the main path soon, and that should make it easier going.'

He was right. The path levelled out and became less rocky as they descended to the side of a stream. The car park was in view, and gradually the vehicles became less like toy ones. Soon, they were crossing the footbridge and back at the car park. The shadows were long and the sun about to sink out of view between the hills and into the sea.

It wasn't a moment too soon. Krys had a blister forming on her little toe, her calves were like jelly and her back ached from carrying the pack.

She was also completely exhilarated.

'I'll drive you home,' he said. 'Unless you fancy a drink at the Bothy on the way?'

She had planned to have a long soak in the tub at the manor but Max's invitation had taken her by surprise.

'Of course, you probably want to be home,' he added.

'No. I mean, yes, but a drink does sound very tempting.' She smiled. 'What will Jake think of you bringing home visitors? Won't he want you to himself?'

'I don't think he'll mind as long as he gets his dinner.'

Jake leapt on Max the moment he opened the door then proceeded to jump up at Krys and dance around her feet.

'Jake!' he ordered. 'Down, boy.'

Amused that Jake didn't take a bit of notice, Krys fussed the dog. 'It's fine. He's happy to see us.'

'Don't let him slobber all over you,' Max said, clearly worried Jake was becoming too enthusiastic. 'I'll let him out for a run and then make a drink.'

'No, I'll put the kettle on while you do that.'

'Thanks.'

While Max took Jake out, Krys made the tea. Having stayed the night, the Bothy felt familiar yet she was still taken aback by its rustic simplicity. The cooker was at least twenty years old; the Belfast sink must have been installed halfway through the last century and the wooden dresser and cupboards looked hand built.

The last time she'd been here, Brett had been sleeping on the sofa, with Max on the floor. He'd let her have his bed and made it a bit too obvious that he wasn't happy to have guests, no matter how well he'd fed and watered them.

Max walked in and Jake ran up to her.

'Have you enjoyed your run? Sorry we left you all day.'

Jake rested his muzzle on her knee. She noticed the sawdust on his paws.

'He wants a treat,' Max said from the sink without turning round. 'But he's only just had his dinner.'

'Oh, your owner is so cruel to you.' Krys stroked Jake's back and her fingers found something in his fur. It was a wood shaving, the kind left behind by a plane or chisel.

'Good boy,' she said, brushing the shaving onto the flagstones by the edge of the sofa.

Max offered to make some food. It was dark outside. She

wasn't relishing going back to the manor. She cradled her mug and Max joined her with two glasses of cordial and a plate of cheese on toast.

'I'll drive you home,' he said.

'Probably best. I'm not sure my legs will ever work again after today.'

He smiled as she crunched down on the toast. 'You might be a bit stiff in the morning.'

'I'm sure I will.'

'It wasn't too awful, though?' His voice rose in hope.

'Not too awful.' She smiled. 'It was totally amazing. More than worth the effort. I wouldn't have missed it for the world.'

The delight in his eyes touched her deeply. A lump found its way into her throat. She'd been privileged to share today with him, but she didn't want to say how much.

After she'd finished the toast, Max took the plates to the sink. She thought of Brett and what he might be doing, and a pang of regret struck her. The fire was warm and she stroked Jake's head for comfort.

Today had given her a fresh perspective on so many things. Not least on herself. It had shown her that there were new places and people, beyond London and her Christmas world, waiting to be explored if she dared . . . *but how did Brett fit into all that?*

'Krys?'

She woke with a start to find Max standing over her. 'Oh!'

'You were nodding off. I should probably take you home. You'll feel worse if you wake up later. Best you get home for a soak and your own bed.'

'Of course. You're right. I'm sorry for falling asleep.'

'It's allowed. You've climbed a mountain.'

'Yes. I have.' She tried to get up off the sofa. 'Ow. Oh.'

He waited while she coaxed her stiff and aching limbs into life. 'OK?'

She groaned. 'Um. Ask me in the morning.'

'It'll be much worse in the morning,' he said with a grin.

He held out his hand and pulled her to her feet. 'Let's get you home before you end up sleeping here again.'

Max drove her home, but Krys was silent, too busy thinking of how Brett would never fit into a life in Thorndale, when he didn't seem to be able to fit into the life they had now.

Chapter Eighteen

Max hadn't wanted Krys to sleep at the Bothy, more for his sake than hers. He might have ended up awake all night, listening to her breathing, longing to . . . well, he didn't like to delve too deeply into what he longed for. It scared him. It didn't fit with the hermit narrative, that was for sure, and it didn't fit with the pledge he'd made not to look at another woman again.

That vow was unravelling by the second, a fraying rope that, if it broke, could send him crashing into oblivion. Even *if* Max was ready for a new adventure, Krys was in a relationship, no matter how much Max thought Brett didn't deserve her.

Over the following few days, Max didn't see Krys again. He told himself that was by accident and he had had more to occupy him than usual. He'd had to go over to Bannerdale several times for some ice climbing and helicopter evac training with other Lakeland teams but he didn't want to be too close to her and endure thoughts and desires that could never be fulfilled.

When he was alone in the Bothy, and night fell, he'd felt the loneliness more keenly than for a long time. He hated to admit it but he *missed* Krys. He'd loved sharing a special place with her, helping her to enjoy it safely and seeing the wonder and delight on her face at reaching the top, when she might not have thought it possible. He'd actually enjoyed teaching her some new skills and in return, she'd reminded him that there was so much out there to enjoy and celebrate.

It was a new feeling and he liked it more than he dared to admit.

Immediately, the pleasure was tinged with pain . . . pleasure in being in Krys's company and the pain that always came when he was reminded of the loss of the woman he once loved – who he still loved.

Erin. His wife.

No one in Thorndale knew about Erin, apart from Amina. Max had never wanted to share and he still didn't and yet Krys had come closest to tempting him to talk about the indescribable pain and loss.

It had eased over time but every so often, a reminder would sting him.

A few days previously, he'd received a letter relating to the legacy his wife had left him. It had come from the managers of the charity trust that Max had set up after her death when he'd sold most of his assets and moved to the Bothy. The cash had been invested and was used to support various good causes. Some of it had already gone to help the MRT build a new base, not that they knew the real source.

The funds he had remaining had come from the sale of the house he and Erin had owned together. These had been invested to cover his day to day living expenses, modest as they were. He'd also had a legacy from his grandfather which he drew on from time to time.

He was aware how very fortunate he was and lately had begun to think that being able to withdraw from society and live an off-grid lifestyle was a huge luxury in itself.

In fact . . . he'd seen the way Krys had looked at him when he'd had her and Brett to stay overnight at the Bothy. A rather odd recluse, she'd probably thought, and actually she'd be right. Surely he was no different to the eccentric aristo hiding away in his decaying castle while the world moved on around him?

The thought niggled at him: joining the mountain rescue team was at least a way of making himself useful, without actually being part of the rat race again.

'Sorry, you'll have to move, mate,' he said, gently removing Jake from his feet and crossing to the kitchen drawer where he'd put the letter. He would have to do something about it soon, but he'd conveniently 'forgotten' about it while he was enjoying Krys's company.

The letter related to the distribution of the money, asking for his approval to make a large donation. Erin's sister, Laurel, was one of its trustees, along with Max himself, and he was surprised that she hadn't been in touch about it before.

With a sigh, he put it away again, Out of sight was out of mind. He'd deal with it tomorrow maybe.

He went along to the next MRT meeting, after completing a casualty resuscitation workshop run by Hector and Katya.

With her MRT mug in hand, Krys was chattering to Nikki, looking every inch as if she was one of the team already. She'd messaged him to say that the sore limbs had lasted three days and she blamed him. He'd sent a devilish smiley back but hadn't called her. Should he have even gone that far? Had it been banter between friends or venturing into something more . . . something dangerously like the teasing of lovers?

He'd wanted to. He'd wanted to head straight round to the manor but hadn't trusted himself in case he did something stupid like asking her for another walk, this time one that ended in a meal at the pub, or dinner – both of which might sound like an actual date. That would surely be the end of their friendship.

His attention was hauled back to the present by Hazel calling them to order and running through a list of incidents. Only two that week. A 'missing' couple who'd turned up safe and sound at their B&B very late, having changed their minds about climbing the Pike but forgotten to inform the landlady of the fact. As a result, the team had turned out for an hour on a freezing evening, for no reason.

'Far better than the alternative,' Hazel said. 'Though we do wish people would let their contact know they decided to go and see the new Marvel action movie in Keswick instead of being benighted on the fells.'

The laughter was rather muted.

The other shout was to help a farmer whose sheep had got itself into a very precarious position on a ledge. The team had helped rescue the animal out of compassion and to prevent the farmer from risking his own safety.

Max listened, shared the laughter about the sheep leading Davy a merry dance and the unspoken satisfaction and pride that came from helping people and perhaps saving a life. The talk then turned to the ball, now not much more than a week away: Max had no part in that activity but he stayed to listen to the preparations, especially as Krys was involved.

'So, you'll be here on the afternoon to start decorating the base? I've rounded up four of us in total, so that should be enough.'

'Great. Can't wait! Brett's looking forward to it too. I can't wait to see him.'

Max listened with a pang. He had enjoyed having her to himself, so to speak. Part of him had hoped Brett might stay in the US but then he would never wish that on Krys.

Any vague notions of inviting her on another walk or to the pub vanished. Their mountain adventure had clearly been a one-off. He was merely someone to pass the time with until Brett returned: she'd made it very obvious that she was looking forward to his return and why not?

Max had subsided into gloomy reverie as the meeting was winding up, when a call came through. Two hikers had become benighted on the lower slopes of a nearby fell. They weren't injured but needed help to get off the hills safely in the deteriorating conditions.

Hazel quickly marshalled a small team that included Nikki and Hector.

'We don't need a full crew tonight,' she said to the rest of the team.

'Should we stay and help here?' Max asked.

'No, you can stand down, but thanks for offering. I appreciate it.'

Shrugging on her backpack, Nikki came over. 'Sorry, have to go. Will you be OK to get home?' she said, obviously to Krys.

'Don't worry about me. I'll be fine,' she said.

Without even thinking, Max dived in. 'I can walk with you to the manor if you like? Not that you need an escort, of course,' he added hastily.

'I don't,' said Krys.

'Oh,' Nikki said, and Max winced.

'Though I haven't brought a torch with me so maybe it's a good idea,' Krys said. 'Can't have me getting lost and falling into a stream, can we?'

'There's no chance of that, but good idea to have company.' Nikki was obviously relieved to have a solution to 'abandoning' Krys. 'I'll call you about the ball!'

'It's a horrible night,' Max said when it started raining as soon as they left the base. As it had been dry when he'd walked there and Krys had been given a lift, neither had proper water-proof gear on.

'Yes,' she said.

'What have you been up to over the past week?' he asked, hoping for some kind of response as they trudged along.

'Walking. I went over to Ambleside for a look around and met a friend I once worked with at a garden centre. She's manager of the big one in the town.'

'I know it. Huge place.'

'Yes. Looks fabulous at this time of year. I also caught up with friends, went round to Amina's one evening . . . What about you?'

Max got the message that Krys was busy and didn't need 'looking after'.

'This and that,' he said. 'Training with the Bannerdale team. You know . . .' He stopped short of saying how long he'd spent moping around the Bothy.

'Yes.'

The weather cut short their sparse conversation. The wind had increased and was driving the rain into their faces. They trudged into the driveway of the manor. Jake ran to the front door, sniffing around the steps. Owls hooted, and above the clouds, Max knew the sky would be awash with stars. It was a beautiful spot but very lonely. How crazy it seemed that they were both isolated in this stunning place . . . like those stars that seemed so close to each other yet were light years apart.

'Night, then,' Max said, struck by a deep feeling of despair.

'Night. Thanks for the escort.'

'Unwanted?' he said wryly.

'Oh no. Not really. Sorry, I didn't mean to be rude at the base.'

Max smiled, as water dripped off his hood and down his nose. 'It's OK. I shouldn't have assumed you needed company.'

He expected her to hurry inside and was amazed when she said: 'Want to come in for a nightcap?'

Every rational cell in his brain screamed at him to say: 'Thank you for the invitation, but I'd better go home in the pouring rain, have a hot shower and spend the evening alone in my rustic hideaway, where I can congratulate myself on not having been tempted to spend the night with a gorgeous woman drinking whisky in front of a cosy fire.'

'I – I have Jake with me.'

'He's very welcome. Look, he's already waiting by the door.' There was just enough uplift in Krys's tone to tell Max that she really did want him to come inside. 'And maybe this storm will blow over while you're in here.'

Maybe pigs would fly, Max thought. This rain was set in until the early hours.

'We're both very wet,' he said.

'Then why don't you shelter for a while.'

The lights glowed and there was warmth in her eyes. 'OK. A quick one.'

He followed her into the manor. Jake's claws clattered on the parquet floor and water dripped off Max's jacket, soaking into the hall rug.

Krys took off her wet coat and hug it on the peg. 'Boy, am I glad to be back here. My jeans are soaked. I'll have to go and get changed.'

Max shrugged off his own jacket. She took it and hung it

next to hers, then took off her boots. He did the same. Jake trotted off to sniff the base of the grandfather clock next to the stairs.

'I'll be back down in a minute if you want to put the kettle on. Is instant OK? I'm out of pods for the machine.'

It was way more than OK. 'It's fine.'

'Great.' She scooted upstairs while he wandered into the kitchen. The house's cosy grandeur still surprised and impressed him. It really was a beautiful house. In other circumstances he might have imagined living there, albeit it was far too big for one person. Krys must really be feeling that at the moment. Perhaps that was why she'd been so desperate to have some company.

He'd hardly put up much of a fight.

He found the kettle and switched it on. Two mugs were upturned on the drainer of the Belfast sink so he put them next to the kettle.

She padded into the kitchen, wearing faded skinny jeans and a soft cream sweater, her bare feet pushed into sheepskin mules. Max found the whole ensemble unbearably sexy.

'Oh, good, you found the mugs.' She grabbed a coffee jar. 'Here you go. Spoons in that drawer. I'll get the milk and something to make the coffee more interesting.'

Jake sat by her feet, gazing up hopefully. 'OK, boy,' she said, clearly amused. 'I think there are some dog treats in the cupboard. You won't miss out.'

'You spoil him,' Max said.

'I don't mind, if Jake doesn't.'

Max laughed, trying not to admire the way her jeans fitted so snugly as she reached up to get the treats from the cupboard. Christ, this was bad. He should never have agreed to come in. An icy cold shower, courtesy of the Lake District clouds, was exactly what he needed.

Having made the coffee, he carried the mugs through to the sitting room, sandwiched between Jake and Krys, who was following with a bottle of bourbon. He wondered if she was admiring his behind, in his very attractive dog-haired cargo trousers. He doubted that very much.

They sat down. She handed him a drink. 'It's only Jack Daniel's. I bought it for Brett.'

'It'll do fine.'

She tipped a slug of bourbon into each mug.

'Thanks.'

He sat down on the chair. Jake made himself at home on the rug in front of the fire. Krys tucked her feet up on the sofa. It was all very cosy. He could feel at home.

Max tore his eyes away from the damp tendrils of hair curling softy around her face. The way she blew them out of her eyes through soft lips. The slender legs tucked under her. He could imagine sitting here, sharing his evenings with Krys, in front of the fire.

He refocused his attention on the room where a solitary card stood by the side of the clock on the mantelpiece. He wondered who it was from.

'What?' she asked.

'Oh . . . nothing really . . . still no decorations?'

'I – I keep thinking of it but I haven't been in the party mood and most of them will be needed for the MRT ball.' She held his gaze steadily. 'Have you decided to go?'

'Let's just say I haven't been measured for my DJ yet.'

She nodded and Max was plunged into desolation again. It was his choice not to go to the ball, and even if he had wanted to, he certainly couldn't bear to see Krys there on the arm of Brett.

He thought of her all alone at the manor and his anger at the man flared into life. Krys really was better off without the guy, in Max's opinion. She deserved so much better: someone who would treasure her, respect her strength, value her – love her? That sounded so arrogant, even in his head.

Who was he to say what Krys needed? He barely knew her and yet . . . love kindled in the most unexpected places and when it caught fire, it was almost impossible to extinguish.

He decided to ask her a question that had bothered him for some time, and to which he didn't know the answer. He was going to ask anyway, if only to quench some of those wild fantasies of spending more time with her.

'After Christmas, after you leave here,' he said, 'what will you do next?'

'Start this new contract with a big store chain. Go to the Christmas trade shows.' To Max's surprise, she sounded quite weary.

'Planning next Christmas when this one is barely over,' he murmured.

'Hazard of the job.' She stroked Jake who'd lain his nose on the cushion next to her. 'Did you know they even have grottos for dogs in some stores.'

Max swore under his breath.

'I can see it might not be for Jake.'

'On the contrary, if it involved dog treats and fawning attention, I'm sure he'd love it.'

They both laughed and the boozy coffee did its trick; he relaxed into the chair and his limbs felt heavy. The walk home in the icy rain became less appealing by the minute and by the look of Jake snoozing by the hearth, he might be walking home alone.

'Did you know I've been asked to help with the Christmas party at the Outdoor Centre?' she said.

'No. I didn't.'

'Oh? I thought Amina might have mentioned it.'

Max was puzzled. 'No, she hasn't. That's going to keep you busy.'

'Yes, and I was in two minds about doing it. It's the same place that I stayed in when I was little . . . how could I refuse, though? I really want to help them out.'

'I'm sure they'll be very grateful.'

'They don't need to be,' she declared. 'I want to . . . put something back, if that doesn't sound corny. My main problem is living up to their – and my own – expectations.'

'They won't have expectations. They'll be glad of the help. I know some of the staff from rescues and they work so hard that any help will be welcome.'

'Yes, but I want to make it *really* special, although there's a budget. I've called in some favours from friends and clients for donations of decorations and the children are making their own with the help of a local artist. I've already ordered a polar bear and a penguin for the outside of the grotto. They should be a big surprise for the kids. With the straw bales, lighting and Hector in his finest, the grotto should look good . . .'

Her voice tailed off and a small frown appeared between her eyes.

'Sounds great to me,' Max said encouragingly. 'The kids will love it.'

'I hope so. The thing is, I wanted to pull out all the stops to give them a fantastic time. The younger ones especially have been through so much. I wanted something with a massive wow factor.'

'And Hector and an illuminated penguin don't cut it?'

'I'm sure Hector will be fabulous,' she said.

Max was sure Hector would be fabulous too but he knew what Krys meant. His heartstrings were well and truly tugged, though he didn't need the idea of vulnerable young people to do that. He had his own private reasons for wanting the children to have a great time. Different to Krys, but maybe just as strong.

'I have an idea. Leave it with me.'

She was instantly on the alert. 'What do you mean, "leave it with you"? What are you thinking, Max?'

He tapped the side of his nose. 'It's just an idea at the moment. I won't say more. It might not come off.'

They spoke about the party and the centre for a while and before he knew it, Max had accepted a second slug of bourbon, this time without the coffee.

Which meant he really should leave. 'I suppose I'd better be going.'

Jake let out a sigh.

'Jake doesn't want to.'

'It's not terribly appealing in this weather, I'll admit.'

Krys hesitated long enough for Max to rise to his feet. Jake lifted his snout from his paws and stared at him with an expression that said: You have to be kidding me?

'Then don't go,' she said, softly. 'I mean, don't go out in this weather.'

He imagined himself heading out into the storm, trudging home, wind-blown and soaked to the skin, while Krys nestled down in a warm bed.

'You could stay the night?' she added.

The very phrase was like a punch to the gut, even though he knew she wasn't offering anything more than shelter. The same battle raged in him as when he'd agreed to come in for coffee: between what he wanted to do and what he should do.

He hesitated a moment too long. 'I could, but . . .'

'You could sleep in one of the spare rooms,' she said. 'It's a long walk back to the Bothy. I just don't like the thought of you going out into the storm. Or Jake, of course.'

'I've been out in worse weather.'

'I'm sure you have.' She smiled. 'It's not compulsory. It was only an idea.'

A squall lashed the windows and made the fire dance crazily. Jake whimpered.

'Well, I have to admit, it seems – ah – the practical thing to do, and if you really don't mind us sleeping here?'

'I wouldn't have asked if I did.'

'We'll probably be gone before you wake,' he said as much for his benefit as hers.

Krys showed him to one of the rooms. The fresh linen smell reminded him of the last time he'd slipped between the sheets with Erin. It had been almost three years. Incredible, in this day and age, that he'd never wanted to be close to another woman in that way.

Until tonight.

'Goodnight, then,' she said, her gaze steady, holding his, almost daring him to look away. He wasn't about to; he couldn't if he'd tried. He was mesmerised by this woman who'd arrived out of the blue and was someone else's.

Her eyes clouded with puzzlement. 'Is there anything else you need, Max?'

Everything, Max thought. *So much*. He leaned forward and then immediately cursed himself.

'No thanks,' he said roughly. 'Goodnight.'

With a nod, she closed his door and left him.

He sat for a while, listening to the creaks of the boards and running water until there was silence and the light from the landing was extinguished. When he was certain Krys wouldn't come back, he stripped off his trousers and fleece, and lay on the bed, with Jake on the floor.

Outside, the storm raged. By all practical considerations, it had been the right thing to do to stay. He'd have been soaked by the time he got home and Jake would have been so pissed off, he might have run off and not come back at all.

However, one thing was for sure, no matter how warm and cosy he was in Krys's spare room, with her so close, he'd have had a much better night's sleep at the Bothy.

Chapter Nineteen

Krys froze under the duvet, hearing sounds from the landing. There was someone in the house. Worse, they were running up the stairs!

'Jake!'

A furry bundle launched itself through the bedroom door, knocking it back against the wall with a clatter. In the haze of her dream-like state, she'd forgotten that Jake and Max were staying at the manor.

'Hello, boy!' Laughing, she pushed herself up the pillows.

Jake leapt onto the bed and licked her face. 'Eww.' Krys rubbed his ears and laughed. 'That's what I call a wake-up call.'

Then she remembered that Max had said he'd be gone before she woke. Well, he obviously hadn't left yet. The previous evening flooded back. There had been a moment when they'd said goodnight when she thought he might have been about to kiss her – no, that was ridiculous. There was no way Max would have kissed her, and she was still with Brett. She certainly wouldn't have responded . . . so why was she sitting here, imagining what it would have been like to kiss Max?

'*Jayyyyke!*'

Max's voice carried upstairs but Jake ignored it. There were footsteps on the stairs and Max stood in the doorway. He was barefoot, in boxers and a T-shirt, his hair sticking up. Desire tugged sharply at her. She couldn't take her eyes off his bare legs and his thighs.

'Jake! Come here!' he said sharply, then caught sight of Krys. He seemed lost for words, seeing her sitting up in bed in her cami top. 'Oh, I'm sorry . . . I forgot . . .'

'It's OK. He's fine,' she said.

With an awkward expression, Max kept back from the doorway, as if he might be zapped by lightning if he set foot across the threshold of the bedroom. 'I'm so sorry. I was asleep and the next thing I knew, he'd bolted in here. Jake! Get off that bed, *now.*'

Finally, Jake jumped off the duvet and slunk over to his owner.

'About time, you reprobate,' Max said, grasping the dog's collar. Jake let out a whimper.

'Oh, please don't tell him off. He's excited and in a strange house,' she said.

'He shouldn't have run away.' Relenting, Max stroked Jake's head. 'I expect he's hungry.'

'There's some leftover cooked chicken in the fridge if he'll eat that, and a few dog biscuits in the cupboard. This is marketed as a dog-friendly property, and maybe Jake knows that.'

'Jake assumes every property is dog-friendly. I'll take him downstairs and let him out in the back garden.'

'I'll get dressed and find us all some breakfast.'

Max didn't say no and vanished.

Krys pulled on her fluffy dressing gown over her pyjamas, shoved her feet into slippers and headed down to the kitchen. The sun had just come up but the garden was glistening with the rain from the night before, twigs and leaves littering the lawn.

Now in cargo trousers and his T-shirt, Max stood in the doorway, keeping an eye on Jake.

She put chicken and dog biscuits in a bowl, before making instant coffee and slicing up a farmhouse loaf. They'd have to make do with toast. She was taking the butter out of the fridge when Jake must have smelled his breakfast and came back inside.

Max wiped his paws and Jake tucked in while Max and Krys sat at the breakfast bar drinking coffee and eating toast.

'How was your room?' she asked.

'Very comfortable,' he replied though the dark shadows under his eyes told another story. 'Though Jake's snoring kept me awake. Hope you couldn't hear it through the walls.'

'No – no, I went out like a light,' she lied. She'd spent ages wondering if she should have invited him to stay. Any other guy would have taken it as an invitation to sleep with her, but she'd known Max wouldn't. To him, it was a practical arrangement. Harriet's teasing about Max fancying her had troubled her, however, but Krys had dismissed it. Max wasn't interested in her or any woman.

'Good . . . good . . .' Max sipped his coffee. Jake's dog tag rattled against the bowl. Krys crunched her toast.

'What are you up to today?' he said.

'I'm off to the Outdoor Centre to help clear out the shed for Santa's Grotto.'

A face appeared at the window and a moment later someone knocked on the back door to the kitchen.

'Oh God, I think it's Nikki!'

Max mouthed something unintelligible. Jake, however, started barking and dashed to the kitchen door.

'I'll have to answer it,' Krys said.

'Jake!' he called but it was pointless. Jake had recognised the scent of an old friend and was barking at the door.

With Max barefoot and herself in a fluffy dressing gown, sharing breakfast, there was no hiding the fact that he'd spent the night there. *Unless* he'd been out walking Jake and dropped in and taken off his muddy boots. Now, that was a possibility.

Krys opened the door to Nikki, who had a large bag.

'Morning! Hope it's not too early. Only I'm doing the change-overs and you were first on my rounds. I brought new linen.'

'Great,' Krys said, grinning like an idiot.

'I hope I haven't got you out of bed. It is early . . .'

'No, it's fine. I'll take those, shall I?'

'The bag's heavy. I was going to do a bit of a clean if you liked, at the same time. Bring fresh loo rolls, see if you wanted anything . . .' She frowned. 'Is that Jake?'

A woof rang out and a moment later, a furry presence trotted past Krys and greeted Nikki with a lick on the hand.

'Yeah. Yeah . . . Max dropped in.'

'Oh. Oh, well I can just leave these and come back later.' Nikki was rather red in the face, but Krys was positively dying of embarrassment.

'It's fine. Come in. We were having a quick coffee, as a matter of fact. And um, some toast . . .'

'Sounds lovely. I'll leave these but I won't stay.'

Krys smiled. The last thing she wanted was Nikki poking around the bedrooms.

She came in and put the bag on the floor.

'Morning, Max,' she said, while stroking Jake.

'Morning,' he said.

Krys saw her eyes widen at his bare feet, and the T-shirt.

'Max's boots were muddy . . .' Krys explained, cringing inside. 'And his socks.'

Max's eyes widened in horror at her embellishment of the lie but he clamped his lips together.

'It happens,' Nikki said with a bright smile. 'Shall I leave your linen here? Of course, I can remake your bed if you want to. It's part of the service but maybe you'd rather do it yourself.'

'I'm fine. I'll do it. You must have loads of other cottages to visit.'

'Yes, it's a busy day. OK.' She placed the fresh towels and sheets on the bar stools.

'I'll see you both at MRT next week, then?'

'Yes. I'm hoping to make it,' Krys said, detaching herself from the "you both". 'Though Brett will be back soon so it depends.'

'That will be nice for you,' Nikki said. 'You won't have to rattle round this great big place on your own any longer.'

'No.' Krys smiled. 'I won't.'

'I'll be at the meeting,' Max muttered. 'And I have to be off now, anyway. *Jake!*'

Jake whined.

'See you both around then,' Nikki said cheerfully.

Too cheerfully. She must have sensed the atmosphere, Krys thought, cringing.

'Thanks,' Krys said, walking to the door with her. With Brett working away, Nikki must have made assumptions: here she was cosied up, having breakfast with Max, first thing in the morning. Sleeping with him. It wasn't like that. She was only friends with Max. OK, she admitted she was physically attracted to him, but that was all, wasn't it?

Krys closed the door behind her and heaved a sigh, before joining Max in the kitchen.

'Oh dear. That was bad timing,' she said, trying to make light of things. 'I've a horrible feeling that we might be a bit of a topic for gossip.'

'I was once,' Max said. 'They gave up after the first few months and I'm sure they've far more important stuff to worry about than us now. I'll see you around. No need to see me out.'

He pulled on his boots and strode out into the morning chill with the dog, without so much as a glance back at her.

Chapter Twenty

Max's moods and Nikki's assumptions were the last thing on Krys's mind later that day. She was waiting to hear from Brett, who should be on his way to JFK airport by now for the overnight flight to Heathrow. He was spending a night at the London flat and, after a hopefully soothing night's sleep, he'd head to Thorndale for a weekend reunion.

She had so much to tell him, about the MRT, the Outdoor Centre grotto, about her climb up Scafell . . . or perhaps she might leave that out. However, as for Max staying overnight, Brett definitely *didn't* need to know that. If she was in his position, Krys thought, she would certainly have jumped to conclusions. She'd have to hope he didn't hear about it on the grapevine and, for once, was glad that Brett wasn't inclined to be too sociable with the locals.

In hindsight, she'd begun to think it hadn't been the wisest of invitations, no matter how innocent. Now she'd have to lie to Brett, or at least keep the truth from him. She was relieved he was coming home so they could press the restart button on their relationship and everything could go back to normal again, whatever normal was. This strange period of time on her own had been unsettling, making her rethink so many aspects of her life.

Before she could think any more about the implications of that, a video call came in on her screen, demanding her attention.

It was Brett . . . calling from JFK, no doubt.

'Hi there!' she cried, delighted to hear from him 'in person' at last.

Immediately, she saw that he wasn't in an airport lounge, but in his hotel room. He also looked dreadful. He must have been under so much stress, Krys could forgive him for staying away so long.

'Hi, babe.'

'You're still in the hotel. Are you OK? You're not ill, are you?'

'No, I'm fine . . . physically fine . . .'

'*Physically* fine? Brett . . .' Her skin prickled unpleasantly. 'What's happened?'

'I had to cancel my flight.'

'Oh no! Why?'

'Because . . . I am so sorry, Krys, but I'm not coming home.'

Krys swore, then apologised. 'Sorry, but Brett, I thought it was guaranteed! I thought you'd be on your way now. If you have to stay any longer, it's almost Christmas and I've been looking forward to seeing you, and to the ball . . .' She stopped, aware she sounded needier than she intended to but mostly *angry*, at him. Angry at herself too, for not sensing that her fantasy Christmas had only been that: a dream. She hardened her tone. 'So, when *will* you be back?'

'I'm not sure.'

'Not sure?' Disappointment flooded her. 'Don't say you're going to miss the ball.'

'Yes, I'm afraid we are. At least, I'm going to miss it.' He rubbed his hand over his mouth and she saw again how haggard he looked. Haggard, fearful and *guilty*. Her skin prickled again and her stomach did an unpleasant flip. She felt cold, despite the blazing fire.

'Krys, there's no easy way to say this and I swear, it's the hardest thing I've ever had to do.'

She knew instantly but it was still a heart-squeezing shock. What he meant was it would be hard on her and he wanted her to make it easy for him, but she wasn't going to: not after being strung along and let down so often.

'What do you mean?' she said. 'I need you to tell me what you mean, Brett.'

'I never intended for this to happen but it's the opportunity of a lifetime. I'm so sorry things have to end like this but it's not fair on you – on either of us – so it's best if we make a clean break. I won't be back for a couple of years, possibly ever.'

'Ever?' She ground out the words. 'I don't understand.'

'Babe, I'm trying to process it myself. It's all happened so fast but the client's demanded I stay here in the New York office to make sure everything runs smoothly. They said it's a deal-breaker if I won't take the job.'

'Stay in N-new York?' she stammered, her composure evaporating.

'Yes. And I know it's only a few hours by plane but it's going to be so full on, I won't have much time to hop back and forth. I'll have a hard enough time finding my feet. Krys, I know I'm not the greatest person when it comes to relationships. I'm selfish, I'm not the most reliable. I have been faithful. I'd never have let you down like *that* but keeping a relationship going over such a distance, and time difference – it wouldn't work and it's not fair on you.'

'Not fair on me.' She propped up the phone on a cushion, too shaky to hold it steady. 'You're right, Brett,' she said, speaking slowly and carefully. 'It's not fair on me. It's not fair that you encouraged me to rent this place for two months, promising to spend Christmas with me. It's not fair that you vanished after one weekend. It's not fair that you haven't even the balls to come and tell me face to face that it's over.'

'Now hold on. I did think about it, but it would only have made things worse. Turning up and conning you into thinking everything was OK? That would have been really cruel.'

'Cruel?' She repeated. 'Cruel! This is cruel!'

Brett sucked in a breath before he replied, irritability creeping into his tone. 'Look, I can understand why you're upset. It's a shock but you'll realise it's better this way. I'm only sorry that you're up there, so far away in that draughty old pile, but maybe that's for the best too. If you were in London . . . the memories, places we've been . . .'

'That's enough. Don't try to justify your cowardice. I get that you want this job. I get that you don't even want to try to make the relationship work, but to tell me on the *phone*? Brett, that's just weak.'

'If you say so.' His voice was tight. 'And I haven't forced you to be up there on your own. You wanted that place, Krys. *You* were wedded to the idea of a perfect Christmas. Don't put that on me.'

She stared at the phone as if it were a cobra that had struck, biting down on her and infecting her with its poison.

'I have to go. I've a meeting with the boss. I am truly sorry. Truly. If things had been different, we might have been in this for the long term.'

'The long term? No. No we wouldn't. I already knew that. You look down on people too much. You don't act from the heart. There's a littleness about you that always bothered me. I only just admitted to it.'

'I can see you're upset. Don't leave things like this between us . . . festering. It's better to part on good terms.'

'The only thing that's festering is you. A festering pile of—' She bit back the expletive and said. 'Go to your meeting, Brett. Do your deal. Goodbye.'

Krys threw the phone on the carpet and collapsed back. She simply could not move. She sat until she was too cold to sit any longer then pulled a blanket over her and lay there as the embers of the fire died down to cold ashes.

She didn't remember going to bed but somehow she woke in the dark December morning with gritty eyes. Staring into the inky blackness, she asked herself why she should bother getting out of bed at all.

Then she heard Linda in her ear: 'Get off the bed, get dressed. You've been through worse and he isn't worth it, sweetheart.'

She dragged on the jeans and fleece she'd discarded on the floor the previous evening. The blue sky had gone and drizzle was blowing in off the mountains. Her throat was dry so she went into the kitchen and filled a mug with water and drank it down, though it hurt to swallow.

The accusations she'd thrown at Brett – that he laughed at people, that he was basically a self-centred coward – were true. Yet they had been intimate: not only physically. He had treated her like she'd been special to him. He had been faithful and she believed that if they'd stayed together, he probably always would have been.

Yet hadn't she also known, deep down, that he was always going to put her second when push came to shove? That he was passing through her life, passing by her . . . and would leave her in his wake. She'd been so desperate for stability, for comfort and for love after Linda had died. The rock of her life was gone and she'd been looking for another one: but she'd always sensed that Brett wasn't it.

He would never be a rock for anyone: he was the torrent flowing round it, and he had no intention of stopping for anyone.

Immediately, she heard Linda in her head again: 'You don't need a rock, my darling Krys. *You* are the strong one and you can get through this without him or anyone. You know it, so dig deep: you'll get through this. There's a new adventure waiting.'

Chapter Twenty-One

'Come on, Jake, let's go for a walk.'

Jake jumped to his paws. The moment Max opened the door, the dog shot off. Max followed, collecting a plastic bag from next to the kitchen sink.

On his way to the lake shore, he met no one. No wonder: it was a weekday in December and the forecast was bad. However, this moment was the calm before the storm. It was one of those rare days when the surface was unruffled, yet the reflections in the surface were no picture postcard scene. The screes plunged headlong into black water, and the fell tops were hidden by heavy cloud.

Jake scampered ahead, pausing to sniff various walls and clumps of bracken. Max headed straight for a tiny bay that few ventured near. He pulled the roses out of the bag and touched his lips to the velvety petals.

'I'm sorry, Erin.'

One by one, he tossed the flowers into the water and watched them float away towards the deep.

There. It was done. Another year had passed.

'Come on, Jake.'

He paused. A solitary figure sat on a rock at the edge of the lake, her arms wrapped around her knees and her chin down.

There was something about her pose that gave Max a shiver of foreboding. He recognised that need to curl up as tightly as possible, to become the merest speck in the landscape: to disappear.

Krys certainly didn't seem to want company, yet that didn't mean she didn't *need* it. She looked so desolate that Max couldn't possibly leave her on her own, even though his stomach had knotted with apprehension. There was something about the way she was sitting that reminded him of himself in the early months after Erin had gone.

Before he could even start walking over to her, Jake had made his own decision. He hared off towards Krys, tongue lolling.

'Jake!'

His call went unheeded: Jake had spotted a lost soul and was on a mission to find her, whether she wanted to be found or not.

He jogged after the dog, who'd reached Krys and was barking happily.

She fussed him and seemed pleased to see him, though how she'd react to Max himself was another story.

'Jake!' he called again. 'Behave!'

'It's OK,' Krys said, 'he's not doing any harm.'

At the sight of her, Max did a double take. The word that sprang to mind was 'broken'.

'Are we disturbing you?' he said, maintaining his distance, a few feet away.

'No. Not really.'

She didn't look too convinced. 'Tell us to go away if you want to.'

'No. No . . . I've been here a while. I was thinking of heading back to the manor anyway.'

Max took his cue to walk over, dismayed at her pale face. There were dark smudges under her eyes and they were red from lack of sleep and possibly crying. Wearing only a thin waterproof and no gloves, she must have been freezing. The urge to hold her and comfort her almost overwhelmed him.

'You seemed lost in your thoughts,' he said, simply, hoping to prompt her.

She laughed bitterly. 'You could say that. I've done enough thinking to last a lifetime over the past few days.'

'Am I guessing not in a good way?'

'Brett and I have split up.'

He hadn't expected that.

'I'm very sorry to hear that.' And he was, but only because Krys was clearly devastated. Brett could go to hell.

'I had so many plans for Holly Manor,' she said, a break in her voice. 'So many plans for Christmas . . . And beyond.'

'Everyone has a plan,' Max said, catching sight of the flowers still floating on the water. 'Until they get punched in the face.'

'Who said that?' she asked.

'I forget. Probably not the world's greatest philosopher, I grant you, but in this case, accurate.'

Krys nodded. Jake licked her hand and she rested it on the silky fur of his head. One thing was sure: Jake was better at empathy than Max was. He was so out of practice himself.

'Have you been punched in the face too?' she said.

'I probably ought to have been, many times.'

'No. Don't joke. Tell me, *please*.' There was desperation in her plea and she added: 'Misery loves company.'

'Hmm. Well, that's why I stay away from people.' Or why he used to, he realised. He'd had more interaction with people since

215

Krys had arrived in Thorndale than in the past three years. 'Why I *used* to stay away from people. I'm not doing such a good job of it lately.'

'As in joining the MRT?'

'That. And . . . this.' He looked at Krys, and the pain in her eyes made his chest tighten. 'I do understand what it's like to lose someone. You've had a double blow: your aunt who I can tell you loved deeply and now Brett . . .'

'Brett and I – I don't know if I loved him deeply.' She clasped her hands together. 'Perhaps love wasn't the word for what we had. Or thought we had.'

'No. Perhaps not. Even so, an unexpected knock-back like that coming on top of a grievous loss is enough to floor anyone. I know it's a cliché but please, be kind to yourself.'

'Be kind to *myself*?' she said sharply, before softening. 'Sorry, but I'm not sure you're the one to give me advice when you haven't told me what happened to bring you to this lonely place . . . and I know that something awful *did*. I can see the scars. I can feel them.'

'You're right,' he said, lifting his eyes to the fell tops, finding them obscured by cloud. 'Something awful did happen. My wife died and I'm afraid it was all my fault.'

Max waited. For what, he didn't know. He received only a silence in return and the parting of lips from Krys. 'I shouldn't have chosen now to tell you,' he said. 'It's not your problem, not your burden to add to the ones you're already carrying.'

'No. Now was exactly the moment to tell me.' She touched his arm. 'Please tell me more. I'm *sure* it can't have been your fault.'

'Not directly, perhaps, but I created the circumstances for it to happen.'

The fine drizzle had turned to rain. Krys hugged herself and shivered, forcing Max into a decision.

'The temperature's dropping. The forecast is for sleet and snow on the tops. You must be freezing.'

'Yes, I rushed out in my waterproof. Should have brought more layers. And probably a Kendal Mint Cake. Clearly, I learned nothing at the MRT evening.'

He loved seeing her smile, even though it melted away like snow in May.

'No one is prepared for anything. In the early days after Erin – my wife – died and I came here, I'd set off in just a T-shirt, daring the weather to close in or something to happen. Almost wanting it to. I didn't care what happened to me.'

'And you do now?'

'A bit more than I did before. The other night on the shout, those students were petrified. They had their whole lives ahead of them and they were desperate to survive. I felt . . . selfish for the way I've acted in the past even though my actions made perfect sense at the time.'

'I'm glad you decided to carry on. To live,' she said. 'Or I'd never have known you and that would have been a terrible shame.'

The urge to fold her in his arms, stroke her hair, kiss her was almost overwhelming. It would be the worst thing he could ever do: for himself and more importantly for Krys.

'Look, it's not nice out here and will only get worse.' Jake let out a whine. 'Even Jake wants to be warm and dry. Fancy a brew? If we're going to share our woes, we may as well be comfortable.'

It was only a ten-minute walk back to the Bothy but during that time, the weather worsened, with the cloud base sinking lower by the minute and the wind sharpening. Max quickened his step, mainly to encourage Krys to keep warm and reach shelter as quickly as possible.

Inside the Bothy, the stove was still warm. He put the kettle on while she sat on the sofa with Jake by her side. He thought about adding whisky to their coffees but decided he'd probably have to drive her back to the manor. He found some mince pies that Amina had given him, and a couple of unchipped plates, and settled down in the chair by the fire. Her cheeks were pinker and she seemed brighter. He wondered whether he could get away with not talking any more about himself.

'Thanks.' She cradled the mug in her hands.

'Have a mince pie. Amina gave them to me last time I was in the village. I think they were going out of date.'

'Can mince pies ever go out of date? I never leave them hanging around long enough to find out.' She took one and bit into it. 'They're still nice.'

Max joined her.

Jake gave a hopeful whine.

'No, sorry, boy. Not for you.'

She glanced around the Bothy, almost as if seeing it through new eyes. 'Did you move here after your wife—?'

'Yes, a few months after she died.'

'But why *here*? It's so isolated.'

'That's why I chose it. I was actually born and brought up in the Lakes, although much further south around Cartmel, not in Thorndale.'

She raised an eyebrow. 'Oh? I'd never have guessed. You don't have a Cumbrian accent.'

'Not now. My parents moved down south when I was twelve but my grandparents still lived up here and I used to come back to walk and climb with my university friends.'

'No wonder you know these hills so well.'

'Well enough. Not as well as some.'

'So, what happened when you left uni?' She ate more of the pie which seemed a good sign.

'After a few years working for a big company, I set up my own business designing and manufacturing 3D printing tech. It did well and I made plenty of money. I'm not ashamed to admit that, but there was a heavy price to pay. Even before I met Erin, I was a workaholic. She was the cousin of a climbing buddy, not that I had any time for climbing but we'd stayed in touch.' He broke off, unable to avoid the glow of warmth inside when he recalled that first meeting with Erin.

She'd been a bridesmaid, a vision in a floor-length pale blue gown, glossy black hair piled up and dressed with spring flowers. 'Absolutely not the thing I'd ever have chosen for myself,' she'd told him later in a quiet corner of the hotel bar.

He'd been a bit drunk by then, and replied, 'Yes, but you look beautiful. I haven't been able to take my eyes off you.'

Cringe-inducing as a chat-up line, yet from the heart.

She'd rolled her eyes. 'Tell me that when you're sober.'

'I will.'

And he had. Two days later on a Monday morning, he'd messaged her: *I'm not pissed now and I still feel the same.*

Krys was watching him, the glow of the fire reflected in her eyes. She was nothing like Erin in looks, her hair light brown, tall and willowy, whereas Erin had been petite and curvy, yet he couldn't take his eyes off her.

And he couldn't tell her because she was on the rebound from the man who'd just dumped her.

He refocused on Krys and noted a little pink back in her cheeks. 'I met her at this mate's wedding around eight years ago. We tied the knot ourselves less than a year after that and moved in together near Reading where my business was based. She had a busy job too, but she also had a life. I was always at work and it took over more and more of my life: weekends, late nights. If anything went wrong, the buck stopped with me.'

'I do know how work can consume you. Brett – Brett has been offered a permanent job in New York. He said he had to take it.'

'That's fine, if you love your job and you want to be consumed, but it was affecting our relationship. I never had the time I wanted to spend with Erin. We hardly had any holidays. I realised how it was taking over my whole life but the business was growing and I didn't know how to step off the wheel I'd set in motion. Not without selling the company and leaving the staff to the mercy of strangers.'

'Lately, I feel I've been on the wheel. Brett too. This holiday was meant to force us both to focus on each other. On pleasure, but he obviously didn't want to get off the wheel.'

'Maybe it's best you found out now, before things became even more serious?'

She shook her head. 'He found it so easy to cut me off, I don't think it could ever have become more serious.'

'I'm sorry.'

'Don't be,' she said then turned her gaze on him. 'You were telling me about Erin?'

'Then one November, I'd finally managed to arrange a weekend away in London for the two of us. I'd booked a swanky hotel, theatre tickets, dinner at a top restaurant: the works.'

He stopped. How shallow it all sounded now, how utterly, desperately trivial.

Yet Krys was waiting to hear more so he screwed up his courage and carried on.

'The day before we were meant to go on the trip, we had an issue with the business and I realised I'd have to spend the whole weekend in the office working. I didn't feel I could leave it to the team. I knew Erin would be disappointed but I thought I had no choice.'

'*Thought?*' Krys put in.

'I *did* have a choice, didn't I? You always have a choice. I could have trusted my management team. I could and should have gone with her. If I had, perhaps there would have been a different outcome.'

Krys was intent on him.

His throat was dry but he had to go on now he'd started. 'Erin's sister, Laurel, went with her instead of me and on the way home they were hit by a lorry driver who was on his mobile. Erin was killed instantly and Laurel was badly injured. She's out of a wheelchair now but she'll never be fully fit again.' He swallowed. Laurel hadn't forgiven him. She'd flung the same accusations at him that he'd directed against himself. He'd seldom seen her in person since the funeral.

Her hand flew to her mouth in shock and sympathy. 'I am so very sorry . . . but the same thing might have happened if you'd gone with Erin.'

'I don't know. What matters is that if I'd been driving, the variables would have been different. We might have stayed a little longer, might have driven a little faster, or stopped on the way. All I can think of is that Erin only had to have missed being in the wrong place at the wrong time by a few seconds. And most of all, that even if it had happened, I'd have been with her. She wouldn't have been alone.'

'And neither would you?' she said, catching him off-guard.

'Exactly. Neither would I. I wouldn't have been left in the world wondering how the fuck I would ever survive in it without her. I've had so many thoughts about Erin that didn't make sense. I've given up trying.'

Jake rested his muzzle on Krys's knee. Rain had started to fall outside, drumming on the roof.

'Listen to me. What a pile of misery to lay on you when you've lost someone special to you and just broken up with your boyfriend.'

'I miss Linda and she was taken too soon but we had had many years together, and as for Brett . . . I'll survive.' There was unexpected steel in Krys's voice that touched Max deeply. Trust her to think of him, not herself. 'But to lose Erin in such a cruel and sudden way and to blame yourself. I can't imagine what it must have been like,' she said.

'I wouldn't bother trying, if I were you,' he replied. 'It's not a lot of fun.'

Krys smiled, only briefly, but it filled him with hope that she would heal. Then she frowned. 'Before you came up to me today, I saw you at the end of the lake. You threw something red into the water and at the time, I guessed it was flowers.'

'Oh yes. The roses.'

'It's today, isn't it? The anniversary of the accident. I am so sorry to have brought my troubles to you.'

'No, it isn't anything to do with the accident. It's – it would have been – our eighth wedding anniversary but please don't worry about disturbing me. I've said my piece to Erin, inside my head, thousands of times, but now you can understand why Christmas isn't a happy time for me.'

'Yes. Yes, I can. Now I know why you must think my job is trivial.'

'No, I don't. Erin *loved* Christmas. So did I, when I was a boy. My parents always made it a special time for me and my brother and Erin adored the planning, decorating the house, and all the shopping. It's why I organised the trip. She was so disappointed I couldn't go but still excited . . .' Max broke off, feeling the softness of his wife's lips on his own, and her parting words on the driveway at their house.

'Bye, big man. Don't work too hard.'

'I'll make it up to you when you get back. I swear.'

'I look forward to that.'

That kiss, their final conversation, so banal and so monumental. They were imprinted on his heart.

He looked up to find Krys staring at him, with tears running down her cheeks.

'Oh shit. I shouldn't have said anything. I really shouldn't.'

It was too late. Krys was howling. To add to it, Jake started whining in sympathy.

He hadn't held a woman in his arms since the morning he said goodbye to Erin. Yet he could not leave her. Max went over, sat next to her, put his arms around her and held her, her sobs juddering. They resonated in his own body, each one making his gut tighten. He felt helpless to comfort her: worse than helpless, as he'd actually made her pain worse by joining his own to it.

Jake pawed at his thigh, whimpering.

'It's OK,' he soothed, to the dog. 'It's OK.'

Only it wasn't OK at all. It was very much not OK to have laid such a terrible burden on Krys when she'd needed to unload her troubles. Jesus, this was what happened when you let your guard down.

Gradually, her sobs subsided but he was still holding her. She was so warm in his arms, so vital even in her misery. From feeling awkward, Max began to enjoy the sensation of another human pressed against him: a woman and one he was deeply drawn to. The pleasure was almost immediately replaced by guilt at feeling pleasure when Krys was so unhappy.

As gently as he could, he let go of her and she rubbed her hand over her eyes.

'Oh God, that was embarrassing.'

Embarrassing? Not for him. Losing her physical presence had been a wrench.

He jumped up, grabbed a roll of paper towels from the sink and held it out. 'Here you go.'

'God, sorry, I don't what came over me. I'm no use to anyone. This isn't like me at all. I don't cry. Until lately. Now I've probably made you feel even worse, if that's possible.'

'Not as bad as I've made you feel. But hey, you know what they say: a problem shared is a problem doubled.'

She'd finished her drink. 'Thanks for the coffee and the pie and the chat.'

'You're welcome. I'm not very good at small talk.'

'You've made a start,' she said.

A gust of wind swirled under the door, and the fire flickered. Sleet rattled against the window.

'It's worse than before. I'll give you a lift home.'

'I could walk,' she said. 'But thanks. Next time I'll come out better equipped.'

'See that you do,' he said, sternly, and was rewarded with another fleeting smile.

'It'll get better, I promise you, and you know where I am if you need me.' He wanted to make a specific offer to see her again but knew it wasn't appropriate today.

She followed him out of the door, with Jake her faithful shadow.

Jake darted off, barking, towards the workshop.

'Damn. There's a sheep in the yard. Jake!' he shouted. 'He's only excited but he could hurt it by accident.' Max hurtled after him. 'Jake!' he bellowed. 'Down, you rogue!'

The sheep ran off and Jake dropped to the ground, flattening his ears.

'No. Never do that again!' Max warned, knowing his dog wouldn't understand the words. Jake let out a whine.

'Come here.' He caught the dog's collar and turned to find Krys there.

She was staring in through the workshop door at the lathe, the array of tools and the dust on the floor.

Max hurried forward and closed the door. 'Sorry about that. Jake can be skittish. That's why he failed the search and rescue test.'

'He's still lovely,' she said.

'Sometimes,' Max said, gruffly. 'Come on, let's take you home.'

Chapter Twenty-Two

Krys had thought that telling people about Brett would be hard, yet with Max, it had felt . . . if not easy, then somehow *natural*. He'd come across her in her darkest moment when she'd been overwhelmed by a double loss. Brett's bombshell and a lack of sleep had ripped open the far more painful wound of Linda's passing.

Otherwise, she would never have been so emotional with Max. She couldn't regret it, though, because if he hadn't found her, she would never have found out about Erin.

In her raw state, Krys had shed a few tears on his behalf when she'd been alone at Holly Manor, but since then, she'd rallied. It was strange but most of her thoughts over the past couple of days had been about Max not Brett.

That was one thing she'd failed to mention when she'd called Harriet to break the news. Harriet had been sympathetic and sent a gorgeous bouquet and chocolates but Krys had had the impression her friend wasn't as shocked as she'd expected.

The ball was hastening up fast and it was the last thing

she felt like being involved in. She certainly wasn't going to it, but she'd made a commitment to helping with the decorations that she could not break. Steeling herself for awkward conversations, she put on some make-up and set off for the post office where Nikki and Amina were chatting by the till.

They were both as cheerful and polite as ever but Krys would be deluding herself to imagine that Nikki hadn't told Amina that Max had spent the night. When they heard her news, they were bound to think he had something to do with the split.

'Hello! Just the woman!' Nikki said. 'I bet your ears were burning.'

'Why?' Krys retorted more sharply than she'd meant to.

'We were chatting about the ball,' Amina said, warily. 'And how excited everyone is about the ice palace theme.'

'Oh. Oh – I see . . .' Krys said, managing a smile. 'I hope I can pull it off.'

'Of course you will. We checked out some of the store displays you've been in charge of. They are amazing.'

Krys smiled weakly again.

'How's Brett? He's back now, isn't he? Will he be going to the kids' party as well as the ball?' Amina asked.

'No, I'm afraid not.' Krys braced herself. 'Brett and I . . . I'm afraid we've gone our separate ways.'

Amina opened her mouth in surprise. 'Oh no!'

'I'm so sorry to hear that.' Nikki looked hard at Krys. 'It seems very sudden,' she added.

Krys could hardly bear the sympathy but she had to get used to telling people, and once they knew, it would be over.

'Did Max say anything?' she burst out.

They swapped glances. 'Max? No. Why would he say anything?' Nikki stared at her. She must think Max was the reason they'd split up but that wasn't what Krys had meant at all. She wished she'd never blurted out his name.

'Only that ... I saw him by the lake the other day and mentioned it to him.'

'No. Max said nothing when he came into the post office,' Amina said. 'Though he doesn't gossip.'

'No. I guess not.' She sighed. 'Brett was offered a job in the States and we didn't think we could keep things going across all that distance.'

How odd it was to say 'we' when it had been solely Brett's decision. Yet Krys had her pride: she wasn't going to let on, and anyway ... perhaps, a tiny corner of her conscience had begun to say, it was better that they made a clean break of it.

'I'm really sorry to hear that,' Nikki said. 'Are you OK about it?'

Krys stiffened. 'Yes.' She forced a smile. 'It's not the greatest news I've ever had, but I've been through a lot worse.'

'It sounds like it was sudden, though?'

'In some ways but we've both been very busy for a while now and our jobs have kept us apart,' she said.

Krys had racked her brain to decide if she'd seen any of it coming. Brett was devoted to his work; it meant a lot to him, but she hadn't thought it meant *everything*. Then again, if she'd really wanted to delve into the cracks in their relationship, perhaps she might have foreseen the break-up, if not now then months down the line ...

'Life stinks sometimes,' Amina said.

'It's not been the happiest of weeks but people have gone through far worse. I won't be coming to the ball myself but I'm still *very* happy to do the decorating for that and the Christmas party. In fact I'm off to the Outdoor Centre after lunch.'

Nikki and Amina exchanged glances. 'If you need anything, want a chat . . .' Nikki said.

'Thanks but I'm fine,' Krys said, simply longing to be on her own and wishing she'd never blurted out Max's name.

Determined to lose herself in activity she drove to the Outdoor Centre and spent the morning, helping to clear out old bits of equipment, compost bags and dried grass cuttings. Two of the staff and some of the older teenagers who were staying there joined her, and the time flew by. By lunchtime, the shed was empty and several hay bales had been brought in, courtesy of a nearby farmer.

She'd forced herself to work like a demon, redoubling her efforts to arrange the bales in place, and stopped to admire her and Jo's handiwork. Now that the heavy work had finished, Krys's nose was turning red in the cold. She'd soon rival Rudolph.

'It's spruced up well though I still can't quite imagine it as Santa's grotto,' Jo said.

'Oh, you soon will, I promise! The inflatable figures arrive at the end of the week so I'll be back with those as soon as I get them.'

Jo looked slightly worried. 'I hope the weather's kind to us. We don't want them flying away.'

'Don't worry. They're made of pretty tough material and they come with ground stakes, guy ropes and sandbags. They inflate automatically when they're plugged in and look *amazing* when the inner LED lights are turned on. You can even have a rotating light inside for extra pizazz.'

'Pizazz is a word I'd never thought I'd hear in connection with the centre.' Jo laughed. 'Want to come inside and see how the kids are getting on with the homemade decorations? You can help if you'd like to.'

Some childish play? It sounded exactly the tonic she needed. 'Thanks. Why not?'

They went inside and grabbed hot chocolates from the café before heading into the main hall. The smell was gorgeous, and coming from pine cones, bracken and holly on the tables.

The noise told her that the crafts workshop was in full swing. There were around twenty children and younger teens sitting at tables with the workshop leader, a couple of carers and two of the staff. The air smelled of spray paint and pine, and there were shrieks of excitement and laughter. She was delighted her donation had gone towards such a happy experience.

'We've tried to use some of the natural materials around the centre,' Sasha, the craft leader, explained. 'The kids had a ball gathering them in. We've left some of the cones natural and sprayed others gold or silver and mixed them in bowls with fairy lights and ribbon.'

Krys sat down at a table, and Sasha encouraged the children to show her what they'd made. They'd painted the cones green with white tips for a snowy effect, and arranged them with leaves and cotton wool to create mini winter scenes for table decorations.

'And if we add some battery-operated tealights, we can turn them into candle holders,' Sasha said.

Another group of children were busy decorating and making pennants, while others were using air-dry clay to create mini characters such as snowmen, Santa and penguins. The older ones were creating mini wreath decorations to take home for the tree.

'I've done that with my auntie,' Krys said, filled with nostalgia at watching three little ones creating snowmen from cotton wool and loo roll tubes. The scene transported her to some of the happier moments of her childhood.

'We did it just like that with the head for the lid and filled the inside with a few sweets. We'd decorate the snowmen with felt and buttons that Linda had squirrelled away in her workbox.'

Clearly amused, Sasha held up a loo roll tube. 'You're an old hand at this. Want to help?'

'Yes, please.'

For the next half an hour, Krys reverted to her childhood, rolling up newspaper into a ball and sticking on cotton wool. She made a little hat for her snowman, and it was met with approval from the children on her table. It would have been nice to sit there with her own children one day, she couldn't help thinking, but that seemed as far away as the moon. Being honest, had she ever thought Brett was the fatherly type? She couldn't imagine it.

'OK, everyone. It's time to tidy away all the materials,' Sasha announced to groans from the kids – and Krys had to admit she was quite disappointed herself. One thing was for sure: Brett would never have been seen dead at a kids' party.

Max turned up at the manor the next morning, somewhat to Krys's surprise. He was also without Jake, which was even more puzzling.

'Morning,' he said brusquely when she opened the door. However, Krys wasn't too put off by his taciturn manner. She wondered if his moroseness had become ingrained in him, after so long keeping himself to himself. Now she knew why he'd hidden away from the world, she felt far more understanding and forgiving towards him.

'How are you?' he asked.

'I'm – OK. I went to the Outdoor Centre yesterday, cleared out the stable for the grotto and spent the afternoon making snowmen from loo rolls.'

231

'Sounds . . . different.'

'Yes. Probably not your thing.' She added a smile. 'To what do I owe this honour?'

'Remember the other evening?' he said. 'When I was here . . .'

How could she forget? 'Yes . . .' she said warily.

'I said I had an idea for the children's party.'

'You did but I'd almost forgotten with everything that's been going on.'

'Hmm. Well, that idea has actually come to fruition, shall we say. If you're not busy today, I wondered if you'd like to come out with me.'

'Where?'

'Let's say it's a surprise,' he said mysteriously.

'I've had a few surprises lately,' Krys murmured, itching to know what he was up to.

'Ah, but this is a good one. I can guarantee that.'

'You have to be kidding me?' Krys exclaimed when they reached their destination. 'You've ordered some actual *reindeer*?'

She and Max were standing at the side of an enclosure where a dozen of the creatures were munching grass, against a backdrop of snow-topped fells. He'd refused to say where he was taking her until they'd turned off the road to Keswick into a grand entrance flanked by two stone pillars and marked: Firholme Estate. A handsome Arts and Crafts era house stood in the centre of the grounds, with the reindeer pen situated behind it.

'Yes, and I think they'll be a big hit with the children.'

'But we can't afford them,' Krys said. 'And they'll never be available at such short notice the week before Christmas.'

'There's been a cancellation, according to Zanthe. She looks after them. Apparently, they hold weddings here and one was

232

called off at short notice so the reindeer are now free for the party.'

'And how do you know this Zanthe?' Krys said, holding out some hay to a sweet female reindeer.

'She's in Borrowdale MRT and she's joined us on the odd shout. I phoned her on the off chance. Oh, look, here she is.'

A young woman in jeans and wellies strode up with a bucket of feed.

'They're just adorable,' Krys said, as Zanthe pointed out the bulls and does, and their calves. She explained how two of them were being trained to pull sleighs.

With the snow on top of the mountains behind their enclosure, Krys could almost believe she was in Lapland. She ought to be used to Christmas and all its 'clichés' as Brett termed them, but which she liked to call traditions. However, the reindeer pushed all her festive buttons, and she knew the children would adore them.

Max stood by the fence with her.

'That baby is beyond cute,' she said to Zanthe, her heart melting at the sight of the baby with its tiny antler buds.

'Even I must admit, it's a charmer,' Max said, stroking the calf's back.

'When was it born?' Krys asked.

'Little Cupid arrived back in May, didn't you, sweetheart?' Zanthe said. 'As a matter of fact, I was thinking of bringing her along to the Outdoor Centre with her mum, Eve, and dad, Hengist. How does that sound?'

Krys was buzzing with excitement, imagining Cupid, Eve and Hengist outside the grotto and the kids feeding them and posing for photos. 'I think it sounds amazing,' she said, then brought herself back down to earth. 'Um, how much will it cost?'

Zanthe named an amount.

'You're joking!' Krys blurted out.

'I'm afraid we have to cover our costs, feed, transport, handler's time. We need the funds to carry on the reindeer conservation work.'

'Of course, I wouldn't expect anything else. It isn't that . . . It all seems *very* reasonable.'

Krys stole a peek at Max, but he was busy patting Cupid's back.

Reasonable was an understatement. The price was a fraction of what she'd expected – in fact, she wasn't sure she'd heard correctly. She'd be able to donate the cost herself. 'It's more than fine. I'm very grateful.'

'I know that Outdoor Centre,' Zanthe said. 'They do good work. Happy to help.'

A short while later, arrangements had been made for Zanthe to transport the reindeer to the Outdoor Centre on the morning of the party. They'd remain there while the grotto was open to enable every child to meet them and have their photo taken.

Signs were hung up for a Christmas tree plantation, with banners along the fences advertising that they were now on sale. A powerful twinge of regret and loss struck her, despite the happy afternoon. She had no desire to choose and dress a tree, and anyway, all her decorations were now needed elsewhere.

On the way back to the car, all kinds of questions niggled at her. Max really must have called in a favour, or he knew Zanthe a lot better than he was letting on. There was a third possibility too: he'd persuaded Zanthe to fib about the price and paid the rest himself.

'A reindeer family including a baby. I can't believe they had a slot available . . . and it's a very low price.' Suspiciously low, she thought, vaguely recalling what the garden centre had had to pay even a couple of years ago.

'Don't look a gift reindeer in the mouth,' Max said. 'Shall we have a coffee? I hear the café here is great.'

It was indeed great. They had slices of Christmas cake and cinnamon lattes in the Firholme Café, which overlooked the great bulk of Skiddaw. The grounds of the estate sloped down to the lake where the surrounding mountains were reflected in the surface. It was incredibly beautiful.

Krys slid a glance at Max, standing on the terrace. He'd taken a phone call but now he simply seemed to be standing there, hands in pockets, looking out over the view. What was he thinking?

About Erin? How much he missed her?

Krys's own phone buzzed and she gave a sharp intake of breath when she saw the sender of the message.

How are you?
I'm sorry.
B
XX

It was the first communication she'd had since he'd dropped his bombshell. The cold blast of air took her breath away. It was coming straight off the mountains.

Max joined her.

'Everything OK?'

'Yes. It's – not important.'

'Not important and yet you look like you've seen a ghost?'

'Actually it was Brett. Saying he's sorry.'

His lips parted.

'But not wanting to get back together.'

'You wouldn't do that, would you?' Max blurted out.

Krys was taken aback. 'No, I wouldn't do that. He's had his chance and now – no matter how much it hurts, I know that we're not right for each other. It would be the biggest mistake I could make to go back to him.'

It was true, thought Krys. She'd come to realise she'd been attracted to him because of his ambition. He seemed driven, like her. He'd come from an ordinary background, brought up by his father after his parents' divorce. He hadn't been to university and made his way up through the company training scheme. You'd never know it from his carefully cultivated man-of-the-people accent, a little bit London, but not so you'd know it. With his love of subtle designer labels and his precious Porsche.

You'd think he'd had a privileged upbringing – as Max had admitted to.

She switched off her phone and shoved it in her pocket.

'I'm beginning to think Brett and I were never right for each other,' she said softly. 'And I just don't think I was willing to admit it until he dumped me.'

'Oh?'

'I felt strung along. I think I came to rely on him too much. I feel – foolish, as if I'd pinned my hopes of the perfect Christmas – a perfect life that only exists in magazines and Instagram posts – on him.'

'You could never be foolish,' Max said.

Krys gasped in mock surprise. 'Not even when driving into a flooded stream?'

'Almost never,' he said, with a smile that was so warm, it melted her frozen heart a little. He could be such a kind and generous man, and today he'd revealed a little more about himself. And so, thought Krys, as they walked away from the reindeer pen, had she.

Chapter Twenty-Three

Max battled conflicting emotions: sorrow for Krys's pain and relief that she was coming to see Brett for what he was: weak, selfish and not good enough to lick her boots. None of which he could say, so he simply listened.

'I thought we were kindred spirits: Brett said as much to me,' Krys said. 'I remember the words. "We understand each other, Krys. We've had to fight for what we've achieved. We've earned it and we deserve to be where we are. We're a one of a kind." So I think – I think – he expected me to understand when he broke the news. He expected me to understand that career trumped love. That I would accept and understand that there was collateral damage along the route to the top.'

'And you're the collateral damage . . .' he murmured.

'Yes.'

'We all leave collateral damage at some point,' he said bitterly.

'True, but I don't think it's possible to go through life and avoid hurting someone sometime', she said. 'Not if we want to have relationships. Not if we want to love and be loved. The pain of loss is the price we pay.'

'A heavy price when you love someone very much,' he said.

'I wonder if it was over between us a long time ago. If I should have ended it myself months ago but I wasn't ready for another loss so soon on top of Linda. Now, I feel humiliated and abandoned. It's not the first time . . . It happened a lot when I was little, you see.'

'You don't mention your mother much. Are you still in contact with her?'

'Very rarely. Not since the funeral, and we argued then. My mother once told me that she felt she'd failed me, because Linda had had to step in so many times, when I was young and when my mum met her new partner.'

'It must have been tough. For all of you.'

'It was, but some kids have it have far worse. When I was ten, I came up here on an Outward Bound course. It was organised by some youth foundation and I think the local council or the school must have put me up for it. We stayed in their hostel, with a load of other kids like me who were having a difficult time at home.'

'Was this at Thorndale?' Max said.

'Yes. It's very different now, but at the time I wasn't happy to be there. I felt sorry for some of the other kids. They were in a much worse situation than me. Kids who'd been in and out of care; kids who'd lived on the streets, literally. Some had been physically and emotionally abused; I could hear one crying every night in her sleep. Anyway, I was one of the lucky ones. I didn't feel I should have been sent on it; I was sure I didn't need any special treatment. In fact, I almost resented it, even though everyone was kind.'

'Is this why you wanted to come back to Thorndale? To lay some ghosts to rest?'

'Yes. I remember passing through the village on the minibus.

It hadn't rained that day which was weird because it rained on all the other days.'

Max smiled.

'It was early December . . . The bus dropped us off, we did the walk, and we were all fed up and knackered and waiting for it to collect us.'

Her smile mirrored his.

'What a surprise.'

'I can't remember exactly when we passed through Thorndale and it seemed idyllic, with the cottages and the smoke curling out of the chimneys like in a Beatrix Potter book. And we were bored of waiting for the bus so I decided to explore. There was a big house, with all its lights on, so I went through the gates into the grounds and I peeped in through the window. It was all decorated for Christmas.' She smiled. 'It sounds creepy, spying on other people's houses.'

'And it was Holly Manor?' He could so easily picture the young Krys peering through the window of a house that must have seemed like a fairy tale palace. He felt incredibly moved.

'It *was* Holly Manor though I didn't realise until recently, when I started hunting for a holiday home. Back then, it was like something from a picture book, with a huge tree, tinsel everywhere, a fire in the hearth, so many gifts . . . and that was the day I decided that I wanted to be in that house, sitting by the fire with Auntie Linda – and my mum. I wanted the feeling of having eaten too much, to have too many presents to open, to be too warm . . . to be a proper family. And I vowed I'd have it, somehow, no matter what it took. I was determined to recreate the perfect Christmas I'd never had.'

A proper family. Max had wanted that too. He'd hoped that he and Erin would have children one day and had spiralled down as the weeks and months went by. It was the darkest place he'd ever been to: an abyss with no bottom that he simply kept falling through. Krys did not need to know about that now.

'After I came back from the trip,' Krys went on, 'everything went from bad to worse. Mum lost her job and we couldn't pay the rent so we were evicted – again. The council put us in B&Bs for a while, or we slept on friends' floors. Then she met Gus and I moved in with Linda.'

She smiled.

'That's a happy memory?' Max prompted.

'Yes, it was best for all of us. In the sixth form I loved crafting and had a little business when I was a teenager. When I went to uni, I got a holiday job at the local garden centre and started helping with the displays, especially at Christmas. Turned out I had a bit of a flair for it. Then for some reason, they put me in charge of the Santa's Grotto.' She laughed.

'I can imagine that,' Max said. 'It would be my idea of hell, to be honest.'

'It's not that bad,' Krys said. '*If* you love Christmas, of course.'

Now I'm living in my dream home, even if it's temporary, with another perfect job lined up next year, and I'm Mrs bloody Christmas, but . . .'

She heaved in a sigh. Max was a moment away from holding her in his arms.

'I have everything I always dreamed of but no one to share it with. No Auntie Linda, no Brett. No one special.' She stopped and let out a groan. 'Oh for God's sake, listen to me! I sound so needy and I don't mean to be. It's not *me*.'

Max's heart ached in sympathy. He knew what it was like to not be who you'd once thought you were. 'You don't have to apologise.'

'I *do*,' she said firmly. 'I'm fine, really, and it's a first world problem if ever there was one.'

She moved away, turning her back on him and looking at the view: mountains, lakes, trees.

'It's so beautiful here. What a place to live and work. Look at it.'

She swept her arm extravagantly around, perhaps embarrassed at her display of emotion.

'Yes, it's a bonny place.'

She swung round, a smile on her face.

'"Bonny", that's what the locals say.'

'I know, I am a local now.' He paused, then added, 'Would you like a Christmas tree?'

'A *tree*?'

'Yeah. Spiky green things. There are a lot of them around.'

'I can see that. I did want one but I'm still not in the mood.'

'Me neither but I wondered if the Outdoor Centre would like one? We could take advantage of the Landy and strap it on the roof.'

'You know, that's not a bad idea at all.'

'Let's do it then, before my temporary Christmas spirit evaporates.'

Half an hour later, Max finished strapping the tree to the roof and turned to Krys.

'Ready to go?' he asked.

'You bet.'

They drove off, talking about the tree and the reindeer and the grotto. Max seemed relaxed enough. For a man who hated Christmas. Except, he didn't seem to hate it that much anymore.

'All of this is OK? It must be difficult for you: the reindeer, the tree . . .'

'It ought to be. It was, but this isn't for *me*. It's for the kids at the Outdoor Centre. It's like being part of the MRT. It's for other people.'

'I do get that. I don't want a tree in the house. It seems wasteful and indulgent to buy and dress it only for me.'

'"Wasteful and indulgent"? Is this Mrs Christmas talking?'

'Yeah, I know. Don't record me or quote me: who'd hire a Mrs Christmas who can't be arsed with Christmas? It's not great PR, is it? But it's OK to spend ages choosing the tree because it's for somebody else. It will be enjoyed and give pleasure to a lot of people. Linda used to tell me: "A moment enjoyed is never wasted."'

'You can use that to justify a lot of things.'

Krys frowned. There was a bitter edge to Max's voice that hadn't been there for a while.

'True,' she said softly.

'Ignore me, I'm being a miserable sod again. I know what your auntie meant and Erin would have agreed.'

'Would she also have agreed with you punishing yourself over the past few years?'

'I didn't have a choice,' he said sharply.

A sudden dusk had fallen on their happy mood. He hadn't meant to snap but she'd pushed him too far; probed a wound that he'd thought had begun to heal but was still raw.

Chapter Twenty-Four

'Wow, that is one heck of a tree.'

Outside the Outdoor Centre the next day, Jo stood with her hands on her hips and blew out a breath. Krys had messaged on the way home that they would be bringing the tree but the size of it obviously took Jo aback.

'It's amazing. The kids will love it. I only hope it fits in the room,' Jo said.

'I can cut it down to size if not,' Max offered.

He untied the tree, while Jo and Krys helped unload it.

It had been dark by the time they'd got back to Thorndale the previous evening so Max said he'd keep the tree on the roof of the car and call the Outdoor Centre so he could take it over the next day. Krys said she'd meet him there because she had stuff to do that morning.

Her comment about punishing himself for Erin's death had touched a raw nerve. Lately he'd asked himself the same question, and Krys – like Nikki and his friends – was only trying to help because she cared about him.

The problem was she didn't know the whole story. Only a handful of people on the planet did. None of them were in Thorndale and one of them was dead.

The centre groundsman arrived to lend a hand removing the tree from the roof so Max had to buck up and concentrate on the job.

The staff had already prepared a tree stand, and for the next half an hour, Max was busy sawing off the base and trimming the lower branches before carrying it inside. The sharp pine scent was gorgeous, inevitably reminding him of Christmases past, with all their bittersweet associations. From then on he'd avoided situations and locations where he might have been reminded of the last tragic Christmas.

He'd changed. He'd already been changing before Krys had arrived in Thorndale but she'd turbocharged his re-entry into society . . . and into the festive season. Yet every time she came close, he seemed to push her away.

Once the tree was in place, Max declined the offer of a coffee and politely excused himself, saying he had a lot to do. It looked beautiful, he had to admit, and the staff and children seemed delighted. He was sure that with Krys's help, the kids would love it, but for the moment, his new-found festive spirit had evaporated.

On his way home he called into the post office for supplies. Several locals were queueing to send parcels and Amina's deputy was working behind the screen, looking flustered at the influx of punters.

Max took his groceries to the counter, where Amina rang them up.

Nikki walked in as she was scanning the last couple of items. 'Hi, Max! Hi, Amina. It's heaving in here.'

'Christmas rush has started,' Amina joked and the three of them had a very quick chat about the next MRT meeting.

Nikki left, after leaving a couple of posters about the ball. Max was relieved, half-expecting her to hint at his presence at Holly Manor. However, she didn't allude to it and Amina seemed ignorant of the whole event. Perhaps Nikki had believed Krys's excuse that he'd been drying out after an early morning walk.

The moment he stepped outside the shop, his hopes were dashed because Nikki was waiting for him by her Cottage Care van.

'Max. So glad I caught you. I wanted a quick word.'

'Oh? Is it about the MRT? You could have spoken to me in the post office.'

'I thought it would be more discreet out here. Look, Max, you can tell me to mind my own business . . .'

He frowned. 'Why would I want to do that?'

'Let's call it a pre-emptive strike. I'd like to think you can call me a friend, as well as a colleague. Even when you didn't want friends, you know I was here for you.'

'This sounds serious. Do I need to sit down on a bench?'

She smiled, but her eyes flashed a warning. There would be no escape.

'This is probably the worst thing I've ever done but I'm going to go ahead and say it. If there's something going on between you and Krys . . .'

He folded his arms. 'Something going on? Is this about the other morning?'

'Yeah. If I'm wrong, I apologise.'

'You're not wrong. I stayed the night, if you must know. Krys told a white lie because she was afraid that exactly this would happen: that people would jump to conclusions.'

He faced her down, daring her.

'It's none of my business what you do, but I don't want to see you hurt. I care about you. I was talking to Amina about it.'

Max gasped. 'I'm a topic of conversation, am I? At the post office? Is there a leaflet drop about me to all the holiday homes, along with the clean sheets and guest hampers?'

Nikki flinched. 'Forget I said anything.'

'No. Nikki, I'm sorry. I didn't mean to be so blunt.'

She raised an eyebrow.

'OK, I *did* and I know you're trying to be kind to me.' Kinder than he was himself. 'I don't need you to worry. For what it's worth, I did spend the night at Krys's. In the spare room. I walked home from the base with her, it was filthy weather and we'd been drinking. End of.'

'Like I say, it's none of my business what you did or didn't do. It's only that I care about you. We all do in the team. More than you know. It's been a pleasure – a relief – to see you join in more and more. At one time, you couldn't bear to even say a "hello" in the post office. It's been a joy to see the cloud lifting.'

Max was moved. He couldn't speak. He'd no idea that people had continued to care after his early rejections of them and his rudeness and his moodiness. He'd done more than enough to push everyone away.

'Not only that. I've seen you two grow closer. You like her, don't you?'

Max said nothing. He really didn't like the way this was going.

'I like Krys, too. She's kind, warm and smart,' Nikki said.

He agreed with all of those things and far more. 'I'm sensing a "but",' Max said warily.

'She's also fresh out of a relationship – was still in it until very recently,' Nikki reminded him.

Max knew that things were more complicated than that. Krys had made it clear that she and Brett had been on rocky ground for months and that the trip to the Lakes was meant to give them some time together to focus on their relationship. Clearly, Krys had been ready to make the commitment and Brett hadn't.

Personally, he thought the guy was nuts but he wasn't going to share Krys's private business with anyone, not even Nikki. He steeled himself to be polite: she did care about him, like his buddies in the team did. He felt the same about them: he'd never wish ill on them. He hated the idea that people were gossiping about him – but was far more worried they were gossiping about Krys. She'd be horrified.

'OK, I only wondered if the two of you might be going to the ball? Not necessarily together,' Nikki added hastily. 'Krys is coming over on the morning to decorate the base. If either of you change your mind about coming, all you have to do is let me know. We can always squeeze you in.'

Max softened. 'Thanks. I probably won't . . . and I appreciate that you both care about me, but please don't worry. I'm a big boy now and I know what I'm doing.' His intended wry smile felt like a grimace so he called to the dog. 'Jake! Come on, mate!'

He left, trying to drive off carefully while his thoughts ranged. He was dismayed that she and Amina had interfered and he hated being the subject of village gossip and yet . . . the reason he was so disturbed was because she'd touched a raw nerve.

Even if he did tell Krys how he felt, even if she had been ready – and, by some miracle, felt the same as him . . . what if it ended?

He couldn't face letting someone into his heart and then losing her again to some cruel twist of fate.

Even if he could accept that it was unlikely such a terrible thing would happen twice, he had a deeper underlying fear. He hadn't been able to be the person Erin needed. He's been driven and ambitious, obsessed with making sure they were financially secure.

What if he couldn't give Krys what she needed either?

Chapter Twenty-Five

Krys arrived at the Outdoor Centre later that morning. It was lucky that the party didn't start until three, and she hadn't been required to be there until half-eleven to help finish setting up.

She hadn't had this feeling since she'd peered through the window of the Christmas card house all those years ago.

The manor might be devoid of ornaments but thanks to a team effort between the staff and youngsters, the Outdoor Centre was as charming as any venue she'd ever decorated. With a mix of commercial and homemade garlands, baubles and decorations, it looked knockout.

She had a lump in her throat the moment she walked through the door. How was she going to get through the day? A Christmas party wouldn't solve the problems and challenges many of the kids faced, but if it gave them a couple of hours of unbridled joy – then surely it had been worth it? The most important thing was that the kids and young people themselves had been involved.

Jo accosted her in the reception area.

'Krys. Thank goodness you're here. We need all the help we can get.'

'Is everything OK?'

'Yes, but I've got a staff member off with a bug and one is going to be late so I'm helping our cook with the food.'

'Just tell me what to do, I'll help any way I can.'

'Can you take charge of the grotto on your own? I had to leave it but I really need to be in here.'

'No problem. I'll make sure it's ready.'

Krys's breezy response belied the task at hand. The arch leading up to the grotto was still standing, and looked great with its mesh of coloured lights. The inflatables still hadn't been fixed in place and Krys wasn't totally sure she could inflate, tether and install them all on her own before the children started arriving, yet set to anyway.

In the middle of inflating the snowman, a familiar vehicle drove into the car park. It was the Landy and there could only be one person at the wheel. She wasted no time in rushing over to meet him at the door of his car.

'Max? I didn't think you were coming!'

'What? And miss the reindeer?' He smiled. 'And I thought you might need a hand with setting up.'

She was delighted he seemed in a happier mood.

'Too right. Jo's short-staffed so we're pretty desperate for help.'

'Show me what to do.'

Together, they secured the snowman and polar bear in place at the entrance to the light tunnel. On this brief Lakeland day, one of the shortest of the year, the sun was already slipping towards the horizon, and the shadows were lengthening.

They'd just turned on the internal lights on the figures when a box van pulled up in the car park.

'It's the reindeer!'

Leaving the snowman and polar bear glowing happily outside the grotto, they met Zanthe at the van.

'Looking good,' she said. 'Any chance of helping me with the pen for these guys?'

'You bet,' said Krys.

With Max and Krys's help, Zanthe set up a portable pen for the reindeer by the entrance to the grotto and scattered hay over the ground before leading the baby out of the trailer first.

Krys placed a bucket of feed in front of the family. 'Oh, they are so gorgeous.'

'Even I will admit they are pretty cute,' Max said as the reindeer tucked into their lunch.

Shortly afterwards two more vans arrived, both branded with the Lakeland Reindeer logo.

'Oh, what's this?' Krys asked.

Zanthe smiled. 'Wait and see.'

Max was smiling too; and unlike Krys, didn't seem the least surprised at the addition to the reindeer convoy.

'What on earth is going on?'

Two more staff dropped down from the cabs and proceeded to unload two adult male reindeer and – Krys could hardly believe it – a sleigh. She'd seen reindeer sleds before, of course, but this one was a stunner, decorated with garlands and furnished with Christmas cushions and cosy blankets.

'Is this what I think it is?' Krys said.

'We thought the kids might enjoy seeing Santa arrive on his sleigh,' Zanthe said, while the handlers settled the two male deer in their pen.

'I can't believe it. Thank you so much,' Krys said.

'You're welcome.'

Zanthe went to harness the sleigh, leaving Krys still astonished at the scene in front of her. Beside her, Max was hardly able to contain himself.

Krys had a flash of insight. 'Max, is this your doing?'

'I couldn't possibly say.'

'Hmm.' She gave him a stern look then said, 'It's – very generous of you.'

'When Zanthe called me to say the sleigh was also available this afternoon, I couldn't resist.'

They went to look at the sleigh which had wheels cleverly concealed in its frame. Krys imagined how magical and authentic it would look with Santa sitting in it.

Jo ran out of the centre, and threw her hands over her mouth in disbelief.

'Am I dreaming or is that an actual Santa's sleigh?'

'Yes, it's an actual sleigh,' said Krys.

Jo's excitement infected them all. Max was grinning fit to burst and Zanthe had a knowing smile on her face. She'd seen it all before but nonetheless seemed delighted with the response from the grown-ups. Krystle could hardly wait to see the children's faces.

'We thought we'd get the children gathered around the grotto and arrange for Santa to arrive?' Zanthe suggested. 'Then maybe they can meet the reindeer outside while they wait for their turn to see him?'

'I can't wait to see Hector's face when he gets here,' Krys said.

'That's going to be one of the best moments.' Max had a wicked smile on his face. Krys hadn't seen him so happy since last night.

By the time Max and Krys had added a few more final touches to the grotto, the sleigh was ready. Krys was itching to capture the scene when Hector turned up to see his transport. He'd look magnificent in his full regalia, drawn by the reindeer.

Max's phone rang so he strolled off to take the call. A few minutes later, he came back with a gloomy expression.

'That was the MRT base,' he said.

'Oh no, don't say you've got to go to a rescue?'

'Not me, but Hector has.'

'Hector? I thought he wasn't on call.'

'He wasn't, but there are two shouts at once and they're desperate for experienced teams. I offered to go myself but he's already halfway up the Pike, and besides, they need someone with medical training.'

'Oh no. I hope everyone will be OK.'

'Me too and it can't be helped, but now you have your grotto and reindeer but no Santa.'

Krys immediately went into crisis handling mode, if you could call a missing Santa a crisis. She was used to trouble shooting and she'd deal with this one. Someone would have to step in.

Max and Krys found Jo and explained the situation.

'So we need a new Father Christmas,' Krys said.

'Arghh,' Jo groaned. 'I can't do it. I've got my hands full looking after the kids. We're at the staffing limit for looking after them as it is, even with the volunteers.'

'Can one of the parents or carers do it?' Max suggested.

'I guess we could try but it's a huge ask and they're meant to be having a break too, without being asked to play Santa with no notice. Could one of you do it?' Jo said, a desperate plea in her voice.

Max visibly paled.

Krys stepped in. 'I – I suppose so. It doesn't have to be a man . . .' She began to feel panicky. She had so much to do. 'But I'm meant to be helping at the grotto, greeting the children, keeping an eye on it, soothing the nervous ones, making sure Santa has the right gifts for the right child.'

Out of the corner of her eye she caught Max, eyes wide and lips parted as if he was on the verge of doing something momentous. She held her breath . . . then came the words she thought she'd never hear in a million years.

'OK, I'll do it,' he said. 'I'll be Santa.'

Chapter Twenty-Six

K rys turned to him in astonishment.

'Wh-what did you say?'

'I can do it, but only if you're totally desperate,' he repeated. 'Though I warn you, I'm not old enough, I'm not big enough and I'm definitely not jolly enough.'

She wanted to throw her arms around him. 'None of that matters. You're older than some of the Santas I've booked in the past. You look more like Santa than some of them ever did. When they rocked up, I often used to think I'd made a huge mistake.'

'Maybe you'll still think that. You've more than enough to do here and I'm ready to do it.

'It would be better. We could have a Mrs Christmas but you've got the voice, the height and . . .' Krys clutched at straws, 'the *gravitas*.'

'"Gravitas"? Are you trying to say I'm a miserable sod?'

'Not at all.' Krys frantically backpedalled, still amazed that Max had offered, however reluctantly. 'You have the life experience for a Santa. And I promise you, in the costume, you'll be brilliant.'

'I doubt it very much. I must be out of my mind and I'll probably terrify the kids but I'll do it. But I've never put on a costume or acted a part in my life.'

Jo seemed a little worried. 'Are you sure, Max?'

'He is,' Krys cut in, before turning to Max. 'Don't worry. I'll help you. I've supervised lots of Santa's Grottos and I had a chat with Hector about it the other day too.'

Jo sighed with relief and probably resignation that she had no choice. 'Right. That's settled. Max is Santa. Krys, you're the elf. What about the costume?'

'Hector already thought of that. He's sending his step-daughter over with the suit now.'

'Great. I'll leave you to it. I'm wanted in the party room. Some of the kids have already set out in the minibus.'

She jogged off.

Max pulled a face. 'I feel sick.'

Krys patted him on the back. 'You'll knock it out of the park.'

While they waited for the suit, she distracted him by talking about the sleigh arrival. Max eyed the reindeer. 'I hope they don't bolt. I like them but I never expected to be behind them in a bloody sleigh.'

Privately, despite her morale-boosting pep talk, Krys was wondering if she should have even encouraged him to play Santa. She wasn't worried about him looking the part: the outfit would do all the work; and she was pretty confident that he'd act the part too. Despite his protestations, from what she'd seen when he was out on a shout, he was very good with people – calm, kind and with a dry sense of humour that helped reassure them.

She wasn't sure if the Max she'd seen in that situation was the old Max – the real Max – or Max acting a part.

She knew the children would have a great time and none would guess that Max was only the main man's stand-in. What

255

worried her was the emotional toll on the man himself. She'd been in attendance at some heart-wrenching moments that would test the most resilient of Father Christmases, like the couple who'd decided to split up after Christmas. The Santa knew them personally, and had the children in to see him, knowing that this would be their final Christmas as a family.

Or the time that a young couple with twin boys had visited her grotto, one of whom was terminally ill. The Santa had known that and after his session had sobbed his heart out in Krys's office. Krys had had to hold it together to comfort this big guy who'd been in the Paras before he'd turned to Santa-ing. Only afterwards, at home, had she given way to her own tears and it had taken a while before she could accept that seeing Santa had given that child and his family a moment of pure joy and happy memories before the inevitable happened.

Max would be unaware of the individual circumstances of the kids today: they were confidential. Only Jo had any insight, but Krys ought to prepare him for what he might hear.

Would it be possible for him to set aside his own pain and regrets to do the job?

Twenty minutes later, Jo came outside to tell them the suit had arrived, so they followed her into the office.

'Best I can do as a green room,' she said before flying off again.

There was a large suit carrier plus an oversized canvas sports bag. Max picked the carrier up and staggered. 'It weighs a ton!'

Krys unzipped the sports bag and stifled a giggle. Wait until Max saw inside. Actually, it might not be that funny when he did.

Meanwhile, he'd unzipped the suit carrier and was taking the jacket and trousers out. His face had paled again, to the shade of Santa's beard, as he held the XXXL crimson jacket aloft. The trousers were draped over the hanger.

Max put the jacket down and held the trousers against his slim waist. 'Oh Jesus. I can't do this. I'd need two of me for a start.'

'Yes you can. The outfit is the best part and I think I've found something to help with the trouser situation.'

She delved into the bag and removed a luxuriant wig and beard.

'Oh my God. Are you suggesting I stuff those down my trousers for bulk?'

'No need,' Krys said, patting the bag. 'There's also a false belly to wear under it.'

'You are joking?'

'No.' She hoisted the belly out of the bag, her arms sagging with the weight. She handed it to Max.

Grimacing, he took hold of it. 'My God, this is worse than carrying a full rescue pack up the fell.'

'Good job you're fit, then.' Krys smiled. 'It's pretty heavy but it'll give you the authentic look.'

'With that under my jacket, I'll look as if I ate all the reindeer and the sleigh.'

Krys laughed. Max was nervous but still had his sense of humour. He'd need it.

He picked up the beard and wig. 'This also weighs a ton.'

'Probably because it's real hair.'

Max closed his eyes and swallowed hard. 'I'd better try it on to get used to it. Can't have Santa toppling over under the weight of his own facial hair. The parents might think I've been at the eggnog.'

'Believe me, that has happened,' Krys said, recalling interviewing a Santa who'd seemed suspiciously merry before he'd even been near a grotto.

Max started to hook the straps of the belly over his shoulders.

'It's best if you don't wear all your other clothes under it. It might get quite hot.'

'You mean you want me to strip off?'

'Well, not everything!' she said, blushing. 'Just to your T-shirt . . . and, um, boxer shorts. I can leave,' Krys added, her cheeks warming, again.

'I'm not shy if you're not,' he said gruffly, unzipping his trousers.

Once he was barefoot and bare-thighed, Krys helped him fasten on the belly, ignoring his mutterings.

Max pulled the suit on, cursing under his breath.

Krys winced. 'Want to know my number one tip for being a great Santa?' she said.

'I want to know any tips!' he cried, swearing as he fastened the belt over the belly.

'Try not to swear in front of the children.'

'I think I can do that, but bloody hell, this thing weighs a ton.'

Finally he had the whole suit on and was pulling on the boots, grunting and cursing. Krys helped him on with the wig and beard, adjusting it around his face.

'It's even heavier than the belly,' he muttered, twitching his nose. 'And it itches. How the hell does anyone get down a chimney in this?' Finally, he stood back, hands on hips, a scowl on his face. 'Do. Not. Say. A. Word.'

'I—' Krys had to put her hand over her mouth to stop herself laughing.

'I look ridiculous, don't I?'

'No,' she said firmly. 'You look exactly like Santa.'

'You think?' He frowned. 'That beard tickles.'

She laughed. 'Part of the job,' A rush of pride on his behalf washed over her. 'Thanks for doing this. I know it must be very hard for you. You could easily have said no.'

'I'm doing it for the centre, for the children and for you.'

For *her*?

Krys had no answer to that and now wasn't the time to think about the meaning of his words. He may have meant he was only helping out a friend, or felt sorry for her.

'I need to warn you about a few things,' she went on briskly. 'Being Santa can be emotional. The children can surprise you in ways you can't anticipate.'

'What if they're terrified of me?'

'Their parents and carers will be there to reassure them and we wouldn't force them to do anything they're not happy with. Besides, I'll be with you.'

'I don't think I could do this if you weren't.'

She felt sorry for him. There was genuine fear in his eyes. 'Now, I'm sure you'll be absolutely fine but here's some advice that might help.'

Max tugged at the moustache with irritation. 'Right now, I'll take anything that gets me through this.'

'Your main aim is for the children to think you really are Santa. So don't make the mistake of asking them: What do you want from Santa this year? That means no references to yourself in the third person. For the little ones, you *are* Santa. You're creating magic and you need to take it seriously.'

'No pressure, then.'

High-pitched voices and squeals of excitement pierced the open window of the staff room. Krys's heart started beating faster.

'I think it's almost time to go to your grotto,' she said.

'Can I chicken out? Fly off in my sleigh?' he asked hopefully.

'No, sorry. And you've forgotten these!' She picked up a pair of metal-rimmed specs from a case in the bottom of the bag.

With a groan, Max put them on.

She clapped her hands with delight, partly to wind him up. 'Perfect! You are Father Christmas to the life.'

'Ho-bloody-ho,' Max grumbled, then said, 'Where's your outfit?'

'Hanging on the back of the loo door, apparently. I guess I'd better put it on. The kids will be here any minute.'

'Go on, then. I want to see Santa's Helper.'

There was a knock at the door and Jo's voice trilled from outside. 'Hello! Is Santa ready because I can't keep the kids waiting much longer. They're ready to explode with excitement.'

'Shit,' said Max.

'What did I say about not swearing?'

'Oh golly gosh, yes,' Max muttered then tried another belly laugh before groaning and saying: 'No, I can't do this.'

'Too late,' Krys said and opened the door. 'Santa's ready.'

She encouraged him forward.

Jo's jaw dropped. 'Oh my God. Is that really Max?'

'No, it's the tooth fairy,' he said.

'You look incredible. No one would know it's you.'

'I hope not,' Max muttered. 'Now, would you mind showing me to my grotto, young lady, so I can get ready to meet all the boys and girls?' Max smiled from under his beard. 'I can't wait to meet them. Happy Christmas, everyone!'

Jo collapsed in giggles and Krys had to stop herself from dissolving into gales of laughter.

'That's the spirit, Santa,' she said. 'You go with Jo and I'll get changed and see you make your entrance.'

He was gone, leaving Krys alone in the office, slipping on the elf outfit at top speed. It was by no means the first time she'd dressed up in costume, and she rather enjoyed launching herself into the spirit of things. If Max could play Santa, she could certainly be his helper. She used her lipstick to give herself some red cheeks and pulled on the green hat with its attached ears. A final check in the mirror and she hurried off to the grotto.

This was going to be fun. She only hoped that Max survived it without running away or bursting into tears.

The scene was so utterly perfect; all they needed now was some snow. However, the darkened sky remained crystal clear, as more and more stars revealed themselves and the moon rose.

She thought of Max in the sleigh and the children laughing, and tears came into her eyes. From the depths of misery, today might well turn out to be one of the most magical in her entire life. There was no need for snow, it was already almost perfect.

Chapter Twenty-Seven

'Are you ready, children?'

'Yes!'

Jo put her hand to her ear. 'I can't hear you! Shout louder for Santa!'

'Ye-essssss! Santaaaaaaaa!'

If Max could have flicked a switch and beamed himself up to Mars, he would have done it in a heartbeat. His beard was scratchy and he was squashed into the rear of the sleigh. The reindeer smelled very . . . reindeer-y and one of them had eyed him suspiciously when he'd clambered aboard.

But that was nothing to the febrile buzz of expectation that awaited him in the yard outside his grotto. The lights were twinkling in the late afternoon gloom, the inflatables were glowing and the kids were hyper. With the staff and families there were at least forty people hopping about in excitement as they awaited his grand entrance on his sleigh. Zanthe was in the front seat with the reins, with a helper on either side of the reindeer.

Max was enthroned in the back, resplendent in his crimson

gear, his heart thumping as hard as if he'd been climbing an icy rockface.

'It's time,' Zanthe said.

Max groaned. 'Oh God. Do I look as ridiculous as I feel?'

'Santa is never ridiculous,' Krys warned, joining him by the sleigh. 'It's time for your big moment.'

'Off we go!' said Zanthe.

With a jingle of bells and a clip-clop of hooves, the sleigh moved off from the staff parking area and out into view of the partygoers.

Shrieks and cries went up, followed by applause.

Krys walked beside the sleigh, carefully in her curled elf bootees, but Max had no time to dwell on how cute she looked. He waved at the families, and the cries of delight and wonder brought a massive lump to his throat.

They reached the grotto to calls of:

'Santa!'

'Is that the real Father Christmas?'

'Can I go first?'

And the odd wail of terror. Krys had told him to prepare for that. It was a big deal for some kids. Not as big a deal as it was for Santa though.

Max alighted from the sleigh, just once catching Krys's eye.

'Your grotto awaits,' Jo said with a wink.

'Thank you. Ho ho!' Max muttered rather croakily.

Once inside, Jo followed him in while Max was sitting on the bales as Krys re-arranged his hat and checked his beard for straw. His stomach was churning like a washing machine and he had clammy palms, which was unpleasant for him and potentially revolting for the children.

'Are you ready?' Jo said. 'Our first visitor is *very* excited to meet Santa.'

Max's stomach went on to the spin cycle. He'd never be ready for this but he had to sound confident for Jo. 'Yes. As I'll ever be.'

'You'll be fine,' Jo and Krys chorused at the same time.

'Here we go,' said Krys, hearing chattering and shrieks outside.

The door opened and a little girl shot in like a rocket and immediately leapt onto Max's lap, which he hadn't been expecting. The children were supposed to sit on a hay bale next to him but he was completely floored.

'Hello, Santa-aaaaaa!' she screeched. 'I'm Tasshaaaaa!'

'Um. Hello, Tasha,' said Max, trying to deepen his voice. 'How old are you?'

'Five, but nearly six. I want to be six but Mummy says not to be too keen to look older than I am. She says that she always pretends to be a lot younger than she is. Is your beard real?'

Tasha tugged Max's beard and he was very glad that a. it wasn't real and b. Hector had invested in a top quality one that Krys had firmly fixed in place.

Tasha chattered away, almost doing Max's job for her, and before long, Krys was saying with heavy emphasis:

'Santa, would you like to find a present for Tasha?'

Max took the hint that time was moving on, so he replied: 'Ho, ho, ho, yes!'

Krys had already placed the little girl's gift ready at the top of Santa's sack and when Max handed it over, she looked at him in wonder and said:

'Thank you very much, Santa.'

'You're very welcome,' Max replied in his best gravelly voice.

Tasha seemed thrilled and skipped out, giggling and saying: 'Have a luvly Christmas, Santa!'

Max sat back and gave a huge sigh. 'What a sweetheart. Blimey, though, I hadn't realised they'd really think I *was* Santa.'

'Shh!' Krys admonished. 'You *are* Santa. You have to stay in character until the last child has been to see you and is well out of hearing.'

She crept to the door. 'Next one,' she said. 'A little boy. He looks like an angel, so watch out.'

A child with blond fluffy hair and the face of a cherub walked in, picking his nose.

'This is Jared,' Krys said. 'Would you like to sit by Santa, Jared?'

Jared eyed Max suspiciously. 'Is he the real one?' he asked.

'Of course I am.' Max sounded genuinely offended. 'Ho, ho, ho.'

Jared was unimpressed. 'My brother says Santas aren't real and you don't exist.'

'Does he? Well, didn't you see me arrive on my sleigh?'

Jared left Max waiting before he answered. 'Spose so . . .'

'Where would I get real reindeer if I wasn't real?'

Jared nodded then said grudgingly, 'I want to ask you a question.'

'OK. Anything.'

'I took a pound from my mum's purse when she wasn't looking. Does that mean I won't get my presents when you come down the chimney on Christmas Eve?'

'A pound? What did you want it for?'

'I was saving for some Panini stickers.'

'Oh?' Max said. 'I liked those when I was little.'

He felt Krys stiffen beside him and Max remembered that Santa was supposed to be eternally in his mid-sixties.

'Do they have football at the North Pole?' Jared asked, suspiciously.

'Oh yes. Elves FC verses Lapland City. The Elves are always diving, to be honest. Always in trouble with the ref. Now, have you told your mum you borrowed this money?' he added hastily, seeing himself rapidly about to disappear down a rabbit hole of tortuous lies.

'No,' Jared said.

'Why don't you tell her that and say you're "sorry" and that Santa has reassured you she won't be too mad if you always ask when you need something again.'

Jared nodded. 'OK.'

'Good boy.'

'Now, can I have my present, please?'

Max smiled. 'Let's see what's in the sack, shall we?'

He delved into the bag, pretending to rummage deep inside to keep up the suspense a little while longer. He pulled out the gift and handed it over.

Jared stared at it. 'Thank you, Santa.'

Then he hurried out of the grotto before Santa could change his mind about the forgiveness or the gift.

Max whispered to Krys, 'Jeez, I don't think I can handle the responsibility. I hope his mum won't be mad.'

'Me neither. A pound doesn't sound much but she might have really needed it.'

'Too late now,' Max said. 'It feels weird, telling a pack of porkies about my own existence and the North Pole Football League.'

'It's not lies, it's magic, and reality will bite soon enough for Jared and the rest. These kids need some fairy dust in their lives. Trust me, when Linda took me to see Santa at the shopping centre, I dreamed about it for weeks afterwards. I'll bring the next visitor in but if I were you, I'd stick to one big fat lie at a time.'

After seeing six more children, some lively, some very shy, Max was flagging. Krys supplied a water bottle and straw then it was on to the next batch of little ones. One had a little sister who was desperately ill, another wanted their mummy and daddy together for Christmas after a traumatic divorce. Max felt as if he'd been emotionally battered.

'You're doing incredibly well. I warned you it could be like this and a lot of these kids have had a horrendous time. It's not your regular Santa gig where most of the children are relatively privileged.'

'I must admit I can't take much more. How many are left?'

'One. He's called Thomas.'

'Thank God for that. Show him in.'

Krys brought in a pale boy whose ginger curls stuck out from his bobble hat. 'This is Thomas,' Krys said.

'Hello, Thomas. What would you like for Christmas?' Max asked.

'A car.'

Max had been briefed that the parcel contained an outdoor stunt plane set, so was floored by the request. 'A Car. Wow. You mean like Hot Wheels or Matchbox?' he said, desperately scraping up some brands from his childhood and hoping they were still around.

'No, a big car that my daddy can drive.'

'Oh . . .' Cripes, thought Max. That was a big ask, even for Santa himself. He would have to say it might be too big to fit down the chimney.

'Has your daddy already got a car?' he asked.

'No. He has to get up really early to get the bus. Three whole hours.'

'That sounds tiring,' Max said gently, moved by the innocent little face staring up at him so trustingly.

'Daddy's always tired. He works very hard. My mummy isn't with us anymore. She was poorly and died last year. Daddy is looking after me and my baby sister and I want a car so that she doesn't get so cold when we're walking to Tesco's.'

'Oh. T-Tesco's . . .' Max echoed, struggling to keep his voice from breaking, and notching up an octave. He caught Krys's eye. She had her hand over her mouth. Oh, God. This was awful. He was going to lose it as well as his elf at this rate.

'Well,' he said. 'I can't promise that a large vehicle will fit down the chimney.'

'We don't have a chimney. Can you just leave it on the road outside our house, please?' Thomas said.

The logic stunned Max. 'Erm . . . erm . . . well you see, I can't just leave a car at your house. I'd have to ask your daddy if it was the right car. It might not be one he can drive or he might not like it.'

Max struggled. He knew he had to say, as gently as possible, that he could not promise a car to this child.

'My dad can drive anything. He was a truck driver but he has to work in the council's office now because it's closer.'

'I see,' said Max in desperation. 'I'll see what I can do.'

'Ok. Thank you, Santa.'

He could feel Krys's horror behind him.

'I've also got a present for you,' Max said. 'Just for you.'

'For me?'

'Yes.'

'Thank you. I'll put this by my tree until Christmas morning when you've been. Daddy told me Santa might not be able to deliver too much this year and then we can open our presents together.'

'That's a good idea,' Max said, handing over the gift in its large box, while feeling utterly helpless.

Thomas beamed. 'I love you, Santa.' Then he added, 'As well as the car, could you magic my mummy back from Heaven.'

Max heard a faint squeak from beside him – Krys.

This isn't about you, Max, he told himself. *It's about Thomas and he deserves an honest answer.* 'I wish I could, Thomas,' he said. 'But there are some things that even Santa can't do.' Emotion welled up in his throat, thinking of the bargaining he'd done in his mind, with God, with any supernatural being, to bring Erin back. 'I am sorry you don't have her anymore,' Max went on, gently. 'But I know your daddy loves you very much and he'll do all he can to make Christmas special for you and your baby sister.'

Thomas nodded. 'Daddy said you'd say that if I asked about Mummy. I didn't tell him about the car, so that will make him happy.'

Oh God. Max could barely murmur: 'You're welcome. Happy Christmas.'

'C-come on, T-Thomas,' Krys said, gently ushering him out.

The moment the boy was gone, Max heaved a deep sigh and swore silently over and over. He dug his nails in his palm. His eyes were stinging and his throat was raw. He had no idea how he wasn't going to cry and if he did, he would bawl his heart out until his beard was soggy. He'd been on shouts and seen people in pain, he'd seen dead bodies in gullies when he knew the relatives were waiting at the base.

He had never cried; always managed to stay that tiny step removed so he could help the casualties.

Thomas had tipped him over the edge.

Worse than dealing with his own emotions was the fact he'd committed the number one Santa sin of promising something he couldn't deliver. He'd raised expectations in Thomas that were impossible to fulfil.

Chapter Twenty-Eight

Krys stumbled out of the grotto, ignoring the few parents who were still chattering nearby. Thank goodness Thomas had been the last child, or she'd never had made it through another story like that.

Except it wasn't a story; it was real-life. Real-life pain and agony. Real-life helplessness that she was feeling now.

Oh, Max. Max had been brilliant but he should never have promised the car.

It was too late now. She'd have to have a discreet word with Jo and ask her to speak to Thomas's dad, so he could dampen down the expectations or explain on Christmas Day that some things were impossible for Santa.

The crisp air hit her lungs and made her gasp. She gulped in the air, fanning her face in an attempt to stem the flow of tears. She daren't cry because her mascara would run and she needed to help Santa get out of his costume so he could discreetly return to the party and help with the food and games.

Little Thomas was with his dad by the reindeer pen. His father had the baby in a snow suit in his arms. Thomas still hadn't unwrapped the gift, and was holding it to him tightly.

Outside, the queue of children to the grotto had gone but many were still around the reindeer pen, having their photos taken with the herd and by Santa's sleigh, many still clutching the toys and gifts from the grotto. The parents, carers and staff were smiling and laughing as much as the children. Even some of the teens were posing with the reindeer, and once again, Krys's heart swelled to bursting point. Of all the times she'd organised a Christmas grotto, this was the best by a country mile.

Her breathing calmed a little and her heart rate slowed. She. Was. Going. To. Be. Fine. But she needed to rescue Max. Maybe it would be better if she collected his clothes and he changed in the grotto? He'd be unrecognisable to most people once he was back in his ordinary gear.

The lights of the tunnel and reindeer enclosure twinkled against the night sky. Christmas carols and music were playing on a loop from the speakers.

Krys went back through the tunnel and into the grotto where Max had taken off the beard. She'd told him to be prepared for the day to be emotional, but she hadn't reckoned with the effect it might have on *her*.

'Krys? Are you OK?' he said. 'Stupid question.'

'I – I – had to go outside. S-sorry. Too close to home but I'm OK now. I'm glad it was the last child, or I don't think I could handle this anymore. I've done this so many times before but this one got to me. How did you hold it together?'

'I don't know . . . maybe only because of the stuff I've experienced on the MRT shouts,' he said. 'That kicked in. God knows how or why. I was worried you'd never come back. I thought you were furious with me for giving hope to Thomas about the car. I could kick myself.'

'Don't worry. I'm going to speak to Jo about it and hope she'll speak to his dad . . . Are you sure you're OK? That was so intense. Poor Thomas and his family.'

'I know. I was this far from bawling my eyes out.' He squeezed his thumb and forefingers together. 'I'm so glad he was the last.'

'No matter what went wrong in my life, at least I did have my mum and Linda. Poor Thomas and his father must be feeling so raw this Christmas, and with money problems too, it doesn't bear thinking about.'

'There is no answer to some things,' he said gloomily. 'You were right when you said that Santa couldn't help every child. That's the problem with playing an omnipotent mythical being, I suppose. We probably shouldn't even try.'

'But look at how happy Tasha was and you even cheered up Jared. And the other kids.'

'One of them burst into tears.'

'Oh, yes. She'll be OK, her big sister said she often cries at Santa.'

'I wish I'd known that. I'd have let you take over.'

'No. You were amazing. You really were.' She almost threw her arms around him. 'I'm so proud of you.'

'I'm glad someone is. I could never have done it without my Helper.' He flicked one of her ears. 'Cute.'

'Do you like them?' she said.

'They're your best feature.'

Krys would have laughed were it not for the fact that Max was looking at her in a funny, intense way – exactly the way that Harriet had noticed. She'd have to be a fool not to realise that the look was desire – desire for her. And she felt the same, a fizzing feeling low in her stomach, a strong need to kiss him and be kissed now. Even with the belly between them.

He reached up and touched her cheek with his hand and she drew in a breath. No matter how wrong it might be, she wanted this.

'Max!'

Max froze, and his eyes widened. He sprang away from Krys as if he'd been electrocuted.

Chapter Twenty-Nine

'Jo!'

Krys turned, finding Jo in the doorway gawping at them. 'Is – um – everything OK?'

'Everything's fine. I came to find you. We could do with some help in the party room if you've – um – finished up here?'

'We have,' Max growled. 'I'm going to change and leave you to it.'

'OK.' Jo walked in. 'Max, I have to thank you for stepping up. You were absolutely amazing. I know how much the staff and the parents appreciated it. I've had several of them come up to me and ask me to say thank you to you.'

'I'm surprised they haven't complained.'

Jo rolled her eyes. 'Of course they haven't. You were brilliant.'

'He was,' Krys cut in, still trying to regain her composure after their almost-kiss.

'Yes . . . well . . .' He frowned. 'I'd better get this thing off and take it back to Hector.'

Jo grinned. 'I think it suits you.'

Krys laughed and even Max managed a smile. 'Maybe I could go on a rescue in it.'

'I'm needed at the party now,' Jo said with a glance at Krys.

'I'll come with you. I may as well stay in costume.'

'Good idea.'

'See you later, Max?' Jo said.

'I'm sure you will.'

With her mind still whirling, Krys followed Jo to the centre. She had wanted Max to kiss her very much – and so had he – but how could that be possible when she'd only recently split with Brett? She was surely on the rebound, and Max was still in love with Erin. Neither of them was ready for a new relationship, but the physical attraction couldn't be denied.

And however unsure she was, Max was even more conflicted, judging by his reaction to Jo walking in on them.

After the party, she went home, filling the space until bedtime by channel surfing and calling Harriet, who issued an invitation to spend Christmas Day with her.

In the background, she could hear the distant rumble of traffic, a siren . . . and had a strange longing to be back in London amid the noise and chaos. Holly Manor was only fun with someone to share it with. She really had to decide soon if she was going to return to London for the festive period.

Why was she even hesitating? There was nothing for her here now, with her perfect Christmas in tatters – but first there was the decorating for the ball to get through. She hadn't heard from Max and she didn't intend to message him.

Having managed to scrounge a delivery of surplus stock pre-lit Christmas trees for the ball, she drove over to the base after breakfast because there was no way everything would fit in the car on one journey.

Some of the other team members had also responded to the call for a variety of items that would help to turn the base into a venue fit for a ball. She had a small wobble. While she was used to buying props for events she had no intention of attending, it felt strange to have been so engaged in the process yet not actually go to this one.

By mid-morning, Nikki, Hector, Hazel and two other men had arrived, and were in the process of setting up chairs and tables that had been loaned by a local hotelier. They'd managed to fit in seven tables of eight for the event, and they could be pushed back later for the disco and band.

'This is looking good already,' Krys said, delighted she didn't have to clear the room.

Hector slotted a chair into place. 'We hoped it would leave a blank canvas.'

Hazel beamed. 'Ready for the expert to wave her magic wand,' she said. 'We're so relieved you've offered to sort it all out for us.'

On the verge of denying she was an expert, Krys stopped. Because actually, she *was*. More importantly, Hazel and all these skilled, brave people were standing like kids in front of a teacher, excitedly awaiting instructions. She needed to inspire them with confidence and now was not the time to give anyone the jitters.

'Great,' she said cheerfully. 'The first thing to do is hang the starlight curtains. I've got them in the car, if anyone wants to give me a hand?'

'Starlight curtains' was a grand name for what was basically a black curtain with fairy lights. Krys had ordered them off an online auction site and obtained the lights at cost from a supplier who had some returned stock.

Puzzled faces greeted her when she opened the box with the nondescript material but they cheered up when she assured them it would create a perfect backdrop for the rest of the décor.

'It's a cheap and cheerful trick that I've used lots of times,' she said. 'I'll show you what to do.'

It took a while, but eventually three of the walls had been hung with curtains and some of the fairy lights fixed in place. Bryony, who was an electrician and part-time singer, turned up with some of the band and helped to install and check the lights while Krys returned to the manor for a second batch of props.

Nikki and Hazel came out to the car and were agog when they saw it, packed to the roof with boxes of artificial trees, garlands, swags and baubles, all in an icy palette of white, silver and blue.

'You found all this for us?' Hazel said, in awe.

'Some of it was mine already. The rest I managed to borrow or scrounge.'

'This will be the poshest do we've ever held,' Hazel said. 'Thank you, Krys. It's been a hard year and the team deserves to enjoy a special night. I really appreciate it.'

Embarrassed at being thanked by this remarkable woman, Krys laughed it off. 'You're very welcome. We've got to get it all in place first!'

Back inside, the main lights had been dimmed and the nets of fairy lights were twinkling, thanks to Bryony. It had started to look like a proper venue and not a training room.

'The whole idea is to bring the outdoors in,' Krys said. 'After all, you live and work in a winter wonderland so let's bring that to the ball.'

There was laughter.

There was a lot to get done, but with so many hands, she was confident it would all be finished well before the event and she could escape before the festivities began. She'd also had the idea of dressing the entrance, using a couple of old wooden tables and benches outside. She'd noticed a few upturned logs about so she'd decided to arrange them by the doors and add candles on them.

Hector started assembling the artificial trees, silver ones with fake snow on them, while Krys and Nikki climbed up stepladders to fix glittering garlands to the stage area. Krys had half hoped Max might turn up to help but there was so far no sign of him

Hazel poked her head around the door. 'Guys. There's an elderly man with breathing difficulties by Sourmilk Gill. We're needed to assist until the helicopter can arrive.'

With a grimace, Nikki dropped the garland.

'Sorry. Have to go!'

'Oh . . .'

In half a minute, the room emptied, leaving Krys on the stepladder, amid a sea of sagging garlands and abandoned tinsel. It looked as if the party was already over.

Krys had lost all but one of her helpers, and that was Hector. However, knowing the team were faced with a life and death situation, she had to put on a smile and get on with it. At least it was still early, so hopefully everyone would be back for the ball itself.

'Oh dear. That's a blow,' Hector said with a sigh. 'I'll see if I can find out more about the incident,' he added sympathetically.

'Thanks. Um. What happens if there's a shout tonight?' Krys asked, fearing the reply.

'Well, pretty much everyone who's ever been in the team is coming and no one's on holiday this time of year so we're at full strength. Some of us are on call so we'll be on soft drinks. Others are most definitely off duty and we have Will and some of the Bannerdale team to cover too. So,' Hector held up crossed fingers, 'we should be OK. The best thing we can hope for is that Joe Public stays cosied up by their fires or in the pub.'

Krys nodded. 'We'll have to get on with it.'

'And I'm not going anywhere, babe,' Hector said firmly. 'So let's do this!'

True to his word, Hector was like a demon, pinning up garlands, setting up trees, but there was still tons to do and it was already four p.m. Bryony had had to go home to collect the rest of the band. There was nothing for it but hope they could somehow complete the job or the team would arrive soon. At this rate, the ball guests would be hanging up tinsel and Krys wanted to be well out of there before the festivities themselves started.

It was hot work making a winter wonderland and Krys had to take off her jumper.

Hector brought glasses of squash. 'Come on down from that ladder. Stop for a minute.'

'I'm worried we won't get it finished.'

'Not if you slip off the ladder we won't. Come on, have a break,' he added sternly.

'Better not stop for too long. It's not quite finished yet,' she said, climbing down and accepting the cool glass.

'Well, it looks bloody good to me,' Hector said. 'Good enough for any ball, let alone one in Thorndale.' He pulled a face. 'Shame it's not gin but there'll be plenty of that later, eh?'

'Mmm,' Krys said, realising he expected her to be going to the ball. With an inner sigh, she took a moment to survey their handiwork. Apart from the empty cardboard boxes on the floor and tables, she had to admit the room was almost there.

The starlight curtains glittered like the night sky above the valley, and the pre-lit, pre-decorated trees were straight out of Lapland. Everywhere sparkled with luxurious garlands and tinsel. The tables had been dressed with white cloths, snowflake confetti and battery-operated tealights. With the main lights down, it would be magical.

'It's totally lush,' Hector said with a sigh and unexpectedly put his arm around Krys. 'You should be proud of yourself.'

She blushed. 'We should be proud. I wanted to dress the outside, add some candles to the sawn logs . . .'

'I'll rope in some of the team to do that. They should be back soon. I suggest you go home and put your party frock on.'

'My party frock? Oh, I'm not coming to the ball.'

'Honey, you have got to be kidding!' Hector's eyes widened in horror. 'After all this work? This is your project. You must come to the ball.'

'No, I um . . .'

'Some of us wondered if you might be coming along with Max,' he added.

'Max?' Krys laughed. 'Why would I do that?'

Hector raised an eyebrow. 'You two seem friendly. I've never seen Max so happy. It's as if his own personal storm cloud has finally vanished.'

'Nothing to do with me. Anyway, I only recently broke up with my boyfriend. I'm not looking for anyone else.'

'Hmm,' Hector murmured, obviously unconvinced. 'If I were you, I wouldn't hang around for Mr Right at the Right Time to happen. You can't order love like a pizza and expect it to turn up in time for dinner. Grab it and devour it the moment you see it, I say, even if you've already had a full English breakfast five minutes before.'

Hector had a point, but . . . 'I should probably go on a diet,' she said. 'For a while.'

'Shame,' said Hector. 'But seriously, you really can't control everything in your life. I'm guessing you've been used to doing that: planning so far ahead, wanting everything to be perfect? Now things haven't turned out exactly as you planned but maybe there's a different ending in store?'

'Maybe . . .' she said. Hadn't this whole trip been her trying to plan and curate the perfect Christmas and the perfect life, to make up for when she wasn't able to be in control as a child?

'If you do want to change your mind about the ball, ping me a message and I'll jump in my chariot and pick you up.'

Impulsively, Krys pecked him on the cheek. 'Thanks, and Hector: you're an absolute star for helping.'

With time moving on, and the team members starting to arrive back from the shout, Krys and Hector piled the boxes into a storeroom and she made her escape. She didn't want thanks, and while she'd have dearly loved to see the reaction of the team, she also didn't want to face any more awkward questions of the pizza delivery variety – especially if they involved Max.

Chapter Thirty

Max had been chopping wood in the gently falling snow when his pager went off, buzzing like an angry bee in his pocket. His presence was urgently required and he'd responded immediately. He was already the closest person to the incident, so he'd headed straight to the Pike car park to rendezvous with the others.

Thankfully, the shout had been relatively straightforward as shouts went, and ended much better than it might have. Dr Katya had been almost certain that the casualty was having a panic attack, rather than something more sinister. Nevertheless, it had been very scary for the guy and his wife, and the man had been flown off to hospital for a check-up. His wife had been escorted to her vehicle and was on her own way to the hospital.

Beyond that, the team wouldn't know the full outcome for a while.

They'd returned to the car park in darkness. Nikki hadn't said anything else about Krys, but Max knew she was at the base, from the general chit chat about having to abandon the decorating.

'Poor lass,' said Tyrone, who ran a sawmill in the valley and was the oldest member of the team. 'She'd made such an effort for us and we had to leave her with only Hector as her apprentice.'

Hazel sighed. 'I feel awful about it but it can't be helped. I'm off back there now to see if I can still lend a hand, though the thing starts in just over an hour.'

'I'll come with you,' Nikki added. 'I've brought my glad rags in the van so I can change at the base.'

'I've asked my husband to bring mine over. At least I'm off duty now so I can enjoy the evening.'

'Can we get a lift back to the base?' Nikki asked Max. 'There must be loads still to do. I hope Krys has been OK.'

Max would much rather have driven straight home but he couldn't refuse a request like that, even though it meant listening to a constant stream of 'How amazing Krys is', and 'How awful we had to abandon her'.

By the time they reached the base, he felt as guilty as if he'd been put in the dock and convicted by a jury of two. He should have offered to help with the decorating, even if he had no intention of attending. The fact he'd been called out was no defence: he should have been hanging up streamers and being helpful, not hiding away.

He had to find Krys and apologise for avoiding her since the kids' party. His feelings had overwhelmed him . . . and he should never have made a move on her, in her vulnerable state.

'Wow.'

Hazel and Nikki joined in his gasp of amazement.

'This is spectacular,' Nikki said.

She and Hazel climbed out, leaving Max in the car.

The outside of the base was barely recognisable. Upturned logs had been decorated with candles in jars and the route to the entrance was lined with snowy-topped Christmas trees. At least twenty people were milling around, in a mix of climbing gear and black tie. Max wondered where they'd all come from, because he hadn't seen half the faces before . . . men with their hair gelled, and beards trimmed, and women in cocktail wear and heels.

A banner hung over the doors to the base: Welcome to the Thorndale Winter Ball.

Feeling horribly underdressed, he headed for the entrance, ignored by the tuxedoed throng snapping selfies beside the log candles and posing next to the trees.

'Hey, Max!'

A tap on the shoulder stopped him as he was about to walk into the porch.

'Tyrone? Is that you?' Max was only half-joking.

'Yes.' He rubbed his chin. 'Dashed home and shaved off my beard. My wife and kids have wanted me to for ages so I decided, tonight's the night.'

'Bloody hell.'

'Wait until you see inside. You won't believe it.'

Max crossed the foyer towards the glow of the training room, drawn like a moth to a flame by the lights, the warmth and the excited chatter of people who had turned from level-headed professionals to kids in a sweetie shop.

It was like stepping into fairy land.

The stone walls had vanished, replaced with night skies twinkling with tiny stars. A glitter ball suspended from the rafters threw shards of rainbow light into the space. Tables with snowy cloths held flickering tealights, pale green foliage and balloons. The chairs were bedecked with silver covers, and there were sparkling Christmas trees at the entrance and by the stage area where a DJ was setting up decks next to amps, microphones and a keyboard. Waiting staff were piling a trestle table with plates and cutlery.

The whole room shimmered with silver and icy blue; the fantasy incarnation of an ice queen's palace.

Of Krys, chief architect of the whole magical transformation, there was no sign.

Heart beating faster, Max made his way through the 'ballroom' to the kitchen, where Amina was bent over the fridge in a black cocktail dress, slotting cling-filmed trays of food in the fridge. Professional caterers buzzed in and out, along with team members in tuxes, carting in boxes of wine and beer.

'Where's Krys?' he asked Amina.

'Don't know,' she said. 'She was here earlier decorating, but I've not long arrived. Hector might know.'

'Thanks.'

He discovered Hector outside the rear door, unloading more beer from the van in an electric blue velvet suit and a glittering rainbow tie.

'Hello, Hector. Looking good, mate.'

'Thanks. I almost wore a frock but I've been too busy here to glam up as I'd like to.'

Max smiled. 'You look fabulous as you are. Have you seen Krys?'

'She was here earlier. She decorated the place almost single-handed while everyone was out on the shout. She's gone home now. Probably knackered.'

Max's heart sank.

'Are you staying for the do?'

'I—' Max stopped. 'I wasn't planning to.'

'Shame. It's going to be a great night. Who knew the old place could scrub up?'

'Yeah. I thought I'd landed in another world.'

'Krys did most of it. I helped but I reckon I was more of a hindrance.' Hector laughed.

Max laughed too, but mirth was the last emotion in his heart.

He'd ballsed everything up, not helping with the decoration, blowing hot and mostly cold with Krys. He *had* to tell her how he felt, even if it meant risking rejection and heartache.

'I'd better leave you all to it,' he said, unwilling to go near the festivities of the room again. He couldn't face being so obviously reminded of the effort Krys had gone to and his lack of a part in it.

'So will we see you later?' Hector asked.

'Not sure,' Max mumbled.

'Well, you're leaving it a bit bloody late to decide, mate!' Hector tossed the words at Max's retreating back.

Max left without answering, knowing he deserved every ounce of Hector's scorn and more.

He drove home, beset by regrets and 'what ifs'. While letting Jake out, he saw the base lit up like a Christmas tree and a faint glimmer of light from Holly Manor.

Jake trotted back to him, licking his hand. No one could see him and no one would care that he wasn't at the ball . . . yet they *would* care. His friends would care and worry about him because that was what friends did. They'd despair of him.

Jake nudged the back of his thigh.

'What?'

Jake's ears pricked up.

'Don't look at me like that. I hate myself enough as it is. I know I've messed up.'

Jake let out a low growl.

'Is that meant to be canine for "you total prat"?'

The dog padded to the Bothy doorway, waiting expectantly for Max to follow.

'Oh . . . sod it,' he said. 'OK, I give up!'

*   *   *

286

Twenty minutes after walking into the shower at the Bothy, and throwing on his DJ, Max was ringing the bell at Holly Manor. By the light of the coach lamp, he could see his face reflected in the door knocker, damp hair sticking up, a suspicious blob of red on his chin.

'Oh, sh—'

'Max?'

Krys opened the door in pyjamas and fluffy slippers, which probably wasn't an encouraging sign. Not that she didn't look gorgeous, perhaps not quite ready for a party.

He blurted out his invitation before he had time to change his mind.

'Would you like to come to the ball with me.'

A painful silence, then: 'Did I just hear what I thought I heard?'

'Yes.' He screwed up his courage. 'Come to the ball with me,' he repeated. '*Please*.'

From the expression on her face, anyone would think he'd asked her to parachute off the Pike in a Santa suit.

'It's not compulsory,' he added, more gruffly than he'd meant. 'In fact, it's probably a terrible idea. I'm an antisocial bugger and the last thing you feel like is partying and there's bound to be gossip afterwards. People will jump to conclusions and it'll be a complete pain in the arse for both of us.'

She raised her eyebrows. 'Oh, Max, you make it sound so tempting.'

'I know. How could any woman possibly resist?'

That made her smile, which sparked a flicker of hope.

'You'd better come in,' she said, her expression serious again.

In the hallway Max launched into his pitch again.

'Like I said, it probably is a stupid idea. Only I'm going to feel like a right tit if I go home and spend the evening with Jake in this get-up. And I honestly won't mind if you say no.'

287

'Once again, such an attractive offer.' She folded her arms.

'OK, I *will* mind, quite a bit actually, because I'd enjoy your company. It's selfish of me to even ask, I suppose, only I thought it was a shame that you'd be spending the evening here in this place on your own after you've spent so much time decorating the base. Anyone would think you were Cinderella.'

'I don't need a prince to take me to the ball. If I wanted to go, I'd take myself.'

Blast, this was going downhill faster than a rolling wheel. 'Of course. I understand . . . However, you've forgotten one important point.'

She frowned. 'What's that?'

'I am the furthest any woman could possibly get from Prince Charming.'

She smiled and this time it stuck.

Progress.

'Now, that is the most sensible thing you've said since you turned up at my door.'

Which meant his invitation was not sensible. It was too late to back out now, so he doubled down.

'So, will you think about it?'

'*Think?*' she said incredulously. 'I don't think there's time to think about it. Aren't the drinks and canapés being served around now?'

'Um. Probably. In that case, may I respectfully suggest that we get a move on?'

'I haven't said "yes", yet.' She sighed and held her chin as if deciding. Max was in agonies.

'OK. Give me ten minutes. I'll also look like a right tit if I turn up looking like this.'

Before he had a chance to laugh, she was dashing upstairs, leaving him standing in the middle of the hall. Max felt like a tethered balloon that had suddenly and unexpectedly been released. He was soaring. After all he'd done to screw up his chances of getting to know Krys better, he could barely believe he'd been given a second chance, let alone a third.

There'd be talk, *major* talk, but he didn't give a toss. He couldn't care less about Nikki or anyone else. He was ready to get close to someone else: and it was the worst idea in the world that it was Krys, who was on the rebound from another relationship. It was too late to draw back: he'd passed the point of no return and he had to risk it.

Ten minutes later, she appeared at the top of the stairs, a wrap over one arm and a pair of heels in her hand.

Max caught his breath. He didn't want to do the clichéd thing and tell her that she looked sensational.

Though she absolutely did.

The sight of her in a figure-hugging crimson maxi dress robbed him of breath. It was sleeveless with slim straps that showed off her beautiful shoulders and neck. Her hair was caught up in a glittery clip.

He stared at her, unable to utter a word as she descended to the hallway.

'I'm ready,' she said.

'I can see that . . .'

'Just need my coat.'

'I'll get it.'

He grabbed her puffer jacket from the stand.

'Not that one,' she said, clearly amused at his ineptitude.

'Oh, sorry.'

He reached for the long black wool coat hanging on the peg.

'Thanks.'

He held it out and she let him put it around her shoulders. As he did so, he caught a whiff of her perfume: a fresh and floral fragrance that made him think of spring. Her cheeks shimmered and she had on a pink gloss that enhanced her lips.

'Thank you,' she said, slipping her bare arms into the coat.

'You're welcome.' Max stood back, shoving his hands in the pockets of his trousers, unsure, nervous as a teenager on a first date. Sexual attraction, sure, and the excitement and the danger of new beginnings. A heady cocktail.

Krys tucked the wrap around her neck and fastened the coat. She slipped her feet into knee high boots.

'I'll carry my shoes.'

'Probably wise. The Land Rover's not the cleanest place. There's probably dog hair on the seats.' Looking down at his tux trousers, he realised he'd already picked up a few already. 'Do you have a blanket to put down? I never thought . . .' He hadn't expected her to say yes. 'I wouldn't want to spoil that lovely dress.'

Her smile lit up her eyes. Her diamond earrings sparkled in the lamplight.

'It's fine. Max. A few dog hairs are the last thing I'm worried about.' She threw him a smile that almost made him self-combust. 'Shall we go?'

Chapter Thirty-One

Tongues would wag. The gossip mill would be red-hot. People would think she'd moved on *way* too fast after Brett and to Thorndale's most confirmed singleton.

But 'people' didn't know the whole story. They'd be right, but gossip was the least of Krys's worries as Max drove her through the dark to the MRT base. She should be at home now, in her pyjamas, miserably channel-surfing. Her resistance had crumbled way too fast, but then again, time hadn't been on her side. Perhaps Max had intended that: turning up at the last minute so she'd have to make a snap decision.

No, she didn't really believe that. The Landy, with its muddy footwell and dog-haired seats, showed no signs of being prepared for a carriage. She could well imagine Max agonising over whether to call, then pulling on his dinner suit at the eleventh hour. The shaving cut on his chin was testament to that. His bow tie was also askew, but at least it was a real one. She pictured it hanging loose later in the evening, his dress shirt unbuttoned, and suppressed a shiver.

Come to think of it . . . 'Where did you get the suit?' she asked him.

'I had it sent up from my parents' house a few days ago. I was hedging my bets about the do at the time.'

'Didn't they wonder why you wanted it?'

'They did ask but I was economical with the truth, said it was an MRT awards do for one of the team. They were too relieved that I might actually be going out into the real world again to ask too many questions.'

She could imagine his parents' happiness at their son beginning to recover.

He slowed and the lights ahead told them they'd almost arrived at the base. 'We're here,' he said, turning to her. 'I have to warn you that I kicked up a bit of a fuss at the base earlier, demanding to know where you were. If we walk in there together, in the eyes of Thorndale, there's no going back.'

No going back from *what*, though? she thought while Max jumped out and opened the door for her.

He stood next to her, looking lethally handsome, and held out his hand. 'Are you ready?'

Krys played along, placing her hand in his warm one. His touch sent a thrill through her. The same electric pulse of desire that had made her skin tingle when he'd slipped her coat around her bare shoulders.

She stepped down, transported back for a moment to the fairy tales of her past. The base was glowing with life, music playing, people spilling out. In her eyes it was as glamorous as any fantasy palace – or maybe it was the man holding her hand, transformed from recluse to prince, who made it so magical.

It was a shame fairy tales had to end.

Her boots hit the gravel of the car park. Max went to close the door.

'Stop!'

'What?'

She reached into the footwell for her heels. 'If I'm going to be Cinderella, I'd better not forget my shoe before we've even started.'

It was safe to say that heads turned when Krys and Max walked in. The party was in full swing, with scores of people with drinks in hand, chatting and laughing while the speakers played Christmas tunes. The buffet table was dressed ready for the food by the professional caterers.

Krys could hardly believe the sight: not so much her own handiwork but the bunch of salt-of-the-earth people dressed in their finery, drinking fizz and partying like there was no tomorrow. They deserved a night off and she felt privileged to have helped make it possible.

Max whispered in her ear. 'You did this.'

'I helped.'

'You made it happen. It's fairy land.'

He rested his hand on the small of her back, making her shimmer inside, like the delicate silver fronds of the garlands.

'Well, look at you two.' Nikki greeted both Krys and Max with a kiss and a raised eyebrow. 'I hardly recognised you, Max.'

'Thanks. You scrub up yourself.'

Nikki gave a little bow, and showed off the glittery shoes peeping out from the pants of her rose silk trouser suit.

'That colour looks amazing on you,' Krys said.

'I'm glad you like it. I can't walk in the shoes of course, so I've brought my trainers. I'll probably last until after the buffet then that's it! I'm pleased to see you here. Both of you,' Nikki said. 'It's a bit of a surprise.'

'It's a surprise to me too. Both of us,' Max said.

Davy bore down on them. 'Wow. Who is this strange being who sounds like Max but can't possibly be him?'

'Can I get you a drink?' Max asked.

'Thanks,' said Krys, her stomach still jittery with excitement, nerves – and desire. She could hardly bear to look at Max too often, he was so ridiculously handsome in the tux.

'I'm on orange juice,' Max said. 'I'm driving.'

'You and half the room,' Davy replied. 'The Bannerdale lot are on duty.'

'I'm not,' said Nikki, raising her fizz. 'Cheers!'

Max left to fetch drinks from the tray by the temporary bar, which was staffed by one of the caterers. In the brief time he was away, Nikki chatted to Krys about the way she'd transformed the base into a winter palace, with only Hector's help.

Krys was blushing as so many people came up to congratulate her but maybe they also wanted to see the woman who had finally persuaded Max to emerge from his cave and into the light.

For once, no one went missing, fell into a beck or got lost so everyone could enjoy the party. It seemed as if no one wanted to leave early and miss a magical moment. Krys became overwhelmed by people congratulating and thanking her for making the evening so special. Max had told her to enjoy the compliments.

Maybe some came up so often to try and find out just how close she and Max were. Krys didn't know herself. She would have done without a single thank you, just to see him smiling and chatting to people, and for the occasional touch of his hand on her arm.

Finally, the DJ put on a ballad and announced it was the end of the evening.

His declaration was met with a mix of drunken 'ah's' and 'noooo's', depending on who was keen to take to the floor for a 'last dance'.

Several couples started dancing, holding each other, some holding each other up. Max reached for her hand. She turned to him in shock but didn't withdraw her fingers.

'Do you want to dance?' he said quietly.

Hesitation flickered in her eyes. He still held her hand, for now in the shadows, out of view of everyone else. 'I've no idea what this song is.'

'It's an Ed Sheeran track,' she said, amused.

'Is that a bad thing?'

She laughed. 'I don't think so but half the world does. Do you honestly care?'

'I don't give a toss.'

'And whether we're dancing to an uncool song is probably the least of our worries.'

'True. Shall we?'

She nodded and they rose to their feet. Max held her hand. His jacket had long been abandoned. She rested her head against his shirt, feeling the heat of his chest through it, imagining his heart beating. Ed sang about lovers growing old together and Krys searched Max's face for a trace of regret, but he smiled down at her as she gently moved around the floor under the beams of the glitter ball as the last seconds of the party ticked away.

Chapter Thirty-Two

'What a beautiful night,' Krys said when Max stepped out of the Landy at Holly Manor. 'The stars seemed brighter than I've ever known. So many too. Hard to believe that I'm standing on the same planet as in London. I know they're always here but hidden by the city glare. You only have to turn off the lights to see them.'

Max gazed upwards. 'When I first came here, I didn't even notice them because I didn't care. Yet gradually, as I stayed, I looked up more, and not at my feet. They were calling to me, if that doesn't sound crazy.'

'No. Not crazy at all.'

Krys tilted back her head for a better view of the sky. Max admired her neck and throat, then felt weird about it and forced his eyes heavenwards.

'Wish I knew what they were all called,' she said.

Max knew a few, but the names of stars were far from his mind, apart from the one next to him, who'd appeared from nowhere and shone her brilliant light into his dark little world.

'On a clear night like this, they're mind-blowing. It's a shame these nights are few and far between. It's usually raining. Remember the night I stayed?' he said.

Krys turned to look at him. 'How could I forget? You couldn't see a single star. You couldn't even look up at the sky.'

'Well, it's not raining now, is it?' he murmured.

'What are you trying to say, Max?'

'I don't have to go home. If you don't want me to,' he said, his pulse racing in case he'd made a huge miscalculation. 'If it's a no, I'll walk away now.'

'I'm not sure I can,' she murmured.

'I know. It's too soon for you. I should never have asked. I didn't mean to put you under pressure. It's . . . fine.'

'Hold on. I meant that now you've asked me, I'm not sure I can say no because I don't *want* to.'

'Oh God . . . I – Look, that's wonderful but I haven't kissed anyone in a very long time. I'm out of practice.'

She reached for his hand. 'I'm sure you'll pick it up again.'

He didn't waste a heartbeat. He pulled her into his arms and kissed her. Her mouth was soft and warm, such a contrast to the frosty night and the cold and lonely place he'd dwelled in for so long. He wanted Krys to be the woman who led him out of the shadows but it really was too soon to confess that.

The kiss ended, gently, and he was holding her. 'Wow.'

'Not bad for someone who's forgotten how to kiss.'

'Suddenly it all came back to me.'

She laughed but shivered too. He took her hands in his. 'You're cold.'

'Then let's go inside and get warm.'

He closed the door of the manor behind him. Its warmth enveloped him and the scent of woodsmoke hung in the air. He helped her shed her coat and held her, kissing her again, before, with a smile, she broke away.

'Sorry. I have to take my boots off . . .'

He laughed too, and half thought of jokingly doing a Prince Charming and taking them off for her.

No, that wasn't him. It wasn't Krys either, so he waited impatiently while she removed them, marvelling at what was happening in front of him – *inside* him. A few short weeks ago, he would never have believed it if you'd told him he'd take a woman to a Christmas party. To have asked her to go to bed with him would have been unthinkable.

Krys bending down to unzip the boot from her slender ankle, Krys looking more beautiful than he'd ever seen her. Krys standing in her stockinged feet, walking towards him a smile on her face, her eyes sparkling with pleasure and desire . . .

His heart almost stopped. He couldn't stem the flow of memories: the moment that he'd left for work on the morning Erin had gone to London. They'd made love and he'd kissed her for the last time as he dashed off to work.

'Goodbye. Have a great time. I promise I'll make it up to you when you get back.'

Now he was here, with another woman. *Forgive me,* he said to Erin, silently in his head. Not knowing if he wanted her to be able to hear him or not. Not knowing if he wanted her blessing, or simply wanted her to not know anything at all.

That was a mystery beyond his comprehension, so he pushed it away and let Krys lead him upstairs.

Chapter Thirty-Three

Krys woke to velvety darkness and a strange stillness. She'd become used to it since she'd moved to the manor but this time, it took a few seconds to remember that she wasn't meant to be alone.

Where was Max?

Had she dreamt the ball and the kiss outside the house, with a billion stars shining down on them? Or the joy of him beside her, of them touching each other and making love for the first and second time?

She switched on the bedside lamp and had a moment of panic. It was barely six a.m.

Had he run home, regretting what he'd done?

It was a momentous step for him, but what about her?

What a risk to take, so soon after her break-up with Brett. Even though she now realised that the relationship had already been past saving, it was asking for trouble to become involved with someone else. When that someone else was a man grieving his late wife, bearing a terrible load of guilt – well, it was madness.

OK, she'd only slept with him. Only – if it *had* been simply sex between them, it wouldn't have been so crazy. She might have lain here, thinking: *oh, hey, that was amazing but we both knew it couldn't go anywhere. He lives here; I'm going back to London soon. It's for the best.* That wasn't true when she had much deeper feelings for Max. Overnight, her life had become far more complicated.

'Krys?'

The door opened and Max walked in, wearing his tux trousers, blinking in the lamplight.

'I thought you'd gone.'

'No, I didn't want to wake you so I've been creeping around in the dark.' He picked up his jacket from the chair. 'Believe me, I don't want to go but Jake's expecting me home. I can't leave him much longer.'

'Oh. If it's Jake, that's OK, then.'

Max crossed to the bed, sat down and took her hand. 'Are you OK? With what happened last night? No regrets?'

So many . . . but not enough to outweigh the pleasures. Or was she simply convincing herself that this mad thing she was doing was the right thing?

She'd left him hanging too long awaiting her answer. 'It's early days for me too, Max.'

'I didn't think you were ready. Or ever would be.'

'I – I know. This is new for me. It's more – it's so soon after Brett.'

'I know.'

She squeezed his hand and leaned forward. 'That doesn't mean I wish it hadn't happened. I'm really glad it did.'

'Then perhaps there's a chance of it happening again?'

The thought made her want to drag him back into bed right that second. 'Yes . . . and next time, maybe Jake can stay over too?'

He laughed. 'I'll be sure to bring his bed with me so he can sleep in the kitchen.'

While he put his jacket on, she pulled on a cami and shorts and threw a fluffy robe over them.

'I'll see you off the premises,' Krys said, kissing him.

'Well, don't let me linger too long or I'll never go home.'

The doorbell rang.

'It's probably the postman.'

'Not on a Sunday. I guess it could be Nikki with the fresh linen,' Krys said. 'What will she think?'

'Do you care what she might think?'

'It's so soon after Brett . . .'

'Is it really so soon?' Max asked.

'No. Not if you believe the pizza theory.'

He frowned. 'The pizza theory? What's that?'

'Something Hector said.' Krys smiled. 'And I don't care what Nikki or anyone thinks, if you don't.'

He put his arm around her waist and opened the door. But, it wasn't Nikki, but a short woman with ash blonde hair who Krys had never set eyes on in her life.

Judging by his horrified face, however, Max was all too familiar with her.

'Laurel,' he said.

For a moment, Krys was too shell-shocked to move. Laurel . . . she'd heard the name before . . . then she realised who the woman was, and that Erin's sister had caught Max and herself so obviously a couple. How had she turned up here?

He let go of Krys's waist.

'I thought I'd find you here,' Laurel said icily. 'I heard you were at some Christmas ball last night.'

'I was,' Max replied mechanically.

301

Laurel seemed incredulous – offended even – by the very notion. Then again, anyone who knew Max might well be astonished that he could play such a role.

Krys stepped forward. 'Good morning. You must be Erin's sister. It's good to meet you.' She smiled in an attempt to defuse the tension that she was sure was already doomed to fail.

Laurel stared at Krys. 'Max has told you about my sister, then?'

'Of course he has.'

Max cut in. 'Laurel, if I'd known you were coming, I'd have made arrangements to meet you at the Bothy.'

'Really? You obviously had an important engagement here.' Her gaze swept over Krys who clutched at the tie on her robe, aware she had only her cami set on underneath. Laurel had managed to plunge the temperature to sub-zero in a few seconds.

'How did you find me here?' Max said carefully, as if he were treading on eggshells.

'I went to the Bothy and there was a woman outside in her car. I think she's called Amina and works at the post office. She said she'd called to deliver a Christmas card to you and when I told her how desperate I was to see you, she let slip you might have walked over here.'

Krys cringed, imagining the position Amina must have been in, guessing that Max had spent the night at Holly Manor and wanting to be discreet, but also trapped by Laurel saying she urgently needed to see him.

'Interesting choice of walking gear,' Laurel said.

'Yeah,' Max said, a hint of irritation creeping into his voice.

Krys was desperate not to inflame a situation that struck her as already incendiary, judging by the dismay on Max's face. However, she wasn't going to explain or apologise for Max having stayed overnight. 'I'm Krys,' she said. 'This is a holiday home.'

'It's very – grand,' Laurel ground out, without taking her eyes off Max. 'Well, I'm sorry for intruding but if you can spare a few moments later, Max, I'd like to talk to you at the Bothy.' Her voice wavered, as if she might be about to scream or cry or both at any moment.

'Of course. I was just on my way home anyway,' Max said.

'I'll meet you there then.'

She marched to her car with a curt nod to Krys.

Max shoved his fingers through his hair. 'I'm sorry about this,' he said. 'That's my sister-in-law. I'd no idea she was planning a visit or that she'd ever turn up here.'

'It's OK. You'd better go and talk to her.'

He groaned. 'Jesus. What a mess.'

'A mess?'

'I didn't mean us . . .' he said desperately. 'Not what we *did*. Just, why did Laurel have to come here *now*?' He grew more agitated by the moment. 'I must go after her. I'll – I'll call you.'

He jogged down the steps to the Landy and got in, leaving Krys on the doorstep, shivering in her robe.

Chapter Thirty-Four

Driving back to the Bothy, Max cursed himself, life and the universe.

Why the hell did Laurel have to turn up *now*? At this moment, in this place?

He hadn't seen his sister-in-law for over a year; the last time was at his financial adviser's in London relating to the trust. That must be why she was here: some urgent query about that donation that she had to deal with personally.

But what timing. It could not possibly have been worse: at Christmas, when he was dressed in this garb and clearly having spent the night with Krys.

Laurel's face . . . Shock and horror didn't come into it. She was . . . disgusted.

He'd left Krys so abruptly. What must she be thinking of him and of Laurel?

He was dreading what Laurel would have to say to him. The Bothy came into view and she was outside, arms folded, staring at the fells. It wasn't a good sign and Max was filled with dread but tried to put himself in her shoes: she'd travelled all this way from London to find him having slept with a strange woman. It was hardly the reception she could have been expecting.

Jake started barking from inside the Bothy.

'Laurel?'

'Your dog's been going mad. He was making a dreadful racket when I called earlier.'

'He needs to be let out,' Max muttered.

'I should imagine he does if you've been out all night.'

Jake dashed out of the door, jumping up on Max briefly.

'Sorry, buddy. I'm late . . .'

Laurel stood by, a wire-taut figure with a pursed mouth.

Jake shot off to do his business behind the woodshed.

'Come inside,' Max said to Laurel, dreading what she had in store for him. Once inside, he kissed her on the cheek but she made no attempt to return his gesture of affection.

'It's a shame I wasn't at home but you might have given me some warning. It was a bit of a shock to find you at the manor.'

'I worked that one out.'

'I didn't mean it in that way. I could have arranged to be at home this morning so you weren't running around Thorndale trying to track me down.'

'It wasn't hard. This post mistress woman knew where you were; so does half of Thorndale, I expect.'

Max was stung into a sharper answer than was wise. 'Probably the whole of Thorndale, actually. Krys and I left the ball together.'

Laurel flinched. 'I can see I've touched a raw nerve.'

'Not at all,' he lied. 'You took me by surprise, that's all. Is everything OK? What was so important that you hared up here instead of picking up the phone?'

'You never answer it. You said you don't have a signal most of the time and you don't have your own wi-fi so I can never be sure you'll pick up an email.'

'You could have written,' he said, clutching at straws.

'*Written*? Don't be ridiculous, Max. It's not the Dark Ages and I can't help it if you choose to live like a hermit in a hovel. Or did do. Clearly, things have changed lately.'

Max restrained himself, aware that anything he said would only inflame the situation further. 'So, what *are* you doing here?' he asked as calmly as he could. 'Are Rob and the children OK?' he said, suddenly fearful for his nephews and brother-in-law.

'They're fine. They're in London embroiled in the whole festive merry-go-round, but this isn't about them. It's about you. What possessed you to go to a ball? With that woman – Krys?' Her voice wavered. 'You *swore* to me, Max. You said you'd never look at another woman. Never smile again. You two – you're together, aren't you?'

Before he could even answer, she pushed on, her voice rising with stress by the moment. 'How did you get enmeshed in all of this – this?' She flung her arm out. 'How can you have forgotten Erin? You said yourself it was your fault that she died.'

Max reeled. He'd heard the accusation many times; taken it without flinching, but this time the blow landed hard and shook him. 'I haven't forgotten Erin. How could I?'

'That's not how it seems.'

'I'll never forget her. You can't possibly really believe that I would. But I can't hide away forever. I can't punish myself the rest of my life. It's killing me.'

'I thought – I thought of all people, you *really* meant it when you said you'd never forgive yourself. I thought you wanted to hide away. You said it would be your lasting tribute to Erin.' Laurel's voice cracked. 'It's only been three years. Three.'

'Three years of *hell*,' Max snapped.

Laurel clasped her hands together. Max could see she was on the edge of breaking down. She was a boiling cauldron of emotions. 'I thought – that was what you wanted. To live in hell. You said it after she died!'

'At the start, but I can't do it any longer. Even if I wanted to, there are people who need me.' Max was thinking of the MRT and of the Outdoor Centre.

'You mean you need them?'

'Well, yes. I do. I thought I didn't, but I do.'

'Or one person in particular?' she said tightly. 'A woman you've known five minutes? In such a short time to forget Erin and move on to this stranger? Oh, Max, what would Erin think?'

There. He'd been waiting for that particular blow. His chest tightened with anger and guilt. 'I don't know. I'll never know. I'll regret arranging that trip for the rest of my life, and the loss of Erin and what it's done to you. I don't think I can keep on punishing myself. I've lost Erin, that's punishment enough.'

Silence. Laurel had tears in her eyes. Max felt awful that he'd even put his case instead of meekly accepting Laurel's accusations. He also feared that any response would never placate her in this mood

Laurel lifted her chin. 'I suppose it's down to your conscience, then.'

'My conscience?' Max echoed then bit back his reply. Laurel was still grieving and he should try to understand that. He had tried, for so very long, but he was running out of empathy and that hurt even more. Was he a bad person?

'But why did you come?'

'To see you. There's an issue to be resolved with Erin's trust fund and I could have written or called but I thought you might appreciate a visit in person, especially today. I thought today would be tough on you and you might be feeling it.'

307

'*Today?*'

'Yes.'

Light dawned, and it was the harsh cold light of a search-light flicked on in the darkness. Max flinched, blinking in the realisation.

'Oh God.'

'You'd forgotten, hadn't you?' Laurel spoke so quietly, he could barely hear. Her eyes were liquid.

'No.'

'Don't lie to me, Max. It doesn't suit you.'

He hung his head. Of course he'd forgotten. He'd been so busy, helping at the Outdoor Centre, on the rescue and then taking Krys to the ball . . . and tumbling out of her bed this morning . . . so distracted by the moment that he had forgotten Erin's funeral had been held three years ago that day.

None of these excuses would diminish the hurt and accusation in Laurel's eyes. She was still grieving deeply for her sister and still blaming him.

'I had forgotten, yes.'

And he *had* begun to forgive himself. To tell himself he deserved a second chance at life. His sister-in-law had made him feel like he didn't.

'I – I can't deal with this now and I can see you're in no fit state. I'm staying at the pub in Thorndale. The Cock, it's called. I'll go back there – I've brought the paperwork I need you to sign. *If* you can spare the time, come and see me at the pub. Room four.'

Chapter Thirty-Five

Like a cat on a hot tin roof, Krys couldn't settle, wondering what was going on between Max and Laurel at the Bothy. She expected to hear from him at any moment. Perhaps he'd call round, as he probably had no signal, but still, she'd hoped he'd pick up on one of her calls.

In the afternoon, when there was no reply to any of them, she walked over to the Bothy, dreading what state of mind he might be in after Laurel's visit but needing to know anyway. The woman had been in complete shock when Max and Krys had answered the door.

With a shiver, she tucked her scarf inside her coat. The gunmetal sky was thick with unshed snow, surely about to dump its load on Thorndale.

In the yard outside the Bothy, Jake ran towards her, his coat covered in sawdust. The dog woofed and licked her hand so she stroked him, and tiny puffs of dust flew into the air.

'Where's Max?' she said to Jake.

As soon as she said the words, Max himself strode out of the woodshed, an axe in his hand. He caught sight of her, and stopped in his tracks, making Krys fear he might turn around and walk off.

'Max!' she shouted and he finally joined her.

Yet it wasn't the man she'd spent a passionate night with: this was a different person, broken and ashamed.

'Hi. I came to see how you were,' she said.

He didn't seem surprised, almost as if he'd been expecting her. 'I should have come to the manor. I need to talk to you.'

Her blood seemed to chill, but Max went straight in.

'This – us – it's too soon for me. Laurel reminded me of that. I should have known I could never outrun the guilt. I tried but I can't.'

'I thought you were ready to start again. You seemed more than ready.'

'I know and I was the one pushing you. It was unforgivable of me. I'm sorry.'

His comments sounded so – *final* – but she wasn't about to give up.

'You might not want to hear this but I'm going to say it anyway. Stop punishing yourself. You don't need to take on Laurel's grief as well as your own. It's too much to bear. She's clearly still devastated but you don't have to stay in the darkness.'

He stared at her. 'Yesterday was the anniversary of Erin's funeral. I forgot.'

Her intake of breath was audible. *Erin's funeral.* Now she understood his reaction a little better, yet she still had to say her piece, no matter what the cost.

'I can understand why you're upset but it's not a crime to have forgotten it was a landmark day while you were helping other people. It's OK to be happy. I didn't know Erin, but she sounds like an amazing woman who loved life. Would she want

310

you to beat yourself up like this and destroy your life? Would she want her own sister to live in misery for the rest of her days? Is that what Erin would have wanted?'

'You have no idea what Erin would have wanted!'

Krys recoiled.

'You've no idea. I've no idea and neither has Laurel because Erin is *gone*. She's gone forever. She's not looking down on me, she doesn't know what's happened and she never will. She is dead and that's it.'

'Max, I'm so—'

'You're sorry, I get it. Everyone is sorry! I'm sorry, her family and friends are sorry but no one knows the gaping hole she left *here*.' He thumped his chest. 'The fucking never-ending pain that replaced her presence when she died. It was starting to ease. I was ready to think I would be happy again. I was happy but now – Jesus, I don't know if I can let myself be.' Max pushed his hands through his hair in a gesture of sheer despair. 'Laurel laid the stone back. I don't think I can find the strength to remove it again. It's too heavy.'

'I'd help you if I could. I *want* to help.'

'You can't. Only I can. Don't even try. Just leave me. Don't be dragged down into this pit with me. Go, please. Just leave me, for God's sake!' He threw the axe onto the yard.

Krys was rigid with shock and dismay. Too scared to leave him, yet helpless.

Then somehow, she found the strength to do as he said; turned and walked and then started running, back to her car. Jake followed her, sniffing at her heels.

Bending down, she ruffled his ears. 'You have to stay here and take care of Max.'

He hung around for a few moments until she started the engine before trotting back towards his owner.

Krys drove off, searching deep into her well of experience for a way to deal with this situation. She found only darkness. Linda had told her no one was a lost cause. That no one was beyond help and anyone could pull themselves up out of a hopeless place into the light, but Krys knew differently.

Max had taken a blow that he couldn't shake off. Or he had until Laurel had knocked him down again.

It was impossible. Some causes were lost and she had to accept that.

Back at Holly Manor, she stood in the kitchen, not sure what to do. After the highs of the ball and the kids' party, she'd crashed down to earth with the most brutal of landings.

The doorbell rang. Visitors were the last thing she wanted but it might be Max, having changed his mind and eager to make peace.

She flew to the door to the very last face she'd expected to see.

'May I come in?'

Bundled up in a coat and hat, rubbing her hands nervously, stood Laurel.

Krys didn't have a good feeling about the woman turning up uninvited, but she could hardly close the door in her face and it wasn't her way of dealing with things. Wasn't this a chance to air some things that needed to be said? If she could get through to Laurel, she might be able to find a way back to Max and help him see his way out of the shadows again.

'Of course.'

Laurel marched into the hall, her keen eyes surveying every inch of it.

'Would you like to come into the sitting room?' Krys said. 'I could make us a coffee? You must be cold.'

'No, thank you,' she said tightly. 'I'm not staying.'

Krys's hopes evaporated.

'Is this about Max?' she said.

'Yes. I don't know if he's told you about our conversation this morning. I know you two are close.'

It was no time for white lies, Krys decided. 'We have spoken. I've just come from the Bothy.'

'Oh?' Laurel frowned.

'He seemed pretty upset.'

'He would be. I can't possibly expect you to understand this, but my sister was a special woman. A *very* special woman. Max was devastated when she was killed. We all were, her friends and her family. You've no idea . . .'

'Actually, I do,' Krys said. 'I've recently lost someone very special to me.'

'Oh?' Laurel seemed astonished.

'My auntie . . .'

Laurel snorted. 'Your auntie? Well, I'm very sorry and I'm sure you were upset but that doesn't come close to losing the love of your life . . . a beloved sister and – and . . .' Laurel stopped. 'I didn't mean to sound callous but what Max has endured, what we *all* have, is beyond words.'

Krys was stunned. Stunned by this woman's anger and deeply sorry for her. It was obvious she was far from even starting to deal with the loss of her sister and for some reason was turning all of that on Max.

'I'm very sorry for your loss. You're right, I haven't lost a partner or sister but Linda was the closest to family I've had. She was a second mother to me but this isn't a competition as to who's suffered the most.'

Laurel's jaw dropped. 'How dare you! My sister was unique. I worshipped her and I would have done anything for her. So did Max and he will never ever meet anyone like her again.' Her eyes blazed with indignation. 'I told Max I was here to sort out a financial issue with Erin's trust fund and that's true but I also came to support him because I knew this would be a difficult time for him, with the anniversary of Erin's funeral so close to Christmas. Then I find he's not only forgotten my sister, but moved on!'

There was no point in saying any more. No soothing words would change the mind or ease the pain of this devastated woman so Krys simply went for honesty, however blunt. 'People grieve in different ways and there is no right or wrong way to react. However, you coming here and laying all your grief on Max won't ever make your pain lessen. Laying it on me won't either. I feel deeply sorry for you, Laurel, but I think it would be better if you went back to the pub now and gave yourself some time.'

'Me? Leave? Are *you* telling me to leave?' She pointed a finger at Krys. 'It's *you* who should get out of Thorndale and leave Max as he was. He doesn't want to meet anyone else. He *can't* love anyone else.'

Krys went to the front door and opened it. 'I think I need to be alone myself now.'

Laurel's eyes burned with anger and disbelief then she marched out of the door.

Krys closed it behind her, trembling. She went into the sitting room and collapsed on the sofa, holding out her hand and finding it was trembling. She'd made things far worse for all of them and despite her bravado in standing up to Laurel, the woman's suggestion that she leave Thorndale was sounding more like a good idea by the second.

There was nothing left for her here now.

Chapter Thirty-Six

It was the whisky bottle which had eventually provided solace – or at least temporary oblivion – for Max after Krys had left him. There was a payback, of course, and he'd woken early and dragged himself out of bed into the bathroom with a dry mouth and a thumping head.

He caught sight of himself in the mirror and recoiled. This wasn't the same person who'd looked back at him on the night of the ball. That man had been smart, tidy, well-rested and – yes, happy. This creature was unkempt and haggard, could easily be a decade older than his thirty-seven years.

He hadn't trusted himself to visit Laurel immediately after her visit. He needed to calm down and tame his emotions first. She might even have gone back to London . . . all he really knew was that he dreaded another confrontation with her.

Jake's collar chinked against his bowl in the kitchen, reminding Max that at least one creature was still depending on him. He felt ashamed. He couldn't erase the lines on his face, the years of being out in all weathers, but he could haul himself out of his pit.

After washing down paracetamol with a gallon of coffee, he hauled his carcass into the shower and dragged a comb through his hair, wondering what the hell he was going to do next.

Before the ball, he'd been putting the finishing touches to a special gift he'd made for Krys. He'd nursed a fantasy of inviting her to spend Christmas with him. He'd been hoping she would say yes, and suggest they spent it at Holly Manor, where he would cook dinner and they'd sit in front of the fire with Jake . . . and maybe later, he'd be invited to stay longer . . .

How ridiculous that sounded now.

A nudge on his hand reminded him Jake needed attention. He'd let him out for a run briefly but now the dog deserved a proper walk. No matter how shitty Max felt, he owed him that.

Jake gazed up at him through trusting eyes. He wanted something, of course, but that look reminded him of Thomas and how he'd believed Santa would help; the total trust and faith he'd had in a lie that Max had perpetuated.

Still in limbo about what to do next, if anything, Max returned to the workshop. It was a raw morning, the chill deepening as the day crawled on.

He had to switch on the workshop light.

There on the work bench lay Krys's gift.

He didn't have the heart to work on it now. It was useless coming in here. What was the point, when there was no one to give it to?

No one special. Only strangers.

'Max?'

'Krys?'

A woman was framed in the doorway.

She stepped inside and his heart sank. A trick of the light had fooled him.

'Jo. I hadn't expected you . . .'

Jo looked sheepish. 'I'm sorry to disturb you but I didn't have any other way of contacting you. Krys mentioned you don't have a signal or wi-fi. I'm on my way home so I made a detour.' She held out a cardboard folder. 'These are for you.'

'Me?'

'Well, strictly speaking, they're for Santa, but they are yours, really. We've had a dozen emails from parents and carers since yesterday and two hand-delivered notes. I printed the emails off. I thought you'd like to see them.'

'Thank you.' He took the folder. 'Are you sure they're for me, not the centre staff?'

She laughed. 'We've had some lovely thank you's too and I've passed those on to Krys as well, but these are specifically for *you*.'

'Oh.'

'I'll leave them with you.' She seemed pretty desperate to go. 'The centre is closed for the holidays until New Year. We're all ready for a break. Can't wait for Christmas.'

'No. I bet.'

'Happy Christmas, then,' she said cheerily.

'You too.' Max forced a smile and waved as Jo left the workshop, eager and excited as any of the children she'd been looking after.

He ached for that carefree feeling of anticipation; of looking forward again, not languishing in the past. He could see no way it would ever happen.

After switching off the light, he returned to the Bothy, leaving the workshop as it had been. He made himself a coffee, and settled down on the sofa, steeling himself to read the messages.

He felt he owed it to the children.

They had obviously been written by the kids' parents, or with their help. They told him of the lovely time they'd had, how

317

much they'd loved the grotto – that was Krys's doing – and meeting him. How special it had made Christmas. The words 'magical' had been used.

> Dear Santa, Thank you for the present.
> I now know you are real and there is magic
> in the world.

Max lifted his eyes to the ceiling, telling himself not to pile on any more emotion to a soul already as raw as the day outside.

Unfolding the last piece of paper, he braced himself. It was written in felt tip with drawings of a reindeer and a sleigh. There was a picture of a Santa and his elf. He knew from the enormous ears that it was Krys – and him.

> Dear Santa,
> Thank you for the present from your grotty.
>
> Daddy has told me I shouldnt have aksed for a reel car.
> He says Santa cant arrange it and might be worried im upset on Xmas morning.
> I wont be upset so don't worry.
> Love
> Thomas xx
> PS Thank you saying youll try to get one.

He stared at the paper a good while before it slipped from his fingers onto the floor, all the bones in his body slowly turning to putty. He could not move. All the fight, the spirit, the rage had left him. How long he sat there, he didn't know, but it was growing dark when, finally, Jake licked his hand and whined.

The dog cocked his head on one side. It was almost dusk but it wasn't too late . . . there was still time, if he got a move on.

Jake laid his head on Max's knee, hinting he still hadn't had his walk.

'I think,' Max said to Jake, who would have listened even if he'd been reciting the ingredients on a biscuit packet, 'that I've let down a lot of people lately.' He patted the dog's head. 'And I'm afraid I'm about to do the same to you, boy.'

With life surging back to his limbs, Max took down the lead and grabbed his car keys, causing Jake to spring up and yip in excitement.

'We *are* going out,' he explained as if Jake might have an opinion. 'But maybe not where you expected. Come on. Let's try to repair some of the mess I've created.'

Lights were twinkling in the valley when Max drove back towards Thorndale, feeling that, at least, one small but important burden had been lifted from his shoulders. Now, all he had to do was come to terms with the weight of guilt that had been placed back on them. Laurel was clearly still grieving deeply for her sister.

He would always do that too, but grief could surely be a part of him while not stealing away any more of his future?

On his way back from his errand, he called in at The Cock, hoping to speak to Laurel. Leaving Jake in the car with the windows open, he walked to the residents' entrance. Pints in hand, a few revellers were vaping and singing along to the Christmas music blaring out from the bar.

He passed the deserted reception desk, went straight up the stairs to Laurel's room and knocked.

He heard noises and the door opened.

'Max?' She blew out a breath. 'I thought you wouldn't come. I almost checked out myself.'

This wasn't a good start. 'I'm glad you didn't. Please, can I come in?'

She nodded. 'I suppose you'd better.'

Great, he thought. 'Thanks.'

The room was stifling. The Cock had clearly pushed the heating up off the scale. The bed was covered with clothes and Laurel's suitcase was still half-open on the floor, as if she hadn't been able to decide whether to stay or go. He decided not to bother with any preamble: whatever he said was sure to upset her, but he felt by not being brutally honest, he would do greater harm to them both.

'There's something I have to say, and I'm going to apologise in advance if you're hurt by it. I would never add to your pain for a single moment, but I have to say this. I'll go mad if I don't. I can't go on like I have been.'

She stared at him. God, she looked as if she was going to burst into tears.

'First, I want to you read these. Read them, and tomorrow, if you still want to talk to me, come and fetch me.'

He handed over the folder.

She stared at it. 'What's in it?'

'Letters from some of the local kids. You see, not only did I go to a ball, but the day before that I played Santa at a children's party. The person who was meant to do it couldn't, so I stepped in.'

Her lips parted in astonishment. 'You played Santa . . .'

'Yes, I did, and I'm sorry if you're shocked but I'm not going to apologise for it,' he said firmly. 'In fact it was a privilege, and if you read these letters, I hope you'll see why. Now, I'm going. I'll see you tomorrow.'

She clutched the folder to her body. 'There's no need to wait until tomorrow,' she said. 'I was coming over to the Bothy anyway.'

To berate him? To say she was going home to London? He could do nothing about her decisions.

'I'd like you to read the letters first, then I'll come back after I've walked Jake around the pub.'

Closing the door on the stuffy room, he collected Jake from the car for his walk. The lane outside the pub wasn't an ideal outing for a restless border collie but there were enticing smells, and the darkness held no fear for a dog who knew every inch of his territory.

He tried to home in, if only for a few minutes, on the senses of the night: an owl hooting, woodsmoke on the crisp winter air. It was also impossible to ignore the lights of the pub and the Christmas music from the bar, the people laughing and winding down ready for the holiday.

Leaving Jake in the car again with a treat, he braced himself for another encounter with Laurel. With a heart bursting with things he needed to say, he knocked on the door.

'Max?' She was red-eyed with crying.

He almost faltered but went inside. 'Even if you don't want to talk to me, I need to speak to you.'

He spotted the folder on the bed.

'Have you read them?'

'Yes.'

'And?'

'They're very moving,' she said mechanically. Her tone filled him with profound sadness. If those letters hadn't got through to her, nothing would, but he was going to say his piece anyway.

'Max. I—'

'No, wait. I have to say this and I have to tell you now in case I change my mind, and that would be a tragedy. Someone said to me recently that the way I've been behaving isn't what Erin would have wanted. It's a cliché to say that to the grieving, but in this case, I know it's absolutely true.'

Laurel sat down heavily on the bed. 'Go on.'

'We both know how badly Erin longed for a family and how much she hoped it would happen. I can't change that but I *can* change what I do from now on. I know she would surely have wanted me to embrace the spirit of the children and families who sent those messages. She'd have wanted me to get up off the floor again.' He paused for breath.

'Max . . .'

'She would have wanted me to move on, always loving her in my heart but also making space for other people – for a family – for . . .'

'Krys?'

'Yes. For Krys,' he declared. 'Though I doubt very much she'll make room for me after how I treated her.'

'After I left?'

He nodded. 'It wasn't your fault. It was my decision how I reacted to what you said. I didn't have to pass my own hurt and guilt on to her.'

'It was my fault. I was coming to see you to say I'm sorry for what I said. I have lain awake. I have done something unfor-givable. I was so shocked – so angry for Erin . . .'

'What do you mean? I'm not angry at what you said to me.'

'Oh, Max. It's not what I said to *you*, though that was unfor-givable. It's what I said to Krys.'

He stiffened. 'Krys?'

'I – I went round to the house that she's staying and I told her to – I told her she should stay away from you, that it was disrespectful to Erin and you could never be happy again with anyone else. And now I wish – I wish – I hadn't done it. I was coming over now to warn you and then to apologise to Krys.'

'Oh my God.' He felt sick.

Laurel clutched at his arm. 'I'm so sorry. I've been blinded by grief, but coming here and finding out you'd been to the ball and stayed the night with Krys, and then realising you'd forgotten about the anniversary . . . I thought it meant you'd forgotten Erin and also I was jealous. Jealous that you'd found hope and happiness again. It tipped me over the edge.'

'I'll never forget Erin.'

'I know that. These letters from the children are beautiful and you're right, they do show that you need to go out and enjoy life, live it to the full, help people, be happy.'

'I need to talk to Krys, before it's too late.'

'It might already be too late. I – God forgive me – told her to leave Thorndale.'

'To leave?' He made a decision in a heartbeat. 'I have to go and see her right now.'

'I wish I could unsay everything I threw at her. I wish I could undo a lot of things.'

'Don't we all? But we can't.'

Laurel burst into tears. His own emotions were seething, but he embraced her, soothing her and understanding exactly what she'd been through. 'We can *both* live our lives, I'm not angry with you, only sad for you. But I have to go.'

She nodded. 'Yes, try to find her. Tell her I'm sorry. I'll – I'll go over there myself but you first.'

He jogged down the pub stairs out to his car. He drove faster than he should have through the narrow lanes to Holly Manor, but there wasn't another soul around on this dark night. No stars were visible under the cloudy sky and he thought it might

323

snow. He had to reach Holly Manor and try to repair the damage that had been done. He could only pray that Krys would listen and forgive him.

He shot through the gates and pulled up with a spray of gravel. There was a vehicle on the drive but it wasn't Krys's hire car.

The front door opened and Nikki walked out, with a bag full of rubbish.

Max knew what it meant.

'She's gone, hasn't she?'

Nikki frowned. 'Yes . . . about half an hour ago. She's on the way to London to spend Christmas with a friend.'

Max swore.

'I thought she might have told you,' Nikki said gently.

'No,' he said, then added desperately, 'Is she coming back?'

'I don't think so. The place is rented until the second of January but – all her stuff is gone.'

His groan echoed into the darkness.

'I'm sorry, Max. Can I do anything to help?'

'No. No one can.'

He jumped in the Landy, with Nikki shouting, 'Max! Be careful!'

He'd spent so long trying to avoid getting close to anyone else, he hadn't even thought that when he did, it might end. Not with a tragic loss, but a loss all the same. He wasn't prepared for that. He'd only ever loved one woman; he'd thought he could never be hurt ever again.

He was wrong.

Chapter Thirty-Seven

Krys switched on the wipers. Sticky flakes were blowing at the windscreen, and it was hard to see the white lines on the main road that led to the motorway. It would be past midnight when she reached North London but at least she'd be home. Her *actual* home: not some fantasy Christmas card version that had delivered nothing but pain and disappointment.

But she couldn't think of Holly Manor without remembering the magical moments too. They'd come from the most unexpected sources and not from the Instagram-perfect Christmas she'd envisaged, with its OTT decorations and tree. The real magic had lain in the joy on the children's faces at the grotto, from the friendship of the mountain rescue team and most of all, from Max.

Seeing him emerge from his shell, sharing his bed and finally starting to know the gorgeous, kind man underneath had been magical. She'd been so very close and yet now, even further away than ever.

Laurel's words had stung like salt in a wound, yet Krys had been able to understand where they'd come from: a place of deep grief. It was Max's words that had cut too deeply to recover from. He'd meant them, they were heartfelt and impossible to stop.

So she'd spent some time wallowing, then packed everything up, thrown it in the car and set off.

She switched on the wipers to top speed, as the snow was falling faster.

She was heading south; there would be none there.

No snow, no darkness, no stars to be seen . . .

She hadn't even said goodbye.

The snow was heavier, coating the bonnet. Her headlights picked out the hedgerows and fields, all ghostly white. The fellsides were visible only by the lights of farms scattered over their flanks. Lonely windows glowed at improbable heights, and above them, there was only pitch blackness. She had to imagine the mountains were there.

The satnav told her that it was only ten minutes to the motorway. If she carried on, with a bit of luck, she'd probably be out of the snow and heading south to the safety of the lowlands.

Ahead was a service station, its lights blazing, wood stacked outside. Her fingers hovered over the indicator stalk and a second before it would have been too late, she flipped it left. Soon, she was turning into the forecourt and out again, and then heading back into the driven snow to Thorndale.

Her head told her it was a filthy evening to be making such a long journey in such dangerous conditions. Her head told her that she should go back to Holly Manor and get up at dawn, and start off again.

Her heart told her that she should have, at least, said goodbye to Max.

There were still three days to Christmas; still time to get back and spend the day with Harriet and her family. One more night in Thorndale would hardly matter.

She was almost back in the village when the gritting truck passed her, spraying salt against her car with a rattle. She'd made the right decision: the radio said that conditions on the motorway were hazardous and getting worse. The police had asked people not to travel unless necessary.

She passed the drive of Holly Manor, the wheels slipping in the slush. She'd call Nikki when she got inside and tell her that she would be staying one more night but she'd manage without any linen. Looking at the weather, it would likely be the least of Nikki's worries. For anyone in the emergency services, it was going to be a busy night.

'Max?

She knocked and called before she pushed open the door of the Bothy. She wasn't surprised to find it unlocked; but she was surprised to find it slightly ajar.

So he must be inside. There was no answer so she upped the volume and banged on the wood, but there was still no answer and no bark of welcome from Jake.

'It's me, Krys!' she called. The snow had blown in onto the doormat and beyond onto the flagstones. The hearth was cold but there was the remains of a meal on the table.

Max must be walking the dog, or in the woodshed.

She closed the door behind her and stopped to gather herself. It felt as if she hadn't paused for breath since she'd decided to turn back. Once the decision had been made, she'd felt a terrible sense of urgency to get to Thorndale. She was worried about being stuck in a drift before she reached Max and had the chance to tell him goodbye. Progress had been slow as the roads had become covered in slush and narrowed to a strip. By the time she'd made it out of Thorndale, she was thanking her lucky stars she'd hired the small four-wheel drive because she'd never have made it otherwise.

With the snowstorm becoming wilder, she'd headed straight for the Bothy. If necessary, she could walk home to the manor, after she'd seen Max. However he reacted, she'd have to deal with it. Nothing mattered except seeing him and trying to talk to him one last time – or at least, saying goodbye properly.

Krys went outside to the workshop but found it in darkness.

It was bitterly cold but the snow had eased a little and the wind had dropped. The storm hadn't been forecast – at least not for this far south. Maybe it had already passed.

'Max!' she called. 'Jake!'

There was no answer.

'Evening!'

Krys jumped, turning in relief to greet Max but finding a stocky older man with a shepherd's crook. She recognised him as a farmer from across the dale. It was the bridge to his farm that Brett's Porsche had blocked.

'Oh, hello,' she said. 'I was looking for Max.'

'Saw him an hour or so since. Told me he was off to search for Jake,' the farmer said. 'Dog's gone off on one of his adventures though it's not the best night fer it. I've sheep to bring in out of this.' He nodded at a quad bike with a small trailer loaded with feed.

'No, it's a horrible night . . .' She peered into the darkness, willing Max and Jake to materialise from the gloom. 'Did he say exactly where he'd gone?'

'Said he'd likely try the path to the Pike car park. Daft hound. Mebbe he won't have gone far.'

'I hope not.'

'I'd wait for them in the warm, lass. They'll be back soon.'

'Of course. Thanks.'

He tipped his cap. 'Happy Christmas.'

'Happy Christmas,' Krys said and watched the farmer melt away into the snow.

She took his advice and sat inside the Bothy, alert to every sound. A dozen times, she thought she heard a bark, a dozen times she went to the window or opened the door in the hope of seeing man and dog walking across the yard towards their home.

The snow had stopped, at least, and the moon peeped cautiously from behind a cloud, revealing a hard and glittering landscape. The puddle outside the door was frozen solid, showing that the temperature had plunged under the clearing skies.

She paced the room, not that there was much to pace. It had been two hours since she'd spoken to the farmer, which meant at least three hours since Max had left the house to search for Jake.

It didn't feel right. She didn't know why but there was a stillness and silence that made her flesh crawl. She was sure something was wrong; no matter how experienced Max was, how well he knew the hills, she was worried.

She could call Nikki, or Amina, if only for reassurance.

Then she remembered that there was no signal.

Krys looked through the window. The skies were still clear and the snow didn't appear to be any deeper. She was sick of expecting Max to turn up at any moment, she couldn't keep still a moment longer. Surely it wouldn't do any harm to wrap up warm, grab a torch and see if she could find him?

Immediately the thought came into her head, it was chased away by another: Max telling her not to be so stupid as to go after him on a night like this. He'd be right for once.

Heaving a sigh, Krys turned away from the window but swung back again. She'd heard a noise: faint barking that cut through the still night. She pulled open the door, wincing at the cold blast of air but also shouting in relief.

'Jake!'

He hurtled through the snow to the open door and almost knocked her over.

'Am I glad to see you.' She peered into the darkness, expecting to see Max close behind.

Jake tried to dart out of the door before she could close it. Krys caught hold of his collar and tried to stroke him. He twisted away, barking, almost snarling.

'OK, boy. OK. Are you hurt?'

He stood by the door, barking.

'Where's Max?' she said, fully aware the dog couldn't answer her. Yet he was *trying* to . . . that wasn't a stupid thought.

Whining, he pawed at the closed door.

'You want to go out again?'

She closed her fingers around the door handle and Jake let rip, his barks bouncing off the Bothy walls.

'OK. I get it. You do want to go out. Have you – have you found Max?'

Cocking his head on one side, Jake stared at her. Krys felt stupid, the dog didn't understand her. For all she knew, he'd found a dead rabbit or smelled a fox. Yet he *was* incredibly agitated. It was possible that Max might be in trouble, only metres from the Bothy. Jake might be a failed search and rescue dog but he had gone through some of the training. One thing was for sure: he had a far better chance of finding Max than she did alone.

'OK. Let's have a look around.'

The moment she opened the door, Jake darted into the snow but he'd have to wait a little while longer. She went to her car and found her waterproof trousers, walking boots and gloves. She changed as fast as she could then found a bottle of water, energy bars and an extra coat from the peg, stuffed it all in Max's bag and grabbed his torch.

At the last minute, she checked the top pocket of the pack and saw the survival sack, whistle and a tiny first aid kit. There was also a head torch which she put on over her beanie hat.

All the while, Jake was going wild, barking non-stop, chasing in and out of the Bothy and scratching at the door.

After trying her phone one last time, she found a map and checked the compass in the top of the rucksack. She'd only a rudimentary knowledge of how to use it, gleaned from her climb up the Pike, but had never used one on her own. She hoped she wouldn't need it and that Max would be a short distance away, possibly having twisted his ankle or with some minor injury. The alternative didn't bear thinking about.

'OK. I *am* coming.'

Finally, she walked out of the yard and Jake ran off into the darkness.

'Wait!'

She trudged off after him, sinking into slushy snow, thanking her stars she'd bought decent boots and a coat.

Even so, the darkness was disorientating. Occasionally the moon peeped out from the clouds, illuminating the fellsides, but mostly it was simply black. Only the head torch illuminated her way. She was saving the big torch for when – if – she found Max.

She knew she daren't venture too far. It was probably crazy to even leave the Bothy but Jake clearly thought she should. Ahead of her, he was a pale blur in the gloom. Frustrated by her lack of canine speed and agility, he kept vanishing before running back to her.

'Jake! Slow down!' she shouted, almost tripping over a tree root.

Even though she'd walked the path from the Bothy to the start of the Pike route several times, in darkness it was a completely different matter. Recognising landmarks – a stile or a fallen tree – by torchlight was in a different league of difficulty. She tried her phone again, hoping to reach the base, but there was still no signal.

After walking and stumbling for twenty minutes, she made it to a gate by a wooden waymark to the Pike route. Jake took a jump at the stone wall, scrambled up and over.

Krys fumbled with the latch, having to take off her gloves to undo it. It was freezing but she got through and onto the path. It was well-trodden and surfaced because of its popularity, although it was a few centimetres deep in snow. She slipped a couple of times but managed to make good progress, until she reached the stile that led up the side of the gill.

The moon came out, showing the dark and jagged outline of the Pike against the night sky. Krys's spirits plunged.

'I can't go up there, Jake.'

He butted against the dog gate at the bottom of the stile.

'I just can't. It's too dangerous.'

This was madness, crazy, everything she shouldn't do, every mistake that she could make, yet Jake *was* going wild. Surely Max must be nearby? What if she turned back now and missed him by a few metres? What if he was lying injured, hoping that someone would find him, but also dreading they might not.

What if he was dead?

Casting that terrible prospect aside, she lifted up the dog gate and Jake wriggled through it, surging onward.

'Slow down!' she shouted.

The path soon became more rugged, and she slithered on the slate and loose stones. She had to switch on the big torch, and watch every step as she climbed upwards. The beck tumbled past, a fierce rush that sounded like a raging torrent in the darkness.

'Oh!'

Her heart was in her mouth. She had to grab for a rock to stop herself from stumbling. Her glove saved her from grazing her hand but it still hurt. She paused, breath misting the air, wisps of snow melting on her face.

'I cannot do this,' she said. 'Jake, we *have* to go back. I have to give up and walk to the base to call out the team.'

But Jake was gone, vanished into blackness.

She waited for her heart rate to calm down and hoped he'd come back.

Minutes ticked past, the stream rushing by angrily but no answering bark to her calls. It broke her heart to have to turn back and leave Max out there on his own, almost certainly injured. If he was still alive, he wouldn't have long left in these conditions. She was in some danger herself.

Now, Jake had vanished again too.

One last try. 'Jake! Jake! Come back!'

He still couldn't hear her above the roaring water.

A flash of white, another bark and the dog appeared again, a few metres above her on the pathway.

'Jake. Thank God.' Her torch beam swung over his fur, and then she froze. 'Oh no. No.'

There was red on his coat. Even by torchlight, she knew what it was. Blood.

Her stomach turned over but she knew what it meant. Max must be very close. Injured – possibly worse – but close. She couldn't give up now.

Jake dashed back to her, panting and agitated, probably to make sure she was still following. She scrambled up some steep rocky steps, praying she wouldn't fall, and finally heard a faint cry on the fellside above her.

'Help! Hello!'

Krys froze, straining her ears. Nothing.

She called at the top of her voice: 'Max! Max! Is that you?'

For a heart-stopping moment, there was only silence and the rush of the beck, then a bark and a voice in the darkness.

'Krys? It's me! Over here!'

Chapter Thirty-Eight

'Max! I'm coming.'

She shone her torch in the direction of the cry and saw a pale blur.

'Max!'

Every instinct told her to run to his side, but that was impossible.

'Be careful . . .' he cried, though it was more of a rasp. 'Don't risk yourself.'

It was too late for that. Using the head torch, she stepped off the path and saw him lying on his back, a few metres below her, on a rocky ledge.

'Where's the team?' he called.

'I don't know. I couldn't raise them. I had no signal.'

'You came out here on your own?'

'Yes. Jake led me. I thought you might only be a little way from the Bothy but he kept on coming. He found you.'

Gingerly, Krys left the path and sat down in the wet scrubby grass, letting herself down gently to the ledge where he lay.

'No,' he insisted. 'You must go down, drive to the base and call them out.'

'I'm not leaving you.'

She reached him. He was half sitting and lying with his back against a rock. Jake lay by him and licked his face

'Thanks, buddy,' he said as Jake settled back by his side.

Krys shone the light over his body and saw that the blood was from a gash on his hand. He'd taken off his glove and his head torch had gone.

Crouching beside him, she touched his face. 'Oh, Max. What have you done?'

'Slipped off the path. I was looking for Jake, I wasn't thinking . . . I was stupid and I saw him and then before I knew it, I'd stumbled and fallen.'

'Did you hit your head?'

'No. I rolled a bit, connected with a few boulders and ended up here.'

His body was already mottled with snowflakes. 'Have you broken anything?' she asked.

'My chest's sore and I'm having trouble getting my breath when I move. Could have cracked a couple of ribs and my ankle's not in great shape either.'

Dreading the answer, she asked: 'Have you broken it?'

'Possibly. There was a crack when I fell.'

She felt sick at the thought of him in such pain. 'You're very cold. Where's your glove?'

'I don't know. Jake found me and I took it off then he vanished again.'

Krys shone the light on the stony ground, which was now white with snow. She spotted objects a few feet away and picked them up.

'Your glove and head torch are here. The blood's congealed on your hand. Can you put the glove back on? Or we'll have frostbite to add to your other problems.'

He was in no state to argue, and, wincing, pulled the glove back on.

'Now, we have to get you out of here,' she said. 'Can you walk?'

'Maybe. With help, but you aren't going to do that,' he said firmly. 'You're going to go back to the base.'

'I'm not leaving you. Even if it wasn't snowing again, and it is.' She held out her glove to show him the thick flakes that had started falling.

Max looked into her eyes, pleading. 'Krys, don't waste your life for me. I couldn't bear that.'

'I'm not wasting anyone's life. Don't talk like that. Now, we're going to get you to shelter.'

There was a pause. 'I'm not sure I can make it all the way down.'

'Don't worry,' she said, as reassuringly as she could. 'We'll think of something else.'

Yet the something else was – as blank as the night. Stay out here in the snow, lying beside him and Jake. She knew the two of them would not survive. Maybe she did have no choice but to brave the route back down, leaving him alone. The wind had strengthened and she remembered Max telling her about the down draughts that could knock you clean off your feet.

'I – think I might make it to the box,' he said.

'The box?' Krys thought he was babbling.

'The stretcher box. It's not far from here.'

She almost wept with relief. At least they would have shelter from the elements. 'Good idea. Come on.'

Krys helped him re-fasten his head torch and with great difficulty got him to his feet. His breathing was raspy and he couldn't stifle the groans of pain as she helped him up the short slope to the path.

'I'm sorry,' he kept saying.

'Shh. Save your energy. We're going to make it.'

She *had* to believe it.

Jake scooted ahead and waited on the path, while Krys staggered under Max's weight.

Somehow they made it onto the path and paused for breath. Her arms ached and she was gulping in the air. The cold made her chest tighten. Max was rasping with every breath. She was sure he'd cracked some ribs. Jake shot down the fellside.

'Not that way!' Krys shouted after him. 'Not tonight.'

For once he obeyed and trotted back, gazing up at them.

'That way.' She pointed upwards, sweeping her torch beam over a metal and wooden box on the fellside above them.

On the move again and Max had to lean on her. Every step seemed to take minutes. The snow had become a blizzard, driven by the swirling wind. She was terrified of a down draught blowing them both off the path. Despite her clothing, she was cold and the exposed flesh on her face was frozen.

'N-nearly there,' she said, finally seeing the box a few metres ahead.

Max said nothing: every ounce of his energy was spent.

They staggered on and Max sagged against the box, holding onto it for support.

Now all she had to do was open it.

The metal bolts were stiff and she had to take off her gloves to draw them back, wincing at the pain in her fingers. Eventually they gave way and she held the door back in the wind. Now all they had to do was crawl inside. Goodness knows what further damage that might do to Max, but they had no choice. She could only hope he was right when he'd said he hadn't hit his head.

Eventually, with Krys pushing him, he managed to crawl inside the box and collapsed on his back inside. She took off

338

the pack, pushed it on top of Max before clambering in herself and beckoning Jake.

There was just enough head height to sit upright though it was cosy with the three of them huddled together by torchlight. Cosy was exactly what they needed. The box provided protection from the wind and snow. The question was, would they make it until morning?

Max propped himself up on one elbow, with Krys pressed against the side of the box, face to face with him. Jake settled on their feet.

She was shaking with adrenaline.

'Jesus, I'm an idiot,' he said. 'A stupid bloody idiot.'

He coughed and then for the first time, she saw a smile.

'Have a drink,' she ordered and pulled her pack towards her. She removed a bottle of water and an energy bar.

'Well done,' Max said.

'This stuff is from your rucksack. You left it in the Bothy. Why did you go off like that, without telling anyone?'

'I wasn't thinking straight after Nikki told me you'd left. The weather was fine, I thought I'd find Jake within a few minutes. I didn't bother with my rucksack and I just had to do something right. I'd lost you. I wasn't losing Jake. Krys, I've been very stupid in so many ways.'

'Drink,' she said, holding the bottle under his nose. 'Try to eat something.'

They shared the water and ate the cereal bars, while Jake dozed on their feet.

'At least he's happy,' Krys said. 'I think we might have to stay here until morning.'

'Finally I get to spend the night with you again.' Max said. 'It wasn't quite how I envisaged it, but I thought it might never happen. I'm so sorry I've put you in danger.'

'It doesn't matter now. I'm going to turn off the torch to save the batteries.'

'Good idea.'

They were plunged into the deepest night Krys had ever known, with the wind howling around them. She had trouble believing they were even on this earth.

Max was silent for a while in the darkness.

'While it's confession time, there's something else I need to tell you, Krys.'

He sounded weak and she didn't want him to get even more tired, but she wanted him to stay awake. In truth, she didn't know *what* to do.

She smiled at him even though she couldn't see him. 'That you're "Dave"?'

She only knew he was smiling back because of the humour in his voice. 'Pretty obvious from the start, was it?'

'No. You flat denied it and so I was put off the scent, though I did see the workshop and found a wood shaving on Jake's coat . . . but I didn't dare ask you again and began to think it really wasn't you.'

'I didn't want anyone to know. My work has always been my solace, my escape, a private corner of my life that is mine alone. When you implied that Dave might be in need of money, that sealed it. I was horrified at being thought of as a "project" to be helped and then I let the lie go on too long to tell you.'

'Well, you picked a funny time to tell me!'

He laughed which set off a coughing fit. Krys was worried he had internal injuries.

'Shh,' she said. 'Save your strength.'

'For what? There's not much we can do in here.'

'I don't think it would be the best idea in your condition but maybe we can revisit that when we get out of here.'

340

'You're such an optimist, Krystle.' He clutched her hand.

'Krystle,' she said. 'No one calls me that now – though Auntie Linda did. I – I thought it was a bit naff when I went to university so I changed it. Brett still thinks I'm called Kristine.'

Max laughed and coughed again. 'It's a beautiful name. You're beautiful. Never change.'

He must be delirious, Krys thought but decided that the best thing to do was humour him.

'What you said about not wanting to be helped . . . I've always tried to escape my past, my roots. Linda would have been so ashamed of me, pretending to be something I'm not. I could never get over the teasing at school and the shame of wearing someone else's boots.'

'What do you mean?'

'It sounds trivial. But some of the kids – and the staff – laughed at my trainers at the Outdoor Centre. I had to wear a pair of borrowed boots and they didn't fit. I hated being there at all, feeling like a charity case. I was an ungrateful little madam, wasn't I?'

'No, you were a vulnerable kid who'd had a tough start in life.'

He squeezed her hand, but without the strength he'd had earlier, and then went very quiet. Max was fading fast.

She shook him gently. 'Hey. Hold on, Max. Don't give up.'

He spoke up again. 'I won't because I need to tell you something.'

'Oh?' Krys had a horrible feeling he was hellbent on making some kind of final confession. It chilled her to the bone. 'Why don't you tell me all this when we're back home at the Bothy?'

He grasped her hand, so hard it hurt. 'I need to tell you *now*.'

So, it *was* a confession.

'I want you to know why I felt I had to hide away at the

Bothy after I lost Erin. You see, she was pregnant at the time of the accident.'

She inhaled with shock.

'She was only a few weeks gone and I didn't find out until – until after she'd died.'

Krys's heart broke for him. 'I am so very sorry, Max.'

'She'd felt queasy on the weekend away, done a test and told Laurel. She was planning to tell me too when she got home but she hadn't said a word before . . . We'd wanted to start a family for a long time. In the end we'd had to accept help. Laurel had donated her eggs. That's why – that's why she was doubly devastated when Erin was killed. It was partly her baby, as well as ours. It belonged to us all.'

'Oh, Max, that's heartbreaking. Poor Laurel.'

'It's why she was so upset to see me celebrating Christmas – this time of year only brings back terrible memories for her. It did for me, until I met you.'

Krys squeezed his hand. 'Yet, forgive me, she has children of her own, but she wants you to go on punishing yourself?'

'She thought she did . . . She fixated on it after Erin died. I'm not going to judge her because we all dealt with the situation – or didn't deal with it – in our own way.' He let go of her hand. 'Jesus, I don't know anything any longer and maybe . . . it doesn't matter now what I know, or think or feel.' He started wheezing and coughing again.

Panicking inside, Krys switched on the torch and he squeezed his eyes shut. 'It *does* matter, she said fiercely. 'You're going to get through this and you're going to talk to Laurel and make her understand you need your life back.'

He blinked his eyes open. 'It's a new life I *do* want. A different life. I can't have the old one back. I realise that and I want to start afresh.'

'Then Laurel has to understand that too.'

'She *is* starting to. I went to see her at the pub and told her how I felt about you. She said she was sorry for coming to the manor. What she did was cruel but it came from a very dark, sad place within her. I think she's realised that now and regrets lashing out at you – and me. She's just taken longer to work that out.'

How he felt about her.

Krys waited for him to say more but his eyes had closed. He was asleep and she didn't try to wake him this time because there was no way he'd stay awake until dawn. She checked her phone and his but there was still no signal.

Even if Max slept, she had to stay alert, ready to signal if she heard rescuers, or a helicopter. Jake crept closer, across their thighs. He whimpered softly but still Max didn't stir.

Krys pressed closer to his body, hoping for a miracle. She thought of Erin, and her auntie. She knew she'd be OK, that she'd survive with Jake and Max to keep her warm – for now.

Yet she dreaded Max growing colder, and his warm breath against her cheek, fading away – stopping.

No matter how hard she tried to keep her eyes open, no matter how loud the storm, sleep tempted her into its embrace. She tried to think of decorating a room to stay awake, but she kept drifting back to the window of the house, all those years ago. She was outside again, looking at the fire burning in the hearth, and the lights twinkling, and the family gathered around the tree, cosy and safe and warm.

It was all a fantasy; it always had been. The real world was one of loss and pain, and restless struggle to survive.

And happy endings didn't exist for people like Max. Or people like her.

* * *

'Max! Max!'

Krys woke, not to darkness, but light creeping between the thin cracks in the stretcher box. She'd been in and out of sleep all night, dreaming fitfully, checking on Max and trying to keep warm.

Now, Max lay face up, his eyes closed, his lips pale. Krys's stomach turned over and over and she cried, 'Wake up! No, Max! No, not this. Don't let it end like this.'

Jake's claws dug in her stomach as he squeezed past her shoulder to the box door.

'Ouch!' she shouted. 'Jake! I can't hear Max.'

'Who – what . . .' Max's eyes opened.

'Oh God, you're alive!' Krys rubbed his hands. 'You aren't dead.'

'Not yet. What's up with Jake?'

'I don't know. Maybe he wants a pee.'

'Don't let him pee in here . . .'

'No.' She almost wept with relief. She pushed the door open hard and it flew back, shooting a blast of icy air into the box.

Jake shot out, plunging into snow up to his shoulders. The landscape had changed from grey rocks to pure white and the sudden chill made her gasp for breath. Anyone would think they were in the Himalayas, not the Lake District. A few flakes were flying in the air, lifted by the breeze. The sky was grey, threatening even more snow.

'Don't run off, Jake! I won't be able to find you. Please don't leave us now.'

Ignoring her, he forged forward, leaving a shoulder high tunnel in the snow.

She despaired. 'I'll have to shut the door to keep us warm.'

She pulled the door to, listening for signs of the dog returning, and leaned over Max, trying to keep him warm. Any hope that the snow might have melted and she could find a path down or try to find some climbers was dashed.

'Jake will be OK . . .' Max lifted a hand as if to say it didn't matter before his eyes fluttered.

'Don't go to sleep,' she murmured, fearing that he would never wake again.

'Krys . . .' His breathing sounded raspy. 'Krys, I need to tell you something.' He stopped to breathe but it was obviously a struggle.

For the first time, genuine panic took hold. 'Try not to talk but don't go to sleep.'

Shortness of breath, chest pain, on top of hypothermia . . . Max must have a serious chest injury. Krys remembered over-hearing snatches of a first aid course at the base. It sounded like a pneumothorax – a collapsed lung probably caused by his fall. She was sure he had cracked ribs and that could be life-threatening. What did she mean, 'could be'? It already *was* life-threatening.

'I have to tell you that I—'

'That your chest hurts?' She supplied the words for him.

He grasped her hand so hard it hurt. 'Yeah, but that's . . .' He gasped for breath. 'Not—'

'Shh. Don't talk. Save your breath. But don't go to sleep!'

He opened his lips but no sound came out . . . but she could hear barks.

'It's Jake!' she said. She shook Max gently by the arm. 'He's coming back!'

She pushed open the door but couldn't see Jake, though she could hear him making a racket somewhere. Maybe he'd lost his sense of direction in the snow, but he would surely hear and smell them?

Wriggling to the edge of the box, she bellowed: 'Jake! Come back here!'

More barking. Lots of barking. Jake was going wild.

Then she saw the dog. A black shadow carving a path through the snow towards the box. Except it wasn't Jake. It was Star, with Jake behind her.

'Star! Jake! Over here!' she yelled until her throat hurt. 'Here! We're in the stretcher box!'

Star reached her first and Krys slipped down into the snow to reach the dog. Star stayed a foot away barking but Jake leapt on her, knocking her off her feet.

She picked herself up out of the snow and yelled into the box: 'We're OK! They've found us! We're going to be OK, Max! Max, wake up! Please wake up! It'll be OK. Max, come on.'

She was still saying it, begging it, praying for it when Hector and Nikki arrived to prise her off Max's silent, unmoving body.

Chapter Thirty-Nine

'*W*here's *Krys?*'

Max opened his eyes to light, and faces that swam in and out of focus. He'd been asleep a long time . . . he'd been so cold . . . so terrified that he might lose Krys too . . . and it would be his fault. This time it would genuinely be his fault.

'*She's here.*'

'*I'm here.*'

Two women stood by the bed. One was holding his hand and stroking his hair. The other stood by, stiff-backed, her arms folded.

'What happened?' Max said.

'Don't you remember?' It was Laurel, grim-faced.

'Some – some of it's coming back.'

Dogs barking, Krys shouting at him, his friends from the team pulling him out of the box and strapping him to a stretcher. Someone putting a mask on his face, being carried over bumpy ground, the roar of a helicopter's rotor blades, a flight through the air and then being wheeled into the hospital, and after that . . . nothing much until *now*.

'Stay calm,' Laurel said.

'I am calm!' Max pushed himself up the bed and groaned.

'Laurel's right. Keep still. You've got three broken ribs, and you had a collapsed lung plus exposure and hypothermia.' Krys was looking sternly down on him.

'Shit. That's almost a full house.'

'Don't swear,' Laurel muttered.

Krys exchanged a glance with Max. The two of them were here together, agreeing with each other. Things must have been bad.

'It's not funny,' Laurel said and rolled her eyes. 'Now I know he's obviously back to normal, I'll leave you to it.' She squeezed Max's hand briefly. 'I'm very happy you're OK. I couldn't have done without you.'

They were left alone. Max gazed at Krys as if she might evaporate. He couldn't believe she was here with him: that they were both together, safe and alive. Many, many times during the long night, he'd said his goodbyes in his head, begged for forgiveness for putting her in such terrible danger.

Holding his hand, Krys sat by his bed. 'What can you remember about last night?'

'Not too much after the dogs started barking. What happened exactly? I've been in and out of it for bloody ages.'

'Jake must have heard or smelt the team coming and he and Star led the rescuers to the stretcher box. The Thorndale, Bannerdale and Borrowdale teams were out looking for us. Plus the RAF of course.'

'Oh God. I've created havoc. I am so stupid . . .'

Krys raised an eyebrow but didn't contradict him.

'How did they know where we were?' he added.

'I'd messaged Nikki to say I was staying at the manor for the night. She called round at seven this morning to see if I was

OK and saw I wasn't there. When the place was empty and I didn't answer my phone, she started to worry.

'She couldn't reach either of us so she raised the alarm. It was the local farmer who eventually told the team he'd seen us both at different times last night and thought we might have gone searching for Jake on the Pike.'

'That was bloody lucky. Thank God for Nikki and the farmer.'

'And the MRTs,' she said. 'I'll never forget the relief of hearing Star and the other team members.'

'Yes . . . I'll never live this down, you know.' He closed his eyes. 'Being rescued by your own team. It'll come up on every rescue forever.'

'Better than the alternative,' Krys said.

'There's that,' Max agreed, then frowned. 'Where's Jake now?'

'Staying with Star and Hector.'

Max lay back. 'He's a bloody nuisance, that dog, but I love him.'

'So do I. He kept us warm.'

'So did you. You saved my life.'

'I doubt it.' Her cheeks flushed. Even totally exhausted, she looked more beautiful than ever to him. 'The nurse told us you can probably go home later,' she said briskly.

'Good. I've caused enough trouble.'

'That's true.' Krys laughed. 'She also insisted that you mustn't be left on your own, so I said . . . that you could stay at the manor with me.'

Max was convinced he'd died and gone to heaven: he'd certainly been given a new lease of life, firstly by Krys turning up in Thorndale and again last night. Emotion choked his throat. 'I thought – that you'd gone back to London for good. Why did you come back?'

'Because I didn't want to leave without saying goodbye. I'd almost reached the motorway. Harriet invited me for Christmas.'

'Well, that's very kind of her but I'm glad you changed your mind. If you hadn't turned back, I might not be here at all.'

'Shh,' said Krys. 'Let's not dwell on that. Look, you don't *have* to stay with me but I'm not sure they'll be too happy for you to go home to the Bothy. Not that it would stop you, of course.'

'So I have two choices. Hobble home to the Bothy and spend Christmas Day on my own with only Jake and a piece of cheese on toast.'

'I've no idea what's in your fridge.'

'Or come to the manor and sit by a cosy fire with turkey sandwiches and you by my side,' he said.

'And Jake, too.'

'Of course.'

He grasped Krys's hand tightly, feeling her warm fingers in his. 'I really don't have a choice, do I?'

'You always have a choice, Max.'

'I don't want to be on my own. Not at Christmas. Not afterwards.'

Her eyes glistened but he wasn't going to wait another moment to say what he had to, what he'd almost been prevented from ever telling her.

'It's too soon for you, I know that. Far too soon after Brett, but not for me. I don't want to be on my own a moment longer. I want to be with someone I care about. Someone who means so much to me, I'm too scared to admit it. I've spent so long in the wilderness, so long hiding away and trying to make amends for something that can never be mended.'

'You hiding away could never have changed anything,' Krys said. 'It might have been the right thing for you for a while. It might have been exactly what you needed.'

'Perhaps, but it hasn't been for many, many months now. I wanted to come out of the shadows before you arrived in

Thorndale. People were trying to lure me out; but you gave me the reason to do it. You helped me give myself permission to stop suffering . . . why did you risk everything for me?'

'Because I know you were worth risking it for. That despite what you might have convinced yourself, you were worth saving.' She kissed him, and ignoring the pain from his ribs, Max hugged her to him. He wanted to say the words that had faded from his lips on the mountain: that he loved her, body and soul, but that could wait for now. He would say it one day soon, when the time was right, and she was ready.

But he wouldn't leave it too long. Not very long at all.

Chapter Forty

While Max was waiting for his medication, Laurel found Krys in the hospital café.

Krys hadn't been alone with her to talk yet. Nikki had phoned Laurel at the pub and told her that Max was in hospital. She'd only arrived later that morning, in time to see him come round.

'I bought you a coffee,' Laurel said, handing over a mug. 'It claims to be cappuccino, though I suspect that defies the Trades Descriptions Act.'

'Thanks.' Krys took it though she was awash with coffee already. Dare she hope it was a peace offering?

'I must speak to you,' Laurel said, ushering her to a table in the corner. The place was almost deserted. It was Christmas Eve and also, so it seemed, the season for confessions.

Krys braced herself. 'If it's about Max, I don't want a confrontation,' she replied, ready for a battle. She was going to stand up to Laurel this time: no running away.

'No confrontation. No more conflict. I was very wrong when I told you to leave Thorndale and I was wrong to make Max feel guilty about starting a new relationship. He wouldn't have gone off like that if he hadn't been in the state of mind he was. I made him feel like that.'

'Max had felt so bad, he was ready to believe it,' she said, gently, seeing Laurel was desperate to make her peace.

'You risked your life to save Max, and Erin would have done the same. She loved Max that much. She always worried about him working too hard, always wanted to have more time together. She told me she was pregnant on the trip. She was so excited . . .'

Laurel choked back a sob. Krys didn't know what to do to comfort her or even if she should. Risking everything, she put her hand on Laurel's arm.

Laurel didn't move away.

'I'm so very sorry.'

Laurel wiped her eyes with a tissue. 'Max is special to you, isn't he?' she said.

'He is.' More than she dared admit to anyone, even Max – even herself – yet.

'Then you have my blessing. Though you don't need my permission,' Laurel added. 'I've done enough damage trying to control Max's life and yours.'

Krys touched her arm. 'I'd rather have your blessing anyway.'

By the time Max had been released from hospital, it was early evening so Krys drove him to the Bothy to collect some clothes and pick up Jake from Hector's house, before heading home to the manor.

He slept for twelve hours, with Jake at the foot of the bed, unwilling to let him out of his sight. Laurel was, by now, also safely home with her family, promising to meet up with Max after Christmas – and Krys too.

While Max rested, Krys had called Harriet again, having already let her know she was OK but had been delayed in

Thorndale. She explained that she'd be spending Christmas with Max but would love to visit for New Year when he was feeling better. It took a full hour before her friend was finally satisfied that she'd heard every last detail of Krys's adventures – and about Max, of course.

After she'd spoken with Harriet, she scrolled through her phone to a number she hadn't used since Linda's funeral. It rang out a dozen times before it was answered.

'Mum? Hello, it's me.'

'Krys? Krys? Thank bloody God. I've been trying to get you but your bloody phone was engaged. Gus saw something about a rescue on the BBC website – God knows why he was looking at the northern news – and he said it was you. And I looked and I saw you'd almost died in the snow saving some silly sod and – Krys, for God's sake, are you OK? I know we don't see eye to eye and I'll never win mum of the year but I could never forgive myself if something happened to you and we'd never made our peace.'

Krys heard her mother's tears; she felt them herself.

'I'm f-fine, M-Mum,' she said, not bothering to stem them. 'Fine. And I think the s-same. After Christmas, let's meet up and talk. Properly talk.'

A while later, she wiped her eyes and went upstairs to check on Max, but he was deep in dreamland, dark lashes against his cheeks, sleeping like a man who hadn't a care in the world.

'Have I died and gone to heaven?'

Max gazed up at Krys from the pillow.

'There's no way you'll get into heaven with cheesy lines like that,' she said, kissing him and thinking how much better he was looking for some proper rest. 'It's Christmas Eve, you know,' she said.

'So Santa should be busy,' he said, pushing himself up the pillows with a grimace.

'Doubt it. He's been lying around asleep.'

He laughed. 'Ouch.'

Gingerly, he levered himself out of bed. She helped him dress and make his way downstairs.

'Krys. Will you do something for me? Wait here.'

He limped off to the hallway and returned with an object wrapped in a piece of tissue paper.

'I made this for you.' He gave a wicked grin. 'Or rather, Dave did.'

She unwrapped the tissue. She could not speak for a few seconds, transfixed by the beautiful object in her hand: a turned angel complete with a halo.

'It's made with shades of oak and ash. It's a one-off.'

'It's perfect. It's beautiful.' It was one of the only Christmas decorations she had left – and already one of the most precious.

'I hoped you'd like it. It was meant to be a peace offering for all the trouble I'd caused you.'

She kissed him, meaning the kiss to be gentle, but he drew her closer, deepening the kiss and the connection until she felt they were one person. The angel was warm and smooth in her hand, a token that bound her to him along with the night they'd spent on the mountain, both expecting it would be his last.

She was losing it; she'd shed more tears since she'd arrived in Thorndale than in a lifetime.

'I've made you cry again. This is not good,' Max said.

She laughed. 'They're the right sort of tears, so that's OK.' She balanced the angel in her palm and held it aloft. The last rays of the sun shone onto it. 'It's gorgeous. Thank you.'

'Don't thank me. Thank Dave.'

'While we were on the mountain, you told me that making these was your secret. Do you remember that?'

'Some of it. I didn't want people to know but I've always loved making stuff. My grandad and dad were craftspeople. I was always in their workshops from when I was young. When I went to uni, it didn't seem cool, then I started the business and I was too busy.'

'Yet you started again?'

'Like I said, a few months after I arrived in Thorndale. If you think I was anti-social when you first got here, you should have seen me then. I'd make a visit to the stores every couple of weeks and the rest of the time I holed up at the Bothy like a wounded animal.'

'Which you were.'

'The place was a dump. I had to get the power re-installed and a back-up generator put in. I needed wood for the fire and that's when I found the workshop. Some of the equipment was salvageable. A circular saw, a lathe. I sent for some tools from my parents' place where I'd left them.' He hesitated. 'I've put them through a lot of pain.'

'I can imagine.'

'I didn't want to see them after the funeral. I didn't want to see anyone. Their own grief – and their distress at my grief – it was all too much. They love me, they loved Erin and they only wanted to help. Yet their concern – and all of my friends' concern – was like layer upon layer of responsibility. They wanted me to start to feel better and I didn't want to feel better. I didn't want anyone to witness me in that state.'

He stroked her hair tenderly.

'Anyway, once I had the equipment, I started going in the workshop more and more,' Max said firmly. 'The pain and thoughts didn't go away at first but making stuff gave me something to do other than walking the hills or staring at the stove. At first, I only made useful things for the Bothy. A table, chairs, chopping boards . . . and then when I'd made everything I needed, I started on stuff I didn't need.'

'The spinning tops?'

'I began with those and realised I didn't think about anything else while I was concentrating on making them. It was a relief that turned into a pleasurable obsession. Then as Christmas came last year, I tried some angels, robins and mini trees. Before I knew, I'd built up a stock of Christmas decorations.'

'Maybe you felt you were healing a little?'

'Perhaps, though I'd no intention of being part of any kind of festivities myself. However, I couldn't let all the stuff I'd made go to waste so I had a word with Amina and she agreed to sell them in the post office stores to raise funds for the MRT base.'

'You didn't want anyone to know about it?'

'I'd no plans to go within a million miles of anything to do with Christmas ever again. I just wanted to quietly do what I could and hide away.' He looked at her. 'Until now.'

The kiss went on a long time and when it finally ended, Max kept hold of her hand.

'There's something else too.'

'Not another present?' she asked.

'No. Something I need to ask you. You know when we were in the stretcher box, I was babbling away, wasn't I?'

'Noo . . .'

He raised an eyebrow.

'OK, a bit, but you were struggling for breath and very cold. You probably didn't know what you were saying.'

'Didn't I?' he said.

'I doubt it. You were verging on delirious.'

'Of course. You're probably right.'

She nodded. She did remember.

'What if I wasn't delirious though? What if I do remember what I said to you? Or what I was trying to say to you?'

He sounded so intense that her skin prickled and butterflies took flight in her stomach.

'There was something I had to tell you. It was only because I couldn't speak that I stopped. That's a lie. It was because I didn't think you wanted me to say it; that you suspected what I was going to say. I genuinely thought I was going to breathe my last and I had to get it out. Well, I'm here, as you can see, and I'm still going to say it, no matter what the consequences.'

She was trembling.

'It's way too soon for you. I know that but I can't wait another second. I'm in love with you. There, I've said it.'

She couldn't reply.

'Because no one can predict or choose when they meet the One. It might be years or it might be weeks. It might be the day after one person walked out of your life, it might be a lifetime, it might be never.'

For her and Max, it happened to be now: this moment.

'Have I gone too far?' he said, searching her face. 'Have I made a huge mistake? Krys. Say something, even if it's only to tell me to get out of here.'

'It's now for me too. Right now.'

He sighed and kissed her, before, finally, adding: 'Now, there's just one more thing I need you to do for me.'

Her tears were replaced by laughter. 'Are you sure you're in any fit state for that.'

His eyes gleamed with promise. 'I might be by tomorrow, but it's not what you think.'

Chapter Forty-One

CHRISTMAS DAY

On Christmas morning, Krys drove Max to the Bothy. The fell tops were covered with snow and the bracken was crisp with frost. Church bells rang out in the vale and she thought it was the most beautiful place she'd ever been in.

Max, however, was more excited about the bright red shiny family hatchback that he'd hidden under a tarpaulin in an outbuilding. He'd told her his plans on Christmas Eve but she could still barely believe it.

'It's fantastic,' she said.

'Perfect for the twenty-first century Santa to arrive in, don't you think?'

Krys agreed and went into the Bothy with him, with Jake at their heels.

'Shall we get changed, Mrs Christmas?' he said.

'I think we'd better, Santa.'

In the Bothy, she helped him into the Santa suit. 'Are you sure you're up to this?' she asked twice as he struggled with the beard.

With two cracked ribs and a badly bruised ankle, he'd had to forgo the belly, and hope Thomas would think Santa had lost some weight after his very busy night. After donning the elf outfit, she took the wheel of the hatchback, while Max climbed gingerly into the driver's seat of the Land Rover. Jake, complete with tinsel on his collar, jumped up beside him and they set off in convoy through the melting snow under a sunny Christmas Day sky.

He parked the Landy around the corner from Thomas's house before Krys jumped into the new car's passenger seat. A moment later they stopped outside Thomas's house.

'I'm nervous about this,' she said.

'Not as nervous as me. Come on, then.'

They'd barely got out of the car when the door opened and Thomas emerged, followed by his father and the baby.

'Thomas's dad was expecting us,' Max said. 'I asked his permission and what make and model he needed and eventually he agreed to accept the car.'

'You're a big softy, Santa, do you know that?'

'Maybe, but don't tell anyone. I can't have my reputation ruined. Here's Thomas.'

Thomas's mouth was the biggest, roundest 'o' Krys had ever seen. He stood by the garden gate clutching his dad's hand.

He looked from the car to Santa, to the elf and his father. 'Daddy?' he said. 'Is this for you?'

'I think it's for all of us, Thomas.'

The child's face was a picture of wonder. It reminded her of her own expression gazing back at herself in the window of the Christmas house.

'Would you and your dad and sister like to sit in it?' Max said.

Thomas looked up at his father.

'Go ahead, Tom. I'll be with you.'

Thomas nodded and climbed inside the passenger seat, with his dad and sister beside him. Max stayed outside with Krys

'Dad said Santa wouldn't be able to send us a car,' he said.

'Santa can't do everything,' Max said. 'But he helps if he possibly can.'

Thomas reached across the car to hug Max. 'Thank you, Santa.'

'Y-you're very w-welcome. Thomas.'

'Why are you crying, Santa?'

'Me? Crying? Ho, ho, ho. It's just some dust in my eye.'

Krys exchanged a glance with Thomas's father. He mouthed 'Thank you.' Krys shook her head as firmly as she could to let him know there was no need and anyway, she hadn't arranged the car, Max had done it all himself.

'We'll let you go for a spin in it. I'm sorry it doesn't fly like a sleigh,' Max said in a croaky voice. 'Maybe I'll see you next year, Thomas!'

'Where's your sleigh?' he asked, still in wonder.

'My elf parked it round the corner but I've made it invisible to everyone else. Goodbye.'

With a wave, Max grabbed Krys's hand and hurried away.

'Daddy, why is Santa holding the lady elf's hand?' Krys heard as Max hobbled around the corner.

They never heard the answer. That was one mystery that Thomas's father would have to explain.

They jumped in the Land Rover where Jake let out a whine.

'Shall we?' Max said as Krys took the wheel.

'I think we sh-should.'

The next few moments were given up to unbridled sobs before Santa composed himself and let his elf drive him off towards the snowy mountains.

Epilogue

TEN MONTHS LATER

'Are you ready for this?' Max asked.

'Ready as I'll ever be,' said Krys.

'You'll smash it.'

'I hope not. There are thousands of pounds' worth of baubles in the back of the van.' She blew out a breath, misting the air. 'I hope I've done the right thing.'

Max's hands were warm around her own. He gave her a stern look 'You'll be great. You're Mrs Christmas.'

She nodded, telling herself that she'd been preparing for this moment for a very long time. She'd spent the New Year in London with Max, visiting Harriet and meeting her mother for the longest conversation they'd had for years. Things weren't perfect between them by a way, but at least they'd made a start. Krys felt the door on their relationship that had been bolted was now at least unlocked.

Then it was back to work, to start her new contract. The past ten months had been spent shuttling back and forth between London, Thorndale and the airport. Krys had enjoyed her stint as buyer for the store chain and had been offered a permanent role at the head office. It was all very confidence-boosting but she'd formulated other plans in the spring.

Today, they came to fruition and it was exciting and terrifying.

'Looks good, doesn't it?' Max said, pointing at her new van, waiting on the driveway, with its smart paint job:

THE KRYSTMAS DECORATOR
Spectacular interiors for every season
Commercial. Events. Residential.

'You certainly can't miss me,' she said, admiring the green and gold livery. 'There's no mistaking what I do.'

No mistaking the leap of faith she'd taken in moving up here to the Lakes to start a new life and business. She'd first had the idea while deep in the whirl of Christmas buying at the trade shows. One day, as the snowdrops had pushed through the warming earth in Thorndale, she and Max had had The Conversation. She couldn't even remember who'd said it first; it felt as if they'd both come to the conclusion at the exact same moment:

What about if they found a way to spend more time together? *Lots* more time.

As the first daffodils appeared in Thorndale churchyard, Max started his new job as an instructor at the Outdoor Centre.

'I can't stay here making angels and robins all day long,' he'd said to Krys when he told her he'd got the job. 'I can't think of any better way to spend my time than teaching the kids the skills they need in the outdoors, and best of all, I can take Jake to work with me.'

'Well,' she'd said, 'I think that's an amazing idea but I will also need a supply of your decorations, because I have a plan, too . . .'

'Oh?'

'I've decided to set up in business as a professional Christmas decorator. I've built up the supplier contacts, I can learn the decorating skills. All I'll need is an office and a storage unit – and clients, of course. I've a little money left over from Linda's legacy to invest and I could sell the flat . . .'

Max's eyes lit up. 'You mean . . .'

'If you like the idea, yes. I'd base myself here in the Lakes. Maybe find a unit and a cottage.'

'Yes, we could find a cottage,' he said, thoughtfully.

That wasn't quite how it happened because by the time a sea of bluebells had popped up in the woods at the head of the dale, Max had discovered that Holly Manor had come up for sale. With the money he'd had invested from his old house in London and the sale of Krys's flat, they could stretch to it.

Krys had needed a nanosecond to say yes and they'd moved in when water lilies were blooming like pink roses on Thorndale tarn. He'd renovated the Bothy and let it to a local farm labourer and his family.

Krys had rented a storage unit and office in one of the coastal towns and recruited a small team to help her.

'So, first commission,' Max said, walking with Krys to the new van.

'Yes. The Firholme Estate. Their events manager, Lottie, is on maternity leave so they need help to dress the function rooms and outdoor spaces. It means I get to meet the reindeer again.'

'Next?'

'A large hotel spa – remember the guy who lent the furniture for the Christmas ball? He gave me the commission. Then, Will's wife, Emma, works in PR so she recommended me to one of her clients: a country craft centre near Ambleside. Plus another couple of hotels so I'm afraid you won't see much of me for the next few weeks and then I have to start on people's houses. I've no idea when I'll have time to do ours here at the manor.'

'You could always leave it to me,' Max said.

Krys laughed. 'The man who hates Christmas?'

'The man who *hated* Christmas.' He pulled her to him. 'Who hated it when he was on his own and saw no point in carrying on most days and could never imagine spending it with anyone he loved again.'

'And now?'

'I guess he's stuck with Mrs Christmas.'

'I rather think he is,' Krys said.

With a kiss, she climbed into the car and set off on her new adventure, knowing that the Christmas card house – and Max – would always be waiting when she came home.

THE END

Acknowledgements

One day I may possibly write a book that doesn't require any research – but I doubt it!

Visiting new places, finding fascinating facts and chatting to interesting people is one of the best parts of being an author, but I'm always reliant on the expertise, time and insight of busy people.

For *The Christmas Holiday*, I'm indebted to Lee, Lou and Rachel at The Museum of Cannock Chase who are wizards at running themed events and conjuring up gorgeous festive decorations. They are also huge book lovers and run a regular series of author/reader events. I also want to thank Christine Scippio of Kaleidoscope Communications, for telling me all about the spectacular, trade-only Harrogate Christmas Fair.

For the tips on Christmas crafting, I turned to one of my readers, the freelance journalist Lauren John. You can follow her lifestyle/crafting blog at www.thesecitydays.co.uk.

Big thanks to Lindy and John for taking time to show me the workshop and beautiful turned wooden objects and artwork. My friend Moira Briggs, who used to volunteer for

367

an MRT, also helped with some of the mountain rescue aspects of the story.

Even when a book is written, a whole team has to move in to get it onto the shelves and e-readers. Huge thanks to Cara Chimirri for editing the book and making me smile with her notes in the margin. Thank you to my copy editor, Fran, to my PR, Becci, and everyone at the Avon sales team, who have been knocking it out of the park this year!

My agent Broo has been with me since I sent my debut novel to her and is always ready to congratulate, commiserate, give feedback and provide the odd glass of fizz.

An author is nothing without readers so thank you to all the book bloggers, my social media followers, writing buddies and my Facebook reader group for your support.

Finally, let me not forget that as well as my imaginary world, I also have a 'Real Life' populated by the friends and family who have become more precious than ever to me in these strange times. So I send love to the Friday Floras, Coffee Crew and Party People and my bookseller mate, Janice Hume, to whom this book is dedicated.

And finally, thank you Mum and Dad, John, Charlotte, James and Charles for absolutely everything. ILY x

If you loved *The Christmas Holiday*,
then don't miss this festive romance
by Phillipa Ashley, set in the magical
Lake District . . .

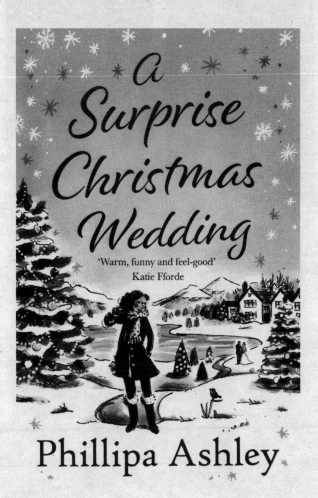

A Surprise Christmas Wedding

'Warm, funny and feel-good'
Katie Fforde

Phillipa Ashley

Explore the beautiful Cornish coast with Phillipa Ashley's beautifully escapist Falford series . . .

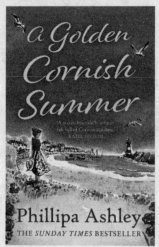

Discover Phillipa Ashley's glorious Porthmellow series . . .

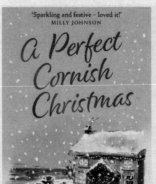

**Escape to the Isles of Scilly
with this glorious trilogy . . .**

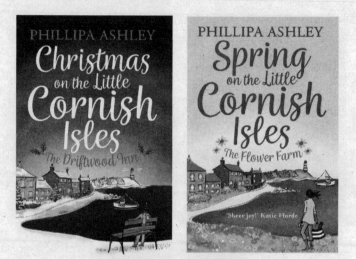

Discover the wonderfully cosy
Cornish Café series . . .